Caffeine Nights Publishing

Snow Kills

RC Bridgestock

Fiction aimed at the heart
and the head..

Published by Caffeine Nights Publishing 2013

Published in Great Britain by Caffeine Nights Publishing

www. caffeine-nights com

British Library Cataloguing in Publication Data.
A CIP catalogue record for this book is available from the British Library

ISBN: 978-1-907565-62-5

Cover design by
Mark (Wills) Williams

Everything else by
Default, Luck and Accident

Acknowledgements

Thank you to our publisher Caffeine Nights Publishing.
The fabulous CEO, Darren Laws, and literary agent, Monika Luukkonen for their continued hard work, support, dedication and tireless enthusiasm. Mark (Wills) Williams, once again, for the brilliant art work for the 'Snow Kills' cover and Gemma Beckwith for her up-to-date knowledge of police procedure. We are also thrilled to welcome on to the DI Dylan series team, Sandra Mangan for 'Snow Kills' – the most proficient editor and proofreader.

We couldn't do it without you!

Dedication

To all our family for their continued love and support.

Our beloved golden retriever Max, who sadly passed away in 2012 at the ripe old age of 15, but still lives on in the DI Dylan series. We're not ready to let go yet, mate...

To those who strive daily to make the world a safer place for everyone, by bringing to justice those individuals who seek to inflict injury and suffering.

The D.I. Dylan Books

Deadly Focus
Consequences
White Lilies

Snow Kills

Preface

'Who am I?' Jack mused as he smiled down at his baby daughter. He put his finger to her rosy red cheek and was rewarded by a lopsided grin. She was snug, warm and sleepy laid in her pram. Dylan looked over his shoulder and back down the forest glade to where he saw Jen admiring snowdrops in flower under the shade of a tree. Sensing his stare, his wife glanced up at him, smiled and rose from her haunches, scurrying towards him as best she could in her wellington boots. Dylan stifled a chuckle – her jerky movements made him think of a newly born deer.

'It always amazes me how anything survives outside in this weather,' she said, expelling warm air from her lips in a mist. She grabbed his arm as an involuntary shiver went through her, even though she was wrapped up in her winter clothing. 'We don't see much of this where I come from,' she said, pointing her gloved hands to the snow filled sky. For a moment, the pair looked to the heavens. Jen watched Dylan close his eyes and screw his nose up as little pinpricks of snow fell on his face. She laughed, put her arm through his and together they watched the snow flurry cross the ever-whitening Yorkshire valley – in silence.

As they walked through Sibden, a strong northerly wind carrying damp snow and sleet blew down the steep hillside. The air was like white sparkling wine. Dylan took a deep breath and put his head down, feeling the cold burning in his lungs as they fought to walk against the rapidly worsening conditions. Jen put her face into his upper arm, closed her eyes and held on tightly, walking blindly.

The sky was full but the snowstorm passed quickly. Dylan looked down, noticing his wife's blonde hair was covered in soft, white snowflakes. Unperturbed by the weather, Max, their Golden Retriever, bounced towards them; a light coating of snow on an ice crusted snow bank was heaven to him. He barked at the top, as though shouting 'I'm king of the castle,' and Dylan put his finger swiftly to his lips. Maisy's eyes flew open and then shut again.

'Shush,' Jen said, crossly. Nevertheless, Max crouched

down in play and barked again. Jen threw a snowball for him to chase and seconds later he was back with more than a dusting of snow on his nose.

'Who'd have thought that five years ago when I was living on the Isle of Wight and engaged to be married to another policeman, when the doctor gave me the news that I'd never have children? Look at me now, three hundred miles away from home, married, and we have Maisy,' she said, with a contented sigh.

'And who'd have thought I'd be a married man? Me, the eternal bachelor, wedded to the job before I met you,' Dylan said. 'I'm not much of a husband when I'm absorbed in an incident though, am I?' he added, as he reached for her and held her tight.

Jen tilted her head up to him, stood on tiptoes and kissed his cheek.

'I miss you, now I don't see you at work,' she said. 'At least when I was at the station and you had a job running I'd see you there... and there is no one else to talk to with Mum gone and Dad so far away,' she mumbled into the breast of his coat. 'Sometimes I feel so alone.'

'Alone? With Maisy?'

Jen cocked her head and gave him a crooked smile.

'When you coming back to work then?'

Jen pulled a face. 'Well, I guess since Maisy is nearly eight months old, I'd better come in and have a chat with Avril Summerfield-Preston soon about my return.'

Max barked louder and the two looked at him in horror. Dylan's phone rang. Maisy started to cry. Jen rolled her watery eyes, and stepped back from their embrace, taking the pram from Dylan and briskly pushing it away. He turned from the force of the wind to take the call.

Who was he?

He was DI Jack Dylan, the officer in charge of Harrowfield CID.

Snow Kills

Chapter 1

Didn't the whole town know it by now? Kayleigh tutted, then sighed, dropping her shoulders as she raised her eyes to the ceiling. Yet another severe weather warning was being broadcast over the airwaves.

Two o'clock prompt – and as always on a Wednesday, the shop door handle turned. This time though, the door juddered over the cardboard on the floor to soak up the wet footprints. As if in slow motion, a snow-covered figure, carrying a suitcase, fell headfirst into the salon. Mavis Beanland lay spread-eagled on the lino.

'I don't know why I'm bothering,' she said, as Kayleigh dashed over. Mavis brushed her away, struggled onto her hands and knees, paused for a moment to untie the Rain Mate that had fallen over her eyes, and pick up a penny. 'See a penny pick it up and all the day you'll have good luck,' she said. 'My hair'll be none the better for doing, you know, by the time I get to my sister's,' she added, puffing and blowing. Kayleigh smiled at her customer and gave a fleeting glance over her shoulder at the busy Harrowfield High Street through the open door. Closing it, she could see the large snowflakes lazily drifting past on an unseen breeze.

'But, I'm here now. Quite a trek from them there moors today it was,' said Mavis, popping the found penny into the charity box on the shop counter next to the till.

'You'll feel better for having it washed,' Kayleigh said, taking the old lady's scarf and gloves as she watched a puddle appear on the floor at Mavis's feet. She took off her coat and hung it up. Unaware of the mess she had made, Mavis padded across the floor towards the basin. With a flick of her plump wrist, she flung her wet fringe out of her eyes and looked at Kayleigh.

'My goodness girl, look at you in them high heeled boots,' she said in mock horror. Kayleigh draped a gown in front of her and Mrs Beanland turned and dropped her head to allow her to tie it. 'They'll be less use than a glass hammer in this weather,' she said, pointing to Kayleigh's footwear. 'And I'll be darned if you don't end up with frostbite on y' ... y' bits,' she added, pointing the same finger a bit higher at a short skirt. 'I wear more in bed,' she said, turning around to sit with a thud on the chair. 'Don't you young 'uns listen to the weather forecast?' she added, shaking her head.

'I wish,' said Kayleigh, turning to the radio sitting on a shelf, as right on cue another severe weather warning rang out, this time with school closures and cancelled public transport notifications. 'And, I'll have you know these boots cost me a week's wages, Mavis,' she said, as she placed a towel around her client's shoulders and turned on the basin taps.

'They did?' Mavis said, pulling a face as her hairdresser's hand expertly guided her head into the wash basin. 'You were robbed. Aren't you worried about getting home? We don't want you breaking a leg now, do we? Who'd do my hair then?' Kayleigh pumped the shampoo from the bottle at the side of the sink into her hand and started massaging Mavis's scalp to form a soapy lather. Kayleigh's favourite client gripped her towel tight to her chest. 'Ooooo, you are a good scrubber,' she said with delight.

'Don't go saying stuff like that; you'll get me a right reputation,' Kayleigh said, laughing. 'People already think that because I'm a blonde and a hairdresser I've nothing between my ears. Aren't you worried about getting to your sister's, Mave?'

'No,' laughed the old lady. 'If the bleeding Germans didn't stop me in the war, a few snowflakes won't.'

'You are a one,' Kayleigh said with a chuckle.

The salon was hot and humid, with condensation running down the windows and Kayleigh could feel sweat beads forming on her top lip. 'Why does everybody want to talk about the weather today?' she said with a sigh, wiping her brow with her forearm.

Unhearing, Mavis went on. 'I hope you aren't wearing those tongue things that I've read about. Kayleigh raised her eyebrows and stifled a giggle. 'If you are, you'll know about it if you go down on your backside, my girl.'

'You mean a thong Mavis, they're called thongs,' laughed Kayleigh, bringing the old lady up from the basin. She patted her wet hair with the towel.

'Call them what you like love, but what you need in this weather is a pair of them there knickers that gathers it all in,' she said. 'Harvest Knickers we used to call them. Not particularly appealing to look at, I grant you that, but...' she said with a nod, looking at Kayleigh through the mirror. 'I tell you what, I'll get you a pair next time I go the market.'

'No, you're alright. They don't sound very ... attractive,' Kayleigh said, screwing up her nose.

'Too bloody cold to be thinking what they look like my girl. Common sense's got to apply on days like these; it's not the middle of summer, you know. Eee ... you'll learn when you get a bit older,' Mavis said, shaking her head.

'You sound like me Mum. Don't cast a clout 'til May passes out, she always says,' Kayleigh mimicked her mother's voice. 'She'd still have me wearing liberty bodices if she had her way.'

'She sounds like a sensible woman your mum ... Ouch!' Mavis flinched as Kayleigh snagged a knot in her hair.

'Concentrate please Kayleigh, tips to roots. How many more times do I have to tell you?' Marlene, Kayleigh's boss said as she walked past, her quick, small feet making a tapping noise on the floor. Kayleigh raised her eyebrows at Mavis in the mirror and the two sniggered like children.

Ten minutes later, Mavis was settled under the dryer, her hair neatly set in curlers, with a cup of tea.

'Look at them and you'll see where I get my ideas from,' Kayleigh said pointing to a page in a magazine. The headline read 'Today's Fashion on a Shoestring'.

Mavis smiled as she took the magazine offered. She visibly relaxed with the soothing noise of the dryer blowing the warm, dry air down on her and for a minute Kayleigh watched her client close her eyes and thought she might fall asleep, as she often did. But within seconds Mavis's eyes flew open and she started to flip through the pages. Kayleigh could hear Mavis humming to herself and couldn't help but smile as she tidied her work station. Gathering an armful of wet towels from the bin, Kayleigh headed for the utility room.

'Kayleigh,' Mavis's shrill voice shouted. She stopped abruptly and pivoted on one foot to face the dryer bank.

'Shh ...You don't have to shout, I can hear you,' she said, a mischievous smile on her lips as she brought her finger to her mouth.

'What did you say love?' Mavis shouted even louder, with her hand cupped to her netted, sponge ear muffs. 'I don't appear to have a biscuit dear,' she said, looking down despairingly at the empty saucer on the wooden arm of her seat. 'Tea without a biscuit is like salt without vinegar on me fish n' chips,' she said. 'Pass us one of them from that box on the counter.'

'You don't miss a trick, Mavis Beanland, do you?' Kayleigh laughed. Picking a Bronte Cafe ginger snap, she passed it to her client.

'Splendid! These look like good dunkers,' Mavis said, nodding to the lady sat next to her, who nodded back in agreement. 'Get one love, I'll pay you for it later.'

Kayleigh smiled fondly at Mavis. 'Thank you, I will,' she said, throwing one in her handbag behind the reception desk.

Thirty minutes later, Kayleigh gently combed Mavis's warm, snuff dry hair round her fingers into little curls, just as she liked it. There was no need for Marlene's expertise with the old lady's coiffure. She held the hand mirror up behind her client's head proudly so that she could also see the rear of her hair. Mavis nodded approvingly and smiled.

'Lovely, dear,' she said, as Kayleigh squeezed a pea sized bit of cream out of the tube of Vitapointe and gently patted it on Mavis's hair. Mavis rose out of her chair with a groan before hobbling to the reception desk. She picked up her wet weather gear and ceremoniously wrapped her scarf around her neck twice before she shrugged into her coat.

'Best thing I ever did was knit this scarf,' she said. 'Do you knit?' she asked Kayleigh, who shook her head.

'Once I start I can't stop,' Mavis said.

'That explains the length of it,' Kayleigh laughed.

'I'll be doing a lot of knitting at my sister's, she doesn't have a telly,' Mavis said with a frown. 'She likes reading. So there's no chance of me keeping up with the soaps for a few weeks,' she added. 'I'll give you a ring to book another appointment when I get back.'

Mavis paid and put a two pound tip into the palm of Kayleigh's hand. 'You're a good kid,' she said with a wink. 'I'll try get you a pair of them Harvest knickers while I'm at my sister's.'

'Thank you, that's very kind,' said Kayleigh, tutting softly, because she knew Mavis would not take no for an answer. 'What would I do without you to look after me?' Mavis squeezed Kayleigh's hand tightly.

'And put that money towards some wellies, never mind that there fashion.' Mavis held Kayleigh's hand in her weather worn arthritic grasp for a moment and, fleetingly closing her eyes, she smiled at the young girl kindly. 'Take care love.'

'You take care, I'll see you soon,' Kayleigh said.

She walked in front of Mavis to the door, opened it and held her hand once again as the old lady precariously negotiated the steps. She watched her tread with trepidation out onto the icy flagstones, which looked treacherous because yet again, the powers-that-be at Harrowfield Council had failed to prepare for the weather that had been long forecast. The wind was stirring the snow into the shop doorway and it was beginning to create snowdrifts that resembled sand dunes against the walls and the door jamb in the porch. The cool air was welcome after the humidity of the salon, and for a moment Kayleigh stood, arms crossed, leaning on the salon window and watching the world go by. It started to snow heavier and she stared at snowflakes like upturned petals floating to the ground. Her eyes lingered on the vehicles at a standstill in a queue of traffic, surrounded by flake-filled air. She looked up at the moving white snow in the grey sky and felt its feather-light cold touch on her forehead. The phone rang and broke her reverie.

'Kayleigh, will you come inside and close that flaming door, or you'll have us all catching our death,' Marlene called. 'The last appointment cancelled, and according to the radio the buses are either stuck en route or suspended until further notice.' Kayleigh hoped and prayed that Mavis would make it to her sister's safely. She knew her friend's bravado hid a fragility she wouldn't dream of admitting to.

'Run the mop quickly over the floor will you, while I cash up? Then you can get off home, otherwise we'll both be spending the night here,' said Marlene. Kayleigh scowled behind her boss's back and shuddered at the thought.

'If it's bad tomorrow I won't be opening up,' Marlene said, crossing the salon floor with the till drawer in her arms. She headed to the staff room to count and deposit the day's takings in the safe.

Kayleigh didn't need telling twice. Within five minutes she had her little white fur jacket on and was heading for the door. 'Bye,' she called out to her boss without a backward glance. She negotiated her first few steps on the compacted snow by holding onto the walls of the building, then slid across the iced pathway and hung onto a lamp post. The surface of the pavement was uneven and she could see parts of it were like a sheet of glass. With a lot of respect, she watched those brave enough to walk on it although they looked as if they were unwitting contestants from a TV show – falling and slipping around in an undignified manner. She negotiated her route via a telegraph pole and a signpost – anything that would help her make it to her car unscathed. Looking back at the salon through the blizzard, she could see a couple of people who looked to be helping Marlene down the steps. She tutted, and Mavis said her boots weren't suitable! She obviously hadn't clapped eyes on Marlene's stilettos.

Walking like an octogenarian, Kayleigh became fascinated by the puzzle of the ice. In the near white-out conditions threatening to paralyse the town, she saw the outline of her car – and as her footsteps eventually cut tracks into the virgin snow around it, she was thankful to spot the orange, rotary, safety light mounted high on the roof of a snow plough coming her way. She looked up at the driver, whose face held no expression, but to her surprise she saw Mavis sat alongside him, chattering away. Mavis was highly delighted to see her, and waved as the gritter came to a standstill.

As Kayleigh waited for the line of traffic to move, the window of the gritter wagon opened, 'Hey Blondie!' the driver shouted. 'You're going up towards the Manchester Road in that little pink monster, Mave here tells me.'

'I'm gonna try,' she shouted back.

'I'm going your way after I've dropped her off at the train station,' he said. 'Follow me and I'll show you the world and anything else you want.' She could hear Mavis chuckling and could only guess at her retort.

It must be dead boring gritting the roads, Kayleigh thought, but if she hurried he was right, she might have more chance of getting home following in his tracks. Looking down at the driver's side door of her car, her hopes were soon dashed. She leaned against the car and moaned; all she had to do now was clear the snow that her knight in shining armour, had pushed against it. Her feet were wet and her toes were numb.

Downhearted, she trudged around the car, scraping off the snow with her bare hands. She looked down at her new boots with despair, for they were surely ruined. Mavis, bless her, was right and she would tell her so when she next saw her. In future, she vowed to keep a pair of wellingtons on hand for days like these. Parked behind her car was a scooter, no doubt Donny Longbottom's. Where was her tormenter when she needed him? Probably at home if he had any sense. He might have a screw or two loose, but even he wouldn't risk riding his bike in these conditions.

Red hands that had been numb began to feel painful at the knuckles as she attempted to rub life back into them. Kayleigh sat for a moment, cold and tired with the exertion.

She picked up her mobile phone. *'Can I come to yours Matt?'* she texted.

'It's Wednesday. I'm at me mate's but you've got a key,' her boyfriend texted back.

'Damn,' she said wiping away a tear that ran down her face.

Kayleigh rang her mum, but the phone went straight onto the answer machine. 'I'm heading for Matt's, mum,' she said. 'Don't worry about me, love you.'

Sighing deeply, Kayleigh threw her phone onto the passenger seat. Surprisingly the little car's engine roared into action and as she waited for the windows to clear she turned on the radio to hear the next weather alert. She set the heater to blow warm air down onto her feet, and wiped the inside of the car windows with a leatherette. Kayleigh hadn't been driving for long and had never driven in snow, but she adored driving her bright pink Ka and she was looking forward to the challenge now she felt a little warmer.

The roads were congested. The daylight was beginning to disappear rapidly and the night was drawing in sooner than expected, due to the grey, low snow clouds. Kayleigh sat patiently in the queue at the start of the Manchester Road. Her windscreen wipers were going ten to the dozen just to clear the driving snow but at least she was heading in the right direction. One minute she was sat in the queue and the next her car slid into the curb as she attempted a corner on a slight incline. 'Flaming hell,' she said out loud, feeling a thread of fear run through her veins. She gripped the steering wheel tighter, pursing her lips together tightly as if trying to whistle, and blew out slowly. 'Thank God it's only six more miles to Matt's.'

Traffic was at a snail's pace. Impatiently she leaned to her right to try to see around the vehicle in front, but all she could spot were brake lights illuminating against the snow-filled backdrop. Moments later the traffic came to a standstill, but Kayleigh wasn't too worried, she kept telling herself that at least she was warm and safe. She shuffled in her seat, in an attempt to make herself comfortable. She sang along to the radio and tapped the steering wheel rhythmically with her finger tips, but the snow didn't abate and after a while she could feel panic starting to rise in her throat. Ironically, she now willed the broadcast to give her the next weather update. Ahead, she could now see, were red lights which reminded her of an airport runway. She looked at her watch. Fifteen minutes went by. The snow continued to fall.

'Beep,' went the radio, followed by an announcement. 'The police report that a wagon has jack-knifed on Manchester Road, causing a collision with a bus. Emergency services are at the scene and ask for your patience,' said the presenter. 'The advice being given out by the police to all motorists is to travel only if it is absolutely crucial. If you're already out on the road, please drive with the utmost care and don't abandon your vehicle unless it is safe to do so – the gritters and snow ploughs need to get through.'

Kayleigh groaned. 'That's all I need,' she said. But the fact that the gritters were out in force gave her hope.

An hour passed and still there was no movement. Kayleigh looked at her watch again. Cars around her were being abandoned. More and more people appeared to be parking up and risking finishing their journey on foot. According to the radio, community centres and churches were being opened to accommodate those in trouble. But that was only for old people, she told herself. *'I'm stuck on Manchester Road, listening to the radio updates,'* she texted Matt. Her phone bleeped. The battery was low.

'I'm at Dave's.'

'Great,' she sighed. *'I might as well try and get home if you're not going to be there,'* she texted.

'Whatever,' he texted back.

Tears welled up in her eyes. Wasn't she more important than his stupid friend and the childish computer games she knew they would be enjoying, sat in a nice warm flat?

The snow was relentless. Her mind was set, she would stay put, even if that meant sleeping in her car. She watched another stream of people walk past after abandoning their vehicles. As time went by, the amount of people passing dwindled and it was only the occasional lonely, snowman-like figure that she saw. She felt alone and began to question her earlier decision. Maybe she should have tagged along with the crowd? The stretch of road she was on had no street lighting and the snow made the night feel eerie as evening quickly turned to dark. There were no houses nearby, but she had passed a couple of cottages set back from the road, close to where she had once dropped Mavis Beanland off. All but one had been in darkness and she assumed that the occupants of the others were stranded elsewhere. Maybe the house with the light on was Mavis's home and she had decided to not attempt the train journey to her sister's after all and the gritter man had dropped her off at home? Kayleigh's spirits rose for a moment, but a sudden bang on the passenger door made her jump. She could see a face squashed up against the window and she quickly hit the button to lock the doors. She grabbed her phone and turned the radio down. She could hear a man's voice laughing, shouting and singing.

'You in there Kay? It's Donny. No mistaking your car, love,' he said. Her heart missed a beat, but she sighed with relief. She opened the window a little, but the strong smell of whisky on his breath hit her. She could see a young lad behind him, who took a quick swig out of a bottle and grimaced before passing it back over Donny's shoulder.

'What the hell are you doing here?' she said through clenched teeth.

'Had to abandon the scooter in town,' he said, shouting against the wind.

'Yes, I saw it.'

'Come with us, we'll see you get home, won't we mate?' he added.

'I'd rather stick pins in my eyes,' she said quietly. 'Go away.'

'What did you say?' he yelled, bending down closer.

'I'll chance my luck in my nice warm car, thank you,' she smiled sweetly.

'Whatever,' he said, swaying in the wind. 'Is that all men could say, whatever?' she fumed, reaching to wind the window up. She heard what sounded like a man's gruff warning bellow in the distance and Donny shrugged his shoulders at her. 'Fuck off!' he called over his shoulder. His friend scarpered.

'Are you lonesome tonight...' she heard Donny singing at the top of his voice as he wandered off into the night laughing like a hyena, oblivious to the cold in his drunken state.

The radio presenter reiterated the advice to motorists to stay in their cars. It was as though he was warning her personally, so isolated did she feel. Her fuel gauge was into the red and her phone beeped low battery for the final time. She fumbled with it in her lap, but the battery was dead. Mindful of her predicament, she steered her car into the side of the road and it slid sideways and jolted to a standstill, into the kerb. She turned off the ignition and sighed heavily.

Inside, the car was almost pitch-black. It was heavily blanketed by snow that was getting thicker by the minute. All was silent. Kayleigh flicked on the internal light and scrabbled in her handbag for something to eat, anything, she was starving. 'Ginger Dunkers,' she said, peeling off the wrapper frenziedly and biting into the grainy biscuit. 'Thank you Mavis.' As she watched the snow continue to build, a wave of sheer panic washed over her. Kayleigh opened the window and gulped a breath of fresh air. She rattled the door, trying to open it more than the few inches the snow would allow. She wanted to run, to escape, to be free from this nightmare. Her heart beat so rapidly she thought it would never again be steady. She closed the window to keep out the cold, closed her eyes and tried to control her breathing. Time passed and she felt as if she was going to die, but then the panic began to subside. She looked again at her watch – she was alone, and now she was beginning to feel very frightened too.

Kayleigh tried to settle in her seat. . Leaning against the door, she turned the radio on low and closed her eyes. Surely sleep would come and blot out this night? Resting her head against the window, she could hear the slightest tapping, so soft that she turned the radio off and sat up. Holding her breath, she listened again, counting the seconds. There was no further sound, but she could sense a presence nearby. Kayleigh shook uncontrollably on seeing a shadowy figure through the snow mottled window. When would the guy take no for an answer? She swallowed hard, but to her horror the tapping increased to a knock, then, when she didn't respond, it became more of a thud. She leant away from the door, listening, looking, her muscles tense, her wits alert. Her hands were in fists and her shoulders hunched. She was trapped, snared like an animal. Her mouth was dry as she gasped for breath. Her legs jumped. The knocking came in pulses, getting louder and louder. Scissors, scissors, where were her scissors? She knew it was only a matter of time before he smashed the window.

Chapter 2

'Like a cuppa? What about a biscuit, love? I bet you're famished.' Kayleigh heard a man's voice against the billowing wind. She wound the car window down as far as it would go, but it still only gave her a post box sized view of the outside world. The Good Samaritan moved closer. 'I saw the light in your car flicker, so I knew someone was inside,' he said. Breathless, and with her hand to her chest, Kayleigh let her head drop back on the headrest. She closed her eyes as she tried to compose herself. She felt dizzy and nauseous. A dog barked and she looked out but couldn't see it. Did she want a drink and a biscuit? Was the pope a Catholic? she thought to herself, happy to see anyone other than the drunken pair outside. The cold night air and snowflakes that blew in onto her face were welcome. The old man, eye sockets dark and hollow, held out a steaming white tin mug. He grinned, an almost toothless smile.

'Sorry,' she said, trying to open the door. 'The window won't open any further either...' The interior light burst into life. The man bent down and leant into her car. She blinked as her eyes reacted to the unaccustomed brightness and she saw him reach into his pocket and retrieve a much coveted Kit Kat.

'What a mess, I live in a cottage down the road, the one with the carriage lamp. See, down yonder? Can I get you anything?'

'No thanks mister, I'll be fine,' Kayleigh said. 'It's very kind of you.' Her hands were still shaking. 'You don't happen to know a Mavis Beanland though, do you?'

'Yes,' he said. 'Known her for years, she lives down there.'

'Oh,' she said, with a downcast look. 'She's a client, a friend of mine. If only she was home.'

'Been watching the cars out here for hours in this horrible weather and thought if there was anyone in them they must be frozen by now.'

Kayleigh looked up. He was wearing a balaclava, which only showed a little of the front of his pinched, frail face, which was wet and weatherworn. His nose was red and cheeks were grey, he looked cold.

'On your own?'

Kayleigh nodded.

'Warm enough?'

She hesitated then, nodded again.

'Sure?' he said.

Kayleigh shuffled in her seat and pulled her little fur jacket around her tight. 'I'll be fine, thanks,' she said, gulping down what remained of the tepid beverage. He took the empty mug from her. 'Thank you,' she said.

'Think on. If you need anything, don't stick fast,' he said, 'you're welcome to come back to our house.'

'That's very kind of you, I'll bear it in mind, but for the time being I think I'll sit tight, thanks. Who knows with the snow ploughs and gritters out, I might get to my boyfriend's after all,' she said half-heartedly.

'He's a lucky lad,' he said, as he left. 'Tarra for now.'

Kayleigh locked the car door. Her seat was damp with the sleet that had sneaked in and the car felt dark and twice as lonely now her visitor had gone. She tore off the biscuit wrapper and peeled the thin tin foil from the two fingers. Kit Kats had been her Dad's favourites. When she was little, they used to race to see who could eat the chocolate off first before eating the wafer underneath. She smiled at the thought as she nibbled at the now chocolate-free wafers. In among the tunes being played on the radio, the broadcaster continued praising people for doing just what the elderly man had done for her. 'Local heroes,' he was calling them. Then he asked, 'Why do we only seem to help our fellow man in adversity, and at any other time we are too busy to even acknowledge each other?' Kayleigh nodded in agreement. It was true. At least now she knew she had an alternative place to go if she felt the need. And he knew Mavis, it somehow eased her mind.

She was refreshed after the nourishment but felt tired and irritable. A friendly face and a warm house were becoming more appealing by the minute. Maybe she could just wait at their house until morning and then try to get home?

She leaned forward, screwed up her eyes and tried to see anything in the darkness outside. The wind had created snowdrifts like big sand dunes against her car. She switched the windscreen wipers on, but in seconds the windscreen was covered in snow again and again. The interior of her car was beginning to feel more and more like a tomb.

She picked up her mobile and growled at the black screen before flinging it onto the floor. 'Thanks a bunch for nothing,' she said. A suffocating feeling of panic rose within her. Swiftly she turned up the radio, 'White Wednesday,' the presenter was saying, and he promised to play music to 'soothe the nerves'. She felt nauseous again, hot and anxious. She had to get out! She closed her eyes and controlled her breathing, and must have drifted off to sleep. When Kayleigh awoke, the radio was announcing the news at ten. Her hands felt wet and clammy, her mouth dry. She could just about see through one side window – the snow was still falling. She switched on the engine and turned on the wipers, but they were useless against the weight of snow that had built up upon the windscreen and just made a dragging, droning noise. She wound her window down slightly to peer out, and a portion of snow fell into her lap. Even in the darkness, she could see the snow had got considerably deeper. Her door wouldn't open at all now and once again panic set in. She really had to get out. Sliding to the passenger seat enabled her to open the door, was it enough to squeeze out? There was no way was she going to be driving anywhere soon and she didn't relish sitting in the car alone all night. Worried that she would be trapped if she stayed there any longer, Kayleigh grabbed her bag to flee. But getting out of the car was no mean feat; she clawed the snow with her bare hands and managed to open the car door wide enough to allow her to alight, albeit with great difficulty.

Stumbling out of the vehicle her legs felt like jelly, and climbing up on the snow drift to shut the door she fell awkwardly onto the top of the door. The pressure on her chest winded her. She turned with difficulty and locked the car door, rubbing her chest frantically. Darn it, no doubt she'd have a bruise there tomorrow. What on earth was she going to look like? The wind took her breath away. 'You can do it, it's not far,' she said, gasping for breath. She put her head down and strode out as best she could. Her feet, that had dried enough to feel only slightly damp, were quickly sodden again as snow came over the top of her boots and melted against the warmth of her legs. Within a few yards the pain of the cold was fierce, but all she could think about was the promise of sanctuary.

Eventually, she saw a snow laden roof and central chimney-stack that billowed smoke. She reached the gate, looked over the snow packed thorn hedge and slid the bolt. A carriage lamp was lit on the outside wall next to the lattice window of the porch. The path had been cleared and grit had been spread on the flagstones. She walked up to the door and saw icicles hung from the gutter. Keyleigh rapped on the door. She turned, rubbed her hands together, blew on them to warm them and looked about her, but she was surrounded by flake-filled air, which didn't allow her to see beyond a few feet back into the garden. Beyond the house she barely made out a building, a garage or a shed perhaps. She waited, but there was no answer. She tried the handle. The porch door was open so she let herself in. She knocked on the interior door, but still no one answered. She tried the handle and again it was open.

'Hello,' she called. 'Hello, is there anyone there?'

She could hear a shuffling noise from within. The hallway was lit by a shadeless bulb hanging from the ceiling. Unaccustomed to the brightness, Kayleigh screwed up her eyes. She could hear a dog woofing and after a few seconds she saw an old lady with irons on her legs making her way down the darkened corridor towards her. 'Tess,' she said, 'for goodness sake gal, give it a rest won't you? Come on lass, in from the cold,' she said, wiping her very red nose with a handkerchief and stuffing it in her apron pocket. Kayleigh stepped over the threshold into the warmth of the stranger's home.

'I am so sorry to bother you. I think I might have the wrong house. A man came to my car with a warm drink and said to come up here if I needed anything. I thought this might be his...'

'That'd have been Norris. Come in, I'm pleased to see you,' she said in a rasping voice, as though she had been suffering with a heavy cold. She coughed and Kayleigh had to smother a laugh as the old lady caught her false teeth in her hanky before pushing them back into place in her mouth. She ushered her visitor inside, and as she did so Kayleigh took stock of the bland looking woman with a curious waxy pallor and bright red rosy cheeks who had a hole in her slipper where her big toe peeped through. Deep furrows ran from her nose to the angles of her mouth and an ill-fitting wig was cocked to one side of her head. Crossing the hall, the woman opened the door and walked in to a room, beckoning Kayleigh to follow.

Kayleigh's first impression was of warmth and shadows. Tess greeted her with a wagging tail and eager old eyes.

'Down.' the old lady commanded in a tone which made Kayleigh jump and the dog drop instantly to the wooden floor with a thump. Kayleigh bent to stroke the animal. 'Oh, no, don't, she's fine,' she said. 'Bless her. I bet she, nor you, expected visitors at this time of night.'

'I'm always glad of visitors. Come on in front of the fire and warm youself,' she said. 'I'll get you a towel.'

'The man, Norris, said my friend Mavis Beanland lived near. Maybe you know her?' Kayleigh called after her, but her words had fallen on deaf ears.

Well at least there was one thing – now she had made the decision to find shelter she wasn't going to be a victim to the weather any more.

The humidity in the lounge reminded Kayleigh of walking into a sauna at her gym when someone had just thrown water over the coals. She perched precariously on the corner of the settee and loosened her clothing. Cushions, books and a pipe lay about and the place seemed absent of any feminine fuss. The musty smell of the cottage made her think of a recent visit to Sibden Hall, with the aroma of medical ointment. Kayleigh stood and stared into dancing flames of the roaring wood fire, mesmerised. The deep, penetrating heat and crackling roar soothed her and on feeling her face burning she sat back down and sank into the velvet cushion of the suite. She drew in her legs to sit up straight. The whole room told of a man's world and as she turned to the shelf next to her she read the titles of books of culture and travel. It reminded her of her grandparent's 'best room', dated and worn but homely. Tess was now contentedly stretched out in front of the tiled hearth. Kayleigh wondered where Norris was, as he must have just knocked his pipe out on the hearth, the red ash had fallen and was still smouldering there. Looking down at the dog in the firelight, she could see her coat was matted and patchy and as she yawned Kayleigh saw signs of ageing in her almost toothless mouth; reminding her of the dog's owner. Kayleigh regarded her surroundings, lit only by the fire and an old standard lamp in the back corner near the dresser and heard a faint ring as if a phone had just been put on a receiver.

It was a while before her host returned. 'Too hot for you?' the old lady said, handing her a threadbare, large old discoloured towel that smelt of mildew. Kayleigh shook her head and smiled into the firelight. 'No, it's lovely, thank you.'

'Brandy, it'll warm you,' the old woman said, thrusting a rose coloured plastic tumbler into her hand. Kayleigh sipped from it, screwing up her nose as she did so. 'Whoa,' she said, coughing fitfully. If age told the strength of the liquor, then this was as old as the lady offering it. Unspeaking, the woman pointed to Kayleigh's boots and she stood and watched Kayleigh slip them off her feet. She wished she had a change of footwear and once again Mavis's words of wisdom came back to haunt her. She lifted her head and caught the old lady giving her a hard stare.

'You know my friend, Mavis Beanland?' Kayleigh asked.

'Yes, I do,' she said.

'Maybe you could get word to her I'm here? She might have got to her sister's, but she might not.'

'Not tonight my girl, it's far too late. Tomorrow?' she said more kindly.

Kayleigh nodded and stared at the fire before looking back up at the old woman. 'Do you have a telephone that I could use please? So that I can let my mum and Matt know I'm okay,' she asked. 'They'll be worried,' she added as a way of explanation to the blank response as she rubbed her feet with the towel.

'I thought the same but the lines are down, I've just checked,' the woman said, rolling her eyes before turning unsteadily in her leg irons and disappearing out of the room with Kayleigh's boots. 'I'll get these dried by the Aga in the kitchen,' she called in her wake.

The house was quiet and still except for the occasional log crackling on the fire. Kayleigh couldn't hear a radio or see a television. Time passed and there was no sign of the old woman or Norris. All there was to do was gaze into the fire. She felt sleepy. Just as she was about to lay her head on the arm of the sofa and close her eyes, the old man who had come to her aid hobbled into the room carrying a plate in his hand and a bottle under his arm. He wore a big baggy jumper with thick cord trousers. Kayleigh smiled and stood to greet him.

'Now then lass. You must be famished,' he said, cheerily.

'Norris! That's very kind of you,' she said. 'I really don't want to be nuisance. I'm just so grateful to you and your...,' said Kayleigh.

'Nelly,' Norris said, pushing the plate towards her. The firelight caught his perspiring brow and as he bent down Kayleigh could see that he too was wearing a wig – and not a very good one at that. 'Do you want some cake?,' he said, with a smile. 'It's homemade' He pointed to Kayleigh's glass. She held it out and he filled it to the brim. 'I'll get you a blanket, then you best settle down for the night.'

Kayleigh stared at him with gritty eyes. 'That's very kind,' she said eventually, not knowing whether to laugh or cry at the predicament she found herself in and the peculiar couple she had unwittingly come across.

Kayleigh hadn't realised just hungry she was until she looked down at the thick slab of the Yorkshire gingerbread. She picked it up with both hands and took a huge bite. 'Urgh!' she said, choking. 'What on earth?' she said spitting the contents of her mouth out onto her hand. It tasted of nothing but fat and salt and there was a whole egg baked in the middle. She picked up her glass and drank quickly in an attempt to wash away the flavour. The drink was sharp, strong and hit the back of her throat. It reminded her of the first time Matt had introduced her to tequila shots. He told her to lick the salt from the back of her hand and throw the drink to the back of her throat. She had been very quickly wasted that night and he had to carry her home. No time to reminisce, she told herself, shaking her head to clear the fog inside. She looked around. The dog lifted its head. Should she give the rest of it to her or throw it on the back of the fire?

The food hissed and sizzled. The old man hobbled back into the room and put a brown blanket at her side before going directly to the fire and poking it aimlessly. 'That'll help burn it,' he said.

'Oh no,' she groaned. He turned to look at her and she felt her face flush crimson. She grimaced. Whether he noticed the burning food or not he didn't say, but he threw a large log on the fire that caused smoke to billow back into the room.

'That should keep you warm. A log of cedar will burn 'til the morning. Happen the weather will have 'baited by then. Is there anything else I can get you before I turn in?'

'Perhaps I could use your bathroom?' she said, tentatively.

'Follow me,' he said. 'It's down the hallway,' Kayleigh followed him down the dimly lit narrow hallway in the direction he pointed, running her hand on the embossed wallpaper. Feeling disorientated. she had to swerve to miss the old fashioned phone that featured on the wall and in doing so grabbed the lead that dangled aimlessly to the floor. Guess there was no point in it being plugged in if it wasn't working, she thought.

'It's to your right,' the old man said. Luckily, there was a handrail along the wall. Gratefully, she held it as she passed the old man. Shyly she looked down at the floor and at the hole in his slipper where his toe peeped through. She couldn't help but smile to herself.

'You'll find your way back?' he said.

She nodded. 'Night,' she said, 'and ... and thanks for everything.'

Norris grunted.

Stepping into the toilet, she closed the door behind her. The room was so cold she looked around for a gap in the wall to the outside. There was no lock. She could hear creaking floorboards outside. Was he still there? No, she had watched too many films with Matt, that was her trouble.

The room was so small that she was able to sit on the toilet and place her foot against the door. The door was made up of large random width vertical planks, she noted. Flushing the toilet, the cistern made enough noise to disturb the dead. 'Damn it,' she said as her sleeve caught on the head-high chain. She yanked her arm free. Opening the door to the dimly lit corridor and seeing the coast was clear, she tiptoed back to the lounge and closed the door behind her, before taking her place again on the sofa in front of the fire. Finishing the drink she had been given, she sighed. 'Waste not, want not,' she said, raising her glass to Tess, and pulled the blanket up under her armpits. If the brandy made her sleep, then sooner it would be morning and she could be on her way. Her eyes were heavy in minutes and she snuggled up, turned and looked into the flames of the fire that were faintly soothing. Funny how other people lived, wasn't it?

Kayleigh lay soundless and as her limbs relaxed, her eyes began to close and she felt her shoulders droop. She heard Tess get to her feet and walk towards her, and Kayleigh looked directly into her wide, dark eyes. Tess paused for a few moments as if waiting for permission before jumping up to sit upright in Kayleigh's curves. The touch of the dog's tongue on her hand was comforting and she stroked the animal's head and rubbed the back of her ears, whispering soothingly. Tess circled and pawed the blanket before moaning and lying as close to Kayleigh as she could get, setting down eventually with a big sigh. Kayleigh placed an arm around her and gave her a fleeting hug and in turn the dog put up her muzzle and licked under her chin, groaning again. Suddenly, the dog's ears flew up and her head was erect and alert. There was an almighty thud. Kayleigh sat bolt upright.

'What the hell was that?' she said out loud. Tess growled,

then flew off the sofa and under the table whimpering loudly.

'Hello, who's there?' she called, pulling the blanket up tightly to her face. Was it the wind? No, the motive force was human.

At the opening of the door, Kayleigh let rip a piercing scream.

Chapter 3

The snow continued to fall from dense, heavy clouds, quite unlike any snow Harrowfield had seen in years. Telephone wires were torn down by the weight of the ice and snow fall. Pipes were frozen and public transport was at a standstill. The weather forecasters were warning of more severe weather before there was a thaw. Children and grown-ups alike spent dawn 'til dusk sledding down the snow covered steep hills Yorkshire is known for, and within days normality started to resume. The main routes were the first to be passable with care. The majority of white snow, on the main roads, turned hour by hour to a dirty black slush. The gritters' work wasn't done, as they continued to spread sand and rock salt to keep the ice at bay at night and remove the heaps of solid snow with their ploughs during the day.

Marlene had been trying to contact Kayleigh all morning via her mobile phone and in frustration rang the landline at her home. The shop had been closed long enough. The phone was answered immediately. 'Hello,' said a hesitant voice.

'Kim, its Marlene, how are you? ' she said brightly.

'Oh, I'm alright. Better than the weather. Worst we've had for twenty years, or so they're saying on the news.'

'Yeah, and the Council still doesn't deal with it any better, do they? There has been as much disruption now as there was back then, if my memory serves me right. The reason why I'm ringing is to let Kayleigh know that I'm opening the salon tomorrow. I'm sure she'll be just as glad to get back to work as me.'

'Well, I'll tell her when I speak to her, but to be honest you're the first person to get through on this line for a week. I'd almost forgotten what the sound of the phone ringing was like; it's been as dead as a doornail since the afternoon of the heavy snowfall and I haven't heard a peep from our Kayleigh since she left a message on the answering machine to say she was heading to Matt's. I'll try and get hold of her now and pass your message on.'

'Her mobile's dead, that's why I rang you,' replied Marlene.

'Oh dear, her battery is probably flat by now. Matt hasn't a landline, I haven't a mobile. What're we like?' Kim paused for a moment and stroked her chin, deep in thought. 'I'll see if I can find Matt's number and give him a ring,' she said.

Putting the phone on its cradle, Kim Harwood headed up the stairs to Kayleigh's bedroom and set about searching for her address book. Eventually, after fumbling under the sweet papers, fashion magazines and used post it notes, she found it in her bedside cabinet. There was no reference to his phone number under 'M' for Matt or 'P' for Prentice, so sitting down on her daughter's bed she started at the beginning and patiently fingered through the book systematically. 'B for boyfriend,' she said with a sigh. 'I should have known that of our Kayleigh.'

It took a few rings before the phone was answered. Matt's voice caught in his throat and the words that came out were a croak. 'Hell ... o?'

'Matt, is that you?' said Kim. 'You sound terrible. Don't bother speaking, just put our Kayleigh on, will you?'

'Sor ...ry? Kay ... leigh's not here. I haven't seen or heard from her since last Wednesday.' Matt said before he sneezed loudly.

Kim's heart leapt into her mouth. She sat down on the nearest chair and cleared her throat. 'You haven't heard from her?' Kim felt her stomach clench. 'Where is she then?' she faltered. 'I thought she was with you,' she said, her voice rising.

'I thought she was at home,' he said, straining his voice.

'Last time she texted me, she said she was stuck on the Manchester Road,' Matt said.

'Oh my God, I'm calling the police. What's happened to her? We need to find her. I'll come pick you up. We'll go to Manchester Road,' said Kim, slamming the phone down before he could answer.

Kim Harwood made a 999 call in a fever of impatience. She gazed around the room at the pictures of Kayleigh and, snatching a photograph off the sideboard, she held it tight. Unchecked tears rolled down her cheeks and she found it hard to talk when the telephone was answered at the other end. 'It's Kayleigh, my daughter,' she said. 'She's missing.'

The person taking the details asked her what seemed to Kim to be pointless questions. 'Just find her. You've got to find her,' she said hysterically.

'Mrs Harwood,' said the operator with an air of impatience. 'Please try and calm yourself. If you could cooperate by getting your daughter's relevant motor documents for us and ring back on the non-emergency number 0845 6060606 when you are in possession of them, that would be very useful. This line is for emergencies only.'

'But, this is an emergency. Wait there, I'll go get them.'

'No please, ring back on the number I gave you when you have them to hand,' said the woman firmly, before abruptly ending their conversation.

Kim listened to the dialling tone in astonishment. She took a deep breath as she felt panic surge within her. Her legs shook as she stumbled up the steps, and with fumbling hands she rummaged through her daughter's drawer once more. Once the details were in her grasp, she picked up the phone and with trembling fingers dialled the number she had been given.

'How many pink Kas can there be?' she screamed at the operator.

'The car's registration number please, Mrs Harwood?' the police civilian staff member said calmly.

'S241 AWW. Can you just get someone to check Manchester Road please? That was the last place we believe she was.'

This time the person at the other end of the phone was more sympathetic and tried to reassure her that Police 4x4 vehicles had patrolled the area, especially the main routes along with the AA, to ensure people were not stranded in their cars for excessive periods. 'It highly unlikely that your daughter is still in the car, but in a place of safety,' he said. 'Many shelters are still open. I'll send out a message now to all patrol cars to check in the vicinity of Manchester Road for you and locate her vehicle if it's there. Try not to worry.'

Kim shuddered as goose bumps rose all over her body.

'I'm afraid I'm going to have to ask you to come into the police station, Mrs Harwood, to file a missing person report for your daughter. It would be really helpful if you could bring along an up-to-date photograph of Kayleigh too.'

Kim silently nodded as she searched the face of her daughter on her driving licence. 'Where are you?' she whispered.

'Mrs Harwood?'

'Huh?'

'It would be most helpful if you could do that as soon as possible.'

'Yes, yes of course.'

'And your phone number Mrs Harwood is?'

'01422 ... 8831976.'

'Your mobile number please, Mrs Harwood?'

'I don't have one... but Matt, her boyfriend, does and he will be with me.'

'And it is?'

'It's er... 08927405210.'

Kim hadn't gained the comfort from the call to the police that she had expected. If Kayleigh had got out of the car and started walking in the extreme weather conditions, who knows what had become of her? She shivered again. That didn't bear thinking about.

Racing to the door, she snatched the photo of Kayleigh from the chair where she had left it. It was the most recent image of her daughter, taken at college. In a panic, she set off to Matt's flat. The roads were passable, but sleet was falling and the roads were very slippery. Her mind was not on her driving and although the journey took twenty minutes, drawing up outside his home, she realised she didn't remember driving through one traffic light or crossing a single road junction. Kim impatiently sounded the car horn. Time was of the essence if they were to find Kayleigh's car before darkness fell. Her heart raced until she felt dizzy and she feared her anxiety might be out of control. Kim's skin was burning. Her mind screamed, yet her voice was silent. After waiting a few moments and with no sign of Matt, she blasted the horn again. 'Come on, come on, come on,' she screamed. Rhythmically, she tapped the steering wheel.

Matt looked pale and dishevelled as he emerged from the flat's entrance. Donning his hoodie, he stumbled unsteadily towards the car. His long, unkempt, dark curly hair was draped over his eyes in a long fringe and his jeans hung off his almost skeletal frame. 'Fashion?' she tutted, but Kayleigh loved every bone in his body, and that was all that mattered.

'Where's your coat?' she snapped. 'Do you want to catch your death?' He looked at her blankly and proceeded to put on his seatbelt.

'You smell like a brewery,' said Kim, looking in her rear-view mirror.

'Sorry,' he sniffled.

'Where the hell is she?' Kim said, signalling to pull out.

'I thought she was with you,' he said.

'What were you thinking, not getting in touch with her before now? You've never been out of touch for a whole week since you've been going out,' Kim snapped, remembering the hours her daughter spent on the phone to him on the few occasions they weren't together.

Matt shook his head and shrugged his shoulders.

'Well?'

'I've been ill.'

Kim cocked her head and looked at him out of the corner of her eyes.

'Okay, I thought she had the hump with me. She could've rung me?'

'Why would she have the hump with you?'

'She asked if she could come to mine. I said I was at Dave's. Why didn't you ring her anyway?'

'Our phone's been out of order. If Marlene hadn't rang me, I wouldn't have known it was working today. You know I don't have a mobile. Forget it! It's no good arguing, we need to find her.'

Chapter 4

Kim and Matt were driving slowly down the Manchester Road when they saw a stationary police car with its hazard lights flashing. 'Kayleigh's car,' screamed Kim, slamming on the brakes as she drew in behind it. The pair jumped out and bounded towards the uniformed police officer who stood next to the coveted pink Ka.

'It's my daughter's,' she said, as her eyes frantically searched for a sign of Kayleigh inside.

'PC Alan Hughes, Mrs ...'

'Harwood,' she said, disregarding the officer and leaning forward, her hands cupped around her eyes in an attempt to peer through the windows.

'Please,' he said, holding out an arm to stop her from touching the car. Kim moved back as if she'd been burned. 'Don't,' he said. 'It might have to be fingerprinted at some stage.'

'Fingerprinted? Why?' she said raising her voice. PC Hughes saw her soft hazel eyes were full of anxiety.

'I know this is very hard Mrs Harwood, but please try to stay calm. The vehicle is secure and it appears that it's been parked as near as your daughter could probably get it to the kerb, under the circumstances,' he said 'Everything seems to suggest that your daughter left it here.'

Matt had his face firmly squashed to the passenger door window. PC Alan Hughes sighed.

'Her mobile, it's there in the foot well,' shouted Matt.

'I said don't... touch the vehicle, sir,' the officer said putting his gloved hand to his brow. 'And you are, sir?' he demanded, taking out his pocket book.

'Matt, Kayleigh's boyfriend,' said Kim.

'Matt what sir?'

'Matt Prentice, why?'

'So when I'm filling out my report I can say who touched the vehicle,' he said in an accusing tone. 'I'll need your fingerprints for elimination.'

'Look Constable, I know Kayleigh and she wouldn't have left her mobile phone if she left the car of her own accord,' Kim said, as she did a three hundred and sixty degree scan of the area.

'Unless her battery was flat,' Matt said thoughtfully.

'If she did leave the vehicle to set off walking, which way do you think your daughter would go? Or did she get a lift?'

'No,' said Matt.

'If someone picked her up they would have needed a four by four and they'd still have struggled to get through up here, that night,' said the officer. 'It's hardly passable now.'

'God, where is she?' Kim said, her teeth chattering. PC Hughes couldn't tell if it was with the shock, fear, or cold.

'Do you know if she knows anyone around here?' said the officer.

'No,' Matt and Kim said, shaking their heads in unison.

'What was she wearing when you last saw her?' PC Alan Hughes said, his pen hovering over a clean page of his pocket notebook.

'She left the house to go to work. Her new boots, a skirt and her white fur jacket,' said Kim. 'You know what young girls are like, even if the weather is bad they still wear next to nothing.'

'I do indeed,' the officer said nodding in agreement. 'I have a teenage daughter myself.'

'I was told to take a recent photo of Kayleigh to the police station.'

'That's a good idea, we can get it circulated. By the sound of it, your daughter wasn't dressed for the weather,' the constable said pensively. 'So it's highly unlikely she would have set off walking far in the conditions that night. I'll have a walk around the immediate area and make some house to house enquiries. There are only a few properties within walking distance when you reach this part of Manchester Road. It's bleak up here at the best of times.'

Kim and Matt walked forlornly up and down the road for a while, looking over the dry stone walls and into the fields but their efforts were futile. They passed PC Hughes, who was walking up the path of the first property he had come upon, as they headed in the car for the police station.

The nearest house was an obvious starting point to the officer and the occupants of Ivy Cottage would be the subject of his first inquiry. He opened the porch door and stepped inside, but before he could rap the door knocker a dog barked from within and the door was opened.

'Sorry to trouble you madam,' said PC Alan Hughes. 'I'm just making enquiries into the owners of abandoned cars on the roadside.' The woman nodded her head. 'There's a pink

Ka parked further up the road and there are concerns for the driver, who hasn't been seen since the 7th January.'

'Down!' the old lady commanded of the Collie who dropped to the floor. 'Ee lad, you must be perished. Would you like to come in out of the cold and have a brew?'

'Thank you, that's very good of you madam,' he said.

'Put wood in't ole after y' then.'

'Don't you lock your door madam?' he said following the old lady down the corridor.

'They'd have to bring it in to thieve it,' she laughed like a drain.

'Yes, quite,' PC Hughes said as he moved to the side of the light bulb that hung low from the heavily nicotine-stained ceiling. He took off his hat. 'A cuppa tea would be very welcome, thank you,' he said, wiping his hands on his handkerchief as she showed him into the lounge.

The room housed a welcoming fire and he stood admiringly at the newly cut wood piled against an old fireback. The dancing flames reflected off the stripes on his luminous jacket. As he looked around the room, he could see that the wall paper had been there for a generation, but the dust was forgotten as he walked around to survey the antiques and the china in the dresser. As he stood warming his hands, the old lady reappeared with a cup and saucer. Gingerly, and rattling it in shaking hands, she passed it to PC Hughes without a drop spilt.

'Many of them stuck?' she asked the constable, nodding her head towards the outside.

'Yes, there're a few cars still there.'

'We were warned early enough about it,' she said, shaking her head wisely. 'The last time it were so bad was, let me see,' she said pulling on a hair or two on her chin. 'It must be over twenty years ago. Same thing happened then, it came down just as quick and fast that they were stood on the snowdrifts with their arms resting on the top of that lamp posts out there.'

'You haven't got a television?'

'I don't bother, with that or newspapers. There's nothing but bad news these days.'

'I agree.' he smiled.

'We've got a young girl missing.'

'Yes, I heard something about that on the radio. Any news?'

'No, sadly nothing. She appears to have vanished into thin

air.'

The old lady nodded her head. 'Doesn't sound good, does it I've been listening out for the updates.'

'Do you live here alone Mrs ...? '

'Call me Nelly, yes it's just us now, isn't it girl?' she said, patting the dog's head.

PC Alan Hughes thanked her for the warm drink as he contemplated his host's frail and transparent face. 'Before I go, I couldn't use your bathroom could I?' he said.

'Down the corridor on the right,' she said with the flick of her wrist in the direction of the closet.

He chuckled to himself as he looked up at the top box cistern, and when he pulled on the chain it made a loud noise.

'Thank you for your hospitality, Nelly,' he said as he shook her bony old hand, and stepped back out into the porch.

'You're more than welcome son. I hope you find her soon.'

'You know what the young 'uns are like today,' he said, standing on the garden path. 'If she's anything like my daughter, she'll probably turn up at her friend's.'

'Make your arms ache when they're young and your heart ache when they grow up,' she said as the top set of dentures fell down and she used her tongue to click them back into place.

PC Hughes walked down the path, tittering to himself. He unbolted the gate, turned to wave to the old woman who stood at the window of the porch and strode out in the direction of next door.

'Don't bother, Mavis's away at her sister's,' Nelly called. 'Don't know when she's back either. She never tells me anything these days.'

'Thanks for that,' said the officer, turning back towards his car. 'You've saved me a journey.'

At Harrowfield Police station, Kim and Matt had almost completed filling in the Missing Persons report form that the front desk officer required of them.

'Is there a possibility that someone she knows could live in the area?' PC Jackie May said.

Matt shook his head and Kim shrugged. 'We've been asked that before, but we don't think so.'

'They don't have to be anyone that she's particularly close to, just someone she might think to take refuge with.'

'I don't know of anyone, but one thing I do know is that if she had stayed over somewhere she would have at least tried to ring me, or Matt.'

'I still live at home Mrs Harwood,' said the constable gently, 'but I don't always ring my mum to let her know if I'm staying over at friends'.'

'But that's just it. It's not just one night, is it? It's been a week and still not a word. We've seen her mobile phone inside her abandoned car, so we know she couldn't use that, but Kayleigh would've found a telephone by now and made contact with one of us if she could. Something's not right. I just know it ...' Kim said, her voice rising as she aired her worst fears, trying desperately to hold back the tears. The officer saw her lip start to tremble and her chin wobble. Tears filled her eyes and began rolling down her cheeks. 'Please find her, please,' Kim begged, grabbing hold of Jackie's hand and holding it tightly. 'You don't understand. You see, since her dad died, she's all I've got. She knows how I fret.' Matt put an arm around her shoulder and hugged Kim tightly.

'Tell you what, why don't I get you both a nice warm drink and I'll try to contact PC Hughes to see if he's got any news for us, eh?' said Jackie kindly. PC May made the call, but it appeared that Kayleigh Harwood had vanished. Call it a police officer's gut instinct, but something didn't feel right to Jackie either. She bit her lip in thought before turning to Kim and Matt.

'I think it's about time we got hold of the Search and Rescue team,' she told them. 'In the meantime, I want you to check with everyone you know, to see if they have heard from her, okay?'

Kim nodded, glad at last that someone was taking her fears seriously, and that she had something to distract her over-active imagination.

'I'll contact you if I get any news and vice-versa, yes?'

Kim nodded again as she wiped her eyes.

PC May patted Kim's hand comfortingly. 'We'll find her, I promise,' she said.

Chapter 5

Twenty four hours passed and there was still no news. Kim had been to the salon to see Marlene, and together she and Matt had rung all the telephone numbers in Kayleigh's address book, but to no avail. A queasy feeling of dread engulfed Matt as he put down his phone on the kitchen table and his dark, deep set eyes met Kim's. He rested his head on top of his folded arms, feeling dizzy and sick. Sweat poured from his brow and the gagging feeling in his throat was still there.

Kim reached out and touched his arm. 'What are we going to do?' she said.

He looked up and gave her the closest thing to a reassuring look he could muster. 'Don't worry, we'll find her – like the police woman said.'

As dawn broke, the search and rescue team started their planned search of the area where Kayleigh's car had been found. The team leaders and their colleagues swept outwards from the vehicle, combing every inch of their predetermined patch. The news spread and civilians from far and wide offered their support.

PC Jackie May understood that Kayleigh wasn't the sort of person that would usually be classed as vulnerable, but there was nothing to suggest that she wanted to disappear either. If there had been an accident, where was her body? The officer was aware that thousands of people went missing every year and some were never found, but she didn't want that to be the case with Kayleigh. She decided to seek the advice of Harrowfield's Criminal Investigation Department (CID). She wondered what their views would be on the facts that she had so far and hoped that they could suggest what she should do next. She was out of her depth.

To Jackie, the CID office had always been intimidating. To the young female, the male dominated arena was like walking into a public house, in the middle of town, at night and alone.

She closed her eyes momentarily as she reached the heavy grey fire door, took a deep breath and raised her hand to knock, then decided otherwise. Taking hold of the door handle, she put her shoulders behind it and walked in. As a rookie, she remembered being shown round the police station and the police officers in plain clothes staring at her from behind their desks had made her feel uncomfortable.

Jackie knew the head of the CID department, Detective Inspector Jack Dylan, by sight. He'd just got married to Jennifer Jones from the admin department and they had had a little girl called Maisy. Their affair had been the talk of the police station at the time – no one thought Dylan, the career detective and hostage negotiator, and Harrowfield's perpetual bachelor, would ever succumb to the proverbial ball and chain. As if thinking about him conjured him up, she spotted Dylan standing at the end of the office, in his shirt sleeves, with his back to her studying a dry wipe board that was full of evidence and drawn links to photographs and minute sheets. Dylan was in his late thirties, she would have a guessed, thick set and around six foot tall. The sort of person you wouldn't want to upset, she thought as he turned around at the sound of the door shutting and glanced at her before continuing with the job in hand. Jackie shivered, pulled herself up to her five foot four inch height and clutched the Misper report for Kayleigh Harwood tightly. Instead of scanning the room, she headed straight down the middle of the desks to where DC Vicky Hardacre sat. Vicky stood up and smiled. Everyone knew Vicky in the nick for her breast implants, which gave her a figure to die for. This was a woman who wasn't intimidated or embarrassed by anyone and Jackie aspired to be just like her one day, as she blushed, a fuchsia shade of pink.

'Hi Jackie, what you got there love? A job for us?' she said.

'She wants to know how much it costs for a boob job like yours,' quipped a chubby bloke with crisp, curly black hair and dark eyes who rested lazily upon one arm on his desk.

Vicky swung round and gave him a slap on the back of his head with the palm of her hand.

'You'll be applying for some dentures if you don't back off,' she said, winking at Jackie. 'Ignore him kid, every office has one.'

Normally at moments like this Jackie would have been praying for the ground to open up and swallow her but to her surprise, she laughed instead. Vicky was cool.

'Come over to my desk, in the corner, we won't be disturbed there mate. Do you fancy a drink? Kettle's just boiled,' she said.

'A coffee would be great, thanks,' she said, shyly. In her experience, detectives told her to go and put the kettle on, they didn't make a drink for her – she was pleasantly surprised.

'Milk, sugar?' Vicky enquired as she spooned the coffee powder out of the jar into two cups.

'Both thanks.' Jackie said.

'Mine's black,' called the detective.

Vicky flashed him her middle finger, 'Ned,' she said. He cocked his head. 'Swivel. Now, what's up love?' she added, smiling as she slid in behind her desk and invited Jackie to sit opposite her.

'Ned?' said Jackie with a frown as she took the mug from Vicky.

'DC Duncan Granger.'

'So why Ned?' she said taking a small sip of her drink.

'Hung like a donkey, or so they say.'

Jackie coughed, took another sip and coughed again mid-swallow, choking on the hot liquid.

'But I wouldn't put it past him starting the rumour himself,' said Vicky, in a loud whisper that DC Granger couldn't help but hear. He flashed her a V sign without lifting his head from the tabloid he was reading.

'Really?' Jackie said wiping the tears from her eyes.

Vicky cocked an eyebrow at the young police officer, who cleared her throat and proceeded to shuffle the papers in her hand.

Jackie cleared her throat. 'I'm concerned about this girl that's gone missing. To be honest, I don't know what else I can do that I haven't done already to try to locate her. Any ideas... I'd be really grateful?' she said, handing Vicky the report.

Vicky sat quietly for a moment or two, taking a mouthful of her coffee as she read the paperwork. Jackie looked around her and her eyes locked in on another man in a suit who sat nearby. She smiled, timidly and he winked at her. She looked quickly away.

'Well, it's certainly a mystery,' Vicky said, scratching her head and gaining Jackie's attention once more. 'Anything else of relevance come in that night?

'Not really, just a male flasher at a house in Harrowfield about tea time.'

'Wonder he didn't freeze his bollocks off,' Vicky laughed. 'You haven't searched her home, her boyfriend's or her workplace yet?'

Jackie shook her head.

'We can't leave anything to chance and we have to be sure about those close to her, or the last person to physically speak to her, before we move on. As the boss would say, we must clear the ground beneath our feet first.' Vicky smiled as she looked in Dylan's direction.

'The rescue teams are out there, so if she is a victim of the weather, they'll find her, I'm confident about that,' said Jackie.

'Good,' Vicky nodded. 'Impressed.'

Jackie sat and listened to the friendly blonde twenty seven year old Detective, who made everything sound so simple.

'I think we had better inform the DI. He likes to be told about anything that CID might be involved in. Have you worked with Dylan before?'

'No, just heard about him,' she said, clasping her hand together tightly in her lap and moving to the edge of her seat. 'He's a bit scary, isn't he?'

Vicky laughed. 'Dylan? Don't you believe all you hear, Dylan's a good boss but he doesn't suffer fools gladly and I suspect it's those who think that he's scary. Work hard, make a good brew,' she said, raising her cup in the air, 'and he'll be putty in your hands. Look, he's just gone in his office. There's no time like the present, let's introduce you to him and see what he has to say about the missing girl.'

'Now?' Jackie gulped. 'You mean just walk in without making an appointment with his secretary?'

'He's a Detective Inspector,' Vicky said, shaking her head as she stood up and walked towards Dylan's office. 'Oh my, you've a lot to learn. CID isn't like uniform. You're treated like real people in here and we don't get any luxuries like secretaries in CID.' Jackie tagged behind, in trepidation. Vicky knocked on Dylan's door and entered without waiting to be invited in, but to Jackie's surprise he looked up from his paperwork, put his pen down and smiled at them.

'Boss, this is PC Jackie May from Harrowfield patrol. She's dealing with a report of an eighteen year old female Misper who disappeared on White Wednesday.' Dylan held out his hand and invited them to sit opposite him.

'Okay, tell me what you know PC May,' he said. Dylan was still smiling, and there was something about his smile that made her feel at ease. The atmosphere was relaxed and she felt comfortable as she went through the circumstances of the case.

'Very thorough and concise,' Dylan said. 'So what else do you think we can do?'

Jackie's mouth was dry and as she wriggled in her seat she looked sideways at Vicky for support.

'We thought perhaps we should search the home, the boyfriend's flat and her work place to confirm that she isn't in any of the obvious places first,' Vicky said.

'Well we should be able to do that with consent, I would have thought, and if anyone objects, we'll deal with that when it arises,' said Dylan, slamming the palms of his hands on his desk as he stood. 'How would you like to come and work with us for a few days in plain clothes Jackie... that's if your Sergeant will allow it?'

'Would I, Sir?' she said, her eyes wide with excitement.

'I'll speak to him boss,' Vicky said.

'Okay, keep me posted. I don't like it when young girls go missing. Vicky, any problems with Jackie's Sergeant let me know, because technically this is still a Uniform job.'

'Don't worry boss, I'll use my charm,' she said with a wink.

'That's what worries me,' Dylan replied as he followed them to the door.

'Thank you, sir,' Jackie said as she stopped and looked up at him.

'You're more than welcome,' Dylan said. 'Thank you for bringing the matter to our attention.'

'Come on. Let's put your Sarg under pressure, he'll be no match for us both,' Vicky said as she marched through the CID office like a woman on a mission.

'Dylan's nice, isn't he?' said Jackie running behind Vicky to keep up.

'Told you he was,' she said, then seeing the look on Jackie's face, like a schoolgirl with a crush, Vicky raised her eyes to the ceiling. 'Oh, no not again,' she said with a groan.

Chapter 6

Dylan passed Kayleigh Harwood's misper details to Claire Rose in the press office. His approach was to ask Kayleigh to make contact, as well as appealing for anyone who had seen her, or who was in the area of Manchester Road on White Wednesday.

Virginia Mason, Editor of the Harrowfield Courier, was soon on the phone to him, so he knew the appeal had gone out directly. 'What else can you tell me Jack?'

Dylan smiled. The direct approach of the young, bubbly brunette, always made him smile.

'Well, while there are obvious concerns for her welfare, V,' he said. 'There could be a legitimate reason for a young girl not contacting family or friends. However, because of the horrendous weather conditions on that night, we are obviously anxious about her safety. Anyone in the area will see we have search and rescue teams combing the surrounding locality where her car was found.'

'Do you suspect she's been abducted... murdered?' Virginia said.

'Kayleigh appears to be a sensible girl, but at the moment her disappearance is unexplained. There's not a lot more I can tell you. I want to hear from anyone who was in the area last Wednesday, the 7th January, so if you can make the appeal in the Harrowfield Courier for us, that would be a start.'

Dylan was always careful not to use the past tense when talking about a misper. It could suggest that he believed them already dead, and when he gave an appeal like this, he hoped with all his being that the missing person was still alive. He waited for further calls from the press. All the editors wanted a headline, that's what sold their newspaper and kept their journalists in work. He was always grateful for their support – and luckily for Dylan, the editors of today were journalists with whom he had been brought up in his early days in the job.

Vicky had managed to get Jackie May attached to CID for a few days. But she'd be weekend off before having to return for their nightshift cover. The two returned to inform Dylan.

'I've given the incident some thought and I'm going to let you have Ned Granger and DC Andy Wormald to assist you.'

Dylan told the pair. 'Let's see if we can get any indications as to what's happened to Kayleigh. I'll speak to you in a bit, but first I have to make a few phone calls.'

'Don't look so worried kid, you'll be fine. Stick with me and I'll show you the world,' Vicky said, placing an arm around Jackie's shoulders and giving her a motherly hug.

Jackie smiled, yet to be convinced. She would be sticking to Vicky like superglue.

Dylan walked into the general office and gave the pair a list of enquiries that needed to be carried out, with a request for an ongoing log to be kept of what was being done by whom and when.

'I want to ensure enquiries into Kayleigh's disappearance are not only diligent but documented. Let Ned and Andy go and talk to her employer and search the hairdresser's. Tell them I want names and addresses of her customers. We're going to have to speak to them at some point. You two, go to Mrs Harwood's house and gather what you can intelligence wise from her, will you? We'll need something of Kayleigh's that we can get a DNA profile from.' Dylan's eyebrows knitted together in a scowl. 'You know the sort of thing, hairbrush, toothbrush etcetera. Then when you get back, I want you two to research the list of customers that the lads have obtained, and I want them to go see the boyfriend and rattle his cage, see what drops out, and make sure she isn't there. Any questions?'

They shook their heads. 'No, seems straightforward.'

'Let's get her found – and don't forget. Keep me updated,' he said, already heading back to his office.

Dylan stopped and turned on his heels at his door, 'In the meantime, if the search and rescue or their body dog turns anything up, I'll let you know.'

'Cheers, boss,' said Vicky.

Jackie smiled.

Detectives Andy Wormald and Ned Granger were directed to the hairdressing salon by force control. Marlene made them a cup of coffee before asking if they minded waiting while she combed out her elderly client's curls.

The two men sat at the dryer bank next to the window.

Marlene Schofield was a slim woman in her thirties. Dressed in a black roll neck jumper, shorter than knee length skirt and high heeled black patent court shoes, her burgundy hair was cut in a neat, short bob. Ned nodded in her direction and winked at Andy. 'Drink on a stick?' he said with a wink.

'Are you for real?' Andy whispered. 'She's way out of your league.'

'I'm sorry about that,' Marlene said apologetically, when she'd seen her customer through the door. She picked up a book from the desk, pulled up a chair and sat opposite the detectives. 'But they still expect their hair doing, no matter what's happening.' She crossed her legs, appearing slightly flustered as she opened the appointment book and ran her finger down a list of clients. 'I thought she hadn't rung me because she wanted time off with Matt. I understand, to a point,' she said, looking at the detectives, her head on one side. 'I was young once, contrary to Kayleigh's beliefs of course, and I'd still love a lie-in after a night on the tiles, but I'm running a business. You'd think youngsters these days would be pleased to have a job when there's so much unemployment round here, wouldn't you?'

'Has she gone missing before?' asked Andy.

'Not that I know of, but Matt does ring her in sick on occasions – and annoyingly, it's always on our busiest days. But that's kids today for you,' she said, shaking her head. 'They'll take responsibility for nothing or no one.'

'He didn't ring you this time then?' said Ned.

'No. Not this time. I tried to ring Kayleigh to let her know I was opening up again after the snow had been cleared some. Her mobile phone wasn't responding and so I ended up calling her home and spoke to her mum.'

'Fortunately, you're not busy,' said Ned, looking around the empty salon.

'You've caught me in-between appointments, that's all. A lot of our clients don't know we're open again. Being on my own means I haven't got around to phoning all our regulars yet.'

'I could do with a trim. Any chance?' said Ned, running his fingers through his hair.

'Suppose so,' Marlene said, getting up from her chair and pointing to the empty chair in front of the wall full of mirrors, as she reached for a gown from the peg on the wall.

Ned moved in quickly and raised an eyebrow to Andy.

Marlene placed a maroon nylon smock around his ample frame and expertly tied the ribbons in a bow at the nape of his neck, to stop any hair falling onto his suit. Next she draped a towel around his shoulders. 'It could do with a bit of a wash,' she said, screwing up her nose as she held up a greasy lock.

Andy sniggered.

'Go on then,' Ned said with a forced smile at Andy.

Marlene took DC Granger over to the bowl.

'What was Kayleigh wearing when you last saw her?' said Andy.

Marlene thought long and hard. 'Nothing appropriate for the weather,' she scoffed. 'In fact, a customer remarked on it: short skirt and high heel boots.'

'I can't understand ...' said Ned, but before he could finish Marlene had pushed his head lower into the sink as she smiled at Andy, who sniggered. 'Bit rough aren't you?' It was Andy's turn to smile at Marlene through the mirror.

'What colour were her boots?' Andy said, suppressing a chuckle.

'Black with a gold ankle strap; they weren't cheap. She doesn't do cheap, our Kayleigh. All these questions... you'd think something bad had happened to her.' Marlene stopped in her tracks. 'You don't think... do you?' Her face was full of concern.

Andy shrugged. 'We don't know. We're just making enquiries with anyone that knows her or saw her Wednesday 7th January for now. Tell me, was she in a good mood? She didn't seem agitated or upset about anything, did she?'

'No,' Marlene said, shaking her head. 'One thing about Kayleigh is she wears her heart on her sleeve. She would have said if there was anything bothering her. You've got me worried now. I feel awful, I thought she just skiving. Just a trim?' she said, turning to Ned as she ruffled his hair dry with a towel.

Ned was quiet. He closed his eyes and noticeably relaxed in the hairdresser's hands. Snip, snip, snip went the scissors.

'Any customers that were a bit over-friendly or showed too much attention towards Kayleigh?' Andy said.

'Well she's popular with the men, as you'd imagine, being young, blonde, attractive and with a figure to die for,' she said.

DC Granger's eyes shot open. Marlene pushed his head down.

'But I suppose the only customer that I consider is a bit of a pest to her is a lad called Donny. He's in his early twenties, I would have said. Dresses like a Teddy boy. You know, skin-tight jeans, big soled shoes and has his hair styled in a big wave at the front of his head. If he's not in here asking her for an appointment to get his hair trimmed with her, he's sitting on that wall opposite with his flaming scooter, drooling.' She pointed across the road to a turning circle in the road. 'I'm not sure if he's a bit, you know, slow, if I'm honest, so I may be being a bit unkind, but the customers and I tease her about him.'

'Don't suppose you've got Danny's number?' asked Andy.

'No, sorry,' she said.

Ned's arm fell from the armrest, his head jerked, momentarily he had fallen asleep.

'Hey, keep your head still,' Marlene scolded. 'Otherwise you'll be minus an ear. I once had an accident and cut through an old lady's hearing aid wire when she did that,' she said. Andy sniggered. Ned opened his eyes wide.

'This lad's about often, then?' Andy said.

'Oh, all the time. But saying that, I haven't seen him since the snow came down.' Marlene put her finger under Ned's chin and lifted his head. She concentrated hard as she ran the scissors along his forehead to cut his fringe.

'Do you have a list of customers' names and addresses that we could see?'

'You can have my customer index, but I only have telephone contact details of our regulars.'

'Any live Manchester Road area?'

'Don't know, like I said we only take telephone numbers. You can help yourself to the cards,' she said pointing to the reception desk. 'Why you asking?'

'We know that's how far Kayleigh managed to drive before parking her car – it's still there.'

'Now you are worrying me. This is serious isn't it?' Marlene said, softly.

'Who was her last customer?' said Andy.

Marlene studied for a moment or two, picked up the appointment book once more, scissors and comb still in her hands and turned the pages. 'Er... Mavis Beanland,' she said. 'And the lad I was talking about, his name is Longbottom, Donny Longbottom.'

'Great. We'll need to speak to Mavis. Have you got her details?'

'Her number'll be in the box,' she said looking suddenly pale. 'But she was going away...'

'Try not to worry, not yet anyway. But if the Teddy Boy turns up, could you give us a call and we'll come round and check him out,' Andy said getting to his feet and placing his calling card down on the dressing table where she was working. Marlene proceeded to brush the small hairs from Ned's neck with a soft brush and untied his gown.

'Bloody hell mate!' Andy said, with a whistle as she turned his colleague round to face him. 'Ned, me old son, I've never seen you looking so darn... smart.'

Ned smiled smugly back at his image in the mirror.

'We do our best. Miracles take a little longer,' Marlene said to Andy, without looking up from the index cards she was fanning through at the counter. She handed them to Andy. Ned took a small bottle of aftershave from his pocket, sprayed in on his hands and slapped his face.

'That's six-fifty,' Marlene said, holding out her hand. Ned looked at her. 'Six-fifty? I don't want to buy the bleeding shop. Anyway you should be paying me, you could sell that lot to stuff a cushion,' he said pointing to the hair that covered the floor around the chair.

'Unreal,' whispered Andy as his colleague turned his pockets out to show they were empty. 'The last time he had a haircut it probably cost him one and six.'

Andy reached inside his jacket for his wallet and took out a ten pound note. He handed it to Marlene.

'Forget it,' she said with a smile. 'Just make sure you find Kayleigh safe and well for me, eh?'

'Well, now that's mighty generous of you love,' said Ned.

Andy looked to the ceiling. 'We will do our best. You really shouldn't though, but I suppose it saves us getting attacked from the moths in his wallet,' he said, clearly annoyed at his colleague. 'Would it be okay if we did a visual search of the premises?' he asked.

Marlene nodded. 'Yeah, of course, if you think it'll help.'

'We just need to be sure, for ourselves that she isn't here.'

'I haven't noticed anything has been disturbed, but she does have her own set of keys, just in case I ever need her to open up for me – you know, that odd late night on the tiles we spoke about,' she said, her eyes downcast.

'You and your better half?' Andy said, nodding towards the ring on her finger.

'Il haven't got a 'better half', as you put it,' she said.

'Oh, you haven't?' said Ned. 'So which tiles do you tread when you go out then?'

'None in particular,' she said. The corners of her mouth curled up in a smile.

'Well you've got my number if you fancy a night out?' he

said, laying his calling card on the reception desk.

'Yeah, sure, that'd be er... nice,' she said, lifting her eyebrows as she smiled knowingly at Andy.

Andy closed his eyes momentarily and shook his head in disbelief.

The officers walked through into the back of the shop and, satisfied that Kayleigh wasn't there, they took the index cards and made their way back to the car.

'She can't wait to get m' kit off?' said Ned.

'You think so do you? I'm not sure your lass would be too pleased at you taking Marlene out, do you?'

'Ah, what she doesn't know, me old son, won't hurt her, will it? Come on Mr Grumpy,' Ned laughed, 'You're just jealous because she fancies me.'

'Whatever,' said Andy as he opened the car door and jumped inside.

Chapter 7

Jackie and Vicky were at the Harwood house, carefully going through Kayleigh's personal belongings in her bedroom. Watching them from the doorway, Kim leant against the door jamb for support, pulling an oversized angora cardigan tight around her tiny frame.

'I know I've already given you a picture of Kayleigh, but this one is a particular favourite of mine,' she said, removing a glossy picture from a dark wooden frame and wiping a tear away. 'It was only taken recently; a reception at the hairdressing college. She won first prize in the Fantasy Style class and she was so proud,' she said touching her daughter's image. 'The Principal presented her with a necklace that had a pair of golden scissors on it.' Vicky reached for it, Kim pulled back. 'You won't lose it, will you?' she said, clutching the picture to her chest as panic flashed into her eyes.

Vicky stepped forward, put a soothing hand on her shoulder and took the photo. Kim lowered her gaze, making a soft whimpering sound.

'I promise, we'll take good care of it,' Vicky said softly. She put a finger under Kim's chin and, tilting it upwards, she smiled into her weary, tear-stained face. 'Go make a cup of tea eh? I'm sure Jackie would like one and I definitely won't say no.'

Kim's smile was weak but she turned on her heels and left them alone. Jackie frowned at Vicky. Quietly and industriously they continued to search through the teenagers things. Vicky placed a comb in a see-through evidence bag and sealed it, just as Kim walked back into the room with a tray of tea and a plate of biscuits.

'I'm sorry, but we do need to take some items away with us, just in case ...' said Vicky, when she saw the look on her face. The tray wobbled in Kim's hands and the cups slid to one side but luckily Jackie was on hand to grab it from her, and gently she helped her put the tray on the top of a set of drawers.

Kim sat on the corner of Kayleigh's bed, taking deep breaths. In between, she sighed heavily. Jackie put an arm around her and rubbed her back soothingly. 'Please don't say... I can't bear to think that something awful has happened. I keep getting this terrible feeling of foreboding. Is this how it's going to end?' Kim said. She flapped her hand in front of her face, and then swallowed hard, choking back the tears. 'Oh, don't mind me. Just do what you need to do.'

Vicky picked up a cup of tea from the tray and placed it in Kim's hands. 'Drink this; it'll make you feel better.'

There was only one way to deal with this situation and that was to continue with as little fuss as possible. They took Kayleigh's toothbrush, handheld mirror and her laptop. Vicky sat and busied herself tagging the bags. The quicker they got this task over with, the better. Hopefully, these few objects would give them a DNA sample, fingerprints and hair sample they needed and they would be able to check her use of the internet.

All finished, the three women looked at each other, each immersed in their own thoughts. Kim Harwood broke the silence and talked about her daughter and how difficult it had been bringing her up on her own since her husband had died. 'They were devoted to each other, you know ... I lost her dad,' she said, wearily. 'I can't lose Kayleigh too. Please find her for me, please,' she whispered as she looked into the eyes of each of the officers in turn. Tears ran down her cheeks and she bravely brushed them away. 'I'm sorry, I just want her home,' she sobbed.

Jackie knelt in front of Kim to comfort her. 'We'll find her for you. We will...'

'Kim, we need to search the rest of the house. It's routine just to ensure she is nowhere here, no matter how ridiculous that might sound. An attic, a garage, a greenhouse or even an outhouse... people turn up in the strangest of places,' Vicky said.

Kim nodded and wiped her face with her handkerchief.

'This shoe box, do you know if it relates to the boots she was wearing on the day she went missing?' Vicky said.

'Yes. She loves them; hasn't had them off her feet since she bought them. Goodness knows how she wears them heels when she's on her feet all day,' Kim half smiled.

'We'll take that with us if you don't mind, it will help us identify the type of boot and if the receipt is inside...' she said taking off the lid and retrieving a small piece of paper which she waved in front of her, 'this tells us when and where she purchased them and even who served her.'

'My goodness, you don't leave anything to chance, do you?' said Kim.

'We can't. Our boss's favourite saying is clear the ground beneath your feet first, and that's what we all do. We'll be checking out anyone and everyone that she has had contact with lately.'

'Well,' Kim sighed. 'All I can say is thank you so very much from the bottom of my heart for everything you're doing.'

'All part of the service,' smiled Vicky as she reached out and gave Kim a brief hug before leaving.

'Oh no,' she said. 'It's so much more than that.'

Dylan was in his office, wading through the endless heap of paperwork that came with modern day policing. He stopped for a moment, yawned and sighed, deep in thought. What he would give to be home with Jen and Maisy right now.

'Pen-pusher to pram-pusher,' he texted. *'How're my favourite girls? Cheer me up. Monthly stats are doing my head in.'*

'Little Maisy is fast asleep and she's snoring her head off, just like her daddy.'

Dylan smiled.

'Walking around Sibden Park with Max. He's pulling the pram up the hill for me while I text. ✍

'Fancy being jealous of a dog! x'

'Don't be late tonight then! Love you x' Jen replied.

Dylan's desk phone rang. He was so deep in thought, it made him jump. 'Dylan,' he snapped.

'Yes sir, Sgt Simon Clegg, I'm with the search and rescue team and I thought I'd let you know that we've found a lady's fur jacket on the outskirts of the woods above the old Cragg quarry, about three miles as the crow flies from where the young lady left her car.'

'Is the jacket still in situ?' asked Dylan with a furrowed brow.

'For now sir. My officers are continuing to search around it, and I've arranged for SOCO to come and photograph.'

'Good. I'll get my all-weather gear and be with you in about twenty minutes. I have your location.'

A thought crossed his mind. Scenes of Crimes Officers would very soon be renamed Crime Scene Investigators in West Yorkshire, he had read. How American was that going to sound when officers were telling him CSI were on their way?

The day was one of sailing clouds and splashes of sunlight. The main road was still littered with the odd abandoned vehicle, haphazardly parked. As Dylan turned into the entrance of the unmade road leading to the quarry, he slowed. The snow was too compacted to hold his wheels. The car lurched, wallowed, skidded and stuck. The back wheels spun on the ice. A few yards beyond the clearing, the track died away and the rough terrain beyond would have been impossible to negotiate over the moorland in his vehicle, even in good weather. Dylan knew he would never get as close as the search and rescue vehicles. This was a solitary place to separate a man from bricks and mortar, he thought as he got out of his vehicle. Pulling on his wellingtons from the boot of his car, he considered his walk down the uneven man-made footpath. The sun intermittently broke through the fast moving cirrostratus cloud cover to form black shadows on the ground. The wind picked up as he marched across the stark moorland. He took his gloves out of his pockets and put them on. The path snaked its way downwards amid thickening bracken, heather and a tangle of old laurels, covered in more places than not with thick, solid, packed snow mounds. He slipped and stumbled along the way, and where the snow was light, dead wood crackled under his feet.

The wind was in his hair and billowing out his coat and he fought to pull it tightly around him. The quarry itself was screened by banks and trees. Dylan walked toward the police Land Rover and soon he could make out steep, sloping layers with benches in the rock faces that looked like giant flat steps in the quarry. Dylan strode out with purpose towards a group of officers, putting his hands in his pockets and screwing up his face as the wind sprayed snow at him on the breeze. A chill ran down his spine. He remembered only too well the difficulties they had had in the past getting down to the waters. He could see a large overgrown hole excavated into the rock. The colours within the steep layers were incredibly stark, grey, pink, red, yellow and black. As he neared, he passed a few old, rusty remnants of machinery, diggers, scrapers and transporting dumper trucks that had been left there to rot. The murky waters now in sight were estimated to be about ten foot deep, if his sources were correct. It had been thought an ideal place to hide a body back in the summer of 2003 when the tired, disillusioned police officers had discarded their wet gear here to dry out on the overgrown rhododendron bushes. The suggestion was then that a car dealer's body had been dumped there after an alleged contract killing. Nothing was ever found; now would it have to be searched again – but with success this time? Only time would tell.

Dylan approached Sgt Clegg, who was looking intently at what turned out to be a mass of snow covered fern that had piled itself like a small tent, around the trunk of a fir. In this sheltered place the air was like deep water. He nodded. The officers were beating the hedges in an attempt to find Kayleigh Harwood. Dylan stood still, watching the approaching men from the base of the quarry. Now and again one of them would peer under the spreading branches of a thorn. Suddenly, everyone's attention was diverted in the direction of an English springer spaniel that had begun circling the ground about a hundred yards away. 'Sir,' Clegg nodded to Dylan. 'Best have a look, it may be something of relevance. Vegas's usually very good. Three years old, but has one hell of a nose,' he said. Dylan walked silently alongside the sergeant towards a solid looking liver and white bitch.

'She certainly seems to be excited about something,' said Dylan, his face suddenly illuminated.

Chapter 8

Andy and Ned arrived at Matt Prentice's flat and were invited in. With trained eyes, they analysed his replies to their questioning about Kayleigh and studied his body language closely.

Kayleigh's boyfriend was co-operative and came across as genuine and very concerned about his girlfriend. But if he was so fond of her, as much as he professed, why would he let a week pass without contact, wondered Andy?

Matt apologised for the state of the apartment. He picked up clothing strewn over the furniture so they could sit down. 'Sorry, I haven't had chance to clear up.' He sniffed, his chest still congested.

'You don't need to bother for us,' Ned said, looking at the amount of personal belongings also on the bedroom floor that could be seen though the open door of the lounge. It was no different from the majority of young people's flats they saw, but he would put his wages on Matt being able to lay his hands on any specific item if it was needed.

'Any of this Kayleigh's?' asked Andy.

'Most of it,' he said, plucking a cardigan from the back of the chair he was sitting in and holding it against him. 'She spends more time here than she does at home these days,' he said, before turning his head. He sneezed into his hand and then sneezed again into the air.

'So, tell us about Wednesday 7th January, what happened?' said Ned.

'Excuse me,' Matt said, blowing his nose on a crumpled tissue. 'I don't usually see Kayleigh on a Wednesday, it's the one day a week she goes home to blow dry her mum's hair. But that night I received a text from her asking if she could come here because of the snow. As if she needed to ask. I told her that I was at Dave's,' he said, with a shrug. 'She texted me later to say she was stuck in the snow but listening to the radio for advice on what to do. I guess, quite rightly so, she was miffed with me because I was in the warm, at m' mates. She'd guess we were playing computer games.'

'Is that the last time you heard from her?' Andy said, making notes in his pocket book.

'Yeah. Look, Kayleigh has her own key; if, she had got here she could have let herself in. What else could I do? If she was stuck, then I'd have got stuck too if I'd attempted to get to her. I stayed at Dave's for the night. Then I started with this lot,' he said, grabbing another tissue from the box, blowing his nose loudly and throwing both tissues in the direction of the rattan bin. 'I thought she'd just gone home until Kim rang me and told me otherwise.'

'So you were at Dave's all night?' said Ned.

'Yeah, we finished off a bottle of vodka he had left over from Christmas,' he laughed, half-heartedly. 'I couldn't stand up. I felt so ill the next day, what with the drink and this lot. When I did make it home, I just about managed to crawl into bed and then slept the clock round. I feel bad now. You don't think something serious has happened to her, do you? Like this is just routine procedure for somebody that's missing? You think she'll be okay, don't you?'

'We hope so, but we do need to trace her. I don't need to tell you how bad the weather was that night. If she set off walking, who knows where she ended up?' said Andy.

'She wouldn't have set off walking. I know Kayleigh, she doesn't do walking unless it's round the shops. She'd have stayed in her car, I'm sure. She wouldn't have risked ruining her new boots for anything.'

'Do you think she'd accept a lift?' said Andy.

'Not unless she knew the person offering. She's not stupid. She was the most sensible person I know... Kayleigh's street-wise, but it is unlike her not to be in touch. Is there anything I can do? I feel so frigging useless just sat here.'

'You can compile a list of everyone you both know for us – and I mean everyone. No matter how trivial the connection – friends, work colleagues, etcetera, absolutely anyone you can think of. We'll need your mate Dave's details too, to check out your story,' Andy said.

'Why would I lie?' Matt said, looking bemused. 'I know when girls go missing, you lot and everyone else automatically suspects the boyfriend, but honestly, I swear I didn't see her that night.'

'Didn't say you've lied, but some do and so we have to verify everything anybody says.' said Ned.

'She's my girl, you know,' he said, his voice choked with emotion.

Obtaining the necessary details and ensuring that Kayleigh was nowhere on the premises the two detectives headed back to the police station.

'He seemed straight enough,' said Ned.

'Yeah but you noticed like I did that he used the past tense about Kayleigh when he said. '*She was the most sensible person...'* didn't you?' said Andy.

'What you saying?' said Ned.

'I think we should never assume,' said Andy, with a grim face.

Sgt Clegg managed to curtail Vegas's barking at the edge of Cragg Quarry. The Springer Spaniel had found a lady's black boot and was over-excited.

Dylan dropped to his haunches to take a closer look, put his hands in his pockets and was alone with his thoughts as he stared at the item of footwear. The boot was of the same description as the one Kayleigh had been wearing on the day she had gone missing. He could see part of a sale label still stuck in the arch of the sole. He looked around him but there was no sign of other clothing or footwear. Dylan glanced down the precipice into the depths of the dank quarry through the broken, rusty metal mesh fence directly ahead. Had she taken that fall? Was she at the bottom in the dark waters? If so, there was one thing for certain, she was never coming back alive.

The logistics for the search team would be a nightmare, with that steep climb down. But then, and only then could the water beneath be searched. He didn't envy the Operational Support Team, but he knew he could rely on them to do a thorough job. When he got back to the station he would make the request for the location to be searched. Somebody would be doing a detailed risk assessment for Health and Safety issues, but thankfully not him. Now the right boot that had been found, it would be photographed in situ, then bagged and tagged with the chance of forensics getting DNA from inside it. He would hope and keep positive, for while there was a chance of Forensics coming up trumps he couldn't miss the opportunity to use it, no matter what the financial cost.

The prospect of finding Kayleigh alive was not looking good. The severe weather conditions, the revelation of a fur jacket and now a boot turning up were inconclusive. He was well aware that hypothermia caused people to discard clothing, so it didn't always follow that there had been foul play. He had dealt with naked bodies found outside with clothing strewn about them, which he had learned very early on in his career was a reaction to nothing sinister, just the extreme cold that made the victims feel hot – and at this point they would remove their clothing. But it was more than likely that Kayleigh was dead. He would never assume, but this missing girl had got his full attention.

Chapter 9

The briefing was about to start. Dylan had invited Sgt Clegg from OSU, who was in charge of the team instructed to search Cragg Quarry and the waters at its base.

'Judging by Ned's new look, boss, I think it's pretty obvious where he's been today don't you?' said Vicky as she ruffled her colleague's hair.

'Give up,' he said, awkwardly.

'You pay for that Ned?' Dylan said as he passed on his way to the front of the room, knowing full well what detectives were like.

'I offered,' he replied, and taking a new comb from his breast pocket, he ran it through his newly styled hair.

Andy looked the other way; Dylan noticed and shook his head.

'Right!' Dylan said, clapping his hands to get the team's attention. 'Vicky, what've you got for us?'

'We've obtained another photo of Kayleigh, and also seized her toothbrush, comb, hairbrush for potential DNA samples as well as a hand mirror she used, from which hopefully we can get her fingerprints. Her laptop is there,' she said, pointing to her desk. 'Jackie and I searched the house. Kim, Kayleigh's mum, is distraught and kept reinforcing to us that her not being in contact is totally out of character.'

Andy cleared his throat. 'That was echoed by Kayleigh's boyfriend, Matt Prentice. He told us that in his opinion she was streetwise and wouldn't accept a lift from a stranger, neither did he think she'd get out of the car and set off walking. He firmly believes she would have stayed in her car and adhered to the advice that was being given over the radio.'

'We've collected the index cards with the names and telephone numbers of regular customers at the hairdressers where she works, but it's also what you'd call a 'drop in' salon, so people do call in as casual customers,' Ned said. 'Mavis Beanland was her last customer on the day she went missing.'

Andy interrupted. 'Marlene, the shop owner, did mention a bit of a strange character who dresses like a Teddy boy and sits outside the shop. He calls in regularly for Kayleigh to trim his hair. His name is Donny Longbottom and she tells us that the regulars tease her about him as he appears to have a bit of a crush. He's possibly in his early twenties, she thinks.'

'Do we know how to get hold of him?'

'We don't have contact details, but we're told he's outside the salon most days. She says she'll let us know when he appears again,' said Andy.

'Is he known to us? Check him out with the Intelligence office – I want him tracing. We also need to speak to Mavis Beanland and any other customers we can get hold of to see if they've seen her. Who knows, one of them may have offered her a lift or shelter that night. The houses near to the abandoned car, I want them checking and searching if need be and what about the shelters set up near by?'

'PC Alan Hughes has done a bit of a house to house sir,' said Jackie. 'There aren't many dwellings in the immediate vicinity.'

'I know he has, but I want us to visit again. We've found a fur jacket and a lady's right black boot, both of these are possibly Kayleigh's. They were found near to Cragg Quarry and yes, before you ask, it's going to be searched – although I'm fully aware it will be a difficult task, Simon.' Dylan nodded apologetically in Sergeant Clegg's direction. 'Vicky, Jackie, I want you to show the items that we have found to Kayleigh's mum and her boyfriend to see if we get a positive ID before we send them to the forensic lab.'

'The continued search by the team has not revealed the left boot,' Sergeant Clegg told the assembled team.

'Ned, Andy can you get on with compiling a list of properties in that area, giving priority to the nearest to her car and working outwards? I want them searching ASAP,' Dylan said. 'I'll get onto the press office and let them have Kayleigh's latest picture to put another appeal out to the public for anyone who saw her that evening or since to come forward. Do we know if any money has been withdrawn from her bank account and have we got her mobile phone being checked out?'

'Battery was flat. I found in the foot well on the passenger side of her car,' said PC Hughes. 'It's in the property store sir.'

'What the hell are you playing at? Get it sent to the hi-tech department immediately for them to download the data. It doesn't matter if the battery's bloody flat, you shouldn't be trying to turn it on. We can get the incoming and outgoing data via a charter application.'

'Point taken, boss,' Ned said, looking directly at the sheepish PC. 'I'll chase that one up.'

'Bank account?'

'Nothing withdrawn boss,' said Andy.

Briefing over, Dylan telephoned the force press office to renew the appeal for Kayleigh, stating that there were concerns for her welfare due to the fact that she had not been seen or heard from by family or friends since White Wednesday, when it appears she, along with others, abandoned their cars at the roadside on the Manchester Road, due to the extreme weather conditions. 'The Police, along with Search and Rescue Teams, are combing the surrounding area and countryside,' he said to Claire Rose. 'And I want to hear from anyone using Manchester Road that night or parking their vehicles up on that road due to the extreme weather conditions too.'

He put the phone down and picked it straight up again to telephone Jen.

'Hello,' a quiet, sleepy voice said.

'Jen? Everything alright?'

'Fine, I must have nodded off. Maisy had a bad night.'

'Did she?' Dylan grinned sheepishly. 'Sorry, didn't mean to wake you. I just wanted to make sure everything is okay.'

'Anything happening at your end?' Jen said, yawning.

'They've found a shoe and a jacket which looks like it's the missing girl's near to Cragg Quarry. So it's going to have to be searched'.

'Not sounding good then?

'No...' he sighed.

'Home on time?'

'So far, so good'

'See you then, love you.'

'Love you more,' Dylan said. With a smile, he hung up.

Jen sighed with contentment. Ever since Maisy's birth, Dylan had stuck to his promise to her. She could see he was making a real effort to get home at a reasonable time and keeping in touch with her. He hadn't been called out as often as before her birth either and he was sleeping through, even if Maisy wasn't. She hoped thinking about her good fortune wasn't going to tempt fate.

'Editor of the Harrowfield Courier, on the phone for you boss!'

shouted Vicky from the main CID office.

'Inspector Dylan.'

'Virginia!' Dylan said brightly.

'Tell me,' she said quietly. 'Do you think there is any connection with the girl who went missing twenty years ago on a similar winter's night on Manchester Road? I can't find anything to suggest she was ever heard from since. Is history repeating itself, do you think?'

Dylan raised his eyebrows. 'Hey, slow down. Firstly that was before I joined up and don't forget there are thousands of people go missing every year. What was the girl's name, incidentally?'

'Tina Walker. My sources say she was twenty years old and was last seen riding her bike along Manchester Road, on her way home from work. She was a bobbin winder at Standeven Woollen Mill in Ovenden at the time.'

'I'll dig out our reports on the case, but let's not start upsetting the family unnecessarily. Kayleigh Harwood may turn up safe and well yet – and by God I hope she does.'

'Will her Mum talk to me, do you think? You know the kind of interview I'm looking for, from the heart. That should get the readers involved. It's every mother's nightmare, a child going missing, no matter how old they are, isn't it? It'll be sure to get some interest for you from an article.'

'I'll ask, you're right, it'll help keep the interest of the public going but I have to emphasise it's her decision, not mine. In the meantime, let's not blow this all out of proportion. If or when there are any developments, as usual, I'll make sure you're aware.'

'Thanks. Will you be speaking to her Mum today?'

Dylan smiled to himself. 'I'll make sure someone speaks to Mrs Harwood today for you. Will that do you?'

'Thank you Dylan, much appreciated,' she said.

Dylan put down the phone. Virginia had him thinking. Would there be any police files still in existence relating to the disappearance of Tina Walker? The reporter had obviously done her digging – but then he didn't expect anything else from the dedicated local newspaper editor who was as keen as mustard. He was curious, more than anything. If there was any evidence found at the time of Tina's disappearance and it was thought that it could have led to a murder enquiry, then he knew nothing would have been destroyed. He walked along the corridor to the intelligence office to see if PC Norman Tempest, the local intelligence officer, could throw some light on the incident. Norman was working on the thirty plus scheme, which meant he had over thirty years of police service, so he would have been in the job at the time of Tina Walker's disappearance. Would he have been working the area at the time? Dylan knew it was more than likely, Bobbies weren't moved around for the sake of it in those days. Not that long ago, all police officers knew their beat and its community like the back of their hands. Criminals may be undesirable, but nevertheless they were part of the community, as were informers. Officers of that era told how they saw the criminals of their early years have children and grandchildren who followed in their footsteps. What else had they to inspire to?

Today's Think Tank recommended moving officers around regularly to avoid corruption. These people had never worked the streets and their advice was absolute rubbish in Dylan's eyes.

'Eyup, just stretching your legs, or have you come to pick our brains?'

'Bit of both Norman, to be honest,' Dylan said.

'Fancy a brew?' he asked.

'Why not,' Dylan smiled broadly at his elder. He outlined the facts on the recent disappearance of Kayleigh Harwood and the call from Virginia asking if he thought the recent case could be linked to the disappearance of Tina Walker.

'Tina Walker? Tina Walker, God above, you're going back some years there, boss. A young lass who, if I remember rightly, used to cycle to Standeven Mill and back on Manchester Road. Strange job that. She was never found, neither was her bike. CID of the day looked into it, in fact it nearly saw the SIO off, but nothing came of it and there's been nothing come to light to this day, that I know of. It was a real mystery. Aye, Barry 'Razor' Sharpe was the boss at that time. He had an eye for detail, a bit like you, if I might say so? Nothing normally got past him, hence the name,' he said with a chuckle. 'He still lives local. I see him on occasions at retirement do's and funerals... sadly; it's a sign of our age.'

Dylan rolled his eyes.

'You'll come to it,' he laughed. 'Barry still lives and breathes that job, though. He's the one to talk to. It's the one crime that pestered him all the way to his retirement and now beyond.'

'They say there's always one that hurts an SIO more than any other, don't they? Do you remember if there were any major suspects at the time?'

'No, not that I remember anyhow,' Norman's eyes crinkled at the corners. 'Razor left no stone unturned, as I recall. He was gutted once all lines of enquiry were exhausted and he had no prisoner to show for all the hard work of the team. It was his only undetected job in his thirty year CID led career. If anyone went missing in them days and didn't turn up, it was believed that they'd gone to London. If that had been right, London must have been downright full of missing people,' he chuckled.

'The days before computers,' said Dylan thoughtfully. 'So somewhere there should be an odd paper file stashed away I guess. I'll try get hold of it and have a read,' said Dylan.

'I'd look at Tandam Bridge, in the attic. I seem to think that's where the undetected murder files are kept, these days. That's if Beaky in admin has kept her bloody hands off them, she's always moving them around.'

Dylan raised his eyebrows. 'Ah, so that's what she does.'

'Quite,' Norman said with a nod of his head. 'There maybe more than an odd file boss. Should be a few shelves full of boxes and exhibits in relation to that job, I'm sure Barry'd be happy to talk you through the enquiry.'

'If he were called Razor, I dread to think what they call me.'

'You don't want to know boss?' he said.

'Probably better I don't,' said Dylan. 'Thanks for the chat and the coffee. I knew if anyone would know about the case it'd be you, mate.'

'By gum you've got me thinking, weren't they just the good ole days? Hey, lad I'm glad to be of some help. You're not much use to anyone when you get to my age. I don't know what I'll do when they retire me out to grass. I always thought I'd do this job 'til I died, especially since I lost our lass.'

'Nonsense, Norman. I say you can't beat experience in this job. Why would they get rid of the people with your knowledge and experience? The most effective policing yet has to be the village Bobby who was everybody's confidant,' Dylan said, as he took his leave.

Dylan knew his next stop was to try to locate the file on Tina Walker. He set one of the incident room staff on its trail. It may or may not have any bearing on the recent disappearance of Kayleigh, but Virginia and Norman had whetted his investigative appetite. He was excited about looking at the pieces of this puzzle and putting them into a picture.

It wasn't long before a property store clerk appeared at Dylan's office door with a rather large, old, battered, and dusty box.

'Tina Walker file sir? There's a lot more where this came from, if you want it, sir,' he said.

Dylan nodded eagerly.

'Sign here,' Trevor said, handing Dylan a form and a pen that he had wedged behind his ear. Trevor stood tall in his brown button-through overall, resting the delivery on the corner of Dylan's desk.

'Thank you,' Dylan said, scribbling his signature as his eyes strayed to the parcel. 'Yes, bring me the rest will you, and as soon as you can.'

'All of it?' Trevor said. 'In here?' he said, looking about him. He got his handkerchief out of his pocket and mopped the sweat from his face.

'Yes,' Dylan said placing the coveted box on the desk in front of him. What information would the papers within hold, he wondered as his hand hovered over them like a blind man touching Braille.

'Well, if you're sure. You're the boss,' Trevor said, shrugging his shoulders before leaving, trailing the empty trolley behind him.

Dylan closed the office door behind him to savour the moment in peace. Carefully and with some trepidation, he opened the cardboard box and lifted from it a large, faded file tied with string. The paper was yellow, even golden, in places. The edges were roughed up and the corners curled and brittle. Dylan sneezed loudly as he brushed the top, worn, moss green cardboard cover with the palm of his hand. 'The unexplained disappearance of Tina Walker, MURDER?' he read aloud.

The papers and police forms were partially handwritten and partially typed, some in duplicate with the typewriter carbon paper still attached. Adrenaline started coursing through Dylan's veins as he eagerly started to read. Tina Walker was just an ordinary girl who had been wearing fashionable clothing of the day and likewise unsuitable for the weather – acid washed denim jacket, stretchy short black mini skirt, bat winged pink polo neck jumper, bright pink and black striped leg warmers and a pink headband with beads and jelly bangles on her arm to complete the look of that era. There was a picture of her and photographs of clothing identical to that she had been wearing.

A knock came at his door and without looking up, he shouted, 'Come in.' Boxes piled high upon an upright trolley were steered in. Dylan kept reading as Trevor positioned them strategically round him.

'You sure you want it all?' Trevor asked.

Still without looking up, Dylan nodded, absorbed as he was in the covering summary. Box after box continued to arrive.

Chapter 10

Donny Longbottom, the would-be Teddy boy, hadn't been hard to trace, although he hadn't shown up outside the hairdressers. He was nineteen years old and had already been brought to the attention of the Local Intelligence Officer for an incident of indecent exposure.

Ned and Andy asked to speak to him in the presence of his mother, with whom he lived in a semi detached council house on the Greenaway Estate. The officers needed a parent or guardian there, as his police record showed a responsible adult needed to be in attendance. They hoped the responsible adult didn't turn out to be a contradiction in terms.

Ned knocked on the door of the address they had been given.

'Mrs Longbottom,' he said as the door opened and he was faced with a scowling, middle-aged, bespectacled woman. He showed her his warrant card.

'What's he done now?' Donny's mother said.

It wasn't a good start.

'He's hardly been out of the house with the weather being so bad,' protested Christine Longbottom as Andy showed her his warrant card and she waved them inside.

Andy explained that Donny had been reported as a client of the missing hairdresser, as well as having often been seen sitting on the wall outside the shop where she worked.

'That isn't a crime, is it?' she said. 'Well, at least we know his medication's working,' she added, grabbing a packet of cigarettes from the hallway table.

Andy and Ned looked at each other.

'Well, if he's only looking...' she said, taking a cigarette out of the packet. 'Look, I can't watch him every minute of the day can I? He's a grown man. D o n n y,' she screeched at the top of her voice from the bottom of the stairs. 'Get your backside down, here; the Police want to see you.'

The house was unexpectedly neat and tidy. Christine Longbottom led them into the lounge. In an armchair, in the conservatory beyond the patio doors they could see an elderly woman who appeared to be asleep. Her head was on the headrest and her mouth wide open.

'She's deaf as a bleedin' doornail,' Christine said,

beckoning them to take a seat. She walked over to put the cigarette packet on the fireplace and placed the cigarette in the corner of her mouth but continued to talk. 'Where is the little shit?' The cigarette bounced up and down to the rhythms of her speech. She took a lighter out of a well-worn leather case and lit it. Taking a long hard drag, she called her son again, 'Donny, will you come down here now?' She exhaled the smoke through her nose, like a smoking chimney, then removed the cigarette from her mouth and pursed her lips, flouncing over to the door to the hallway. The two men heard a burring sound and turned in time to see Christine rushing to the foot of the stairs.

'Get off your Gran's stair lift, before I knock you off the bloody thing,' she yelled, striking her son across his head with the palm of her hand.

Donny walked into the room in front of his mother, somewhat subdued and rubbing the back of his head. He was dressed in black skin-tight jeans and a red checked shirt, with nothing on his feet. Without acknowledging the visitors, he walked straight to the mirror over the fireplace and started to comb his wet hair with a fine-toothed comb from his back pocket.

'DC Wormald and DC Granger,' Andy said.'We're investigating the disappearance of a young woman you know from Envy Hair and Beauty.'

Donny calmly continued to coiffure his hairstyle into a quiff at the front and then with great precision expertly combed the hair at the back and around the sides of his head into a DA.

'Kayleigh, your hairdresser, she's missing,' said Ned.

Donny stopped what he was doing and stared at the men through the mirror, but said nothing.

'You know who we mean, don't you Donny?'

'Yeah,' he said turning to face them. 'I'm not stupid. The one with the nice tits,' he said, raising an eyebrow at the officers.

'Do you want a crack?' Christine said. She tutted, 'just for once, can't you just answer the officer in a civil manner?' she said leaning forward and stubbing out her cigarette in a large green onyx ashtray on a glass table in the centre of the lounge.

'Have you ever seen her anywhere other than at the hairdressers?' Andy asked.

'Why would I?'

'You'd better bloody not have been pestering that girl,'

Christine said under her breath.

Donny suddenly lunged at his mother. 'Shut you're cake'ole,' he said. Mother and son were face to face, nose to nose, but she pushed him away, apparently unfazed by his outburst.

'I saw something in the paper. When did she go missing?' asked Christine.

'White Wednesday,' Ned said.

'You had an appointment at the doctor's that day, didn't you? One of them repeat prescriptions that he has to see you for, do you remember? You were in the back garden that afternoon building a snowman with that other lad, weren't you?' she said to Donny, then looked at the officers. 'I remember it because I had to bollock him because they'd given the snowman a dick with the carrot I'd given them for the nose – and stupid as he is, he thought it was hilarious, rolling around in the snow. Wet through, he was. There's times, believe you me, I wish I could do to him what I did to that carrot. Solve a lot of problems that would, I'll tell you,' she said.

Donny smirked. 'As if!'

'So, you behaving yourself these days Donny?' said Andy.

'Yeah,' he replied, rubbing his bare foot frantically on the nylon carpet. He reached out to his mum and she jumped in shock at the positive static electric charge he passed to her.

'You bloody idiot, stop that,' she said. Donny laughed raucously, ran over to the doors of the conservatory and once again rubbed his foot on the carpet furiously.

'Party trick,' she said apologetically.

'With your consent, we'll have a quick look around Donny's bedroom, Mrs Longbottom?' She nodded. 'Top of the stairs, first door on the left.' The old woman in the conservatory let out a scream.

'Donny, for fuck's sake. Give up, will you? You'll bloody kill your Gran doing that one of these days.'

'Well, at least we know grandma's alive,' said Ned, sniggering as he walked behind Andy up the stairs.

There were a lot of DVDs and magazines in Donny Longbottom's bedroom but nothing that seemed out of place in a teenager's room. Andy pointed out a few risky ones to Ned, but he screwed up his face and they decided to leave them in situ.

Thanking Mrs Longbottom, the officers left the house.

'I honestly thought she wasn't breathing, you know,' said Andy.

'What? The Gran? Me neither. I wouldn't bet she was when we first went in. Maybe the shock brought her back to life?' Ned laughed.

'I wouldn't want a daughter of mine bringing a Donny Longbottom home, would you?' said Andy.

'Or a son!'

'His hairstyle's not bad though, in fact it's nearly as good as yours,' Andy said as he put the car into first gear and looked in his rear view mirror before driving the CID car away from the kerb.

'Cheeky twat,' said Ned.

Dylan sat in his office digesting the information in the file and imagining the detectives of the day with their afro hairstyles, moustaches, trilby hats and weather-worn raincoats, for wasn't that the dress code back then? Tina, along with her dark green coloured 21" frame Raleigh Cameo lady's bike, seemed to have disappeared into thin air too after her shift at the mill on that snowy night. Standeven Mill was now a collection of business units and luxury flats. The file showed that everyone at the Mill at the time was spoken to over a period of a few weeks but nothing was gleaned from the interviews and extensive searches. The investigation had been thorough, there was no doubt. The workers had been checked, as had strangers to the mill who had made deliveries that day. Detectives had spoken to anyone and everyone who they thought may have had any information, which was apparent from the amount of paperwork, and they had used every tool available to them at that time. The only comparison with the Kayleigh Harwood case was that a young girl had gone missing in the same area and in the same weather conditions. Dylan was sad that there weren't any other striking similarities. He would speak with Barry Sharpe, he didn't consider it urgent but he was intrigued.

The team were updated at the day's debrief in respect of Donny Longbottom and the resemblances in the case to that of the disappearance of Tina Walker. Dylan told the assembled group that although he was aware of it, there was no evidence so far to support a link to the recent disappearance of Kayleigh Harwood.

Vicky confirmed that the shoe and jacket had been identified by Kayleigh's mum and boyfriend as identical to the ones Kayleigh owned and was wearing on the day she went missing. 'I've tried to convince them boss that she might just have dumped them because of hypothermia but they weren't having none of it. They are obviously distraught at the finds.'

Vicky and Jackie had also visited some of the customers of the hairdressing salon where Kayleigh worked, but there was nothing of relevance to report. Dylan emphasised the need to trace people who were in the area on the night in question, even if they were only stranded for a short time. 'We should be able to trace some from the abandoned cars, surely?' he said. 'The difference between Kayleigh going missing and Tina Walker twenty years ago is that we'll find her, I'm sure of that,' he told his team before they left. 'Vicky, did you speak to Mavis Beanland yet or anyone at the nearby shelter?'

'No sir. Mavis is not home yet and no one can tell us where her sister lives, but she is still on our list to see, as are the people at the shelters.'

'Let me know when you've spoken to her, them.'

Vicky nodded.

Dylan was on the way home. Tomorrow was another day. Just for tonight he wanted to get home and hold Jen and Maisy in his arms. Maisy was growing daily. Gone were the days of just caring for her, she was becoming a real little character. A bit more hair, fewer wrinkles and she was noticing more about the world around her. He held her as Jen made the evening meal, Maisy's tiny chubby hand gripped onto his long index finger and the connection ran all the way to the core of his being. She chuckled when he nibbled her foot or tickled her under the chin.

Jen listened to Dylan talking to his daughter soothingly, then all went quiet and when she put her head around the living room door, she found them both fast asleep. Dylan's head had fallen back onto the cushion and Maisy was sprawled out on his flattened chest. Tears came into her eyes. She wished her mum could see how happy she was. That reminded her – she must ring dad.

'I'll just change her nappy before we eat, Jen,' called Dylan, fifteen minutes later.

'She was only changed just before you arrived home,' she shouted back.

'Well she certainly needs changing again, don't you gorgeous?' he said holding her away from him and curling up his nose as he walked into the kitchen, with Maisy in his outstretched arms. 'Pooh,' he said and she chuckled. 'Just like your Mummy.'

Jen watched him carefully change Maisy's nappy. He was a natural. Comfortable and warm, Maisy fell instantly back to sleep in her Moses basket, which gave them a chance to have their meal in peace.

'I was speaking to Norman in LIO today. He says they make your arms ache when they're babies and your heart ache when they grow up,' said Dylan looking at Maisy adoringly.

'Yes, and we'll worry just as much about her brothers and sisters when they came along,' she said, quietly kissing him on his cheek as she stood to take the dirty dishes to the sink.

Jack's face was a picture and she stifled a laugh.

'Isn't it about time you were going back to work?' he said.

Jen screwed up her face. 'No, I'm thinking I might take a career break,' she said. 'And Jack?'

'Yes.'

'Maisy takes after you, not me,' she said, smiling broadly.

Chapter 11

The search of the quarry and its waters had been carefully carried out. The OSU team was satisfied that there were no bodies or other items of Kayleigh's clothing in their depths.

'Although to get down to the water was a nightmare, believe it or not once in it was quite clear. I'm sorry we didn't get a result for you, sir,' Sgt Clegg said to Dylan.

He shook his head. 'No, thank you for your hard work, and pass on my thanks to the rest of the team. I'm very grateful we can eliminate that line of enquiry.'

She wasn't there, so where is she? pondered Dylan, as he sat at his desk, hands folded together and his chin resting on his knuckles.

'Vicky!' he shouted. 'Get an aerial search done to look for any geological changes on the moors, will you.'

'What you thinking, shallow grave?' she asked as she stood at his door.

'Perhaps,' he said shrugging his shoulders. 'I'm off to Barry Sharpe to see if I can glean any more of what happened when Tina Walker went missing.'

'Back to basics?'

'It can't do any harm,' Dylan sighed, picking up his jacket and putting relevant paperwork in his briefcase. He wasn't happy that only one of Kayleigh's boots and her coat had been found – it didn't feel right. He would have expected to have found both boots together if she'd discarded them. Were the garments left there by someone to throw them off a scent, he wondered? Had she got into someone's car that night and been taken there, or had she started walking home and hypothermia set in? Would they ever know?

Dylan drove up onto the Manchester Road and stood quietly where Kayleigh's car had been parked. He looked across the moors. Kayleigh knew the area. She would have known that by travelling further along Manchester Road in the direction she was heading that it would take her out onto nothing but bleak moorland, so common sense told him that if she had headed anywhere that night, on foot, it would have been back in the direction from which she had come and towards nearby dwellings. Providing of course she was in control of her own movements, he conceded.

He could just see the roof of the nearest house a short

distance away. He walked a little closer to the building. When he got back to the police station, he would ensure physical searches were done there and the occupiers checked out. A call and a chat were not good enough at this stage of the enquiry. He needed to be sure she wasn't being kept somewhere against her will. He knew from experience that predators struck in all types of weather and circumstances, usually when victims were at their most vulnerable, making them easy prey.

Dylan took out his mobile and rang Barry Sharpe's number. Thirty minutes later, he was shown into his dining room which looked out onto a large flat perfectly manicured lawn.

Dylan sat down opposite his tired, dishevelled looking predecessor. 'Dylan,' he said holding out his hand. Barry gripped it tightly.

'It's good to see you mate,' he said.

'Tea and biscuits, Detective Inspector Dylan?' asked Barry's wife Trish. 'I haven't seen Barry so enthused about a meeting in a long number of years,' she said with a smile. 'He's been busy up in the attic digging out all his old paperwork since you rang,' she added, ruffling the few remaining hairs on her husband's head.

Barry's hands were resting protectively upon a pile of papers. 'Well it's not often people are as interested as I am in the Tina Walker case these days,' he said.

Trish put a loving arm around her husband's shoulders and squeezed him tight. 'It's not, is it dear?' she said, planting a kiss on the top of his head.

Barry squirmed. 'If it's the last thing I do I'll find the bugger that abducted her,' he said with a hint of fire in his eyes.

'I thought at one time that investigation would be the last thing he ever did do,' Trish said seriously to Dylan.

'Baloney woman, you fret too much,' said Barry.

'Coffee would be lovely, thank you Mrs Sharpe. It would be great to get a positive connection in the two cases,' said Dylan.

'It troubles me even now. Did we miss something? Was it me that was off the boil? Did I have tunnel vision? I was so determined to get the culprit for this one... We never found her, her clothing or her bike. It was as though she just vanished into thin air that day.' Barry's stare was steady and unblinking as he looked at Dylan and beyond. 'There was another girl went missing just over the border not long afore in the snow, y' know. She was never found either, but because she was a member of the travelling fraternity, it was deemed she might have moved on. They called her Defiance ... Diffy for short.'

Dylan smiled. 'If Jen heard you right now, she'd say you sounded just like me,' he chuckled.

'Then I don't envy your wife one bit,' Trish said, raising her eyebrows as she took leave of the two men to make the drinks.

'I'm sure you did the best you could with the technology you had back then, Barry. Don't be too hard on yourself. And Tina's disappearance might not even be connected to Kayleigh, so I don't want you getting your hopes up, but we will revisit the investigation to see if there is any similarities and if they are connected or not.'

Barry's eyes lit up. 'But you suspect the worst don't you? Just like I did, don't you?' he said.

'The facts speak for themselves, unfortunately. She's a young girl, pretty, supposedly street wise, but she suddenly goes missing in atrocious weather, body not found. You of all people know the types of predators out there, somebody will highly likely have taken advantage of her situation – and unfortunately, if they have, she's become their victim. I just hope we get some leads, otherwise some detective might be coming to see me in a few years time to see what I know, as I have with you.'

'I hope you solve it Dylan, not just for her family but, selfishly, for me too... If we get a result then I'll go back into my garden in peace this year,' he said, pointing towards his sanctuary.

'Like I said, Kayleigh's disappearance may have nothing to do with Tina Walker's but if it has we'll do our damnedest to find the connection. You obviously have green fingers. It's like a park out there,' Dylan said looking out to the garden.

'Ah, not at this time of year but it's good exercise, so the wife tells me,' he said with a nod of his head in her direction. 'You can see the results almost instantly when you do a bit of work out there – and that's what I like these days.'

'I don't get much time for gardening,' said Dylan, thoughtfully. 'It's like everything else, left to Jen, especially when a job's running.'

'Neither did I back then, but God willing you will. The years fly past. Before you know it your thirty years will have gone too and you can pick up the threads of your home life, if you've still got one that is. There were many officers I worked with who didn't see their retirement or hang onto their marriages or children. I was lucky,' he said, smiling in Trish's direction. 'So it's zero tolerance for the weeds now, but just like criminals they keep on coming back generation after generation,' he laughed.

As Dylan drove back to the station with Barry Sharpe's files safely locked in the boot of his car, he thought how nice it was to see one of his forerunners enjoying their well-earned retirement. He had known a hell of a lot of colleagues who had never made it there too, for one reason or another. His phone rang and he pulled into a lay-by to answer it.

'Avril Summerfield-Preston,' Beaky said in a cool, curt voice. 'Divisional Administrator, Harrowfield.'

Dylan smiled. 'I know who you are Avril. You don't have to tell me every time you ring me.'

'I like to keep it professional, Detective Inspector Dylan. I'm ringing to tell you that from tomorrow you'll be sharing the CID office with a DI Turner and his officers from Hampshire Constabulary who are coming up to do some investigations on a cold case enquiry.'

'And where may I ask are they going to sit, on our bloody knees?' Dylan snapped. His brows furrowed.

'There is no margin for discussion. Chief Superintendent Hugo-Watkins says... Well, let's just say the decision has been made.'

'I might have known. Does that pompous, supercilious git actually know how many people work out our office already? Oh no, silly me, how could he, he doesn't honour the likes of us mere mortals with his bloody presence.' Dylan cut the call without saying goodbye, threw his head back on the headrest, closed his eyes and inhaled deeply. He texted Jen, *'I need some fresh air – how about a bit of pram pushing? Ten minutes suit you?'*

'We'll be ready and waiting,' she texted back immediately. Dylan taking time out, there must be something wrong, she thought as she dressed Maisy to go out in the cold afternoon sun. 'One thing for sure my lovely girl, we are about to find out what's up,' she said to Maisy as she sat the baby in the pram. Maisy had become unusually calm over the past few days, instead of needing Jen's attention for most of every waking hour, she was now beginning to amuse herself for short periods.

Jen watched Dylan as he got out of the car in the driveway

from the living room window, his face was like thunder.

Maisy squealed with delight as her daddy walked in the door and Jen saw his face instantly soften. He crept across the room grinning and bent down, waving his fingers in front of her. She threw her teddy out of the pram and Dylan picked it up. Handing it back to her, he kissed the top of her head and stood up. Instantly she threw the teddy out again and Dylan bent down to pick it up once more.

'I'll have that, young lady,' Jen said, seizing the toy. 'Otherwise we'll be here all day playing that little game.' Maisy howled. Dylan put his finger in the palm of her hand and she grasped it tightly, still whimpering miserably. He took hold of the pram and negotiated it expertly out of the door. Maisy's face was solemn for a minute or two, but as soon as they stepped outside Dylan was rewarded with a smile. Max stood beside the pram, panting with excitement. In silence they strolled towards Sibden Park. Jen hooked up to Dylan's arm, reaching down intermittently to stop and throw a stick for Max to fetch. Dylan took a few deep breaths and turned to look at his wife. 'I've been to see a retired SIO this morning about another girl who went missing in the same area twenty years ago.'

'You think it may be linked?'

'Well, Tina Walker did disappear a long time ago...,' he said. 'Albeit it was in the same weather conditions... but my gut instinct is saying where the hell has the perpetrator been, if it is the same person or persons, since? Surely whoever abducted Tina Walker, if that is what happened to her, hasn't waited twenty years to do it again?'

'You'd better get it sorted mister. I don't want any detectives coming around pestering us when you've retired. I want us to leave all this well and truly behind us.'

'Me too Jen, me too,' he nodded.

'Something he said made you cross?'

Dylan smiled. 'You know me too well my girl,' he said. 'Hell no! It's Hugo...'

'Watkins,' she smiled knowingly.

'The hierarchy as usual,' Dylan said with a sigh. 'He's only told a group of officers from Hampshire that they can use our office while they're up here on a cold case enquiry.'

'Oh,' she grimaced. 'Linked?'

'Don't know anything else yet. I put the phone down on Beaky.'

'Ouch. You didn't! Don't go upsetting her. I need her to

agree to my back to work terms or my career-break...' she smiled apprehensively.

'Well... She rubs me up the wrong way. What you thinking about returning?'

'Arh, I'm just thinking about it...' she said thoughtfully. 'You're not going to get into trouble for walking out with us are you?' Jen said reaching forward to pull Maisy's knitted bonnet away from her eyes.

'Well let's see, I have my mobile with me. If anyone wants me, they can get hold of me. I'm the boss. So, if I don't tell myself off, then I guess I'm okay,' he said, forcing a smile. 'But there again, if it had been someone else's wife I was with, pushing a pram, then I guess I'd be in trouble, right?'

'No, you'd be in hospital and I'd be at the police station admitting the assault.'

'That's one thing you'll never have to worry about with me, Jen. There is only room for two girls in my life and I'm with them,' he said, smiling lovingly down at Maisy, who was fast asleep, her pretty little head tilted with her chin upon her chest.

'She's her father's daughter,' Jen said, surveying Maisy closely.

'Because she's cute with kissable lips?' he gave an almost noiseless laugh.

'No because she snores and can fall asleep on a washing line, as my mum used to say.' Jen smiled up into his eyes and kissed him on the lips.

Dylan felt much better as he strolled back into the CID office an hour later. Looking around, he could see that Avril had already had desks moved and placed in a square, to accommodate their visitors. Trust her to do it while he was out.

'Who was about on the evening of White Wednesday, DC Granger? Have all the nearby houses been checked, DC Wormald?' he said with renewed vigour. The officers didn't look up from their work. 'Ned, Andy, you listening to me?' Dylan shouted. 'Well?'

'A lady phoned the office this morning in response to the appeal saying that her and her husband had abandoned their vehicle in the same area that night. The only people they saw were two young lads who were drinking and being quite loud and boisterous. Oh, and a person was seen carrying hot drinks to stranded drivers. The aforementioned lady has been given priority to be seen and the person seen carrying the hot drinks has yet to be found,' said Vicky.

'Make sure it's recorded on the HOLMES computer system. The amount of information coming in is becoming too much for paper records and we need it on the system for quick cross-referencing. Arrange for the file of Tina Walker to be typed on as a linked category to show the extent of background research at this time, but also so it is immediately retrievable. It's in my office and I've picked up retired Detective Superintendent Barry Sharpe's paperwork this morning that I want going through. It's only a matter of time before Kayleigh's body turns up,' said Dylan.

'That's what it is...' said Vicky looking over Dylan's shoulder into his office that was stacked high with boxes. 'Shall I get it removed now?'

'Bloody hell! They've found more?'

'Yes, Trevor put the last of the boxes on your desk and chair this morning, there was nowhere else to put them.'

'Barry Sharpe mentioned another misper from just over the border too, about the same time as Tina Walker went missing, but it was thought she might have moved on, part of the travelling fraternity, he said. Maybe worth getting hold of that information from GMP?'

'There's still a remote chance she'll turn up alive, isn't there sir?' said Jackie.

'As much as Ned or Andy over there going out today and finding rocking horse shit, there is,' said Vicky.

'Vicky...' scolded Dylan.

Chapter 12

Dylan appealed on the radio and in all the local newspapers, asking anyone who had been good Samaritans on the evening of White Wednesday and particularly those who took hot drinks to stranded drivers in the Manchester Road area, to contact Harrowfield Police Station. He also called for the two young men who were seen on that same evening, on Manchester Road in the vicinity of the nearest houses to where Kayleigh's car was found, who he believed were drinking, to come forward. He stressed it was to eliminate people seen in the area, so that the team working on the case could piece together the last sighting of Kayleigh Harwood. He also requested that anyone who had not come forward before, for whatever reason, to do so now as their information might just be the piece missing in the jigsaw.

He kept returning to the surrounding area and the houses nearest to where her car had been parked and his old motto of 'clear the ground beneath your feet', kept going round and round in his head.

'Our initial focus must be on the nearby houses, their occupants and outbuildings,' Dylan told the assembled group at the later pre-arranged briefing, 'to see if anyone saw Kayleigh on that night, or indeed anything untoward. The person who was out offering drinks to the stranded can't live far away. Now we've found a boot and a coat identical to those worn by her nearby, I want local premises thoroughly searched, including attics, garages, sheds, in fact anywhere that a body could be hidden. A body can be located in the smallest of spaces. Bodies, and living people, have been discovered inside hollowed out settees, under beds, in cupboards, suitcases, even animal cages. Nothing must be overlooked on this search.'

'The nearest house to where Kayleigh parked her car – who lives there, do we know?'

PC Alan Hughes raised his hand, 'I made initial enquiries there. The house is called Ivy Cottage. The owner is an old lady who lives there alone. You've gotta feel sorry for them, haven't you, stuck up there in the middle of nowhere in that weather? I didn't look around the property, I wasn't told to check it out at that point. My instruction at the time was to seek information.'

'That's fine. Tomorrow it's a priority – it's the nearest house, so we search it.'

The team was all ears.

'I want her checking out, her home and any garage or outbuildings she may have. I want us to be absolutely sure Kayleigh wasn't or isn't there. I'll arrange a search team as well as an interview team and then we move to the next house and the next until we get more information.'

'I'm sure she'll be glad of the company, boss,' PC Alan Hughes said, with a curl of his lip and a shrug of his shoulders.

'In the meantime...' Dylan said irritably. 'Vicky, can you do some in-depth research on her and the address and when we move to the next property I want the same doing again.'

There was no good news for PC Jackie May. She had to return to uniform. Dylan tried to keep her but he lost the argument with her uniform Inspector as they were short staffed on the night shift.

'Even if you had a body and it was a murder investigation, I couldn't release her to you, Dylan. You know what it's like for Christ's sake, I'm below our minimum number of personnel for patrol with courses, PSU commitments, holidays and sickness as it is,' Inspector Mark Baggs said, genuinely upset. 'You can have her back as soon as I can manage without her, I promise.'

Dylan didn't push the matter with him.

'It would have been good experience working with CID throughout the enquiry, Jackie,' Dylan said. 'But Mark has promised me you can come back as soon as he can release you,' he told the very disappointed officer at the debrief. 'Moving on, the team from CID will consist of DC Vicky Hardacre, DC Andy Wormald and DC Duncan Granger for now. Ned, are you bloody listening, that's you!' he yelled. Ned jumped.

'Yes sir,' he said yawning, as he raised his head from where it had been laid on his folded arms upon his desk.

'Keeping you up, are we?' Dylan snapped. 'The rolling house search programme, as I said, will take you from the abandoned car outwards. I'll meet you at any property where you have any problems or concerns and we will be supported by a dedicated search team from OSU.'

PS Clegg nodded, 'Affirmative.'

'I can't stress enough the importance of this stage of the

enquiry. Any house searched could be a potential murder scene and the body or evidence could still be there. Be aware that the perpetrator may have kept something of relevance as a trophy. If any of the properties have gardens or outbuildings, I repeat these MUST be searched thoroughly.'

'I've already checked the Electoral Roll for Ivy Cottage, boss, and it shows an N Regan – and that's confirmed with Council Tax and Benefits Office,' Vicky said.

Dylan acknowledged her comment. 'I want recent prison releases and sex offenders registered in the area to become priority enquiries. What about the emergency service vehicles that were about that night and the council workers?'

'Waiting for a definitive list from the council of ad-hoc workers that night, because basically anyone with a wagon, tractor etcetera in the area that can spread grit or move snow apparently was called upon,' said Andy.

'If they got cash in hand they aren't gonna 'fess up are they?' said Ned.

'I'm not bothered about the back-handers. We just need details of who was out there on that night, especially in the vicinity of Manchester Road.'

'I'll tell them, sir,' said Andy.

Dylan arrived home on time and looked forward to savouring a quite night in. He opened the door to pandemonium.

'She won't stop crying,' said a tearful Jen as she paced the floor, babe in arms. Dylan looked down at the screaming, red faced, drooling child who was gnawing ravenously at her chubby fist.

Chapter 13

It was 9 am and Vicky, Andy and Ned stood at the door of the first cottage, supported by a team of six operational support officers.

'Not much of a gardener is she?' Ned remarked, surveying the jungle surrounding the house. The path and flowerbeds were weedy and the lawn uncut, which could be seen even though the snow was still present. The gate needed a lick of paint, as did the lattice near the porch. As he touched it, a piece snapped off in his hand. He grimaced at Vicky and stood upright with hands behind his back, whistling quietly.

A dog was making a persistent woof, woof, woof sound from inside but no one answered.

Andy held the door knocker high and rapped loudly, and only then did the inner door slowly begin to open. The old lady hesitated, as if frightened of what might be there. She was dressed in baggy clothes and her thick head of hair was ruffled, resembling a mop.

'It's open.' she yelled. 'What do you want?'

Vicky stepped forward, showed her warrant card and introduced herself and her companions.

'Can we come in?' she asked politely. 'We are looking to speak to the householder.'

'That's me,' she said, looking slightly confused.

All three officers noticed the leg irons she wore. She walked a short distance ahead of them down the corridor with a limp and jerk of the opposite shoulder.

'Mrs?'

The old lady stopped and turned to face them.

'Regan,' she muttered, pulling her right sleeve up above her elbow.

'Mrs Regan, we need to have a look around your property, inside and out I'm afraid,' Vicky said, with a furrowed brow as she stared inquisitively at the old lady's hairy arm.

She turned to her companions and frowned. The three followed the woman into the lounge where a large open fire blazed. She picked up the poker and stabbed at the coals vigorously. The search team were outside waiting patiently for the instruction from the officers inside that they could begin.

'Well is it? Is that what you would have us call you?' Vicky

said.

There was a pregnant pause. Andy coughed.

'You can call me Nelly. Nelly Regan.'

Ned gasped.

'Really?' Vicky said. The old woman stood very still, cocking her head, as she stroked her Adam's apple.

'Alright, my name's Norris, Norris Regan but everyone calls me Nelly,' the man said in a husky voice, as he flopped into a chair and pulled off his wig.

Andy and Ned remained silent, but looked bemused as they stifled a chuckle.

'Do you dress as a woman often?' Vicky said.

'Yes,' he said.

'Right, Norris Regan then?' Vicky said.

He nodded.

'We have a team of officers here and we need to search your property to be sure the missing girl Kayleigh Harwood isn't here. Can we have your consent to do that?'

'You can but it'd be a waste of time, she in't here.'

Vicky nodded to Andy and he left the room. Vicky and Ned sat down. Almost immediately, footsteps could be heard running up the stairs and the team's fluorescent jackets brushed noisily on the walls as they moved down the narrow hallway.

'Do you go out dressed like that, or is it just something you do in your own home?' said Vicky.

'This is how everyone knows me round here,' he said, pointing to the callipers with shiny steel, supports. His thighs and calves were encased in leather, with buckles and straps galore. 'I aren't disabled. The irons were mother's. I wear them because it makes me feel... Well, I like wearing them,' Norris swallowed. 'You see, I'm what you'd call a calliper devotee,' he said quietly, closing his eyes for a brief moment.

'A what?' said Vicky, her voice rising to a high pitch.

'There aren't a lot a people around these days that have to don them. Don't get me wrong, I'm glad that most of the world is rid of polio and the likes, but it poses a problem for folk like me. Today, it's a memorable day for me to see someone in irons. When I was a child, it was a common sight.'

'Can you tell me when all this started, so we can perhaps begin to understand?' said Vicky.

Above them, the creaking of floorboards and movement of the search team shifting furniture rumbled like thunder.

'Me and Mother were close, you see. She was mithered keeping the secret all them years but she did it, because it was her fault I'm like this,' he said, in a relieved manner.

'Oh, yeah, how come?' said Ned looking to the ceiling.

'My cousin had polio and wore the irons. He were dead chuffed o'course when Mother mollycoddled him and I saw and felt his pleasure in her favouritism. She knew it made me mardy but she still pandered to his every whim. I used to watch her don the callipers and doff 'em when she had to wear them and I know it sounds bizarre but it excited me. As I got older it became pleasurable. After all this time I'm less convinced that disability, as such, is so important. I take pleasure in seeing people wearing the apparatus and my mum fulfilled that need for me. When she died... well I wear them now.'

'When did she die?' said Vicky.

'A few years ago.'

'Why do you wear her clothes?' said Vicky.

'Because I like to, is that good enough for you?' he said looking straight into her eyes.

Vicky stomach turned. Ned looked on, but Vicky's face showed no sign of emotion.

'So everybody round here calls you Nelly Regan,' he said. 'But they know?'

Norris shrugged his shoulders.

'So, is it a sexual thing, a fetish, is that right?' said Ned.

'Suppose you could call it that.'

'Have you kept all your Mum's things?' Vicky said, daring to glance at Ned for the first time since the interview had begun. He seemed totally disbelieving of what he was seeing and hearing.

'That way she's still here, with us, isn't she girl?' he said, patting the dog.

'Have you ever had any medical treatment for the problem?' Ned asked, with a look of disgust.

'What problem? I loved my mother, don't you?'

'Obviously not like you do,' Ned said with a stifled little cough.

'We had a special bond, me and Mother, but I don't expect you to understand.'

Vicky felt a shudder go down her spine. She had to keep him talking.

'You mentioned people round here... When it snowed heavy on the 7th January, White Wednesday the media are calling it. Do you remember that night?'

Norris stared past Vicky to the wall, as if constructing images upon it. He nodded.

'Did you have anyone call on you?'

He screwed up his eyes and put a finger to his lips.

Vicky coughed but he dreamed on. 'It must get very lonely up here sometimes?' she said, in attempt to break the silence. 'Especially in bad weather.'

Ned stood and started to pace the room like a caged animal.

'You see, some kind souls took hot drinks out to stranded motorists and I wondered if maybe they came to check on you too?' There was no reply.

'Well?' Ned said, as he bent down and leaned heavily on the arm of Norris's chair. 'The lady is asking you a question.' Norris flinched and reached out to grab the wig to stop it from falling off the chair arm. Ignoring Ned, he took hold of it and spun it around in his hands as if considering putting it back on his head.

'Did you, or did you not, see people taking hot drinks out to stranded motorists?' demanded Ned, impatiently. 'And stop playing with that flaming rug rat,' he said, taking it.

Vicky caught his eye and scowled. 'It was a lovely thing for people to do. You seem like a kind sort of person to me,' said Vicky. Ned walked around the back of Norris's chair and raised his eyebrows at Vicky. 'Eh?' he mouthed.

'Do you remember what you did that night? Did you go out?' Vicky asked in a softer tone.

'It snowed really heavy, I got wet.'

'So you did go out?' Ned said eagerly as he sat back down next to Vicky and threw the wig back at Regan.

Norris didn't reply, but he stuck the wig back on his head haphazardly.

'What DC Granger means is did you go out in the awful weather on White Wednesday or did some kind person come and see if you were okay that night and maybe bring you a hot drink?' Vicky said, stamping her heel firmly on the toe of Ned's shoe.

'Ouch.' Ned muffled a cry. Norris looked at Ned insolently, his lips thin.

'I'd like to help you if I can. Mother and I always helped out in the community.' Norris smiled to himself, his eyes narrowed.

'So did you take drinks out that night? Did anyone accept a

drink from you?' Ned said.

Norris Regan remained silent.

'Did you go out in the leg braces?' Vicky continued to dig into his ribs.

'Don't be daft. You can't walk in that kind of snow in these,' Norris said, his glance fell away from Vicky's face, like a hand being furtively withdrawn.

'Did you see or speak to anyone that night, Norris?' Vicky wasn't going to let his manner hinder her questioning and she raised her eyebrows at him in expectation of an answer.

'Yes, I shovelled the snow off the path.'

'Didn't you hear the lady? Did you speak to anyone?'

Norris looked in Ned's direction but avoided eye contact.

'If your mother was so God fearing, what did she do to you when you told a lie?' Ned leaned forward and put his face close to Norris's.

'I haven't lied,' he said, putting his hand to his head. He caressed the hair of his wig, softly.

Chapter 14

'Holly, West Control Room, sir.'

'Go ahead Holly,' said Dylan.

'Chief Superintendent Hugo-Watkins is requesting your attendance at the scene of a major incident, sir.' Jack Dylan's shoulders dropped and he idly twiddled his pen between his thumb and forefinger. He stifled a yawn.

'Is this an exercise Holly? I haven't got time to be laiking about with him today. If he's not asking us to fill in his blasted forms for the Home Office, he wants us to do some flaming role play instead of real police work, just to tick his box for promotion.'

'I'm pretty sure this isn't, sir. The Chief Super has called out the helicopter, Force Support Team, Dogs, Scenes of Crime Supervisor and the press office.'

'Holy shit Holly, what's the cause of him calling the circus out?'

'There's a skull been found on moorland near a lay-by on the Manchester Road. A wagon driver rang the information in about an hour ago. Seemingly the poor guy had got out of his cab to relieve himself, when he saw it at the bottom of the grass banking.'

'So Mr Watkins has taken charge has he? Just decided that it might be a crime, and is only now contacting me?' Dylan raised his voice, his face getting redder by the minute. He threw his pen across the desk and clenched his fist. Lisa looked up from her typing to see what the commotion was.

'There's a rumour, he's saying that he thinks it might be your missing hairdresser that's been found.'

'What? How the hell does he come to that conclusion? Since when did he qualify to be a flaming pathologist?'

'Don't know sir, I'm only repeating what's been said to me. I'm sure he'll tell you himself when you get there. I'll let him know you have been informed, and en route, shall I?'

'There's no rush, is there? The skull's not going anywhere, is it?' Dylan said.

He hung up in a rage, then sat back and breathed in deeply. Hugo-Watkins knew the rules. Dylan was the man in charge of crime for the Division, so why had he decided to take control? Dylan had a real urge to leave him to cope with the entourage he'd called upon. It was obvious he was trying to raise his profile by taking charge of the incident, another tick in a box maybe? Were interviews for promotion boards due? Dylan wasn't sure. Had Hugo-Watkins just had his personal performance review? Either way, he would let him stew in his own juices for a while.

Dylan picked up the phone.

'How's my favourite girls?' he said.

'What's up?' said Jen. 'You're going to be late home aren't you?'

'Why do you say that?'

'I can just tell by the tone of your voice.'

'Well, I've just been summoned to a crime scene by our leader.'

'Hugo-Watkins at a crime scene? No...'

'Exactly. You okay? You sound tired.'

'Oh, it's nothing,' she said. 'Maisy's temperature isn't going down, so I'm taking her to the doctor. Just a minute, there's something ... on the radio,' she said, turning up the volume. *'Grim discovery, Chief Supt Hugo-Watkins takes charge of a major investigation into the gruesome finding of a skull near to the border with Greater Manchester. Full report on the lunchtime news.'*

Dylan gasped, 'You're joking. This is the man that sealed off the area after witnesses saw a man jump to his death and had left a note apologising for what he was about to do, because he thought it might be suspicious! God give me strength, Jen. What time you at the doctor's with Maisy and I'll try to be there.'

'No need Jack, I'll sort it – and think on, don't be too hard on the egotistical soul, he makes you look good,' she said with a half-hearted laugh. 'The tooth's through by the way.'

'Tooth?'

'Your daughter's teething? Remember, another sleepless night? Or it was for me anyway,' Jen said as she wiped Maisy's running nose.

'Oh, yeah,' he said. 'You know me love, I could sleep on a park bench.'

'And have done before now, I dare say.'

'There are a lot worse places to get your head down when you're doing observations, I'll tell you. When I was a baby I slept in a drawer at the bottom of my mum and dad's bed with a coat over me to keep me warm.'

'Oh, they were the good old days Maisy. Did you hear your Dada?'

Dylan laughed. 'I'll try resist being too smug when I get to the scene, but it won't be easy.'

'Oh, get on with you. The sooner you go, the sooner you'll be home.'

'You're right. I'm going,' he said, smiling. 'Love you.'

No sooner had he hung up, the phone rang again. He sighed.

'Sir. Holly. Two requests, one from Chief Superintendent Hugo-Watkins who wants to know your E.T.A. and believe it or not you have been requested to attend – and wait for this ... the discovery of two more skulls, near to the footbridge crossing the beck at Ovenden. Just for your information, there was a manslaughter there some years back.'

'Yeah, I remember it well. I lived nearby at the time. I know the location so I'll head there first. Could you inform Mr Hugo-Watkins that I've been diverted, the finding of two skulls out-trumps his one for now.'

'Will do sir,' she said. 'He's not going to be pleased.' Dylan could hear the caution in her voice. 'Uniform are at the scene with the elderly couple who came across the skulls and rang it in. You do realise this brings a totally different meaning to the graveyard shift, don't you boss?'

He smiled to himself as he went to his car. Chief Superintendent Hugo-Watkins would have to cope with his self-induced spectacle a little longer. 'Builders,' Dylan thought as he drove towards Ovenden. It was probably someone building an extension and didn't want delays after accidentally unearthing some old skulls. 'Never assume, Dylan,' he scolded himself. Only time would tell if his prophecy was correct.

Fifteen minutes later he was in Ovenden and liaising with the two uniformed officers on the footbridge. With the recent heavy snow and increase in water levels, the beck had been at its highest for a long while, although it had subsided considerably in the past two days or so, he was informed. A visual check up and down the now shallow stream showed there had been collapses on the banking, and there was a small housing development taking place about a mile up-stream at the bottom of Ovenden Way. The nearest he could get to view the skulls was about six yards from a very muddy bank. They were devoid of flesh and hair and to Dylan's untrained eye they looked old. However, Forensic would examine them to ensure neither displayed any obvious signs of foul play, such as the bullet hole in the forehead, a broken jaw or a fractured skull. An archaeologist could also age them.

'Right lads, get scenes of crime to photograph them in situ for me, will you? Then they need recovering into exhibit bags for the forensic pathologist and archaeologist to look at over in the Sheffield lab. Will you also do a visual check further up and down stream for any other skeletal remains? They could have been washed up here or dumped. That we may never know, but let's do what we can to find out, shall we? Once we have an idea just how old these are, we should hopefully have a better idea of how they got here.'

Twenty five minutes later, Dylan arrived at the moorland scene. It was a darn sight colder on the tops, Dylan thought, pulling up the collar on his leather coat as he got out of the car. He shivered. The 'CRIME SCENE DO NOT CROSS' blue and white tape flapped merrily in the wind. It seemed to be everywhere he turned, and so were the media.

Chief Superintendent Hugo-Watkins stood in front of an audience. He continually wiped a moustache that was slightly greyer than his dyed hair. In his right gloved hand he was holding up a clear plastic bag containing what looked like the remains of a skull. Dylan couldn't believe his eyes or ears.

'Alas poor Yorick,' Dylan heard a uniformed colleague say to Riley the reporter. Dylan dreaded what the headlines would be in the Harrowfield Express.

'Hamlet, he was meditating on the fragility of life,' said Riley, studiously. The policeman looked at him, confused.

'I don't think the Chief Superintendent is playing the right part here, Riley,' said Dylan. Riley sniggered.

'No, he's more like the bloody court jester,' he said. It was Dylan's turn to snigger.

'Victoria Whittam, Calendar News: Is it true two other skulls have been found in your Division today? Are they connected and should people be worried?'

Dylan was very tempted to stand by and let Hugo-Watkins reap what he had already started to sow, but he knew the press would have a field day with him and in the cold wind he could see him look decidedly hot under the collar. Dylan stepped forward and stood at his boss's side, to his obvious relief.

'Ladies and Gents, let me first of all clarify one or two things for you, as I am sure you all have deadlines to meet.' There was a rumble of agreement and a shuffle of getting pen to paper.

Dylan went on. 'Firstly, while you have been shown the skull, I can't confirm to you by looking at it that it is even human. Please don't use any pictures you may have taken here today of the find.' Dylan pointed to the skull in the bag. 'It won't help identify who the person was, but could cause distress. Remember whoever this person was, if in fact it is human, he or she had relatives that may still be alive. Secondly, the location where it was found and the circumstances it was found in suggest to me that it wasn't buried there. It could have been that an animal has dropped it or someone might have discarded it, having found it elsewhere. They might have foreseen all the attention we have, here today. In due course, which may be weeks rather than days, we will probably have an approximate age of the skull. You will be informed of this, along with any other relevant information. As for the other two skulls. I have just been to the scene and let me assure there is no evidence to connect them. Finally, pre-empting the question, no they are not and I repeat not connected to the recent disappearance of local girl Kayleigh Harwood. The skulls are far too decomposed. Thank you ladies and gents. As you can imagine, we have a lot of work to do.'

'Yes quite,' endorsed Chief Superintendent Hugo-Watkins. 'And DI Dylan is a very busy man, move on,' he said, ushering the reporters to the side as he walked through the crowd.

'It's a bit like Moses parting the Red Sea,' Riley said, laughing.

'Now he only has to stop the Sun, like Joshua did, to get people to take him seriously,' laughed the police officer.

'You've been in the business too long Riley,' Dylan whispered out the side of his mouth.

Satisfied with what they had and with deadlines to meet, the media started to disperse.

'Chief Superintendent, I think we need to speak when we get back to the station,' said Dylan, holding his car door ajar.

Hugo-Watkins put his window down 'Yes, we do Inspector, my office four p.m. Can you finish off here please,' he said, handing the bagged skull to Dylan, who kept his hands in his pockets. Louisa Edwards, the Scene of Crime Officer, stepped forward and took hold of the bag. Dylan winked at her. 'I thought he was never going to let it go, boss,' she said, as they walked back to the scene together for one last look.

'Thank-you sir.'

Dylan headed back to the office at Harrowfield. He would be steeled and ready for his four o'clock meeting. Would Hugo-Watkins remain aloof and arrogant? Dylan told himself to keep calm whatever.

Chapter 15

Ned nodded for Vicky to leave the room. He wanted to be alone with Mr Regan, but she was having none of his bully boy tactics. That wasn't going to get them anywhere. She stood her ground.

'Do you want to see how the search team are doing, DC Granger?' she said. He was a distraction.

'No, I'm more interested in what Tranny's got to say,' he said, settling himself next to her once more.

'DC Granger, that's enough. Go.' Vicky scowled at her colleague.

'Norris, we were quite rude to you before and I apologise. What was your mum's name?' said Vicky, moving to the edge of her seat and turning her back on Ned.

'Nelly Regan that's N for November, e for echo, l for lima, l for lima and y for yankee ...' said Norris looking pleased with himself.

'And W is for wanker,' said Ned under his breath.

'Whisky,' hissed Vicky.

'Couldn't we all do with one of those right now?' said Ned. 'What the fuck are you doing? So he can do a bit of the frenetic alphabet. Where're you going with this? '

'Thank you, Mr Regan,' said Vicky, sharply. 'Thank you.' She glared at Ned. 'I'm sure if your mother was here, she would want you to help us the best you can, don't you?'

'Oh yes, she would've done anything to help anybody, she really would. She was a good woman, my mother was.'

'Is there anything more that you can tell us, Norris, that you think might be helpful to our investigation?' said Vicky, softly.

'I'm thinking,' he said, tapping his front teeth with his fingernail.

'Well, while you're sat here thinking, we'll just go and see how the search team are doing, together shall we?' Vicky said, getting to her feet and pulling Ned to his. 'Can I use your bathroom?'

'Down the corridor on the right.'

Ned didn't take his eyes off Norris, but putting her hand behind his back Vicky pushed him out of the room. As soon as the door shut behind them Ned turned. 'What's with the high and mighty stuff? He's a bloody perv, a weirdo. I'm not playing his bleedin' games any more.'

'He isn't responding to your aggression, can't you see that, you idiot? You're being totally unprofessional and you're fucking annoying me. So quit it, and sharp.'

'Don't try tell me what to do, you're not my bloody boss,' said Ned, indignantly. 'Give me five minutes on my own with him and he'll tell me what he's done, no worries.'

'Good job I'm not your boss or you'd be off the fucking enquiry as quick as you could say 'ow's y' father. All you're gonna do with an attitude like that is wreck the case.'

'I'm not that stupid. I don't know about you, but I'm looking for a missing girl and time's crucial right now, so if you think I'm pussy-footing around some mentalist you're mistaken. It's him Vicky. For fuck's sake, it's him, I just know it, so will you stop sucking up to him and let's get him banged up.'

'If Dylan heard you right now he'd rip your fucking head off. How many times have you heard him say, never assume? Anyway if you didn't notice, all we're short of here, dick head, and before we can arrest him is that little thing called evidence,' she hissed. 'So how about you check with the others and see if they've found anything to incriminate him, while I nip to the loo.'

'I told you, don't tell me what to do,' he said through gritted teeth.

'You can thank God I'm not your boss right now, but what an incentive to go for the boards...fucking grow up?' she said pushing him against the wall as she passed him on the narrow corridor.

'You threatening me?' he said.

'Whatever,' she said.

Standing at the little grubby sink, Vicky stared into the mirror above. Her teeth were clenched, she breathed heavily through flared nostrils, her face was red and her lips were pale – that always happened when she got angry. There was no warm water and the soap was hard and old and smelt of carbolic. She laid her hand on the thin, stained, linen towel briefly, heard raised voices and cocked her head to one side to listen. 'Good God,' she screeched, frantically trying to open the door.

Ned had returned to the lounge. 'Right, you perverted bastard. What have you done with her?' he shouted. He was nose to nose with Norris, who cowered in silence, his arms protecting his face. Ned grabbed the wig from his head and held it for a moment in his fist under Norris's chin.

Vicky flew down the hallway, banging her head on the

telephone fixed to the wall. 'Ouch,' she cried.

'Where the fuck is she?' Ned screamed, just as she arrived at the door. Ned stepped back, turned slightly and threw the wig onto the seat of a nearby chair.

Vicky threw the door open wide, and saw the back of Ned's hunched figure. Norris smiled up at him momentarily, then he threw himself out of his chair and onto the floor.

'What the fuck?' she cried, running to aid of the calliper clad man, who lay on the floor of his lounge, sobbing. 'What the hell's going on?' she screamed.

'Whoever gave you that scar on the top of your head didn't hit you fucking hard enough,' Ned said, his face contorted in anger. Then he stepped back further, hands in the air. 'I never touched him. I never laid a finger on him Vicky, I swear. The little prick threw himself on the floor,' he said.

Vicky knew her colleague mouthed off and played the hard man, but to her knowledge he had never hit out before. Had Norris pushed him over the edge? She took in the scene before her. 'How did that happen?' she said pointing to the wig strewn like a rabbit skin on the chair.

'Tell her the truth, tell her,' Ned demanded. Vicky helped Norris back into his chair and offered him a tissue from her bag. He moaned.

'Are you okay Mr Regan? A glass of water Ned please, now!' she shouted, glaring in Ned's direction. 'It might help,' she said to him her eyes wide and staring.

'Bollocks, absolute bollocks!' Ned said, storming out of the room. He was quickly back with a cup in his hand.

Norris sipped the water. Ned cheeks were red and his ego inflamed. He hadn't liked the look of Norris Regan to start with, but now he knew how devious he was too.

'Feeling better?' said Vicky, soothingly. She knelt down beside Norris and took the cup from the old man's shaking hands.

'Yes, thank you, but please don't leave me alone again with him again,' he said, leaning to one side in the chair and rubbing his leg.

Ned for once remained silent, but stared at his prey, wishing looks could kill.

'We just need to know, Norris. If did you go out that night, did you see anything that may help us? It is so important for us to find the young girl that has gone missing. Her mum is very worried, as you can imagine – just like your mum would have been if you'd gone missing when you were a teenager.

Kayleigh was just trying to get home from work that night. She lives with her mum, just like you used to. The snow came down so fast she got stuck in her car, just up the road from here. Can you help us find her, please?'

'I, I remember. I did go out.'

Ned nodded, smugly and eyeballed Vicky.

Vicky closed her eyes for an instant and sighed. Norris Regan appeared to have calmed down and was co-operating.

'I was carrying a hot drink, but I saw two ruffians banging on a car shouting to be let in. I came back inside very quickly.'

'Did you go back out again?'

'I would have given them a good hiding once upon a time, but not now.'

'What did they look like, these ruffians. Can you give us a description?'

'I don't know, it was dark and snowing but they sounded as if they'd been drinking,' he said, scratching his stubbly chin.

'Can you remember anything else about them at all? It's really important.'

There was a knock at the door and Andy walked in. 'Can I just have a quick word?' he said, beckoning Ned out of the room.

'Call me if you want me. I'm not far,' he said to Vicky. She nodded and turned back to Norris.

Ned disappeared behind the closing door.

'Come with me, I want you to look at something,' Andy whispered. 'You're never gonna believe this.'

'He lives here on his own and dresses in his dead mother's clothes,' said Ned as he followed Andy along the hallway and up the stairs. 'I think I'd believe anything about this weirdo right now.'

Chapter 16

Andy took Ned up the dark threadbare carpeted staircase that led into the bedroom.

'Fucking hell, what's that smell?' Ned said, gagging into his cupped hand. He fumbled for his handkerchief. 'No self respecting rat would venture up here.'

'Should've warned you,' Andy grinned. 'You'll get used to it after a while. Be careful you don't trip over the cess pot,' he said pointing to the potty directly in front of him. The rug at the side of the bed was heavily stained. 'But that's not what I've brought you up here to show you,' he said looking at the wall. 'Look at them.'

Ned was chuckling.

'What the hell is there to laugh about?' said Andy.

'I was just remembering a tale my tutor once told me. He'd been called to a disturbance. A crowd had gathered around a house in a terrace he was passing on his beat. Peering through the window, they could see the old guy who lived there slumped in a chair. The corpse was mysteriously wet through and the house reeked, beside him there was a cast iron pot. They called the coroner, as you do, and a sudden-death investigation got under way. They interviewed the other people who lived in the house and took statements from all and sundry and in the end it was ascertained that the guy's death was misfortune but not suspicious.'

'And what's that to do with the price of fish?'

'Wait on ... Seemingly the guy used to keep a cess pot next to his bed like our man downstairs, and over the months it had become too heavy to lift so he'd let it spill over. It had soaked into the floorboards and they'd rotted. The bloody pot had only fallen through the ceiling and killed the old man as he sat in his armchair watching television that day.'

'Jesus Christ, straight up?'

'Straight up!'

Ned walked around the cess pot to look at the pictures on the wall. 'Do you see anything odd?'

Ned screwed up his face and shrugged his shoulders. 'Nothing surprises me about that weirdo downstairs.'

'But can't you see? Among the family portraits of him and his mother, the others are all wearing leg irons, why?'

'It's a fetish. The leg irons he's got on, they're his mother's, and guess what? The sad bastard says they turn him on!'

'Nah, come on, you're winding me up,' Andy said, his eyes as round as plates.

'He's what they call a calliper devotee, or so he says.'

'Bloody hell, just when you think you've seen it all.' Andy reached over the bed. 'Down there's his bedtime reading. Orthopaedic Appliances Atlas, Novel Approach to Sexuality and Disability with a special piece regarding Devotee Attraction,' he read, picking just a few from the top of the pile with his gloved hands. 'Now this lot is beginning to make more sense.'

'And there's the mucky mags. He's serious wanker alright...'

'In more ways than one.'

'And he's not as daft as he's cabbage looking either. I raised my voice to him when Vicky was out of the room, to try and get a reaction and I got one alright, he threw himself on the soddin' floor, making out I'd pushed him.'

'What? Vicky knows you better than that,' Andy said.

'Yeah, but she's still gonna tell the boss isn't she? And it doesn't look good, does it?'

Andy stood at the chest of drawers that still had the lady of the house's dressing table set laid out on a crochet mat and looked through the mirror above. He slowly turned to look about the room. 'Have you seen anything more crazy than that?' he said pointing to the bell screwed to the bed head. 'I wonder if that's what his mother used when she wanted room service?'

'Could've been,' Ned said, sniggering.

'We're going to be here a while. You've only got to look at the state of this place to see we've a lot more digging to do, and it appears it might be worth a thorough look, don't you agree?'

'He was too close to his mother, it's unhealthy. I watched a programme on TV the other day and kids who were still being breast fed at twelve years old. You don't think?'

'How does your mind work? Worryingly, you're probably on this weirdo's wavelength.'

Ned was still laughing as he ran down the stairs and, without knocking, he let himself into the lounge.

Vicky and Norris were sat chatting amiably.

'We've just been going through Norris's early life, haven't we?' Vicky said turning to acknowledge Ned's entrance. 'A bit of background on how mum brought him up on her own,' she said quietly. 'He doesn't remember his dad ever being around, in fact he doesn't know who his dad is, do you Norris?' she said.

Ned watched Norris Regan's body language as he sat opposite him. Vicky talked. Norris crossed his arms and legs, changing his stance into a defensive mode towards Ned as he replied. He made no eye contact at all with either officer but preferred to fiddle with a bit of ribbon on the edge of his apron.

Ned spoke in a softer tone, which made Vicky wonder what he was up to. 'Were you a bottle fed baby, or were you one of the lucky ones?' he said, his voice, gentle and hesitant to start with, gradually rose in pitch and volume.

Vicky looked at Ned as if he'd just declared he'd seen a flying pig. Norris raised his head slightly to look at him but said nothing.

'A simple question Norris, not embarrassed or ashamed are we?' Ned raised his voice further as speaking to a man who was hard of hearing.

Vicky sat still, one brow curled up, her mouth opened in a perfect 'O'. Where the hell was Ned's line of questioning going? What had Andy shown him upstairs?

'You certainly like your reading material don't you? The devotee phenomenon, Admirer, Devotee & Pretenders r i s k y...' Ned said, watching Norris's face intently.

Vicky breathed in through her nose sharply, sat up straight and pulled her jacket tightly around her.

'No TV?' Ned frowned. 'So that's how you get your kicks is it? That's what turns you on?'

Norris was shifting in his seat as if he had sand in his blouse. 'I'm an adult. It's not illegal. I want to make a complaint,' he said looking directly at Vicky. 'I thought you lot weren't supposed to be prejudiced?' He turned back to Ned. 'I want you to leave my house now,' he shouted as he tried to stand quickly but his heavy metal callipers stopped him. He staggered, wobbled and flopped down once again into the chair.

'Sit down please,' Vicky said calmly. 'We just want your co-operation. We're losing sight of what we're here for. We're trying to piece together the last known movements of a missing young girl, whose car we have found abandoned a short distance from your home, aren't we?' she said, turning to Ned quickly, her eyes like daggers. 'Now Norris, you told us on the night in question you did go outside but, came back in because you saw a couple of drunken lads? How old do you think these lads were?'

Vicky had managed to regain his attention. He screwed up his eyes and thought long and hard before answering. 'Teenagers, early twenties I'd say. It was dark and snowing, how the hell am I supposed to know?' he said, disgruntled.

'Let's cut to the chase. Did you see a pink car or the young girl that was driving it?' Ned said.

'I can't help you,' Norris said flatly.

'Just talking to us and letting us search your house has helped already to try to eliminate any involvement you may have,' said Vicky.

'Well she isn't here. You're wasting your time with me,' he said pulling himself to the edge of the chair and with effort he pushed himself up to a standing position and took a hesitant step forward.

Vicky and Ned looked at each other, both noticing how confident he was. The most confident he had been since they arrived.

'One more question?'

Norris looked at Ned.

'Do you have a bike?'

Vicky again looked bemused.

'What would I want a bike for when I wear these,' he said bending down and tapping the leg irons with his knuckles.'

'But theoretically they aren't really yours are they? You don't actually need them.'

'After wearing them for so long, my doctor thinks I probably do,' he said, his head jutted forward and his eyeballs bulged like a toad.

Vicky studied the pair closely.

'Did you ever own a bike?' Ned said.

'Now you've got me baffled. Why are you asking me about a bicycle? I thought the girl that went missing had a car?'

Norris appeared to be gaining more confidence, Vicky noted.

'The bell on the bedpost – where'd that come from?'

Norris shrugged his shoulders.

'It looks old,' said Ned.

Vicky sat quietly and observed.

'That's why I asked if you had a bike, see.'

Norris looked thoughtful but remained silent.

'Where did you get the bell from?'

'I don't know,' he said, with a dismissive wave of his hand.

It was Ned's turn to nod his head.

'Mother might have picked it up from a jumble sale, she was always going to them.'

'Yeah, but it's not the sort of thing you'd pick up if you don't have a bike, is it?'

Norris cocked his head to one side and grimaced.

'Okay let's move on. You have a telephone don't you?'

'Yes,' he sighed heavily.

'You like to help people don't you?

'Yes.'

'So, why didn't you use your phone to report the teenagers you saw banging on a car on White Wednesday? Didn't you think that there might have been someone inside that might've been scared?'

Norris Regan looked shaken. 'Oh, I... I didn't want to be involved. They might have come here. Anyway the phone wasn't working.'

'Ah. Not working you say?'

'How do you know? Did you try to ring someone?'

'No, they said on the radio that the lines were down,' he said. 'I picked it up to see. Look, I'm tired now. I don't want to talk to you any more.'

Chapter 17

Dylan telephoned Jen. 'I'm just off to see Hugo-Watkins.'

'Why bother? Look what happened last time? If you go for him again, he's bound to report you this time.'

'I'm not going in for an argument Jen, unless he goes off on one,' he said, with a lopsided grin. 'But I have to tell him what a balls he made out there.'

'He'll know that already.'

'But he shouldn't meddle in what he knows bugger all about, should he?'

'We all know that Jack. Be nice to him for once eh? You wouldn't want his flaming job – and you know what they say, hold your friends close but your enemies even closer.'

'Like you do with Beaky?'

Jen sighed. 'Touché.'

'But he's not the enemy Jen, that's just it, we're supposed to be on the same flaming side. He just keeps on putting his size eleven graduate entry feet in it and involves himself in stuff that he doesn't need to, for the glory, not for the good of the job. What with his Grecian 2000 dyed black hair and matching coloured moustache that's groomed to perfection. He's got fuck all else to do... or rather won't take ownership of fuck all else. It's the victims that matter, not his bloody ego and what the Chief Constable thinks of him.'

'Jack. You, me, we all know a lot of the top brass that are like that... Why do you still allow them to eat away at you? Think about us... Try get home for Maisy's bath time, will you? That's more important, isn't it? What do you fancy for tea, corned beef hash, pasta, gammon?'

'Gammon with two eggs, sunny side up?' he said. 'See you later.'

'Mmm,' Jen said, with a frown, 'and let's hope Daddy still has a job when he comes home, eh Maisy?' she said rattling a soft bunny rattle in front of their daughter who was happily sat in her baby seat, oblivious to the outburst.

Dylan walked along the corridor to the Chief Superintendent's office. The station was warm – or at least the top corridor where the hierarchy had their offices was. He stood tall. 'Rise above it,' he said, smiling at Janet, Hugo-Watkins' secretary and she smiled back quizzically. This wasn't Dylan's normal approach when heading into the boss's office and she knew it. What was he up to?

Dylan knocked at the door, listened for a minute and knocked again. He glanced back at Janet and she was still looking at him, her lovely long fingers, with perfectly French manicured nails, poised hesitantly over the computer keyboard.

'Come in Dylan,' Hugo-Watkins shouted. Dylan raised his eyebrows at Janet and smiled. He opened the office door and as he stepped inside he heard her typing.

Hugo-Watkins' coffee percolator was nosily bubbling away and Dylan's favourite pure chocolate cookies with a crispy edge and a chewy centre were waiting on a plate on the coffee table. Hugo-Watkins had predicted his imminent arrival – or Janet had, Dylan thought.

'Take a seat and help yourself to the refreshments,' Hugo-Watkins said, as he got up from behind his desk. He straightened the black clip on, uniform tie that lay neatly upon his crisp white shirt and settled himself opposite Dylan on the big cushioned two-seater leather settee that smelt like a saddle. The walnut coffee table was the only barrier between them now.

Dylan poured a drink and ignored his boss's staring eyes. The office was cosy, with richly decorated wood-panelled walls, thick carpet and ornately trimmed furnishings, with expensive paintings more suited to a plush hotel room than to the office of the officer in charge of Harrowfield police station. The en-suite bathroom door to the office was slightly open. The room was tasteful and reflected the image of authority that Hugo-Watkins sought to portray. Dylan sat back and took the cup to his lips before making eye contact. Hugo-Watkins held up his hand.

'Before you say anything, I have something to say. I know we haven't seen eye to eye in the past, and right now I imagine I'm your least favourite person in this force.'

'Try the service,' Dylan said, his lips still touching the cup.

'Alright, I deserve that, but I have a job to do, just like you. Headquarters monitor me, not just on the Divisional performance but also on my personal development and that was the purpose of my involvement today – management of major incidents and taking an interest in crime, my latest instruction.'

'Okay, I understand that and can imagine how hard it is for people at your level, since you don't actually go out into the real world to get the ticks in the boxes that allow you to climb the ranks. But I have the overall responsibility for the investigation of serious crime in the area, which includes this division, so it would have been nice to hear about the discovery of skull when it happened, not over an hour later. If you wanted to speak to the media I could have advised you regarding the crime scene, and as for picking up the skull for a photo...' Dylan shook his head. 'Well, it's not a good idea, even if you know what you're doing.'

'It was in a bag,' Hugo-Watkins said, looking at Dylan imploringly.

'It was a flaming see-through bag,' Dylan said.

'Point taken. I know, I haven't got experience in these matters and I never will have if I don't try, now will I?'

'You could use your common sense, go on a course, or just ask!'

Hugo-Watkins sighed heavily. The room was silent. Dylan could hear Janet stop typing and the wall clock ticking. He sat forward and put his cup on the table. 'Look, tell you what,' said Dylan. 'The next major incident room I run, why don't you take the ride with the incident team? Come to the briefings. I'll take you through the process and then you might gain some background to the extent of the work that goes on, in a major investigation?'

'I don't want to get in the way.'

'You won't.... You can make coffee, can't you?' he said. Hugo-Watkins smiled, saw Dylan's serious face, looked horrified and nodded. Dylan smiled. 'There then. The team will actually be pleased, believe it or not, to see some senior management showing their support instead of what they normally do, harass them over budgets, overtime and expenses,' he said.

'You know that resources and funding are a nightmare for us all Dylan. But I know you do very well getting funding from the centre for most of your jobs.'

'Well if we didn't, the first murder at division would take you straight into the red.'

'That's true,' he said, with a nod of acceptance. 'You've been a Detective Inspector for some years now, doesn't promotion interest you?' Hugo-Watkins asked, with what seemed like genuine interest.

'There's no fear of you getting rid of me that way,' Dylan said with a snort.

'No, no I didn't mean...'

'Quit while you're ahead.'

'I just wondered if it was something you'd be looking at in the future. Difficult objectives, Jack.'

'Not on your life. You know what they say, the higher up the tree you go, the more of your arse you show – and with the size of mine, I think I'm high enough,' Dylan said, shaking his head. 'I don't want to get stuck behind a desk all day. I'd go stir crazy, like the rest of you.'

'Quite,' said Hugo-Watkins, lifting his cup to his mouth. His pinky finger stuck up and Dylan had an urge to laugh at the mannerism but thought better of it. He coughed into his hand instead. 'You chaps have a meeting for everything and never get anything bloody done. That's not for me,' he said. 'The bottom line is that I still enjoy the thrill of the chase and the satisfaction when I feel a collar.' Dylan screwed his hand into a fist and held it high, looking at it intently as if imagining a criminal hanging from his grasp.

'But as you get older and after all those horrific sights you've witnessed, maybe at some stage you'll want a change, a quieter existence,' said Hugo-Watkins, leaning forward and pouring another drink from the pot. He offered a refill to Dylan, who covered the cup with his hand. 'Just think Dylan, one day you could be in charge of a Division and get hassle from your own DI,' he said, pouring the remaining dark brown liquid into Dylan's empty cup nonetheless.

'Now that would be a challenge,' Dylan smiled. The shrill tone of his mobile phone interrupted them. He took it from his pocket, looked at the screen and then back at Hugo-Watkins. 'I've gotta take this,' he said. Hugo-Watkins nodded.

'Dylan,' he said.

'Boss I need to speak to you regarding Nelly Regan. Search team are still here, but I think Ned and I could do with a chat with you about her... him.'

His head tilted, his eyes narrowed and his nose wrinkled as if he'd smelled something funny. 'What?'

'I think it would be easier to explain face to face. Can we meet you back at the nick in about fifteen minutes?'

'I'll see you both in my office,' he said.

'Problem?' asked Hugo-Watkins

'The team have been searching a house near where Kayleigh Harwood went missing.'

'Do you smell a rat?' asked Hugo-Watkins with interest.

'You could say that, we're sure she didn't want to disappear and I'm sure the stats would suggest foul play, murder even...

Like I said, you, might want to drop in at one of the incident room briefings sooner rather than later.'

'Yes, I might just do that, if I get the time,' Hugo-Watkins stood up and extended his right arm to shake Dylan's hand. Dylan took it with a firm grip.

'I'm glad we've managed to have this little chat. We should do it more often,' he said.

Dylan nodded his head and smiled at Hugo-Watkins, who pressed his thumb over the knuckle joint of his middle finger where it met his hand. 'And, thank you for your assistance today, I'd dug myself into a bloody big hole that seemed to be getting deeper until you arrived,' he added, releasing his grip. 'Keep me informed Jack. Believe it or not, I am interested.'

'Thanks for the coffee,' said Dylan. He left the office, walked along the corridor and down the stairs to his own. Was he getting soft in his old age, thinking that Hugo Watkins wasn't such a bad bloke after all? His handshake was weak – and then it clicked, Hugo was testing Dylan to see if he was a Freemason by shaking his hand in that particular way. He sensed another invitation to one of the local Lodge's social functions. He couldn't be doing with all that rolling up of the trouser leg and baring of the chest. He didn't have the time to see his own daughter have a bath, for God's sake!

'I'll phone you when I'm setting off, Jen,' Dylan said into the phone, just as his office door opened. Vicky almost fell inside. He put his hand in the air to stop her and she put her finger to her lips, giggled, and backed out, closing his door quietly. She did her best impression of making a drink of coffee through the window and Dylan nodded the affirmative.

'Okay, don't keep me in suspense. How did it go with the Chief Super? Tell me you kept calm ... you didn't thump him?' Jen said.

'No,' he said, laughing. 'Me and Hugo, we're like that,' he said, crossing his fingers, 'bestie mates.'

'You see? I told you everyone has a good side, if only you take the time to look for it.'

'Not everybody Jen, you can be so bloody naïve. What do you think about me joining the Freemasons?'

'Oh no, not the handshake? Not in a thousand years. There's only one set of breasts you like and if you're late it's your own fault if you don't see them,' she chuckled.

'Naughty,' Dylan smiled. 'But nice... Gotta go. Ned and Vicky are waiting to speak to me.'

'Remember, I'll be waiting to see you practise the initiation,' she said, laughing as she hung up.

Vicky put an overflowing mug of coffee on his desk. 'Good job you're good at your job,' Dylan said as he looked into the deep dark liquid. 'I had better upstairs.'

'What?'

'Nothing.'

'Someone, who will remain nameless, got that cheap own brand crap from the pound shop.' Vicky scowled. 'Anyhow, it'll keep you awake, urgh,' she said, frowning as she took her first sip. She shuddered. 'You won't believe what's just happened to us,' she added, her eyes wide.

'Go on,' Dylan said, taking a sip.

'I've met some weirdos in my time, but it wouldn't surprise me if this one knows something about Kayleigh's disappearance.'

'He's nowhere near as stupid as he makes out either,' said Ned,

'And he dresses up in women's clothes and wears his mother's leg irons, which by the way, he says excites him,' Vicky said, lips pursed.

'He's what I believe they call a calliper devotee,' Ned said.

Dylan bit on his lower lip, 'Slow down, let's start again. Vicky, set the scene, then you can add your two penn'orth Ned. Describe this character to me.'

Chapter 18

'I wouldn't even wear my mum's clothes,' said Vicky. 'never mind him! Get this, he even wears her bloody wig. He answered the door wearing the whole regalia and at first he told us he was her ... but the Adam's apple gives it away for me every time.' She leaned forward and half cupped her hand around her mouth. 'Then the hairy arms and big feet; not sure he realised it though boss,' she winked, jerking her thumb over her shoulder towards Ned. 'Good job 'Nelly' wasn't in a night club when you'd had a few Ned, eh?'

'Clever sod. The lighting was poor and some women have Adam's apples.'

'Get away! None, I know of and not as big as his is,' Vicky said.

'Maybe you should have yours removed? They house the vocal cords, in case you didn't know,' he said. 'Go on, tell him about the leg irons,' Ned said.

'Okay, so, we establish that N Regan is actually Norris Regan, who is the only occupant and owner of the property. His mum Nelly is dead and he wears her clothes and wig because...'

Ned couldn't hold back, 'Because they turn him on,' he said.

Dylan sat in stunned silence. 'Well, it's not often I'm stuck for words...'

'The leg irons are the old fashioned heavy kind with metal leg braces that come up to just above the knee. He's a masochist. They must be so bloody painful to wear. He's talking, but didn't like Ned's aggressive tact,' Vicky scowled over at her partner.

'He annoyed me.'

'He frightens you.'

'I shouted at him to get a reaction and he threw himself down on the floor and told Vicky that I'd thumped him.'

'Tell me you didn't?' said Dylan, with a grimace.

'It was very tempting. But no, I didn't. The wall in his bedroom is covered with pictures of him and his mum and calliper clad Anothers and there's a great pile of calliper devotee type literature at the side of his bed.'

'Well that's a new one on me. Makes a change from the plastic sheet brigade, or the shoe fetish lot,' said Dylan, raising an eyebrow. 'So let's get down to the nitty gritty. Did he see Kayleigh? Was she there?'

'At first he denied going out on White Wednesday, but when we pushed him he admits to shovelling away the snow on his path and having the intention of offering hot drinks to stranded drivers, but he tells us he saw two guys who he thought may have been drunk banging on a car and shouting not far from his house, which put him off,' Vicky said.

'And he didn't report the incident to us?'

'No, I asked him why and he said his phone wasn't working.'

'Do we believe him?' Ned added, smacking his lips. 'Nope!'

'One thing is for sure is he's agitated one minute and gives us the silent treatment the next. There's more to him than meets the eye, I'm sure of that, and it's not just his weird sexual habits,' Vicky said.

'He lived in that house for years, just him and his mum... His mother must have been almost bedridden before she died. She even had the bell on the bed headboard to call him, and it's still there.'

'A bell?' Dylan said.

'Yes, an old bike bell,' Ned said.

'We weren't gonna get any more from him today. He told us he was fed up of talking to us, which became more apparent when we asked about White Wednesday and him seeing Kayleigh, so we decided to come away and seek your views as to where to go from here,' said Vicky.

'I think we should have him in, boss. I'm certain he knows more than he's telling us,' Ned said, licking his lips.

'I appreciate your enthusiasm, but on what grounds, that he's weird? What evidence have you got? Give him a solicitor and he won't speak a word to us. Get Andy to seize the bell.'

'The bell?' said Vicky. 'Why?'

'Because it's a simple request that might be all that is needed for him to agree to let us have it at this stage.'

'But, there were no identifying marks on it as far as I could see,' said Ned. 'It is just an old bike bell.'

'Just do it. Yes, I agree, we need to talk to him more. Will they finish the search today, do you think?'

'You're joking. They still have a jungle of a garden to search. I'd think it'd take them at least a couple of days to do it justice,' said Vicky.

'He's consenting to the search then?' said Dylan.

'Yeah, he seems quite happy to have the search team

there. Doesn't seem bothered about them at all. But let's face it, he's had plenty of chance to get rid of ought if he wanted to, hasn't he?' Vicky said.

'Right, so for now we continue to do everything with his consent. If that changes, we'll need to get a warrant. I want more research done on him to try put him in or out of the frame once and for all. After all, his property is the nearest dwelling to where Kayleigh's car was parked. We also need to identify the two drinkers who were seen banging on that car. If they exist, that is. I'll give the press office a push to put a fresh appeal for witnesses out and in the meantime keep Andy up to speed with our decision regarding the search. Anything else?'

'Nope, Ned wanted to hoist him, but like you say on what grounds? I guess there is always theft of his mother's leg irons? Let's face it, we've not got anything else on him.'

'A spell in a cell might get some straight talking out of him. I have a feeling about the weird bastard. He's been hiding behind the charade of being his own mother, so what else is he capable of lying about or covering up besides his weird fetish?'

'Hey Ned, dial it back,' said Vicky. Ned glared at her.

'She's right mate, patience. Find some evidence, or at least show me something that proves his story isn't true. Then you might get your wish. Remember the old bull young bull...' Dylan smiled.

Vicky and Ned looked at each other. 'You've lost us,' Vicky said.

'Have you never heard that saying before about the old bull and the young bull looking at a field full of cows? The young bull says, 'let's run down there and shag one of those cows.' The wise old bull winked at the young bull. 'Let's walk down and shag 'em all",' Dylan heartily laughed at his own joke. Ned's face softened and he smiled.

'You're so funny,' Vicky said sliding off her chair. Ned stood a broad grin on his face. 'I like that.' He walked out of the office mumbling the words of the joke and laughing to himself.

'If you didn't laugh you'd cry Vicky, you should have learnt that by now,' Dylan said. She sauntered back into the CID office. Dylan picked up the phone still chuckling and rang Jen to tell her he was on his way home. Just when he thought nothing could surprise him any more, he was proved wrong. 'Never assume,' he said quietly. Wasn't this what he loved about his job, the unexpected, the unforeseen and the unknown? Jen would be amazed at this latest revelation, she'd had her eyes opened since she had met Dylan and he hoped she learned a thing or two and was a lot less trusting of people these days.

Norris Regan was certainly of interest to the enquiry, and to Dylan.

Chapter 19

Dylan was in the station early next morning. DI Turner and his team were already busy working away. He raised his hand in acknowledgement, 'Morning lads,' he called. 'Alright?'

'Moving forward somewhen,' said Shaun Turner. 'Once we've got the swabbing done, we should be wrapped up.'

'Somewhen?' said Dylan. Somewhen? An Isle of Wight-ism if ever he heard one, a word Jen still used often. He turned into his office and switched on the fluorescent light to be faced again by the mountain of boxes he'd asked Trevor to fetch. He chortled to himself. What was he thinking when he had asked him to bring ALL the files and exhibits appertaining to the missing Tina Walker? Trevor stood behind him. 'Ah, Just the man,' he said.

'Been told they want moving back.' Trevor huffed and puffed.

'Yes well, the files need to go to the HOLMES indexers,' Dylan said sheepishly, taking off his jacket and putting it on the back of his chair. He helped Trevor to lift the boxes from his desk onto the trolley. Once clear, he unpacked his briefcase and set his fruit in his drawer before turning on his computer. He raised his head suddenly as Trevor banged his trolley blindly into the door frame. Dylan looked through the window to see if he could catch Lisa's attention to guide him out but caught Shaun Turner, not for the first time, staring in at him very oddly. It gave him a prickling at the base of his neck. Shaun picked up the phone and swivelled his chair round, deliberately it seemed, so that his back was to Dylan.

Nonplussed, Dylan scanned the detailed information on the incidents that had occurred within the Force in the past twenty four hours, before starting on his in box.

Vicky breezed into his office with a brew in her hand, 'Morning boss, little Maisy waking you up these days or are you just an early riser?' she said with one of her cheeky grins.

'Good job you brought me a drink lady, otherwise I'd have bollocked you for suggestive remarks,' he said, not taking his eyes from the computer screen. He raised an eyebrow but showed no other sign of emotion.

'Now you tell me. A severe reprimand from you sounds like a good start to the day to me,' she purred at the menacing look being thrown her way. Vicky winked at Dylan and turned on her heels. Dylan couldn't help but smile in her wake. 'Tell whoever asked Trevor to remove the boxes back to store thanks, will you?'

'It was me.'

'Thanks,' he said flatly. 'Vicky?' he called.

'Yes.'

'What do you think about Regan?' he said.

She stopped and walked back to stand in the doorway. 'I wouldn't trust him as far as I could throw him.'

'In your opinion, is he our man?'

She pondered.

'Don't sit on the fence. Has he seen Kayleigh off, do you think?'

Dylan knew the likelihood of finding the young hairdresser alive had diminished.

'Honestly?' she said. 'I've no idea.'

'Stop behaving like a bloody politician. It's me you're talking to. Answer the question, is he, or could he be, in your opinion, a murderer?'

'He lives in his own little world.' Vicky bit her lip. 'Let's just say years ago they'd have hung, drawn and quartered him on his appearance alone.' She stopped, brought her hand to her chin and rubbed it thoughtfully. 'I think he's capable of something, but what I don't know...'

'So is that a Yes?'

'A definite maybe.'

'All we need now is a motive and evidence.' Dylan groaned loudly, put his head in his hands and scratched his scalp with his fingertips.

'What do you always tell us? If the evidence is there then we'll find it. I'm going over to his house later. Andy is over there now with the search team and Ned's on his way.'

Dylan turned to face her. 'Good, let's put him in or out of the frame once and for all today if we can. Do we know what happened to his mother? If they've lived there for a long time they'd have been about when Tina Walker went missing, wouldn't they?'

'And that bike bell? I've known people have all sorts of stuff on their bedposts, but, that's a strange one.'

'I think so too,' Dylan said.

'You'll be telling me you wear cycle clips over your P J bottoms next.'

'Pyjamas?' he said with a cock of his head. 'What's them

then?'

'Way too much information,' she said as she left his office.

Dylan looked at the carpet. From the door to his desk was a trail of mud. He looked down at his shoes, no doubt from taking Max out for his morning walk. He'd made an extra effort to get up earlier and take the dog out since the arrival of Maisy. Poor Max hadn't been getting as many walks as he used to, but it seemed that he and Jen were now getting slowly but surely back into a routine and the dog wasn't getting any younger so he didn't need as much exercise as he used to. Dylan was wiping dirt from his shoes with a tissue when Vicky stuck her head around the door, she looked at him oddly.

'I know we deal with some shit boss, but it hasn't got that deep has it?' she grimaced.

'Just letting you know uniform have locked up Donny Longbottom this morning for an indecent assault on a sixteen year old girl, so I'm just going to find out what the score is.'

'The would be Teddy boy who has the hots for Kayleigh?' said Dylan.

'That's one and the same.'

'Another that we need to put in or out of the frame. So what're you waiting for?' Dylan growled.

'I'm gone,' Vicky called, as she vanished into the bowels of the CID office.

There was no time to spare, this needed to go onto HOLMES immediately. The computerised major crime system would help him, as the SIO, direct and control the course of the enquiry. The information that was coming in needed cross-referencing and the last thing he wanted to do was miss or overlook anything of importance. The success of any major investigation requires an organised and methodical approach and the Major Incident Room (MIR) is central to any enquiry. It is where all the information is gathered from members of the public, enquiry officers and any other available source. This information is documented and managed, using a set of proven administrative procedures. Was it only twenty years since UK Police Forces starting using it? 'How on earth did Razor Sharpe and the likes manage without it?' he thought as he picked up his phone.

'Custody Officer, please,' he said, with authority.

'Speaking.'

'Jack Dylan. Can you ask the officers dealing with

Longbottom to liaise with me about the circumstances of his arrest please?'

'Of course, sir,' said the Sergeant.

Dylan picked up his mobile and distractedly turned it around in his hand. He texted Jen.

'What're my two lovely girls up to?'

'Your daughter's creating and I've just dealt with the most disgusting nappy. I feel like death warmed up this morning.'

'Normal day then?'

'Ha ha! You're not the only one that deals with crap. Did you just phone?'

'No why?' Dylan scowled.

'I missed a withheld number and it's one of a few in the last couple of days, that's all. Maisy's screaming the place down and Max is hiding under the table – poor fella,' she wrote.

'Sounds like fun. Speak later,' Dylan texted before tossing the phone down onto his blotter.

The office phone rang and he grabbed it. 'Dylan,' he said.

'Detective Inspector Jack Dylan, Harrowfield CID?' said a female voice.

'That's right, to whom am I speaking?'

'Maggie Jones at the forensic lab. You've sent us some skulls to examine?'

'Yeah that's right Maggie, they're a bit like buses and policemen, you don't see any for ages and then they all come along at once,' Dylan said.

'I wish I could say that,' she said. 'I'll send you the detail in hard copy, but for now each of the three skulls have been given separate identification numbers, and what I can tell you from my visual examination is the one found on the moorland is around a hundred years old, quite well preserved, nothing sinister like fractures or holes to suggest foul play. However, the other two are more recent. I'd say as an educated guess no older than twenty-five to thirty-years, at the very most. One of them is damaged quite badly, but that's been caused recently looking at the clean edges, again nothing to suggest anything sinister at the moment. There is a little bit of scar tissue on the other but nothing that suggests a major head injury.

'I'm really grateful for the quick response. In respect of the latter two skulls, perhaps we need to do some further investigations?' Dylan said, rubbing his chin. 'Do you think they may be from a grave disturbance, which was my initial thought?'

'I can't tell you that, but the good news is that we can do further work to age them more accurately. There is sand wedged deep in the eye sockets of one, so we'll analyse samples taken from that. The bonus is that they still have teeth intact. I will contact a forensic ondontologist who will examine and evaluate them for you and hopefully you will be able to corroborate the dental evidence. Should you require it, he will be able to present his evidence in court for you at a later stage. We should get DNA that will be preserved in the teeth and if need be we can do craniofacial reconstructions so we should be able to give you a biological profile.'

'That's excellent,' Dylan said, brightly.

'Bad news is that everything takes time and costs money.'

'How much?'

Maggie Jones whistled through her teeth. 'How big's your budget? I can guess from experience it's not enough.'

'It's not gonna happen is it? Not with the funds we're allocated. I was hoping they were all going to be a hundred years old. Trouble is, now I may have no choice but to look at them more closely, no matter what the cost. The reconstruction can wait, but it'd be helpful if you can get on with the other examinations – and hopefully we'll solve the mystery before cost becomes an issue. Obviously if we find that official graves have been disturbed, or any other information comes to light in the meantime, we'll let you know.'

'That's my job. It's fascinating for me to unravel mysteries in this way, I'll be in touch in due course.'

Forensics might be excited about the find, but Dylan would have to get a team together to start tracing any further remains and the origin of the skulls already found. He knew the media would love the story. It was the stuff that sold papers for them. However it wasn't thrilling to him, it was more work on the already stretched manpower, but his inquisitive nature that made him want to be an investigator in the first place would drive him on to get a result.

He turned to his computer, selected a pro forma for an internal blank Minute Sheet and typed a note to Chief Superintendent Walter Hugo-Watkins, updating him and informing him that he would start an investigation into the younger two skulls.

The response was immediate. *'Thank you for the update. I would like to be in the loop and I'm sure HQ will watch the story with interest. Leave it with you,'* he said.

'I'll obviously require more staff, which will need to come from Division in these early days,' Dylan responded.

'Speak to the Chief Inspector Operations. I will message him. Thank you. Walter.'

See, big buddies Jen? Dylan thought, and smiled to himself.

Someone coughed behind him and he turned to look over his shoulder. There were two uniformed officers at his door.

'Come in,' said Dylan.

'You wanted to see us sir, regarding Donny Longbottom?'

'Yes,' he said. 'Please take a seat.'

Chapter 20

Five foot eight, blond and muscle bound, PS Hornby didn't need any introduction to DI Dylan, he knew of him previously from working as a DC in his office. During his time in CID he had continually parked his black Peugeot in Dylan's private parking space. If he concentrated on his work as much as he did on his sports, Dylan had once told him, he would make a bloody good police officer. It seemed Hornby might have taken that advice on board as he sat before him with stripes on his uniform and a desire to move back into CID when the selection boards for the Criminal Investigation Department came around.

Hornby was the taller and younger of the two men. 'We've had a complaint from a sixteen year old girl sir,' he said. 'She's alleging that she was on her way to work this morning, at the Piece Hall, when a lad indecently assaulted her. He told her to be quiet as he tried to drag her back into the bushes but she screamed and kicked out at him, which to be honest probably saved her from actually being raped. Lucky for her, some people were walking towards Harrowfield on the main road nearby and heard her cries for help.'

'What time did the incident happen?'

'About half-seven. She had walked through People's Park from the north-west direction, across the terrace, past the statues and round by the side of the lake, nearest to Harrowfield Road. She was just nearing the entrance by Park Road swimming baths when the attack took place.'

'Where is she now?' said Dylan.

'She's with the specialist unit who are looking after her and I've contacted her mum who is en route. Acting Inspector Dawn Farren is dealing.'

'What's the girl's name?'

'Sharon Manning, boss,' said PC Charlie Brook, with a scowl on his fat, round face. 'She said she caught a glimpse of him as he turned on her before running away and was sure she'd seen him hanging around the Piece Hall.'

'So how did we latch onto Longbottom?' said Dylan.

'A passerby who'd gone to help her called 999 and as luck would have it we were just around the corner. We calmed her down, got the description and circulated it. Then, in the car as were on our way to the unit, she screamed so loud it almost burst our eardrums, pointing to Longbottom who was peering into the window of a shop on the roundabout in town. I pulled around the corner of Lord Street, Sergeant Hornby got out and lifted him and we called for a unit to come and transport him to the station.'

'Did he say anything?'

'His exact words were...' he stopped briefly, flicking to the appropriate page in his pocket book. 'Were... Leave me alone. I haven't done anything wrong. I'm off to get a tattoo,' he said, looking back at Dylan.

'We've locked him up for indecent assault, clothing bagged etcetera. He looks like he hasn't a care in the world, sitting, swinging his legs from the bed in his cell,' said PS Hornby.

'He's come into the enquiry of the missing hairdresser Kayleigh Harwood. We've spoken to him but nothing to connect him, nor to eliminate either...' Dylan said. 'Are you two alright to interview him for this one?'

'Certainly, boss,' replied Hornby.' He needs taking off the streets. In my mind he's the classic indecency man. According to intelligence he's got form for flashing, now indecent assault – and who knows what else?'

'He needs bloody castrating if you ask me,' Charlie said under his breath.

'Let me know how you get on. And when you've finished, I'd like a couple of our team to speak to him again regarding the Harwood girl.'

'Will do, boss.'

'Cheers lads, and by the way good lock up. Well done on the stripes Hornby, I can see I'd better look out for my parking space.'

'Thanks boss,' said PS Hornby. 'Appreciated, I've grown up a bit since then...' he added awkwardly.

'Good to hear.'

Dylan picked up his phone, but the telephone rang for a while before it was picked up by the Child Protection Unit. 'Inspector Dawn Farren, CPU,' Dawn said.

'You don't happen to have one of those lovely embroidered hankies that I'm partial to in your pocket?' he said in a deep Yorkshire drawl.

'Jack Dylan, I'd know that fetish anywhere. It seems ages. How y'doin?'

'Sleepless nights, mostly wind... and that's just Jen,' Dylan laughed.

'You are awful,' she said. 'What's up?'

'You've just had a young lass brought in called Sharon Manning, and uniform have locked up a Donny Longbottom who features in the Kayleigh Harwood enquiry. Tell you what, put the kettle on and I'll drive over to see you.'

'You wouldn't be passing Thomas's Bakery would you?'

'Why?'

'Bring a couple of vanilla slices with you and I'm all yours.'

'A cream cake and you're anyone's Dawn,' Dylan smiled at the familiarity of his old friend and colleague.

'Don't tell everyone,' she laughed. Dylan could visualise the round cheery face and rosy complexion framed by her dark bobbed hair.

'I'm leaving this minute,' he said, picking up the paperwork as he stood and grabbing his coat from the back of his chair.

Dylan saw Chief Superintendent Hugo-Watkins in the yard talking to John Benjamin and put up his hand to acknowledge them. What a feeble, insignificant looking man he was, standing beside the big, black, athletic-looking detective. After his stint at Training School, John was back in the CID office as a substantive Detective Sergeant – and was just the presence needed on the skulls enquiry.

Dylan arrived at the Child Protection Unit armed with the requested goodies. He stood for a moment at the front of the new building, taking in its impressive frontage. As he walked towards the large glass revolving doors he could see Dawn inside at the reception desk speaking with DI Turner. As soon as she saw him her face lit up and Shaun Turner watched her leave and go straight into Dylan's open arms.

'Great to see you,' said Dylan, as he hugged Dawn. She held him tight for a moment or two.

'Ooo it's so good to see you too, long time no see,' she said patting him on his back in a motherly fashion.

'I think you might have an admirer there,' Dylan said, nodding over her shoulder towards the DI.

'Well, you've either got it or you haven't,' she said wiggling her voluptuous hips.

'How's the girl?' he said.

'Not great, her lip's a mess and she bit her tongue quite badly,' she grimaced.

'You working with the Hampshire lads?' he said, with a nod once again in DI Turner's direction.

'Just a familial DNA job, but it hasn't come to anything on

our patch. I presumed they were working with you too?'

'Me?'

'Yes.'

'No, they're working out of our office but that's it.'

'Ah, that's why he wanted the lowdown on you,' she said, satisfied.

Dylan shrugged. 'He's a detective isn't he, we're all bloody nosey. You okay now?' he asked.

'Getting there, I didn't realise how much having Violet would affect me. I truly thought I was going mad until the doctors diagnosed the post natal depression,' she said.

Dylan looked at Dawn in mock horror. 'You didn't need a psychiatrist to tell me you're stark raving bonkers,' he laughed. She slapped him, playfully.

'How are Violet and Ralph?'

'Violet is running us ragged. Got her dad wrapped around her little finger and he has been so busy at the restaurant over Christmas that he had to take on extra staff.'

'That's good, isn't it?'

She nodded. 'Mmm...' she said.

'Thank goodness they finally got it together to replace the temporary unit,' Dylan said, arm around her as he ushered her forward and towards the doors of the new structure.

'The new facility is unbelievable, such a step forward for us and it's brilliant to have a team of key staff here that have immediate access to each other, especially with ongoing enquiries.'

'It's much better having a private environment for the survivors of horrendous crimes. A police station wasn't the right place and the temporary unit ... well, now that was nothing more than a dismal excuse given to us by the Force. Although they are threatening to dissect the unit and rename us again,' she looked skywards.

Dylan raised his eyebrows, 'And the flavour of the month being?'

'Police Safeguarding Unit, believe it or not?'

Entry to the building was via an intercom and Dawn let them in. Dylan gave a nod to Shaun Turner, who was leaning on the reception desk. He followed Dawn up a small flight of stairs and into her modern and comfortable office with all the up to date systems on the new power desk.

'This makes my office look dire. I'm dead impressed,' he said with a low whistle. 'About time they constructed buildings that are built for purpose and not just bought any old place that's up for sale and have us make do. I wish to God they'd do the same with the computer systems.'

'Well it's a start, and very nice to work in,' she said, 'but not entirely thought through, we've no bloody parking,' she said looking about him for where the cream cakes might be secreted. 'Did you get the ...?'

'You are so darn predictable,' he said holding up his briefcase. 'Sounds about right for the Think Tank'.

'Oh, no. They'll be squashed,' she said, raising her hand in mock horror.

'Squashed or not, I'm sure you'll enjoy them,' Dylan said as he watched her reach for her handkerchief in her skirt pocket and dab her mouth. He sighed, put his briefcase on the desk and opened it wide. Dawn's eyes lit up. She took the cellophane container that housed the cakes, opened it and screwed up her face like the cat that had got the cream.

'What's up now?' he said raising his voice.

'Which is the biggest, do you think?' she said puckering her lips.

'I don't care. Take your pick.'

'You might not be bothered, but I am,' she said picking up a slice and putting it to her lips. 'Mmm..' she moaned with delight through a mouthful of puff pastry and vanilla custard. She sat down in her chair with a thud and moaned again loudly. 'You certainly know how to spoil a girl.' Her eyes flew open as she licked the icing from the top. 'What was with them poxy Jaffa cake biscuits you brought me when Violet was born?' she said, words muffled through the mouthful of pastry. 'Now, if you'd have brought me one of these,' she said, eyeing up the second vanilla slice that remained untouched, 'I might've got better a whole lot quicker,' she said through another mouthful.

Dylan laughed heartily. It was so good to have the old Dawn back. He had worried that she wouldn't conquer her depression after numerous miscarriages and the birth of a much-wanted daughter. She had been the life and soul of his enquiries in the past. His very own Dawn French lookalike; there would never be another Dawn Farren.

'I thought I'd lost you to the depths of despair at one time.'

'We got the statue like you suggested, in the garden, to remember the babies that didn't make it. It helps ... thank you,' she said covering his hand with hers. He looked at her plump white hands, with soft, blunt fingertips and smiled weakly. Tears sprang to her eyes as she gazed into his. She paused for a moment in reflection. The door opened. DI Turner stood before them.

'Dawn?' said Shaun Turner.

Dylan and Dawn turned to face him. Dawn wiped a tear from her eye and withdrew her hand from Dylan's quickly.

'Sorry, to interrupt,' he said with a discreet little cough. There was a brief moment of embarrassment on his part. 'I'm, off...,' he said, nodding his head at them both and not waiting for a reply, he promptly shut the door.

Dawn and Dylan looked at each other and burst out laughing. 'Oops! Guess that's another rumour started,' she said.

Her face turned serious and her eyes met his. 'Tell me, how you coping with being a dad? I must admit you had me and Jen questioning whether you were living for this job and nothing else.'

'Actually you might be surprised to hear that our dear departed colleague Larry Banks actually had something to do with the metamorphosis.'

'Really?'

'Yes, he wrote me a note, given to me by his solicitor after they found his body and his exact words were that I should work to live, not live to work.'

'Pity he had to get a poor young woman killed and leave a little girl orphaned to realise that little gem of wisdom, and make a significant impact on your life. Anyway, enough about our dear departed, bent colleague. There is more to life... Maisy?'

Dylan's face lit up at the mention of his daughter's name.

'She's amazing... she's going on eight months now,' he said grappling in his jacket pocket for his wallet and a well thumbed picture to show off.

'Oh, my God, she's gorgeous and blonde curly hair.'

'She takes after her mother, thankfully.'

'Quite,' she said raising her eyebrows. 'You must come around and see us sometime and let Ralph cook you a meal. Mawingo is quiet at this time of year, so it will give my gorgeous hubby a chance to try out his new dishes on you, and give his staff at the restaurant something useful to occupy their idle hands.'

'That sounds ominous.'

'Don't ask.'

'Well it sounds good to me – sure Ralph won't mind? I bet

the snowdrops are out now, aren't they? Is that carpet of crocus in the grounds in bloom yet?'

'Snowdrops are out but I haven't seen anything of the crocus yet this year. I think the cold snap and heavy snowfall held them back a bit but I wouldn't be surprised if they aren't out soon.'

'I love the Sibden Valley, it's always picturesque no matter what season we're in,' he said dreamily.

'Yeah, until someone like Larry Banks decides to help get someone torched there. I don't think the grass will ever grow back in the bottom car park.'

'That's the consequence isn't it, I know. Did you have a good Christmas?'

'Yeah, we did thanks. Violet actually enjoyed it this year, and you?'

'Maisy played with the boxes and loved the crinkly wrapping paper and Max's new dog chain, believe it or not. Jen was frazzled, I got called out during Christmas Eve to a hostage situation and a domestic stabbing on Christmas lunchtime so I was knackered by the time I got back and they were both in bed.' Dylan shrugged, 'Well you know what it's like...'

'You mean you were doing a Scrooge impersonation?' she said.

Dylan looked sheepish. 'More like Jacob Marley's ghost.'

'Moody eh?' she said, with a flick of her head.

'Seldom seen and yes, moody sounds an apt description,' he said with a wry smile. 'To make it worse Cyril, Jen's Dad, couldn't make it because he was a bit under the weather. She worries about him being on the Isle of Wight alone and I think she misses the work banter too.'

'Well, her Dad's not exactly around the corner for her to visit, is he?'

'I know, that's what she says. Maybe I can fix that though. I've just had a good idea,' he raised an eyebrow and smiled.

'Poor Jen, knowing you that smile means she's hot-footing it back to work,' Dawn said, her brows furrowing.

'She is threatening... but no, maybe an impromptu visit to her dad's though,' he said.

'God willing there'll be lots more Christmases for you all. Why do you think there's always an increase in domestic violence over Christmas and New Year period?'

'Ah, I don't know. How long's a piece of string?' Dylan shrugged. 'Between December 17th and 4thJanuary I was called to three bodies, all related to domestic violence.'

'I wish you'd learn to say no, try the next mug,' she said.

'What, me?' he said.

'Yes, they're only little once you know. Before you know it, Maisy will be having kids of her own. I finish at three o'clock these days, every day,' she said.

'You do?' Dylan said. 'Like I said, you're not the first one to tell me to slow down and enjoy life.'

Dawn raised both eyebrows. 'I'm not?'

'Larry...'

'Not him again,' she sighed. 'You'll be having him cast as a bloody saint before long,' she said.

'No, when Larry wrote to me to try to explain what had happened...'

'What lies did he manage to spin for that web then?' she said with indifference.

'He said he knew the drink was his downfall.'

'You don't have to be the brightest button to know that.'

'And he said he wanted me to know the truth. He didn't think for a minute that the blackmailer would carry out the threats he made. He said he was sorry for letting the team down and asked for forgiveness.'

Dawn shook her head. 'Well that sounds about right for him, thinking about himself as per usual.'

'He was prepared to die. He knew Liz's husband would be out to get revenge once he knew he was involved.'

'Big of him,' she said, flatly.

'If I can't trust my own team Dawn, who the hell can I trust?' he said with a sigh. 'It seems like a lifetime ago now and her husband Malcolm is still missing. I guess he'll turn up eventually, one day. His little girl is an orphan until he does.'

Dawn shuddered. 'Let's hope he does. Well, by the sound of it Sharon Manning was flaming lucky this morning. The girls are just video interviewing her now,' she said.

'It's a good job people were about at the time,' Dylan said.

'And prepared to get involved. Her scalp is very sore where he pulled her hair out.'

'They've got him in for indecent assault at the moment but we'll run him or for attempted rape or maybe even abduction. That was his intention, after all.'

'He apparently told her he wouldn't harm her, he just wanted to give her one.'

'Well that declaration from her should get him remanded so he can't attack anyone else. How's Sharon coping?'

'How does anyone cope?' She'll have nightmares for years to come, poor thing. I was only talking to a lady the other day at a meeting who had been attacked in much the same way sixteen years ago and she still won't go out on her own. While the wanker who attacked her feeds on the fantasy, she'll have to cope with the fear. Not fair, is it?'

'No, but all we can do is our best to get him put away, and for a long time.'

'I'll get them to update you later.'

Dylan's mobile buzzed and Dawn's office phone started ringing.

'Do you think somebody is trying to tell us something?' Dylan said with the tilt of his head and half a smile. He answered his phone.

'Boss, just thought you would like to know someone has rang in to say they think they know who the two lads were, seen banging on the car the night Kayleigh Harwood went missing, but they'll only speak to the man in charge of the investigation.'

'I'm on my way, have you got contact details?'

'Yes.'

'I'll call them from the office.'

'Okay, boss.

'Would it be a crank or a genuine call?' Dylan wondered as he collected his coat, picked up his briefcase and waved Dawn a silent goodbye.

DI Shaun Turner sat in the coffee bar considering his options. He had thought of Jen every day since he'd learned she had left the Island, compartmentalising the guilt and blaming it on his misguided youth, when the doctor had delivered the blow that his fiancée at that time would never be able to have his child and he ran away. However, the second he'd seen her again with Maisy visiting Harrowfield police station, he knew his feelings for her were as strong as ever. He knew Dylan was dedicated to the Force by the long hours he spent at work, or was dedication the wrong word? Could he have other reasons for staying at work? The girls were awful flirty with him – and look at the predicament he'd found him in today with Dawn Farren. Dawn had given him Dylan's home number and he truly believed at the time when he called that hearing Jen's voice, however briefly, when she picked up, would be enough for him. But now he realised it wasn't, he had to see her and tell her how he felt before he went back home to his loveless, childless marriage. He took his phone out of his pocket and dialled Dylan and Jen's number.

'Jen,' he said. 'It's Shaun. I have to see you.'

Chapter 21

A Harrowfield telephone number had been scrawled across a pink post-it-note and was stuck to his computer screen. Dylan picked up the phone and dialled it hurriedly but it rang out over and over again on deaf ears, as his mum would have said. He put the phone on its cradle, sat down, sighed and checked the written numerals before dialling more carefully this time. A female voice answered this time, taking him by surprise,

'Hello?' she said, hesitantly.

'Detective Inspector Jack Dylan, I'm the man in charge of the Kayleigh Harwood enquiry. I've been told you want to speak to me?'

'To be honest I was in two minds whether I should ring. I think I know who the two boys are that you are appealing for.'

'You do? Who am I speaking to?'

'Yes, but I need you to promise me that no one will know it was me that told you.'

'I can assure you of absolute confidentiality Mrs...?'

There was silence.

'There's nothing at the moment to suggest that these two have done anything wrong. We just know that they were in the area at the time... But we would very much like to speak to them Mrs..?'

'You can say that now, but you see it all the time in the papers, don't you? People get called a Grass and others make their lives hell. I couldn't cope with that. No. I can't. I'm sorry to have bothered you. I wish I hadn't rung.'

All was quiet but the caller hadn't hung up.

'No,' Dylan said as he stared out of the window. He saw DI Turner, head bowed, strolling across the yard with his hands in his trouser pockets. He swivelled his chair back to face his desk. 'You've done the right thing. We desperately need people like you to come forward. Without calls like yours we may never get to the truth.'

The caller appeared to be hanging on hesitantly, but she was still silent.

'Please...'

'If these lads were drinking under age, would they be in trouble and have to go to court?' she said. 'No, let me assure you that they wouldn't go to court. That's not the purpose of our investigation. We are trying to trace a missing girl. Not, I repeat not under aged drinkers. You obviously know who the lads are, are you related?'

'I won't protect either of them if they've done anything wrong. I'm a mother...'

'So, do you want to tell me who you are? Who they are? Or do you want someone to come and see you? I can arrange for my officers to come to your home address or meet you elsewhere?'

'I'll tell you, but promise me,' she begged. 'Promise me, I won't have to go to Court as a witness because I don't want anyone to know it was me who told on them.'

'I promise you, you won't have to go to Court and no one will ever know from me it was you who told us. Now...'

'One of them may have been my son... You see I overheard him on the phone talking.'

'Your son's name?'

'Ryan, Ryan Merryfield. He's never been in trouble before, Mr Dylan. Ryan's a good kid but he's always been easily led and I'm worried he's getting in with the wrong crowd.'

'You understand that we are going to have to speak to Ryan, don't you?' There was further silence.

'What will you say?' she asked anxiously.

'We'll tell him that we believe that he is one of the people we have been appealing for, and ask him what he can tell us about the night in question. Is that okay?'

'Yes. You won't lock him up, will you?'

'No, I can assure you that he won't be locked up. We just want to know if he was there, who he was with, and what he saw.'

'When will you be coming round tomorrow? I'm off work tomorrow afternoon.'

'Does Ryan go to school,? Work?'

'No, I'm hoping this might make him think twice about the people he is hanging around with.'

Dylan picked up his pen. 'Your name and address, Mrs...?'

'Number five, Wainhouse Road and my name is Mrs Merryfield. Mary Merryfield.'

'Thank you for the call. I know it's not an easy thing to do, but it is appreciated. I'll arrange for two of my officers to come round and have a chat with Ryan.'

'I've put my trust in you, Mr Dylan. Please don't let me down.'

'I won't – and thank you for calling me. You've done the

right thing.'

Dylan had a fire in his eyes, Lisa the office girl noted as he walked out of his office. 'Vicky?' he called as he scanned the office.

'Still at the Regan house,' she said.

'What about Ned and Andy?'

'Same, do you want me to get hold of her?'

'No, I'll do it,' he said as he turned and swiftly walked back into his own office with long strides. 'I'd love a brew though,' he shouted over his shoulder.

Lisa smiled and shook her head in mock surprise. Dressed, as always, in black, her long black hair fell about her young, thin face.

'Vicky,' Dylan's voice rose as the answering message bleeped at the start of its recording. 'There've been some interesting developments this end. We'll have a scrum down tomorrow morning to review where we are and what our priorities have to be. See you first thing, unless you need me in the meantime. I'll be on my mobile.' He hung up. His phone rang, it was Vicky.

'Sorry boss, just missed you. Sounds interesting. There's nothing new here. This moron gets weirder and weirder. He isn't talking to us any more, so we're getting on with the search. Ned wants to kick seven bells out of him – but don't worry, Andy's got him under control.'

Lisa walked in and placed a mug of coffee on Dylan's desk as he put down the receiver. 'You look all in'.

'Do I?' he said. 'Cheers for the coffee. You on a twelve, eight shift?'

She nodded and pulled a face.

'Why don't you get off? I'm going in a minute and the team won't be back for ages.'

'I might just do that,' she said. 'Thanks.'

Dylan sat back in his traditional old leather office chair. He felt glad that he hadn't let Beaky throw it out when she'd refurbished. The CID office was empty. He sighed and picked up his phone and telephoned Jen. His head was banging and his stomach was rumbling. 'I'm setting off now so I can bath my little girl.'

'You've missed it, and if you want to see her before she goes to bed you better get your skates on. It is nearly seven o'clock.'

Dylan looked at his watch. 'So it is. Blimey! I thought it was six.'

'Guess it's been quiet there then?'

Dylan laughed half-heartedly. 'Far from it, but what I haven't got done today can wait – tomorrow's another day isn't it? I might get a call from the search team, but that should be all.'

He heard Max bark and Maisy, obviously startled by the sudden noise, let out a long, low wail. 'Tired?'

'Yeah.'

'I'll see you soon,' he said.

Maisy was drifting to sleep in her cot when he looked in on her. The lights were low; her night light shone stars on her ceiling and played a lullaby. She was biting her teething ring like a horse chomping on its bit. Her left cheek was bright red and looked angry.

'It might be a restless night,' Jen whispered as she took the teething ring away and wiped her mouth with a tissue. The baby started to cry. Dylan watched her expertly massage teething gel onto Maisy's gums. Her eyes were puffy with crying but she stopped as suddenly as she'd begun, and she sucked eagerly at Jen's finger. Sobbing pitifully, she gradually calmed down. She could hardly keep her little eyes open.

'I understand you know, don't worry,' he said, stroking his hand gently across Jen's shoulder blades.

'I wish you did,' said Jen, her eyes filled with tears as she turned to look up at him. 'We need to talk.'

'Shh... I know,' he said, pulling her down to the settee. Sitting alongside his wife he put his arm protectively around her shoulders. 'I will try to get home earlier and take some of the pressure off you, when it quietens down, I promise.'

'You don't understand, it's...'

'Course, I understand. It might be good for you to get back to work – but not yet, eh?'

Jen shook her head silently as a lump rose in her throat. Tears ran down her cheeks. 'But...'

'Not now,' he said, stroking her leg. 'You look all in.'

The night was a long one and Jen walked the floor with Maisy tossing and turning in her arms. Her restlessness echoing Jen's inner turmoil, 'Why, Oh why had Shaun called her? After all this time, what on earth did he expect her to say? Didn't he realise how much he'd hurt her? Why would she have left the family that meant everything to her, if she hadn't been able to live with the thought that he didn't want to be with her any more? What did he want from her? She had no intention of seeing him and she'd told him so in no uncertain terms before slamming the phone down.

Just when she thought Maisy was going to settle, Jen's arm cramped and the movement made her stir. Jen held her breath. Her daughter was feverish. 'Please,' she said, putting Maisy over her shoulder and laying back on the sofa, 'please go to sleep, shh..'

At 6.30 the alarm went off and woke Dylan, who looked over at his wife, the baby was sound asleep across her chest, on the settee in their bedroom.

'It can't be morning already,' Jen groaned, croakily.

Dylan reached out to grab hold of the alarm clock.

'Tell me it isn't time to get up,' she said, sleepily. Dylan sat up straight, stretched his arms overhead and interlocked his fingers, turning the palms to the ceiling. He yawned loudly and his jaw clicked.

'Jack...shhh...' she said in a hushed tone. 'You're not going in yet are you? I thought we were going to talk?'

'Tonight?' he said, stumbling over the shoes that he'd discarded at the foot of the bed. He switched the light on and turned the dimmer switch. Maisy stirred once more. Jen closed her eyes.

'Don't... you dare wake her,' she whispered through clenched teeth. She got up with trepidation and lay Maisy down in her cot, in the nursery. The infant remained asleep and she patted her soothingly to make sure. Jen licked her dry lips. She had to talk to Jack now. She had to explain, tell him just who DI Turner was, because Shaun obviously hadn't mentioned it. 'Why not go in a bit later?' she said flopping back down on the settee as he sat down beside her pulling up his socks. She watched him tie his shoe laces, her head in her hands, her fingers grasping her hair.

'You know I can't,' he said, impatiently. 'We've got a lot on.'

She sighed. 'I guess I better go and make a brew,' she said, making a huge effort to get to her feet. She bent over him, put her hand on the nape of his bare neck and kissed the top of his head.

'Do you remember once upon a time when we used to do breakfast together?' he said, as he watched her walk out of the bedroom door.

'Yes,' she said stopping for a moment and looking over her shoulder at him. 'I do, and it seems like a lifetime ago,' she said sadly. Her eyes felt gritty. A glance in the hallway mirror as she stepped over Max's prone body showed a pale face with dark circles under her eyes. Max moaned and rolled over on his back for her to stroke his belly. She smiled at him. 'It's alright for you mate,' she said, bending down to pay him some attention. 'You want some breakfast too?' she whispered and Max ambled to his feet and padded after her into the kitchen. He knew the word 'breakfast' meant food. 'What're we going to do, old fella?' she sighed, putting his dish down on the floor and ruffling the hair behind his ears lovingly.

'Do about what?' Dylan startled Jen by coming up behind her as she stood looking dreamily out of the window as she filled the kettle at the kitchen sink 'Ooh! Don't do that. You nearly made me jump out of my skin.'

'Guilty conscience?' he said with a chuckle.

'No. What made you say that?' she said.

Dylan put his arms around her. 'Why don't you go back to bed?' he said. She shook her head and smiled weakly, handing him a banana, apple, and a bag of sandwiches she'd made last night.

'Worth a try,' he said with a smile. 'Thanks.' He put her offerings in his overstuffed briefcase. 'I used to get little notes too.'

She handed him a steaming mug of coffee. 'Well, you'll just have to do with the food today. See you later,' she said, standing on tiptoes to kiss him on his cheek. She strolled down the hallway and slowly climbed up the stairs. Her legs were like lead and her heart was heavier. The sooner DI Shaun Turner went back from whence he came, the better.

'Bye love,' Dylan called out.

'Jack, don't let the door...' she started and closed her eyes for the inevitable.

The door slammed shut behind him. Jen cringed and held her breath. Max looked up at her quizzically from the bottom of the stairs. Maisy screamed.

It was turned half seven and Dylan was sat in traffic on the ring road when a police car whizzed past, followed by an ambulance. He stopped at the traffic lights to let them pass, even though they were at green. Others tried to nip out in front of him but Dylan knew the urgency of that call and what the noise of the sirens getting nearer would mean to someone in trouble.

Chapter 22

'Substantive Detective Sergeant John Benjamin. It's great, to see you back, mate,' Dylan said loudly and with heartfelt enthusiasm. 'What's with the new haircut?' he called over the CID office to his colleague. The team looked up from what they were doing and stared at John.

'Nits going round the school, boss,' he said, scratching his head. 'I asked Luigi for a number one for me and Josh,' he laughed. 'Maria and Laura weren't too keen. Haven't the faintest idea why not?'

'Guess I've got that pleasure to come,' Dylan said, wrinkling his nose. 'When I was a kid they used to shave patches of hair off our heads and made us sit at the front of the class if we had head lice. Wouldn't happen these days would it? There would be a hue and cry.'

'Doesn't Nitty Nora still do the rounds?' said Vicky.

John nodded. 'Yeah, think so.'

'We used to queue up for hours in the hall waiting to see the old battleaxe.'

'I can still smell that coal tar soap,' said Andy.

'My mum used to have us bending over a sheet of brown paper as she combed our hair with a nit comb after our bath on a Sunday,' said Ned.

'Jeez, you only had a bath once a week? Suppose it was in a tin bath in front of the coal fire,' said Vicky.

'Hey lady, we were lucky if we got a bath at all in them days. I had two older brothers and two younger sisters, so invariably I didn't get a bath, more of a top and toe,' Dylan said.

'Go on. And I suppose you hid from the rent man and only ate what fell off the back of a lorry? My dad's poor tale is of how they lived off tins of pineapple rings for a whole week.'

'Actually... never mind,' he said.

Lisa walked in with a tray full of mugs of coffee and a plate of warm toast lathered with pork dripping. The smell always reminded Dylan of his childhood. Everyone turned to look in her direction with expectation. 'What?' she said, her face flushing a bright shade of red.

'Grab a chair and put your feet up love. The boss was just telling us a story,' said Vicky.

'The boss wasn't,' Dylan said. 'Get me the updates. I want a meeting in five,' he said, opening his door and switching on his office light.

Dylan sat at the head of the group of desks in the middle of the CID office ten minutes later. Some of the team had to perch on desks, some on stools, others leaned on the corner of filing cabinets. Everyone was quiet. Dylan opened his mouth to talk and his mobile rang.

'Excuse me,' he said.

'Sergeant Hornby, boss. Just to update you regarding Longbottom. Because of what Sharon Manning is saying in her statement, we've updated his arrest status to attempt rape, as well as indecent assault.'

'Rightly so, I was talking to DI Farren yesterday, Is he talking?'

'No, he was a right twat in the first interview. He said the usual, you know, he'd done nothing wrong. He's sticking to his story about going for a tattoo when we stopped him. So we put it to him that he didn't have any money on him when he was arrested, so how was he going to pay? As expected he 'no replied'. We asked him if he had an appointment so we could check out his alibi but he said he hadn't made an appointment. Then he said he wasn't feeling well. So we had no choice but to stop the interview.'

Dylan tutted and raised his eyes to the ceiling.

'The doc's been out since, given him a couple of Paracetamols and says he's fit for interview.'

'Good. What's his custody time clock looking like? It must be twenty four hours since we locked him up.'

'Whoever came up with the bright idea that you can only keep suspects in custody for twenty four hours before you've got to charge or release, eh?'

'Obviously someone who's never interviewed a suspect for a crime,' said Dylan.

'We've had to get the Superintendent's twelve hour extension.'

'Who's his solicitor?'

'Err... it's someone from Perfect and Best.'

Dylan put his hands up to his forehead. 'There's no show without Punch is there?' he said, shaking his head.

'What?'

'Nothing. Do you know who from Perfect and Best?'

'I think it's Lin Perfect. I saw Yvonne heading for the

Magistrates' court.'

'Okay, keep me posted. I want him ultimately charging with attempted rape. Any problems with the Crown Prosecution Service looking to water down the charge to an indecent assault, let me know immediately. This guy's dangerous. We need to keep him off the streets. Let me know when you've finished the next interview. Obviously we need to go for a remand, but CID need to speak to him regarding Kayleigh Harwood's disappearance like I said.'

'No problem boss, I'll be in touch.'

Dylan replaced the receiver.

'No show without punch?' said Vicky, scratching her head with the top of her pen.

'You mean you've never heard that saying before?' he said. The team looked on, each one shaking their heads.

'You must have seen the Punch and Judy shows?'

His audience nodded collectively.

'God, I can't believe you lot have never heard that saying. My granddad used to say it to us kids all the time.'

'In't olden days,' Vicky said, teasingly. 'On Ilkley Moor b'aht 'at,' she sang raucously.

Dylan ignored her. 'You've all seen a puppet show. Punch is the protagonist isn't he, along with his wife Judy, a policeman, a dog, a crocodile and now I think about it possibly several other characters. But the phrase I just used means that it wouldn't be much of a show without the main character. Right, lesson over, let's get on,' he said, rubbing his hands together.

'So who's Punch and Judy in this scenario?' said Vicky, looking slightly bemused.

'Perfect and Best.'

'Ah,' she nodded. 'Okay.'

'Now, back to the job in hand, Longbottom is being interviewed for attempted rape on sixteen year old Sharon Manning yesterday. PS Hornby and PC Brook are dealing and are likely to charge him later today. Mrs Merryfield, Ryan Merryfield's mother says he will be in this afternoon. Are you and Ned able to pick that one up for us, Andy?'

They both nodded in the affirmative. 'Late afternoon?' said Ned.

'Overtime?' said Dylan cocking his head to one side.

'Couple of hours tops,' said Ned. 'Honest.'

'That's fine, but I do need to speak to you before you go. Ryan must not be told his mum rang in. I gave my word.'

'Vicky, you and me will speak to Longbottom together once we know what's what from uniform.'

'Sure,' she said, jumping down from the filing cabinet where she had been perched.

'I'm available boss, once I have shifted some outstanding paperwork,' said John.

'Actually John, I'd like you to look into the discovery of a couple of skulls for me if you will. I'll give you all the info I have on that after this meeting.'

John raised his eyebrows and nodded.

'Okay, Andy, Ned, Vicky what's the consensus of opinion now on Norris Regan then?'

Ned was first to respond. 'He's undeniably one of the strangest people I've ever come across. He makes out he's this weak and feeble little old lady... er, I mean man, I mean lady, but as we know he's devious.'

'I agree with Ned, boss. We may have discovered some strange fetishes of his, but he didn't seem overly concerned about us being all over his house, so I don't think he's hiding anything, not there anyway. I do think he thought that after his disclosure about wearing the women's clothes and the leg irons we'd move on though – and of course we didn't, I think that took him by surprise.'

'He was far too comfortable with talking about his perversions with us. It as though he was getting off on it.'

Dylan looked in Andy's direction.

'I didn't speak to him much boss, but the collection of photographs on the bedroom wall and his preferred reading material are definitely different to anything else I've ever seen.'

'A man wearing women's clothes and leg irons?' asked John.

'Oh, yes! Tell you later big boy,' Vicky said suggestively, stroking his thigh.

John shook his head.

'You're a mad mare,' said Ned.

'Jealousy will get you nowhere son,' she said.

'The bicycle bell on the bed head, now that's of interest to me obviously. What's that about, do you think?' Dylan said, while John continued to look puzzled and amused.

'Totally off the fucking wall, just like him. I think you need to speak to him yourself to see what a weird bastard he really is boss,' said Vicky.

'Vicky you're doing some local background on him, yeah?

And we've seized some belongings we're checking out, right?'

Vicky nodded.

'And there was no objection?'

'Nope, none at all,' said Andy.

'In that case, we have a busy day ahead of us, so let's get on with it. John, my office now,' he said, standing.

'You felt sorry for Norris yesterday didn't you Vicky?' Ned called across the room as everyone started to disperse.

'Are you fucking mad, knob head?' she said with a scowl. 'Everyone knows the way to a man's heart is to keep his stomach full and his balls empty. Regan is strange like you, he gets neither. Back at you weirdo,' she said.

'And on that note,' Dylan shouted. 'Vicky, let's get on. Ned, stop winding her up, will you?'

'Well he chuffin' asked for it,' Vicky said out of the corner of her mouth. 'It's obvious you're well looked after, boss,' she said winking at Dylan as she passed. Andy held the door open for her. Dylan laughed at John and shook his head. DI Shaun Turner looked on from the corner of the room.

'Find me some evidence you lot, assumptions are just that. I want something to support them,' Dylan shouted after them.

Chapter 23

Dylan's day was moving at a pace. He left the office to get some water and walked directly into Shaun Turner.

'Now then, what's new with you?' he said as they stood together at the water fountain. Dylan held a plastic cup under the water spout.

'Almost finished our enquiries, so hopefully we'll all be gone from under your feet by tomorrow.' DI Turner stood with his hands in his pockets. Dylan looked up at him as his cup overflowed.

'Bet you'll be glad to see us go?' he said, offering a napkin.

'So soon?' Dylan said dismissing the offer. He searched for his handkerchief in his trouser pocket and dried his hands. 'How rude of me, we haven't even managed a pint.'

'Don't suppose you and your good lady are free tonight?' Shaun said.

'I would say yes, but I don't know what Jen has planned.'

'No worries, it was just a thought. The others are off back home today, that's all, and I've got one or two loose ends to tie up so I'm not planning on leaving until tomorrow morning.'

Dylan knew what it was like to work away from home.

'Tell you what. Look, why not come round to ours tonight? I'll pick fish and chips up on my way home, it'd be good to have a natter. There's not much time here – as you can see, we're up to our necks in it. I'll meet you here later, yeah?'

'Sounds good to me,' Turner nodded and a smile spread across his face which made him look younger.

'Ah, I'd better warn you now though our little Maisy's teething,' Dylan said apologetically.

DI Turner laughed softly. 'Don't worry, I love children.'

'Any of your own?'

'No, sadly not... Can't...' he said. Dylan thought he caught a glimpse of pain in his eyes.

'I'm sorry,' said Dylan.

'That's life, I guess,' he said with a sigh. 'Funny how things pan out, isn't it?'

Dylan was distracted by the sound of his name being called from the other side of the office. 'PS Hornby on the phone for you, boss.'

'Half seven okay with you?' he said hurriedly.

'Yeah, I'll be waiting,' said Turner.

Dylan walked over to Lisa, Shaun saw him wink and grab the telephone from her.

'Hornby!'

'Looks like a night in the traps did Longbottom good boss, either that or Lin Perfect had a word in his lughole. He's now admitting lying to us. He says he was frightened. He's admitted seeing Sharon in People's Park and talking to her, and he's not denying that he fancied his chances either.'

'But he didn't bother asking her if she fancied him too, I guess?' said Dylan.

'No, exactly. He denies grabbing her by the hair and admits he might have 'accidentally' touched her breast when he tried to put his arm around her, but nothing else. We told him that she was heard screaming at him and so we asked him, since he was a complete stranger to her, what made him think that she liked him? He says she isn't a stranger and that he knows her. He knew she worked at the Piece Hall and he said she'd spoken to him often. According to her, her friendliness towards him was all in his head. He'd spoken to her alright and basically she'd ignored him or told him to fuck off because she thought he was a bit strange. He may have been admiring her from afar before this incident, but this time it looks like he took it a step further. We've taken his clothes of course and nail scrapings since it's alleged he pulled some of her hair out.'

'Good work,' Dylan said. 'What did you put to him?'

'That he'd been watching her before attacking her this morning, taking her by the hair and dragging her into the nearby bushes against her will, hoping to have sex with her. He says that wasn't true. He says she'd been up for it until somebody come along, which is when he says she screamed. We pushed him, but he wasn't for admitting anything. To be fair to his solicitor, Lin Perfect let us get into his ribs, but when we started to go over his story again she reminded us we had already asked him the questions once and wasn't happy for us to repeat them, which is fair enough. In the end she asked for a break. If you agree we'll give him another very short interview and the opportunity to admit the offences put to him, then charge him with the attempted rape and do a remand file for Court tomorrow.'

'Yes, Court'll be over for today,' he said looking at his watch.

'I've spoke to the Custody Sergeant and he's okay with it and Lin Perfect is anticipating that course of action.'

'Well let's not disappoint her; I'd like to see the summary, just to make sure it's strong enough. I don't want CPS watering the charge down, like I said. It's a good lock up, well done. By the way, who is the custody sergeant again?'

'Thumper,' Hornby said. 'I mean Sergeant Maude, boss. We won't have any trouble from him, I've updated him and he's sound.'

'Tell him to liaise with me later and let me know when Longbottom's charged.'

'Will do boss.'

Andy and Ned pulled up outside 5, Wainhouse Road, parked the car on the gable end and walked around on the cobbled road to the front entrance of the end terraced house. Andy stood on the doorstep and rang the bell. Ned tried to peer through the bow window that looked directly onto the street. He pulled a face and shook his head.

'Nets are too thick, can't see a thing,' he whispered.

The pair waited patiently but there was no answer. Without a word to each other, just a nod and a meeting of eyes, Andy stepped off the doorstep and together they walked to the back of the house. At the gate of the small, square back yard, Ned stopped and turned. 'See that?' he said, his hand still on the latch.

'What? The Fire Station?' Andy asked.

'No, Wainhouse tower; I once did a project on that landmark at school. The whole class climbed the 369 steps to the observatory at the top just to be told that it was a myth that you could see Blackpool Tower from it. Evil, our teachers were.'

'I can tell school days weren't among your happiest, were they Ned?' Andy laughed. 'Don't forget it wasn't Mrs Merryfield who told us about her son being on Manchester Road that night,' he whispered as he knocked once again on a door that belonged to the grim looking house. They could hear music this time and a washing machine that sounded as if it was on a spin cycle.

'Hello! Hello! Is there anyone in?' shouted Ned through the letter box. A tall, middle aged, handsome woman came directly to the door and immediately played her role well.

'Mrs Merryfield?'

'DC Andy Wormald and DC Duncan Granger,' Andy said,

showing her his warrant card.

'You'd better come in,' she said loudly. She half lifted her head, giving them permission to enter. Ned flashed his warrant card for her to see as he passed by. 'He's only sixteen. Does that mean I have to be present?' she whispered.

'Yes, that would help,' Andy said to her as they walked through the kitchen diner and out through the passage at the bottom of the stairs towards the front door. There was a closed door to the left and Mrs Merryfield opened it for them to enter. Ryan lay playing a computer game on the TV, the console gripped tightly in his hands. His eyes didn't leave the TV screen.

'Turn that off please. We have guests Ryan,' Mary Merryfield said, brushing his feet off the sofa. The two men sat. 'These are police officers from CID.'

The lounge had flock wallpaper and a tired-looking brown patterned carpet. The settee was reminiscent of a bygone age and was made of durable fabric. The fireplace surround was solid coloured red brick and housed a living flame fire.

Ryan Merryfield obediently stopped what he was doing and shuffled to the edge of his seat. He looked at the officers anxiously.

'Can you confirm to me that you are Ryan Merryfield?'

Ryan nodded. 'And your date of birth is?'

The young lad mumbled his answer and his mother agreed with a nod of her head.

'Where were you on the 7th January, Ryan?' said Andy.

Ryan looked puzzled.

'The night of the heavy snowfall?' said Ned.

Ryan shrugged his shoulders.

'Well, let's try and jog your memory shall we? You might have seen something about a girl going missing on the news,' Ned said.

'White Wednesday, they're calling it?' said Andy.

Ryan shook his head.

Mrs Merryfield flinched. She hesitated and looked puzzled. 'You do know about it. I showed you the article in the newspaper myself, and you watched the news with me, so why are you lying to the officers?'

'I'll ask you again Ryan. Do remember a girl going missing?' said Ned.

'Suppose,' he said, fiddling with the console now loosely held in one hand.

'Who were you out with on that night Ryan?'

'I wasn't.'

Mrs Merryfield looked at him sharply. 'Yes you were Ryan, I heard you talking to someone on the phone about it,' she said.

Ned and Andy looked at Ryan with questioning eyes.

'Donny, Donny Longbottom,' he said reluctantly.

'Longbottom?' said Andy.

'Yes, Donny Longbottom,' said Ryan in a quiet voice, staring down at the carpet. He shut his eyes and ran his fingers through his hair.

'You know Donny Longbottom?' said Andy.

Ryan looked sideways at his mother, then furtively at the detectives.

'Look, you're not in trouble, we just want to know if you know him,' Andy said.

'I sometimes hang out with him. Mum thinks he's a bad influence, though.'

'I can't tell you how many times I've told him I don't want him seeing that lad,' Mary said, staring at her son.

'Would you say he was a mate of yours then?' asked Ned.

'Guess so. He can be a bit strange but he's a laugh too,' he sniggered.

'So, it'd be fair to say that you knock about with him then?' asked Andy.

'Yeah, sometimes.'

'What do you mean by the word strange?' said Ned.

Ryan screwed up his face. 'He's obsessed, with girls you know ...' he stopped and looked at his mum.

'Carry on Ryan, I'm sure you can't shock your mum. She's probably heard it all before,' Ned said. He could see Mary Merryfield twisting the wedding ring around on her finger.

'He thinks every girl he sees fancies him. He follows them about, looking through windows and stuff. He's a bit of a perv – but I wouldn't tell him that, he's a lot bigger than me.'

'You might not be surprised then to know that he's recently been locked up for attacking a young girl and we'll be speaking to him about the girl that went missing on the night we are asking you about.'

Ryan sat up straight. 'No?' he said his eyes wide and disbelieving.

'What did I tell you?' Mary Merryfield gasped, her hooded eyes moved right and up to the ceiling.

'Were you out on Manchester Road with Longbottom on

White Wednesday, Ryan?' said Ned.

'You came home wet through that night, didn't you? Remember, I asked you what you had been doing?'

Ryan looked into his mother's face but said nothing.

'I said, you'll get bloody pneumonia if you didn't start wearing a decent coat instead of that damn denim jacket, remember?' said Mrs Merryfield, before her son had chance to deny it.

'Is that right Ryan?' said Ned.

'Yes,' he said softly.

'Were you drinking? Did you at any point bang on a car on the Manchester Road that night while in drink?' said Andy.

Ryan sat perfectly still and made no reply.

'Well, did you?' said Ned.

'I'm too young to drink,' he said sheepishly.

'Ryan you're not in trouble for drinking, we're more interested in the young girl that went missing that night and we need all the help we can get to find her. We need you to be truthful with us, so we don't have to waste any more of our time coming back to see you again,' said Andy.

Ryan looked down.

'And you don't need to protect Longbottom either, or worry about reprisals because he's locked up, and will be for some time. Come on tell us what happened that night. Where did you meet Longbottom?' said Andy.

'If you know anything Ryan, tell them,' said Mrs Merryfield sternly.

'Okay!' he turned, snapping at her. 'I was with him. We were walking home from Harrowfield. We'd been building a snowman in his garden before going into town to get his medication. I was freezing.'

'Well, whose fault was that?' said Mrs Merryfield. Ned gave her a withering look.

'Go on,' said Andy.

'He gave me a swig out of his bottle of whisky, said it would keep me warm. He told me he'd got it from Akram's Off Licence on the precinct. He said that it were easy to nick it because it was Mr Akram's daughter that was serving on and he reckoned she fancied him,' he said, rolling his eyes.

'Then what?' said Andy.

'We stood chatting in a shop doorway and he was going on about what he'd like to do to Akram's daughter. Then he suggested we go on up the main road home as somebody said there'd been a crash, it was blocked, or sommat. It was snowing like hell and I just wanted to go home because I knew I'd get into bother with her,' he said, looking in his mother's direction. 'I knew she'd go mad.'

'She's the cats mother!' snapped Mrs Merryfield.

'Did you go with him?' said Andy.

'Not far.'

'Why?'

'He started going down people's paths and stuff, looking in their windows. He was trying to catch someone getting undressed, naked and that, he said. At one house he got up the drainpipe onto a porch roof because from the road you could see this woman walking about in her bedroom with what looked like a towel around her from where I was standing.' Ryan sniggered. 'The drainpipe came away from the wall and made a right noise, so I ran off.'

'So you both went to try look at this half-naked woman?' said Andy.

'Well, it wasn't quite like that, but yeah, I suppose we did. Sorry mum,' he said turning towards his mum with a bowed head. 'I think Donny frightened the woman though.'

Mrs Merryfield looked at him with tears in her unblinking eyes.

'How'd you mean?'

'Well when I ran I heard this scream and when he caught up with me he was laughing. He was still buttoning up his flies, so you didn't need to be too clever to guess what he'd done.'

Andy and Ned looked briefly at each other.

'Do you know which house it was?'

Ryan shook his head.

'Okay, let's put it this way, if we asked you to show us, do you think you could?' said Ned.

'Now?'

'No, not just now but another time maybe?'

'I know whereabouts it was and it was the only house with no curtains upstairs. Like I said before, Donny notices stuff like that.'

'So go on, what happened then?' Ned said.

'Snow was really, really heavy. It bothered me, like I say I was cold, wet and hungry by this time. Donny was drinking, a lot.'

'My son's a peeping tom. How am I going to live that down,' Mrs Merryfield said quietly as she wiped away a tear that ran down her cheek with a handkerchief from her apron pocket.

Ryan looked at his mum as she blew her nose loudly.

'Carry on, Ryan. Anything else you can remember from that night?' said Ned.

'There was a car at the side of the road and Donny said he knew whose it was. He banged on it and shouted something to the person inside but I didn't see who it was, I only heard a woman's voice. He thought it was highly amusing. Like I say, he was drunk,' he said by a way of an explanation. 'Then a man shouted at us. He sounded really angry and so we legged it. Donny went one way and I headed home, I'd had enough and that's it. God's honest truth mum, I haven't seen him since.'

'And that's everything you know?' said Andy.

'I swear,' he said, nodding his head.

'You say Longbottom said he knew the person whose car he was banging on?' Andy said.

'He said he did, but he says he knows lots of stuff, just like...'

'He thinks everyone fancies him,' said Ned, nodding.

'I don't know whose it was. The cars were all covered in snow but it was a pink car though, I could see that much.'

'And you don't know who owns the car?' Ned said.

'No, it was a woman's voice, that's all I know.'

'What about the person who shouted at you?'

'It was a man but I didn't stick around to see him, he sounded proper mad. Donny shouted 'run', and I scarpered.'

'We'll need a statement from you, Ryan. It may help us with the girl's movements before she went missing.'

Mrs Merryfield nodded. 'So the girl that's gone missing, that's her car you think?'

'Yes it is,' said Andy.

'There won't be a problem with you giving a statement, will there Ryan?'

'No, mum.'

Andy and Ned were pleased. They had a statement from Ryan Merryfield. It was a few new pieces in the jigsaw puzzle. Donny Longbottom could now be put at the scene and they had no doubt the 'flasher' reported that night had been down to him too. Could it also have been Norris Regan who had shouted at them?

Chapter 24

Dylan picked up his mobile. *'It's gonna be a late one love. One of the lads is coming back for tea, but don't worry, I've warned him it'll be fish and chips,'* he texted Jen.

Dylan's office phone rang. Vicky walked in the office as he picked it up and she stood quietly waiting for him to finish.

'So, Longbottom's charged with attempted rape,' he said, raising his eyes to look at Vicky from where he was seated. 'I want to see the remand summary,' he said before putting the phone down.

Dylan's mobile phone beeped. He sat with it in his hand. 'Longbottom expected to be going home,' he said to Vicky, while reading the text. He closed his eyes momentarily and put the phone back down on his desk. 'Someone else I've upset today,' he said. 'Better make that fish and chips and a big bunch of flowers.'

'Donny Longbottom expected what?' said Vicky.

'He didn't think he'd be staying in for Court.'

'Wait 'til he knows that it'll be recommended that he should be remanded to prison until his trial,' she said.

'Prison is a place he hasn't been yet. I expect his defence team to be making an application for bail.'

Vicky sat down and took off her shoe. 'My bloody feet are killing me,' she said, rubbing the ball of her foot. 'I don't know how I ever walked the beat.'

'You were younger and fitter then,' he laughed.

'Cheeky sod, I haven't put on weight since I've been in CID.'

'Yeah, whatever,' he said, absentmindedly.

'DI Turner about, Lisa?' he called, looking past Vicky and out into the CID office.

'No sir.'

'Get hold of him will you and give him my home address. I'm going to have to call at Court and speak to the solicitor, so it'd be better for him to make his own way there tonight.'

'Will do,' she called back.

Vicky looked at him with a furrowed brow. 'Oh, I've invited him round for tea. The others have gone back today and he was on his own. I felt bad I hadn't even had a drink with them.'

'And how does Jen feel about that? Ah, get it, the big

bunch of flowers...'

'Ah, she'll be fine.'

Vicky shrugged. 'She's a better woman that me, coping with a teething child and entertaining your bloody cronies.'

'That's why I married her and not you Vicky,' he said with a grin. 'It'll be right. He's from down there isn't he? They'll have lots to talk about when she gets over herself. She'll be pleased... she just doesn't know it yet.'

'Changing the subject, I'll tell you what,' Vicky said, quickly. 'They don't miss much in Merton village where I've just come from. I've been to a W.I. meeting at the Church Hall up Manchester Road today and those who knew Mrs Regan and her son from old, said they've been known as a strange pair for as long as any of them can remember. He used to push his mother about in a wheelchair and they'd swap their wigs years back. They say, he thinks they don't know it's him that dresses as his mum but they just accept him as he is.'

'So, he's known as being strange, nothing else?' he said, chewing his lip.

'Well they said that they hadn't seen him as her, oh God you know what I mean, about for a while... but then no one goes out much up there in winter if they don't have to. I've wrote it all up in my pocket book and got all their details, but since I had to go on my own I've got no statements as yet.'

There was a knock at the door. A uniformed Sergeant stood, in his shirt sleeves, with his hand resting on the door handle.

'Can I have a quick word in private?' said the Custody Sergeant.

Dylan looked bemused. 'Of course, Sergeant Maude, come in,' he said.

'I'll make a drink boss,' Vicky said, hopping to the door as she tried to put her boot back on. She squeezed past the Sergeant, who was built like a tank. Maude stepped into the office with a twinkle in his eye and shut the door behind her.

'Take a seat,' Dylan said, 'What can I do for you?' he asked him.

'It's more what I've done for you sir,' he said, tapping the side of his red, bulbous nose. His voice was deep and deliberate with an impressive rasp. 'This Longbottom, what a weirdo. I've just been down to his cell doing a bit of interviewing, off the record like. I thought I'd have a go at him about the Misper; Harwood girl for you. I made him shit himself,' he laughed. 'Uniform said you lot were gonna have a little chat with him later but you don't need to now, I got the cough.'

Dylan could feel anger bubbling to the surface. His fingers held his pencil just that little too tight and it snapped. His arms were rigid but he allowed the officer to continue.

'I had him in tears, nearly crushed his balls. A wrestler would have been proud of that testicular claw,' he snorted. 'He admitted the indecent assault. Yeah, just before one of them bloody civilian gaolers came down the corridor to see what all the fuss was about. I had to look sharpish and get out, but not before I told him we knew he was also a murderer. And do you know, reckons he's a hard knock, he just curled up in a ball and cried like a little baby. Soft bastard kids these days, should be made to do national service,' he sneered.

Dylan stood up, slapping both hands down on his desk and gave an almighty roar that rattled the office window, 'You fucking idiot!' he shouted.

PS Maude jumped in the chair and Dylan's voice dropped to nothing more than a whisper.

'Not only have you broken every rule in the book, you twat, you have assaulted him for no good reason. I've heard it said before, but it's right you shouldn't even be in this job, let alone be a supervisor. You'll go back and record on the detention sheet what you have just told me, now. Do I make myself clear? And I want a duty statement from you. Mark my words, you'll be dealt with for assault. Now get out of my office.'

'But I thought ...' he said.

Dylan picked up the phone but held it to his heaving chest. He stopped. 'That's just it though isn't it? You didn't fucking think. You egoistic prick, you just wanted to get an admission, which is fucking worthless to me. You've crossed the line once too often, Maude – and this time, it's big time.' He dialled a number on his landline. 'Discipline and Complaints please,' he said, giving Sergeant Maude a glare that could have cut steel.

Vicky stopped at the door, tray of drinks in hand. She took a step back and rested it on Lisa's desk. 'If I were going to pick a fight with someone, Lisa, I might choose somebody smaller than Maude,' she said under her breath.

'From what I've heard, it's not Dylan that needs to worry,' Lisa said, pulling a face.

'Get out of my sight,' Dylan roared.

The door flew open and Lisa and Vicky turned away.

'You'll regret this. If I lose my job... if I lose my pension because of you, you'll pay. Mark my words, you'll pay,' Maude said.

'You threatening me, Sergeant?' Dylan shouted after him. Sergeant Maude stormed through the CID office, his face like thunder, slamming the door in his wake. The girls flinched. The door almost came off its hinges as it crashed back into the frame. Dylan's eyes followed Sergeant Maude out of the CID office. He was tempted to go after him and arrest him, but he knew gathering the evidence first was necessary. Maude was the sort of officer that gave the police a bad name. With his length of service, he should know better.

'Guess you're off his Christmas card list then this year,' said Vicky as she cautiously entered Dylan's office waving a white napkin a couple of minutes later.

'No one is above the law, Vicky. D & C have taken charge. I'm required to make a witness statement. Ned called him Thumper didn't he? He's already under investigation. I can't get over the fact that he thought he could simply walk in and interview someone in a case of mine like that.'

Dylan put his pen to paper. 'The sooner the statement's completed, signed and faxed to D & C, the better,' he said.

'Guess our interview with Longbottom will be delayed?'

'It will now,' he said.

Within the hour, rumours were flying around Harrowfield nick, quicker than any intelligence system could ever circulate information. On leaving Dylan's office, Sergeant Maude had picked up his coat and left the police station, telling his supervisor he felt ill. The internal team of D & C were already in the cell area interviewing Donny Longbottom, who confirmed to them what the Sergeant had told Dylan. Longbottom was being medically examined and his injuries would be photographed as evidence.

'It'd be only right to wait, or even do a prison visit to talk to Longbottom after he's remanded tomorrow. An interview now will be frowned upon in the future and seen to be unreliable as well as pressurised,' he said, with venom in his voice.

'Well, Sergeant Maude was always said to be someone you didn't want as an enemy but he met his match with you boss. I know a lot who'd have turned a blind eye.'

'No one frightens me Vicky,' he said. 'One thing I won't do is walk away.' Glancing at his watch, a look of horror crossed his face. 'Oh, my God, I should have left for home half an hour ago. Jen is going to kill me.'

Vicky laughed. 'No one, boss?' Jen had definitely got under the once confirmed bachelor's skin.

Seven o'clock, there was a rap at the front door. Jen had just got Maisy settled and she flew down the steps to avoid further commotion that might wake the sleeping child. She couldn't make out who the person was standing at the other side of the patterned glass but guessed it must be Dylan's guest. She practised her false smile in the hallway mirror as she passed and hoped the make-up she'd applied earlier had survived Maisy's bathtime antics. Once tonight was over, she would speak to Dylan and tell him the truth, the whole truth, and nothing but the truth about her past and DI Shaun Turner.

Opening the door, she gasped. It couldn't be. Her stomach flipped. Max hurtled past her to greet their guest. It was true, dogs didn't forget.

Chapter 25

Andy and Ned arrived back at the nick, just in time to see Dylan jogging out of the building.

'Sir, hold on! We need to speak to you before you go, it's urgent,' shouted Ned.

'Jesus, make it quick, Turner must be on his way to ours by now,' called Dylan.

'I think we'd better go inside boss,' said Andy as they met in the middle of the yard.

'Can't it wait?' Dylan said.

'No sir, it can't.'

The men followed Dylan back into the nick.

'Vicky, here now,' shouted Dylan from the CID office door. Vicky threw down the papers she was reading off the spewing fax machine, took off her coat, tossed it on her desk over her handbag and followed her colleagues into Dylan's office without a word.

'Ryan Merryfield has just put Donny Longbottom on Manchester Road for us the night Kayleigh went missing,' said Ned.

'Never,' said Vicky.

'And not only that, her car...' said Andy. Vicky stared at her workmate wide-eyed.

'Merryfield told us that Longbottom and him went their separate ways, after a man shouted at them when a drunken Longbottom banged on a pink coloured car. He also said Longbottom knew the woman inside the car,' said Andy.

'And it also appears Longbottom might just be the flasher that was reported that night, according to Merryfield,' Ned said.

'So you think the man they heard that night is our man, Norris Regan?' said Vicky.

'It fits in with the timeline,' said Andy.

'And Longbottom, who is already out perving, just happens to come across Kayleigh who he's been stalking for weeks, vulnerable and alone in her car. Coincidence?' said Ned, cocking an eyebrow.

'We can corroborate some of what Merryfield says and we know he did go home afterwards. What I'd like to know is where Longbottom went after he and Merryfield parted company?' Dylan spoke his thoughts out loud.

'We've been faxed a list of Council workers on duty that night who might be able to support what he's saying, although I've noticed there's a couple with previous which might not be a good thing as far as reliable witnesses go,' said Vicky.

'Good work. We need to prioritise the Council workers that were working, however. Vicky will you update these guys regarding recent events here for me? I really have to go,' said Dylan, looking up at the clock. 'God, is that the time?'

'Armitage Arms lads, for a swift one?' said Vicky.

'Sounds good to me,' said Ned.

'Count me in,' said Andy.

'You coming Lisa?' asked Vicky. 'They're buying,' she said throwing the men a glance over her shoulder.

'Yeah, I can give you a quick one if you like,' said Ned as he walked past Lisa's desk. Lisa put one finger up at him without looking in his direction.

'You wish. I've got other fish to fry tonight,' she grinned.

'I'll see you all early tomorrow,' Dylan laughed. 'Talking of frying, I've got to go to the chippie on my way home to get some tea... er supper, now,' Dylan said, looking anxiously at his watch again, 'for Shaun Turner.'

Lisa's hand flew up to her mouth, 'Oh, God,' she said.

'What?' said Dylan.

'I forgot to ring him with your address. He didn't come back to the nick.'

'Well he's not here now, so I guess he must be there?'

Lisa shrugged.

'No worries. He'll have got our address from Dawn.'

Jen could feel her heart beating rapidly against her breastbone. She opened her mouth but found she couldn't utter a word. Her knees buckled and the only reason she didn't fall was because Shaun Turner reached out to hold her upright. She stepped away, forcing him to release her. His smile faltered, but he thrust forward the bunch of freesias he was carrying.

She had a choice, she could slam the door in his face and wait for Dylan to come home and bare her soul, or she could let him back into her life again. Her first instinct was to fall into his arms. She never could resist that smile.

'Your favourites,' Shaun said sheepishly, nodding at the flowers. He laughed a deep laugh that came from the pit of his stomach, amused at her surprise. He leant forward to kiss her cheek. 'And I remembered,' he continued, producing a bottle of Chateauneuf De Pape that he'd hidden under his arm. 'It might help the shock,' he offered. His mouth was upturned and his eyes were dancing, with adorable crinkles at the corners that she had not remembered being there the last time she had seen him. But how could she recall such things? It was nearly a decade since they'd been face to face. She thought time had healed the wounds but she was wrong, her heart still bore the scars – and the longer she looked at him, the more they seemed to open.

Shaun put his unclaimed offerings on the hallway table. 'You look good. Motherhood suits you. Can I come in?' he said awkwardly but with affection. Jen stood resolute. His voice was like a knife turning in her stomach. He stepped forward, and without taking his eyes off her he pushed the door closed gently behind him.

'What the hell are you doing here?' she said in a hushed tone.

'Didn't Dylan tell you I was coming for dinner?' he said.

'Go, please, just go before he gets home,' Jen said quietly. He tried to step around her but she blocked his way.

'I just want the chance to explain. I've waited such a long time for this opportunity and I'm not going to leave without telling you how I feel now.'

'It can't be that important. It's taken you ten years to find me.'

'I'm sorry,' he said softly. 'I was a total asshole.'

'You're right about that. Did you think for one moment what I went through?'

'When I found out you couldn't have chil...'

'Children, go on, you can say the word,' she snapped.

'I thought I couldn't live without having kids... but now, I know it's you I can't live without.'

'Tough,' she said lifting her head defiantly.

'Obviously, big style,' he said, nodding towards Maisy's pram.

'What're you saying?' she said, crossly her voice rising. 'I lied?'

'No of course I know you didn't lie. The doctors were wrong, weren't they? If they hadn't taken... If they hadn't operated?'

'I'd have been dead Shaun, dead. Would you rather that?'

'No, No I didn't mean that, but if the doctor had said you could still conceive, then our lives could be so different now.

We'd still be together, wouldn't we?' he pleaded.

'You don't get it do you? My mum's dead, my dad's three hundred miles away and I'm here, all because of you. If I'd still been living on the Isle of Wight, my Mum... well, she might not be dead.'

'Surely, you can't blame me for your mum being killed?' he pleaded. 'You didn't have to leave the Island because we split up. Look, I couldn't stop thinking about you.'

'And you think I could?'

'I can't live without you...'

'Tough!'

Shaun held her gaze. At least he had the decency to look ashamed. 'If it is any comfort, I was there for your mum that day; I was on duty and went to the scene. I stayed with her until she got to the hospital. I saw you there and watched over you at the funeral. I should have come to talk to you then, I know that now, but it didn't feel it was the right time or the place to come clean about my feelings. Come back with me Jen. I need you. Your dad, he needs you now. I saw him recently, he's been unwell.' Shaun reached to take her hand. Jen pulled away quickly.

'Don't you dare bring my dad into this,' she said, as tears slid down her cheeks. She wiped them away with one swift hand movement and let out a sob.

Shaun could see the door to the lounge was open and slowly he stepped forward. Delicately, he put his hand on her shoulder and guided her into the room. He helped her to the sofa and sat next to her, talking to her softly all the while. Jen sobbed quietly and, handing her his handkerchief, he pulled her to him. She didn't allow her head to fall on his chest but looked ahead so she didn't have to meet his gaze. She stared at the flames dancing in the fire, blocking all the painful thoughts from her mind, but she let him hold her.

There were a lot of things Dylan didn't share with Jen. He didn't want to upset her with the triviality of the office and he wasn't a gossip. Neither did he want to upset her with the gore and detail of some of the incidents he went to, but the incident with Sergeant Maude had infuriated him. Just wait 'til I get home and tell her about it, he thought.

Dylan put his key in the front door and shouted that he was home. He saw the wine on the telephone table next to the clock in the hallway and picked it up. No one came to greet him and, noticing the lounge door closed, he walked straight through to the kitchen where he took the plates out of the cupboard. He heard a noise behind him. Shaun Turner stood in the doorway. His shirt sleeves were rolled up and he looked relaxed.

'Oh, good, you found us then?' Dylan grinned, over his shoulder. He unwrapped the fish and chips. 'I'm sorry I'm late. You know how it is?'

Shaun nodded. 'No worries,' he said, softly.

The food was hot and Dylan blew on his fingers after he scooped a handful of chips onto a plate.

'Chessell Pottery?' Shaun said, nodding towards the distinctive blue star painted Emma Bridgewater crockery on the kitchen worktop.

'Don't know about that mate, they were Jen's before I moved in,' he said. 'Lisa was worried she hadn't given you our address,' he added absentmindedly as he reached back into the cupboard for the mugs.

'I'm a detective aren't I?' he said, tersely. Dylan nodded agreeably.

'Everything has to match,' he said, looking down at the mug in his hand and smiled. 'Where is that lovely lady of mine?'

'Upstairs with the baby,' Shaun said.

'Oh good, you've met them then,' Dylan said, counting out the cutlery from the drawer. He didn't wait for a reply. 'Great choice of wine mate, Jen's favourite. That'll have put her in a good mood. Guess I could do with all the help I can get tonight,' he said as he handed Shaun Turner a tray with a plate full of food upon it. He picked up his meal. 'There's nothing like fish, chips and mushy peas with bits on for tea,' he said.

Shaun looked puzzled.

'Oh, yeah it's dinner where you come from, isn't it mate, not tea?' he said. 'Fancy a beer to go with it?' Dylan added reaching into the fridge and throwing Turner a can with his free hand.

'Thanks,' he said following his host back into the lounge.

Shaun sat in the chair facing the door, Max laid at his feet. He pushed his food around the plate.

'Good?'

'Yes,' he said agreeably as he watched Jen come down the stairs.

'You're honoured,' Dylan said to Shaun as he nodded at Max.

Shaun glanced at Jen as she stood in the doorway. She looked at Shaun. How could he act as if nothing had happened?

Dylan smiled at Jen. 'Yours are in the oven love, warming,' Dylan said, through a mouthful of food.

'I think Max has found a new friend there?' he said indicating Max sat firmly at Shaun's feet.

Jen opened her mouth as if to say something. Shaun's eyes met hers and she closed it again.

'Sorry love, you've met Shaun haven't you?' Dylan said.

'Yes,' was all she could manage before heading for the kitchen to pour herself a large glass of chilled white wine from the fridge, with a trembling hand.

Dylan shrugged his shoulders at Shaun. 'Women?' he mouthed with a grimace. 'I'm late again.' He stood and carried their trays into the kitchen.

Shaun Turner sat alone in the lounge with a coffee in his hand. He stroked Max's head and the outside of the mug he was holding. The mugs that had been an engagement present from his parents. He looked around the comfortable home Jen had created. Her mobile in a bright flowered case was on the hearth to his right and he picked it up and tossed it about in his hands, flicking through her photographs.

Jen stood at the butler kitchen sink, deep in thought. Dylan approached her, unheard.

'Not hungry?' he said tentatively, placing the dirty dishes on the draining board before stopping to drop a kiss on her cheek. Jen didn't look at him but he felt her freeze at his touch.

'Oh, come on,' he said wearily, standing with his back to the units. He felt irritable and tired. 'Okay, I'm sorry I'm late, again, but it wasn't my fault – I really couldn't get away. Don't be like this,' he begged. Seeing her face soften he turned to her and slid his arms around her waist.

The plate she was washing slipped through her fingers and smashed in the basin.

'You've no idea what you've done, have you?' she said, looking into his tired eyes.

'Look, I know it's hard for you.'

'Hard?' she said through gritted teeth. 'Just go, go and see to your... your new matey,' she spat, picking the pieces out of the soapy water and lying them gingerly on the worktop.

Maisy slept through the night without waking. Dylan was annoyed with Jen for sloping off to bed without as much as a by your leave, and his head was fuzzy with the amount of drink he and Shaun had managed to consume. He didn't remember Turner leaving – funny that, how alcohol had a way of switching his mind off, relaxing his body and blotting out the things that seem all too troublesome at the time. But drink had a habit of biting back at him the next morning. 'Ouch,' he moaned, putting his hand to his brow as he turned on the light. He had slept in the spare room. Shaving in the semi-darkness of the en suite, he stared at the gash under his chin. Bloody hell, how had he done that? He gathered his clothes and was at work for 7 am without waking Jen. To his surprise, he saw Shaun's car tail lights heading out of the nick's car park. He must have been OPL last night, and probably still was this morning. Hey, he wasn't his concern. The DI was old enough to know what he was doing.

'Something we said?'

'Huh?' Lisa said, looking up from her typing as he walked in the office.

'Did I just see Shaun's car leaving?'

Lisa looked at him puzzled.

'Turner, has he gone?'

'Yes, he said something about doing what he had come up here to do,' she said looking at him with alarm. 'Looked as though he'd slept on a park bench all night. Must be a long drive for him though,' she said slowly, brow furrowed.

'Yeah, it is. Not surprised – we had a skin full. You okay?' he asked, 'You look peaky?'

'Yeah, I will be,' she said. 'A late night with a bottle of red and another man who was sadly only after what he could get.'

'Mmm..,' he said. 'I know the feeling.'

'Huh?' she said for the second time, frowning.

'The bottle, not the love rat thankfully,' he said. 'Black coffee, paras' he said, reaching into his desk drawer.

'Mmm... You're a life saver,' she moaned as she fumbled the tablets out of the palm of his hand. He took two, she took two.

'Guess it's about the only way I'm going to get any work out of you today.'

She smiled wanly 'I'll get the coffee,' she said, groaning. 'I need to move myself. What've you done to your face?' Don't tell me you were in a fight again last night? The last person who did that to you ended up committing suicide.'

'No, it's nothing like that,' Dylan said. 'At least I don't think so...' he added, rubbing his chin thoughtfully.

By half past Dylan had the full list of Council workers and drivers that the Council hired on an ad hoc basis, and a large mug of black coffee on his desk.

'Thank you Lisa,' he said as she headed for his door. 'I didn't realise there would be so many, nearly three hundred,' he said with a long, low whistle as he flicked through the pages of printouts.

'That's the whole of West Yorkshire – and not all of them were working that night, obviously – but they use anyone available with flat back wagons and tractors on twelve hour shifts in extreme weather conditions too, I'm told. No doubt it's a good earner for the farmers in the region,' she smiled weakly.

'I want the team out on these enquiries today,' he said firmly.

'There were only two Council gritters and an ad hoc covered the Manchester Road area that night, you'll be pleased to know,' she said.

'A good starting-point to trace, identify and eliminate the drivers.'

Lisa nodded.

'I reckon we can do those interviews today if we get our skates on, don't you? We'll get the others moving as soon as they come in.'

DC Vicky Hardacre was down to work with DC Andy Wormald, and by half past eight they were speaking to one of the council operatives at the depot when the other drove in. He halted his lorry in the space directly in front of them and turned his engine off. The cabin door opened with complaint and the rotund driver breathlessly clambered down. Both men looked similar, with rugged faces and cheery smiles. Joe Davis stepped to the side and leant heavily on the door of his mate's lorry.

'Yes, I was on the night shift that night with Bert. We were driving the vehicles with ploughs in front that night, weren't we Bert?'

His friend looked puzzled.

'They've come to talk to us about White Wednesday.'

Joe lifted his chin with a grimace. 'Shall we go up for a brew?' he said, indicating the way to the canteen.

The four drank tea from big white pint ceramic mugs as

they spoke.

'It was the worst weather I've seen for near on twenty years,' said Joe.

'The roads were totally gridlocked at one point,' said Bert. 'Our job was to keep the main arterial route open, at our side of the County. I even had to give Joe a tow, didn't I mate?' he said, loudly, pointing his finger at his friend and laughing heartily.

'We are very concerned about the young girl who got stuck on Manchester Road. As you are probably aware, she hasn't been seen since,' said Vicky.

'Her little pink car was parked that night at the side of the road nearest to Ivy Cottage,' Andy said. 'Did you see it?'

The pair shook their heads from side to side. 'Can't say it rings a bell with me, does it with you?' Bert said.

'Did you see anyone acting suspiciously that night along Manchester Road?'

Again the pair shook their heads.

'The speed the snow came down, that night, meant all we could do was go backwards and forwards on the main road best we could, as far as we could, for abandoned vehicles. The windscreen wipers could hardly cope with the downpour. All the vehicles were covered in snow. I couldn't tell you what colour or make they were. They were all white! I don't know about you Bert but it took me all my time to make out where the road ended and the pavements started.'

'Aye, it was so bad that they had to bring in one of blokes with his lorry onto Manchester Road. A chap called Barrowclough. I don't know what time he started, maybe dinnertime, I believe he gritted the roads from town to over the border into Lancashire too,' Bert said. 'I wish I could help you love, I really do, but it were blizzard conditions,' he added, shrugging his broad, plump shoulders.

'Well you did an excellent job by all accounts,' Vicky said looking down at her list. 'Barrowclough, yeah, he's on our list of people to see. We're off to see a Mr Paul Barrowclough next,' said Vicky.

'That's him. He's a self employed bloke, in his fifties I'd say. We've used him before.'

Andy took Vicky's lead as she stood to leave.

'Before you go,' Bert said. 'I'd better confess that I've been in trouble with you lot before.'

Vicky and Andy raised their eyebrows.

'A bit of a bad lad I was when I was a youngster, burglary

and the like but no more.'

Andy smiled. 'Thanks for being up front mate. It saves us a lot of time, we'll be doing our research,' he said.

The detectives were escorted out of the building.

'The next statement might prove more difficult,' said Vicky, mobile phone to her ear. 'Mr Barrowclough isn't answering his phone.'

'Let's go to the address, it's on our way back anyway, so we've nothing to lose,' said Andy, steering the CID fleet car out of the yard. They drove down the unmade track to The Railyard. The approach was unkempt, furrowed and had deep potholes. Tucked away at the bottom was a ramshackle building next to the disused railway line – hence its name, no doubt. It was like an old scrap yard. There were bits of vehicles, metal poles, frames from old chairs and picture frames. Wooden pallets were stacked ten foot high and there was also countless big rusty barrels with heaps of old tyres. The car crawled slowly forward as Andy looked for a suitable place to stop and park up but within seconds a German Shepherd dog, fur unkempt, came lunging menacingly at the vehicle with bared teeth. He slammed on the brakes. Vicky shrank back in her seat, but suddenly, just before it reached her door the dog came to an abrupt halt. It was fastened to a thick, rusty chain that in turn was attached to a wooden kennel in bad need of repair. The dog reminded her of a bear, except its legs were long and thin. It ran anxiously back and forth, barking incessantly, before coming to a standstill with its feet in its metal food-encrusted bowl and scum-filled water container.

'Poor thing,' she said. She could feel her heart beating frantically.

Andy chuckled. 'You wouldn't have said that if you had been standing out there. I just hope that chain is as secure as it appears. That animal looks mighty hungry to me.'

The pair sat for moment looking about the yard, watching a few hens and an odd scraggy cockerel that crowed relentlessly. Suddenly Vicky let out a piercing scream, cowered in her seat and covered her eyes. Swallowing hard Andy looked aghast as a fox, ran swiftly past the front of the car and snatched the cockerel. All was suddenly quiet. The large wooden doors of big barn to the right juddered slowly open. Vicky looked through splayed fingers and gulped. Nudging Andy, she pointed to the giant of a man in a cloth cap, wearing blue, stained overalls under a worn, dirty jacket, who wiped his foul and slimy oil stained hands on a filthy rag, as he emerged.

'Gerr!' he roared at the dog as he half-heartedly kicked out with his boot. The animal's dark eyes never left his master. Immediately its ears dropped. It lowered its belly to the floor and it slunk into a dark corner. 'Useless swine,' he called out.

Feeling somewhat safer now the dog was out of harm's way, Andy opened his door and Vicky followed, digging deep in their pockets for identification. The man continued to come towards them dragging his steel toe-capped boots on the flagstones. 'They'll be no more fucking chicks this year until I get another,' he mumbled to himself, brandishing the big metal ratchet he held in his hand. 'Whatever you're selling, I don't want any. Clear off. Don't you know you're on private property?' he said.

'Mr Barrowclough, Paul Barrowclough?' Andy said.

'Who's asking?'

'DC Andy Wormald, Harrowfield CID,' he said, holding up his warrant card.

'And DC Hardacre,' Vicky said, with a glare.

'What do you want?' The man was so obese; his neck reminded Vicky of a pair of hotdogs. The stench came from him like a force field, pushing her backwards. She tried to raise a confident smile but struggled to find half a grimace.

'January 7th you worked for Harrowfield Council, helping them grit Manchester Road in the heavy snow, that right?'

'That's right darling'. Not a crime is it? Hey, Tell you what, coppers are better looking now than they were in my day,' he said, turning to Andy.

'And wagon drivers get uglier in my experience,' Vicky muttered under her breath.

'A sense of humour too. I like that,' He held his hands out. 'Cuff me now. I'll admit to anything sweetheart.'

'We're speaking to drivers who were out during the evening of White Wednesday Mr Barrowclough, to see if they can help us with our enquiries,' Andy said.

Barrowclough cocked his head.

'A young girl parked her car, a pink Ka, near to Ivy Cottage on Manchester Road. She hasn't been seen since.'

'Well, that's the vehicle I was using that night, in there,' Barrowclough said, nodding towards the open wooden doors. 'Brake drums seized, probably all that bloody salt. You want to go in and have a look?'

'Should we?' said Andy.

'Thought that's what you lot did, nosey around?'

'We just want to know if you saw the car or a young girl walking alone on Manchester Road that night, or anything else that seemed out of the ordinary that you think might help in the investigation into her disappearance?'

'I saw a lot of bloody cars that night and a lot of bloody people walking in the snow too. Ivy Cottage? Yes, I know the place. Nelly's brewed up for us many a time.'

'Did you go there on White Wednesday?' said Vicky.

'No, too busy,' he said.

'Did you see this girl or the car?' Andrew pressed on, showing him a photograph of Kayleigh.

'No. But I did see some young lads larking around a car. They'd gone by time I headed back to the depot. Can't say I blame them. Nobody in the right mind would stay out in weather like that.'

'You did,' said Vicky with a sneer.

'Pays well darling and I need all the money I can get to treat my ladies.'

'You're not married then?' said Andy.

'Not the marrying kind. Love 'em and leave 'em, that's my motto, always has been,' he said. 'It's been nice talking to you, but I can't stand here all day. Anything else I can help you with?' he said. 'I've got to get the wagon working. It won't earn me anything stuck in that shed.'

'Can you give us a description of the lads you saw messing around the vehicle on Manchester Road that night?' said Andy.

'Yeah,' he said. Vicky looked at Paul Barrowclough, pen poised.

'They looked like bloody snowmen,' he chuckled. 'Got you there, didn't I? Eee it's the way I tell 'em.'

Vicky scowled and put her notebook back in her coat pocket.

'We'll need a statement off you at some point, sir,' Andy said.

'Oh no,' he said, shaking his head. 'I'm not getting involved. I've told you what I can remember, and that's it.'

Andy looked at Vicky.

'Please?' she said, unenthusiastically.

'Not even if you got your top bollocks out, darling.'

'Well that's never going to happen, so before we go, one last question, have you ever been in trouble with the Police?'

'I'm sure you know the answer to that already. So if that's it, I've got other things to do,' he said turning and walking away without a backward glance. Vicky watched the huge doors closing, but not before he gave her a sly wave of his dirty hand.

'Jerk!' she said under her breath as she followed Andy back to the car.

'Small world isn't it? He admits knowing Regan and it's Longbottom and his mate Merryfield he saw, no doubt.' said Andy

'Wonder if he knows Nelly Regan is a man?' said Vicky. 'His eyes are far too close together for my liking. We need to dig deeper with that bastard.'

Andy laughed. 'He's really got to you hasn't he? The top bollocks jibe?'

'No, I used to work with a bloke who always called tits top bollocks, or brace and bits. It's the way he said it, made my skin crawl.' Vicky said shuddering as she rolled up her sleeve.

'See, look at them hairs standing up on my arm.'

'Wonder what he's got previous for?'

'Fiver says it's sex offences.'

'Can't be much, or they're old records that they've weeded out, like the burglaries for matey back at the Council depot. I think it'll be assault or handling and receiving stolen goods – you're on.'

'Hang on, you can only choose one offence.'

'Okay, okay. Assault'.

'No, it's definitely a sex offence. Want to double the bet to a tenner?'

'Have you already seen some Precons?'

'No, if I had seen his previous convictions then I'd have dropped it on his toes. You're not that cocksure now, are you?' she said with a grin.

'A tenner it is,' Andy said holding out his hand for her to shake.

'Easiest tenner I've ever made,' she said with a wink.

Chapter 26

'I think Jen just needs a rest,' said Dylan. 'She needs to get away for a while.'

'And you've as much chance of her wanting to leave you, as you have Hugo-Watkins taking an interest in your missing girl,' said Dawn.

Dylan sat in deep thought.

'I think you're wrong.'

'You're telling me that Jen won't worry about how you are coping, here, alone when you've got this lot on? Well, be it on your head, but I'm telling you now she won't want to go anywhere without you,' said Dawn.

A/Detective Inspector Dawn Farren walked out of his office with an 'I told you so' look upon her face.

Dylan's phone rang and he snatched it up.

'Dylan,' he said.

'I've got good news for you, Inspector Dylan. I'm right, the odontologist I've been talking to says it is highly likely he'll get DNA from the two newest skulls' teeth,' said Maggie Jones.

'What can we do this end?' asked Dylan.

'The odontologist will take a mould of the teeth and then it'll be up to your team to liaise with the local dentist with a view to identifying the deceased. That's of course if their respective records are still maintained over the past three decades.'

'Well that's definitely a positive line of enquiry for us,' said Dylan.

Dylan put the phone down, contemplating her words.

'Odontology?' said John Benjamin.

'Tina Walker, the girl who went missing all them years ago – I wonder,' he pondered as he threw the file over the desk to John. 'Check what information we have about other Mispers around the time that she went missing, will you? Either in our Force area or over the border.'

'Interesting,' he said. 'This investigation is not your run of the mill, is it?'

'No, budget permitting we might even look at craniofacial reconstructions on the skulls. Although they're telling me it's expensive, we might have to see if it's feasible on this.'

'How good would that be though, to see what the two

people who the skulls belong to in 3D?'

'Find out how they lived, find out how they died, or so they say. This investigation will get lots of media attention, John, so it's a real chance for you to get to know the journalists and editors.'

John frowned. 'I don't like doing TV and radio, boss. What if I say something wrong?'

'You won't. I don't like it either but you'll get used to it, it's a necessary part of the job, I'm afraid. We need the media to help us to get the information about the incidents we deal with out there and ensure the appeals go as far and wide as possible. The reporters are your voice, and don't you forget it. They might need us for the information but it's a two-way thing, we need them too. Be nice to them.' Dylan stood quiet for a moment. 'I want to see for myself what's further up the river and on the hillside above where the skulls were found. They might have got washed down with the heavy rain and snow we've had lately. Do you fancy a run out?' he said.

'Yeah, why not? I just hope we don't find any more,' John said.

Dylan grabbed his old leather coat from the coat stand and shrugged into it.

'You and me both, mate. Years ago, they reckon that if the police even had a loose horse near the border of Lancashire they'd frighten it over so the expense and work load would be incurred by our neighbours,' he grinned. 'They may have possibly reciprocated with the skulls on this occasion.'

He stopped at Lisa's desk on their way out and bent down to speak to her quietly. 'Do me a favour, will you? Enquire about times of trains from Harrowfield to Portsmouth for me?'

Lisa frowned. 'One or two tickets?'

'Just get me the times.'

Lisa shrugged. 'Okay.'

John followed Dylan out of the door collecting his radio from his desk as he passed. 'Do you think they did really?' John said as he caught Dylan up at the door.

'What? Move a body from one county to the next? Probably, especially if the officers were due to go off duty. They wouldn't get paid overtime in them days, remember, a bit like Inspectors and above nowadays. It's okay for the desk boffins who approve the legislation, but not for us who work the bloody hours.'

'Some things don't change, do they?' said John.

'Talking about moving bodies reminds me,' Dylan said.

'Going back some time, one of the forensic pathologists working on a case of mine took a head back to the laboratory, from the mortuary for further examination. He had it in a plastic bag on the back seat of his car, not labelled or anything, mind. He'd thrown a car rug over it so it was concealed though. Guess what?' Dylan chuckled.

'What?'

'He only got stopped for speeding on the M62.'

The men had arrived at the car. Dylan pressed the fob to release the locks. Dylan and John opened the doors in unison and got in.

'No.'

'Yeah, and since it was at night and they didn't have a lot on, the traffic lads searched the car and made the gruesome discovery.'

'I guess he would be arrested and questions asked later?'

'Well they thought they'd apprehended a murderer of course. He'd a hell of a job convincing them who he was, and where he had just come from.'

'I bet he never did it again.'

Dylan chuckled. 'What we tend to forget, as police officers, dealing with lying scum day in day out, is that the majority of people are honest, even if they've done something wrong. Like the bloke who parked on double yellows outside the nick and went in to admit that he'd murdered his wife and tell them she was in the boot of his car. Since he was illegally parked, the officer on desk duty told him to go and move the car immediately, otherwise he would get a parking ticket.'

Dylan steered the car from his car parking space in the rear yard and drove out towards Ovenden.

'Never!'

'True as I sit here. As you can imagine, the bloke became really agitated, so the help desk officer called a beat officer in to deal with him. He went to the car with the man, who voluntarily opened his car boot, showed him the body and the officer arrested him for murder.'

'God, how embarrassing. He'd have to make a statement to say the he hadn't believed him.'

'You'd think so wouldn't you? But no, he just asked me if he should include the fact that he was parked contrary to regulations on double yellow lines in the file, so he could get done for that as well,' Dylan laughed.

'Nothing stranger than folk, as they say in Yorkshire, is there?' John said.

'Yes, and you have to include police women in that too. I once knew a long-serving policewoman who was fingerprinting a joiner. His left index finger was missing, so she prints his second finger again in the space provided on the form. Nobody's any wiser about this until the forms come back with a red ink notice and an instruction to take the joiner's fingerprints again as, they pointed out, she'd taken the print of his second finger on left hand twice. She wrote back to the bureau stating the man's forefinger was missing so she thought she'd make use of the space. The report went back and forth to HQ several times. She couldn't see that the problem was that she had shown the defendant with all fingers present. I think the moral is John never underestimate the ability of police officers to cock things up when something should be straightforward.'

'Unbelievable.'

'I've got another one for you. A drunken man walks into the station and tells the officer on the desk, 'I've killed the bitch. She deserved it after all these years. She won't make my life a misery ever again. So here I am to give myself in.' Now, some people are very helpful, or at least they try to be, but in this instance he was sent packing and told, 'Come back when you're sober. I haven't time to listen to your drunken stories today, Fred,' for the officer knew him. Fortunately he got a taxi to the next town and went into the nick there and made his confession again. This time, they checked out his story and found it to be true. He had killed his wife and he was arrested. In the subsequent interview he told them he'd also been to another nick to turn himself in and they'd sent him packing too. Can you imagine if all we had to do was wait at the front desk for people to come in and confess?'

'Yeah, wouldn't life be boring?'

They drove in silence for a while to where the skulls had been found, and then out onto the main Ovenden road above. There was a large lay-by surrounded by a little fence and a small wall. The field beyond sloped steeply down to the stream which in turn continued to flow down to where the skulls were discovered. At one corner of the lay-by was a pile of rock salt, the wall behind it had crumbled and it had spilled over into the field below.

'Council grit store? I've passed it numerous times over the years. The pile is usually bigger than this,' Dylan said.

'Yeah, I pass it most days. It's the lowest I've ever seen it,' said John. 'Perhaps the weight of the recent dump for this year's bad weather explains the wall crumbling?'

'Did the skulls come from here?' he said, kicking the bottom of the remaining pile that was hard and compacted. 'Then did they roll down into the stream? I think we need this grit moved to see if we find any other human remains in it. I bet the tarmac underneath hasn't seen the light of day for donkey's years.'

'I seem to remember when I was a lad there was a grit box in the corner.'

'I wonder if that still exists under this lot?' said Dylan.

'Probably rotted away. But there's only one way to find out, as long as I don't have to move it.'

'I think we'll talk nicely to the Council, John,' Dylan smiled. 'Otherwise, mate, there's a shovel in the boot.'

Chapter 27

It was back to the office for the scrum down. Dylan wondered if the officers had progressed with their individual enquiries; he looked forward to this time of day. The only person that had caused some interest today and was brought to Dylan's attention was Paul Barrowclough.

'We've been to see the most obese, obnoxious, grubby, smelly, man of the century,' said Vicky.

Dylan laughed, 'I can always count on you to say it as it is, can't I? I take it he wasn't your idea of an Adonis?'

'Positively minging. You know me, I aren't picky but... he was a fucking weirdo – and surprise, surprise, the night Kayleigh went missing he was on Manchester Road with his wagon. Furthermore, he says he knows Regan and he also told us he saw two lads making a nuisance of themselves, which fits in nicely with what we already know.'

Andy shook his head in despair of his partner.

'He impressed you then? Maybe he will end up as our star witness?'

'Well, I pity the pair that have to interview him if we have him in for questioning.'

Andy's eyes went up to the ceiling.

'He riled her, boss. He told her he wouldn't make a statement even if she showed her top bollocks, didn't he?' said Ned.

'They are not bollocks, moron. You told him, Andy? Anyway, you'd better get your wallet out, you snitch, you owe me a tenner.'

'So we have established the guy is not on Vicky's favourites list, but what else do we have on him?' said Dylan.

'Barrowclough tells us Ivy Cottage was, is, a coffee spot for him and he has Precons for unlawful sexual intercourse, although to be fair to him, he did admit to being known to us,' Vicky said holding her hand out for the ten pound note Andy offered.

'The brief summary of the USI is, when he was twenty-nine he picked up a fifteen year old girl in his wagon on the pretext of giving her a lift and ended up raping her. He argued consent, saying she had told him she was nineteen and agreed to everything including the anal sex. He pleaded to indecent assault as she didn't want to go to Court. He had his hands slapped, six months imprisonment suspended for two years. I don't think for a minute that this leopard has changed his spots. My theory is he just hasn't been caught since.'

'It's definitely worth more research Vicky, but we need hard evidence. Smelling like a dead rat means nothing to CPS or a jury,' Dylan said. 'But it's very interesting that he knows Ivy Cottage and Regan, very interesting indeed.'

'Well he knows Regan as Nelly... so maybe he doesn't know him that well.'

'Surely he'd have guessed, or is he in on the act?' said Dylan, pulling a face. 'Well, it takes all sorts. John and I also have a theory on the skulls enquiry, and the possibility that they may be linked to the grit stored in the lay-by at Ovenden, above the spot where they were found. While this enquiry seems to be focusing on a small group of people, I am very conscious that we don't put all our eggs in one basket. However, we certainly need to put the people we have now, in, or out, of the enquiry. We also need to speak with Donny Longbottom, I'll speak with Perfect and Best Solicitors for a suitable time and date.

'I want you to look at telephones, Andy, Ned, see if you can show some contact between Barrowclough and Regan. Also, look into their financial background. Let's dig and see if it's at all possible to show anything. John, I want you to stick with the investigation into the skulls. Okay, we are moving it forward and I'm going to increase the HOLMES staff and get the incident room up to maximum strength. A vast amount of information is starting to come in and we don't want to miss anything.'

Dylan was interrupted by the telephone, 'Dylan,' he said.

'You bastard!' he heard a man yell. 'They've suspended me. You'll fucking live to regret it,' the caller said and then hung up.

'Everything okay boss?' Vicky asked.

'Yeah, yeah just a certain Sergeant Maude who isn't very happy with me at the moment,' he said with a sigh.

'Not speaking out of turn boss, but Thumper has always been a bit of a loose cannon. I'd keep looking over your shoulder if I were you,' Ned said.

'Don't worry, there are bigger, uglier men that have threatened me – but, in my experience, it's the quiet ones who hurt you the most.'

After the meeting, Dylan informed Discipline and Complaints

about the telephone call. It would be another nail in the sergeant's coffin. He hated it when police personnel crossed the line, especially when they had had such a long and seemingly unblemished career. For a moment, his mind wandered back to the murder of Detective Sergeant Larry Banks. Larry the 'lad' as he was known had been his colleague – but women, greed and the demon drink had been his downfall. It wasn't good to look back. Police officers had to trust their colleagues implicitly. After all, they put their lives in their hands on many occasions in the line of duty – which is why it hurt so much when it turned out they were bent. The day had been going well, but that call had left a nasty taste in his mouth. How naïve of Sergeant Maude to try to interview and then assault the prisoner in his cell – and why would he think he'd not only please Dylan, but get away with it, these days? Dylan wondered just how many times he had done it in the past. But his tactics wouldn't be condoned – not on Dylan's patch.

Dylan picked up the phone to arrange to interview Donny Longbottom. It would probably mean a visit to Armley Prison where he was on remand, but Dylan needed to know if his solicitor or a representative wanted to be present. He spoke to Yvonne Best.

'I don't think he'll want to speak to anyone at the moment,' she said. 'He's having a hard time in there since the other inmates found out what he was inside for. So he's gone into solitary. What is it you need to talk to him about?'

'Kayleigh Harwood, who went missing on January 7th in that heavy snow.'

'Yes, I read about it, but you don't think he's anything to do with that, do you?' she said. Dylan was open with her, 'Well, he used to go to her for his hair cutting and frequently sat outside the hairdressing shop where she worked, so it is a line of enquiry.'

'But she got stuck in the snow, didn't she?'

'Yes, but I have a statement from Longbottom's mate to say they were both in the area at the time. It's believed he'd been drinking and while in drink he banged on her car roof when she was inside.'

'I can see why then it's important for you to talk to him. She's not been found, has she?'

'No, we were going to have a word with him when he was in the nick for the attempted rape, but with the Custody Sergeant messing up big time that day we still need to speak to him. I personally made a statement against Sergeant Maude for his actions, just for your info.'

'I understand. Lin is diaried to go see him in the next couple of days. Do you want her to ask him if he'll see you? If she tells him it's you who made a statement against the police officer who assaulted him, he might just agree.'

'I'd appreciate it. I need to know whether or not someone wants to be present from your office? If he doesn't want to see us, we will still have to see him as we need to put some questions to him.'

'Better if he's co-operating then. At least that way you'll get some answers. Truthful or not, that's another thing,' she laughed. 'I'll get Lin to give you a call.'

'Thanks for that, Yvonne, I'll wait to hear from her.'

John Benjamin was at the office door waiting for Dylan to finish on the telephone. Dylan waved him in.

'What's on your mind, big fella?'

'I just was just wondering what the possibility was of dentists having records from thirty years ago?'

'I'm sure they will have. Some may have even uploaded the details onto their computerised system, but if it's like here, they'll still have the old paper systems as back up.'

'Looking at her photograph, Tina Walker had a distinctive gap in her two front teeth, so that could be a positive when it comes to the search. We don't have her dental records on file do we?'

'No.'

'And one of the skulls is minus the front teeth, isn't it?'

'Yes. But we're jumping ahead of ourselves. The skulls could belong to anyone, John. It would be interesting if one of them does turn out to be Tina's, but then who does the other belong to if they were dumped in the same place? Actually that may be the bonus and the jigsaw piece that finally unravels the mystery...'

'The problem is that even thirty years ago a hell of a lot of people went missing, just like they do today. I must admit I didn't realise so many people were never traced 'til I started looking into the stats for this case.'

'Treat the skulls a bit like a pebble in a pond, start with them nearest at the centre of your enquiry and work outwards. Keep an open mind, there may be an innocent explanation for those skulls being in that particular location.'

'Yes, I know. Only time will tell,' John smiled. 'I'm

determined to solve it, boss.'

'I'd expect nothing less from you,' said Dylan. 'Just keep me posted.'

Chapter 28

Jen sat listening to the ticking clock in the dark. There was a strong wind blowing and she could hear the rain beating down on the lounge windowpane. Maisy was fast asleep. Her phone beeped. Another message, the sound added to her inward agitation. The days of strain and suspense, never knowing when Shaun was going to try to contact her again, or if indeed Dylan would see one of the hundred messages he had sent, was taking its toll. The room felt chilly all of a sudden and she shivered. She couldn't see the time but she assumed it was around ten o'clock and presumed Dylan would be home soon. Following another deluge of rainfall, she heard a key turn in the lock. She held her breath. The outer door open and closed quietly. She sat up straight. Tonight she would tell him.

Dylan stood in the hallway looking forlorn and jaded, his back to the front door. He looked too weary for words.

'What on earth have you done to your chin?'

'Shaving,' he sighed, bringing his hand up to the cut.

'You look like a drowned rat,' she said smiling through unshed tears at the sight of his pale, wan face.

She took his briefcase and he discarded his coat to the banister before sitting down on the stairs. He reached out for her hand and pulled her onto his knee. 'I'm knackered,' he said, laying his head against her shoulder.

Jen stroked his head lovingly and for an instant she thought he had fallen asleep, until he spoke. 'And I need to find Kayleigh.'

'Why did Mrs Harwood not report Kayleigh missing earlier? She'd been gone for a week, hadn't she, before anyone had noticed she was missing? I couldn't let Maisy out of my radar for that long, no matter how old she was.'

Dylan looked up at her face with a seriousness and helplessness he didn't display to her often. 'Because, when the time comes, we have to let go. Giving the ones we love freedom is a good thing to let them make their own choices, Maisy will always be our child, but like you and me, without freedom she won't be healthy. Freedom is a healthy part of nurturing.'

'That is very profound for this time of night. Bed,' she said, pointing up the stairs. 'I'll go and make you a drink.' With a lump in her throat and a little sigh, she watched Dylan struggle up the stairs. A tear rolled down her cheek and she wiped it way. This was no time to be opening up her heart as he was opening up his to her.

The days rolled by, much to the frustration of Dylan and the team, and time slipped away for him and Jen. Kim Harwood was living a never-ending nightmare that caused her to break down. In contrast, Kayleigh's boyfriend Matt had been spurred into action by her disappearance and, to Dylan's surprise, distributed posters of her, hoping that someone, somewhere, may have seen her and that she would be found alive.

Dylan knew Kayleigh's mother and boyfriend were both eaten up by the fact that they hadn't questioned her absence. He told them that there was no way they could have foreseen what had happened. Hindsight was a wonderful thing, but nevertheless he felt their pain. Even if they had been in touch with each other, would it really have made any difference to what had taken place? He thought not. He did, however, wish that he had some news for them, even if it was bad news. Finding a body would at least help them to move forward with their lives.

It had been almost two weeks before the officers could get a visit to Armley prison. Dylan was taking Vicky with him and Lin Perfect would be there to support her client, she confirmed in a telephone call.

Cold stone, tiled walls, the clinking of chains, doors slamming and locking, seemed to be the incessant background noise within the prison, Dylan noted as he waited with Vicky to be taken to an interview room to see Donny Longbottom.

'Be careful in here Vicky, because in here you're worth a fortune.' Dylan whispered to her.

'You're not funny, boss. This place gives me the heebie jeebies. They're like packs of salivating dogs, it makes m' skin crawl,' she said, staring at a prisoner who was giving her the eye as he went about his duties cleaning the vinyl floor.

'What I'll never understand is how people form friendships from the outside with them,' she said nodding in the staring inmate's direction with distaste.

'And the rest.' said Dylan. 'Trouble is, they're still human beings.' Dylan sighed. 'Just a shame we can't put some of them down like we would do a violent dog. Sorry, but once a bad 'un, always a bad 'un in my experience.'

'And I know you, you'd vote to bring the death penalty back, unless you're going soft on me.'

'Too bloody true, with some of the murderers I've come face to face with,' he said.

A prison officer strode towards them. He opened one of two gates that were locked at each end of the corridor. The peak of his flat cap was slashed so it partly covered his eyes. He was swinging a bunch of keys. 'Ready?' he said. 'I'll take you to see Longbottom, if you follow me.'

No other words were spoken and they obeyed his instruction. He locked the gate again once they were through and unlocked the gate at the far end of the corridor, locking it behind them. They followed him closely across an internal walled yard. Wolf whistles came from the high barred windows. The only thing the officers could see were the inmates' fingers. Their jeers echoed eerily.

'Faceless people living a empty life,' Vicky whispered.

'Make you nervous?' said Dylan.

'Not nervous but vulnerable, I guess. Don't you dare tell Ned I admitted that,' she said.

The next door led into the segregation unit and once inside they were taken into a windowless interview room. Sat at a table were Donny Longbottom and his Solicitor Lin Perfect. The prisoner officer stood guard in silence at the only exit.

Dylan introduced them both to Longbottom and explained that they were investigating the last movements of a missing girl.

The prisoner wasn't looking at Dylan but staring blatantly at Vicky's breasts. 'We have a statement from a Ryan Merryfield to say you were with him during the heavy snow in Manchester Road, the night Kayleigh Harwood went missing. Do you remember that night?'

Longbottom looked spaced out, staring, with his head on one side.

'Donny, are you going to answer the Inspector's questions?' asked Lin Perfect.

'No,' Longbottom said as he lay back slovenly in his chair.

'No you don't remember or no you're not answering the question?' asked Vicky.

He looked up at her face.'You're too nice looking to be a copper,' he said, leaning forward with a lazy smile upon his face.

'And you're being disrespectful.'

'So?'

'So, you going to talk to us?' Vicky said,

He shrugged his shoulders.

'You could start by telling us what you remember about 7th January, White Wednesday, when you were out with Ryan. Or don't you want to because you did something that you shouldn't have that night?'

'I've done nothing wrong. I told that Sergeant in the cells, but he wouldn't believe me. Look where that got me.' Donny Longbottom rubbed his crotch.

'Well, tell us eh? We already know what Ryan says. Shall I read you the statement he's given us,' asked Dylan.

'That would be really helpful, Inspector,' Lin Perfect answered for him. Donny lifted the chair onto two legs and rocked to and fro nonchalantly.

Dylan read Ryan's statement aloud.

'That's a load of crap. I didn't nick that booze,' Longbottom said, raising his voice. 'I just made that up,' he said stopping, himself from rocking by resting his hands on the table.

'The rest's right then? You were peeping through people's windows?'

'Nothing wrong with looking through a window is there?' He rocked once more. 'In't that what windows are made for?'

'Did you know the girl in the car?' said Vicky.

'Might have.'

'She cuts your hair, doesn't she?'

'Might do,' he said putting all four legs of the chair firmly back on the floor with a bang.

'Did you see anything unusual that night that you think might help us find her?' Vicky said.

He considered the question for a moment or two, but so convinced were they that he wouldn't say anything worthy of note neither officer poised their pens above paper.

'I saw a lot of people who looked like snowmen... I saw people on skis... Did I tell you I built a snowman and I used the carrot mum gave us...? That was so funny,' he laughed raucously.

'We're wasting our time, aren't we?' Vicky said.

'Might be, but it gets me out of the cell,' he grinned.

'Will you make a statement about what happened that night, if what you're saying is Ryan is lying?' said Dylan.

'No way, you'd only twist it. It's been nice looking at you Mrs, but I'm bored,' he said standing up.

The interview ended. He was taken away by the prison guard while they waited in their seats.

'I'll try to get through to him later. Do you really think he is involved, or do you think that he just happened to be in the area?' said Lin Perfect.

'At the moment we're keeping an open mind, but it appears he does have a bit of a crush on the girl and had been hanging around the salon where she worked. It seems a bit of a coincidence that on the night she went missing we can put him at the scene where she was last known to be,' said Dylan.

'But Ryan says in his statement that they ran off at the sound of a man's voice and can't confirm that it was Kayleigh in the car or that it was definitely her car,' she said.

'It's not like Kayleigh's car isn't distinctive though, is it? And he also states that he doesn't know where Longbottom went afterwards, so we can't eliminate him.'

'I understand. I have to see him again about the assault. I'll try to get him to speak to you further. It is in his interest.'

'Thanks,' said Dylan. 'Every little helps, as they say.'

Dylan and Vicky headed back to the nick.

'Is he the one?' Dylan asked Vicky.

'No, not for me. He's just a wanker and he's in the right place for it.'

'I wouldn't have put it exactly like that, but I have to agree with you. I don't think it's him either.'

'Barrowclough has gone to the top of my list, followed closely behind by our man Regan.'

'We just need evidence, concrete bloody evidence. The same names keep cropping up into the enquiry – and that can't be a coincidence, no way.'

'Well we'll keep digging – and like you say, if the evidence is there we'll find it. But it doesn't look like we're going to find Kayleigh alive now, does it?' said Vicky sadly.

'We have to be realistic. She didn't go missing because she wanted to, by all accounts and it is looking increasingly like somebody has seized an opportunity when she was at her most vulnerable.'

'Happens all too often doesn't it? Who knows what form predators take? But what sort of moron is out in that sort of weather looking for someone to take advantage of?'

'Looks like somebody was... Normal people get home as quick as they can in weather like that and stay where it's warm and dry. We have to concentrate on the people we know were out there that night, for whatever reason. Check with forensics and fingerprints when we get back regarding her car. In fact, we've heard very little from them so far on this one. That's another thing, her mobile. I haven't seen any results from her phone company, have you? We need to go back over the basics and satisfy ourselves we have done all that we can with what information we have.'

'Will do, boss,' Vicky said as she climbed out of Dylan's car and into the back yard of the police station. 'Your Jen and Maisy okay?' she asked as they walked together towards the CID entrance.

'Yeah, fine why?'

'Oh, nothing, Jen's phone's just been off lately when I've tried to ring her.'

'That's odd,' he said with a puzzled expression crossing his face. 'Maybe it's because she's been busy.'

'Every night?' she said.

Dylan shrugged his shoulders as he checked his pigeonhole for his afternoon mail. There were two letters with his name printed on them, one in capital letters. He looked at the postmark, 'Edinburgh' it read. Curious, he opened it with his letter opener and let the correspondence drop out of the envelope onto his desk. Picking it up by the corner, very gingerly, he could see someone had taken the time to cut letters from a newspaper.

I'D RATHER BE DEAD THAN GO TO PRISON
KEEP LOOKING BEHIND YOU DYLAN

There was no doubt in Dylan's mind it was the work of Sergeant Maude. Was he having a breakdown of some kind? He didn't like the suggestion of suicide.

Dylan put his phone on speaker as he listened to the ringing tone for Discipline and Complaints.

'Put the letter and envelope into separate exhibit bags,' said the guy in their admin department. 'Then send them both on to us.'

Dylan knew Sergeant Maude was suspended. 'He told us not to bother preparing a file against him as it would be a waste of our time,' said the man in D&C.

'What are we doing about it?' asked Dylan.

'Well, between you, me, and the gatepost, there has been a lot going on in his personal life. He left his wife, his girlfriend abandoned him after he assaulted her and he has other allegations against him for which he is under investigation. We've got his car circulated as the usual 'Occupant may have suicidal tendencies. If seen, contact D& C', but there is not a lot more we can do. I'll speak to Edinburgh Police though, now we have a specific location to see if they can help locate him for us.'

'What a sad end to his police career,' Dylan said, flatly.

'He knew what he was doing, Dylan. Sadly, he has only himself to blame. Better go, the other phone is ringing – but be assured, we are doing everything we can.'

Dylan sat for moment after he'd put the phone down and reflected on what the guy at D&C had just said. Policing was a bloody hard job, but who really monitored how it affected the Bobbies? No one. Granted, there was the Occupational Health Unit, but a lot saw going there as a weakness – and more importantly, so did the bosses. He was aware of a few Bobbies who had killed themselves over the years and those who had contemplated suicide. They managed to solve other people's problems, but sadly not their own. It was far from pleasant dealing with a fellow officer who had committed suicide. Dylan didn't like the thought of a life being wasted when there were millions of people desperately fighting to stay alive. Life was for living, in his book, and Carpe Diem his mantra.

He opened the second letter – Jen's ticket for her surprise trip to the Isle of Wight. But was he ready to let her go?

Chapter 29

Dylan gave Maisy a hug and chattered away to her as he fastened her into the high chair for breakfast, as Jen busily prepared her Weetabix. Her phone, laid on the kitchen table, bleeped and he picked it up and looked at the screen. Jen raised her head up to meet his eyes that were full of concern for her.

'It's just a low battery,' he said as he plugged it into the charger. Jen hurriedly crossed the kitchen, unplugged it and slipped it in her pocket.

'We don't want disturbing, do we Maisy?' she said with a forced smile as she sat in front of their daughter. Jen put Maisy's cereal bowl on the tray attached to her chair. Dylan stood behind her. Laying his hands on her shoulders, he massaged her neck lovingly. She closed her eyes momentarily.

'You okay love? You're a little jumpy,' he said, gently bending to kiss her on her cheek.

'I'm fine,' she said. She put a spoon of cereal to Maisy's open mouth. 'Just a bit tired, that's all,' she added shrugging his hands away.

'Vicky said your phone has been turned off recently.'

'Did she?'

Maisy opened her mouth and grinned, which made the food spill down her chin. 'Come on, don't mess me around today little monkey,' Jen said scooping it up expertly with the plastic spoon.

'What's up love?' Dylan asked, seeing her pale, pinched face as if for the first time. 'You're not yourself,' he said, sitting down beside her.

'I told you I'm just tired. Let's talk later, yeah?' she said, her eyes filling with tears as they found his.

Dylan put up his hand to silence her. 'I know and hopefully I can make you feel better. I've got a surprise for you that I think will cheer you up no end.' He smiled a big smile that melted her heart.

Maisy screeched and thrust both hands into the Weetabix bowl. Before Jen knew it, the cereal, spoon and bowl were flying across the kitchen and crashing onto the floor.

'For God's sake Maisy, I can't take my eye off the ball for one second can I?' Jen yelled. Jumping up, she picked a cloth from the drainer and proceeded to wipe up the mess.

Maisy screamed a high pitched wail before the tears came. Jack went to comfort her. Jen turned, hands in the air from her crouched position on the floor.

'Not now Jack,' she yelled. 'Go. We'll talk later.'

'But...'

'Just go to work, will you?' she shouted.

Dylan knew there was no reasoning with Jen in this mood, so he picked up his jacket and briefcase and walked out without looking back.

The door slammed. Maisy stopped crying instantly and started to sob instead. Jen turned and slid down the wall to the floor. Sat with her back to the kitchen units, she wept. Stunned by her mother's tears, Maisy was still.

'Da Da?' she said when silence came. 'Hic!'

Jen looked up at her, smiled through her tears at her daughter and dragged herself off the floor. Taking her out of her high chair, she held Maisy tight and rocked her gently, singing softly until her hiccups went and she fell asleep.

Dylan threw open the CID office door. There were people talking and laughing.

'You won't solve crime sat in here,' he barked as he stormed through the office. Entering his own room, he slammed his office door behind him and sat down, elbows on the desk and head in his hands. A few moments later the door opened slowly and very quietly.

'You okay?' said John hesitantly.

Dylan nodded, looking at Jen's tickets, propped up in front of his computer screen. 'Detective Sergeant Benjamin, what can I do for you?' Dylan said, lifting his head, but not turning to face his colleague. John stood and watched him in silence unpack his briefcase. Dylan held a banana and an apple in one hand. He looked at his colleague questioningly.

'I just thought I'd update you before I went out, sir.'

'Take a seat, I won't be a minute,' he said, calmer as he placed the fruit in his drawer.

'I'm seeing a Roger Clarke, the head guy at the Council services this morning. He's worked there for thirty three years. He tells me he sited the first grit bin in that lay-by. Apparently, it's an overflow storage unit which they fill from purchases made from councils over the border if extra grit is required. This agreement stops unnecessary pre-planned outlay if we have a mild winter.'

'Good, tell him about the skulls and ask him if he could move the rock salt or grit, or whatever he calls it. We need to search the area for other human remains, as soon as possible.' Dylan was sombre, his mobile beeped. He looked at it.

I'm sorry. It's not you it's me. I love you. Jen x he read. He closed his eyes for a moment and bit his bottom lip. Dylan looked at John and raised his eyebrows.

'Will do boss. Also Odontology have informed me they have the necessary from the first skull for me this morning, so I'll start visiting the local dentists.'

Dylan nodded. 'If we need more staff on it to get it done quickly, let me know.'

'There are only seven dental practices in the immediate area, so I'll work outwards from the scene. If none of the enquiries prove fruitful, I might have a further twenty or so to visit.'

'Okay, okay, keep me updated,' Dylan said absent-mindedly. John walked to the door. 'You sure you're okay, sir?'

'Fine. Send Vicky, Andy and Ned in, will you?'

Vicky idly flipped a pen through her fingers as they waited in Dylan's office, in silence, for Ned.

'So what's the update on the Kayleigh Harwood enquiry?' asked Dylan. 'You got anything for me?'

Vicky shook her head. Ned entered the office and sat down with a groan. His face looked like a blancmange.

'Anything yet on Regan and Barrowclough's phone numbers?' Dylan asked Andy.

'Got Regan's but Barrowclough's is flagged on Intel according to the system so I am waiting for supervision to give me the nod when they have assessed the information, boss.'

'For fuck's sake.'

Ned flinched. 'Bit fragile this morning?' Dylan said, scowling. 'Late night? Your problem. Don't let it affect your work, not on my team, or you'll be on your way. Do I make myself understood, DC Granger?'

'Yes boss, I'm on with it,' he said getting up from his chair and leaving the office at speed. It was Vicky's turn to raise her eyebrows to Andy.

'Andy, have we got any more from Marlene at the salon?'

Andy shook his head.

'What no gossip, nothing?'

'No, I'll call again this morning,' he said.

'The bicycle bell? Any news on its age, make?'

'I've got an appointment with a bicycle dealer later today. There aren't any markings on the bell but I thought it worth a shot. He's been recommended; an old guy, been in the job years, but about as much of an expert as I think I'll get on this one.'

'Good work. Vicky I want Jackie May back. Have a word with her Inspector, Mark Baggs, today will you? We need more hands to the pumps. Tell them that Chief Superintendent Hugo-Watkins has okayed it.'

'He has?' she said, her eyes the widest he'd seen them this morning.

'He will. He was supposed to be coming to our briefings to show his support, but he hasn't. It's the least he can do for us.'

'I want you or Jackie to keep Mrs Harwood and Kayleigh's boyfriend updated.'

'Will do boss. I've got some good news for you.'

'Good, I could do with it.'

'Fingerprints are running the biscuit wrappers we found in Kayleigh's car through the metal deposition machine to see if they can come up with any prints for us. They've managed to lift Kayleigh's from the mirror we seized from her bedroom.'

'For God's sake, are they only just doing that? I thought they'd cleared her car, printed it and found nothing other than her fingerprints there,' he said through clenched teeth.

'There were Matt's and her mum's too, we got their elims.'

'Yeah, course,' he said, tetchily. 'So when will we know?'

'Hopefully today. I asked them to let you know A.S.A.P. To be fair, they have been working systematically through items in the car.'

'We need that data back from her mobile.'

'Today boss. Okay, if I get on?' said Andy.

Dylan nodded. 'Tell Lisa to get hold of Perfect and Best will you? I want to know if Longbottom's told them anything else, on or off the record.'

'Better get you some more caffeine before you burn out this morning, boss,' said Vicky.

'We've got to move this investigation forward. It feels like it's stagnating,' Dylan snarled.

'A bit like whatever you last had in this mug on the window sill. Are you growing penicillin?' she said, screwing up her nose.

Dylan sat looking at the screen of his mobile phone, contemplating calling Jen, but his office phone rang before he got the chance.

'Now then,' said a big bright, cheery voice.

'Dawn,' he said with a sigh and half a smile.

'What you up to?' she asked.

'Trying to move forward with the missing girl enquiry, although it feels like I'm walking though treacle; you haven't heard from Jen have you?'

'No, why?'

'I've got the tickets...'

'You're going ahead with the plan then? Look, I've been thinking about what you said. You don't think she might be suffering from post natal depression, do you? Something I learned is that the symptoms don't always show up directly after birth, like they did with me, but they can come on months after baby's arrival.'

'I don't know what's wrong,' he said with a sigh. 'I wish I did.'

'Well, if you think I can help, remember I've been there, bought the T-shirt and worn the socks as they say. I was going to ask you if you'd heard any more from Shaun Turner?'

'No. Why should I?'

'Did you know he knew Jen before?'

'Before when?' Dylan's brow furrowed.

'Before, when they both lived on the Isle of Wight?'

'No, no I didn't ...' he said feeling little shivers of cold down his back. 'Why didn't they say?'

Chapter 30

Lisa knocked at the door. She could see Dylan sat perfectly still, gazing out of the window.

The room was overheated, outside was a bleak, brittle and dark day. His mind was blank, his stare fixed. He felt dreadfully alone.

'Come in,' he called distractedly.

'Lin Perfect on the phone for you, boss,' she said, popping her head around the door. Dylan looked round at her vacantly. 'She couldn't get through, your phone's off the hook,' she said pointing to the receiver in his hand.

'Sorry,' he said with a shake of his head as he replaced it on its cradle.

'Donny Longbottom, for what it's worth, tells me that he saw someone speaking to Kayleigh as she sat in her car that night, an older guy he guessed, but he couldn't give me a description,' said Lin.

Dylan sighed deeply. 'So he's admitting to seeing Kayleigh in her car that night on Manchester Road?'

'Yes, but the bad news is that he isn't up for making a statement to that effect.'

'Right, thanks anyway.'

'I'm on holiday for the next three weeks, so if you need anything you'll need to speak to Yvonne, I've brought her up to speed with the case.'

'Lucky you,' he said before putting the phone down.

Lin Perfect stared at the telephone in her hand. 'Well, thank you Lin for all your trouble,' she said out loud.

Dylan's mind was in a spin. Why hadn't Jen told him she knew Shaun Turner, if she did? The thought moved him to an unexpected emotion. Why didn't DI Turner tell him he knew her? It didn't make sense. He couldn't process the news that Dawn had sprung on him and for once his methodical mind couldn't work through the thick fog that descended upon him. Could it be true, Shaun Turner and Jen shared a secret? It would explain why she was acting so oddly. Dylan suddenly realised an insecurity and vulnerability he had never experienced since being a teenager. He wasn't young, he wasn't naïve but he had for good reason chosen to live the life of a bachelor – until Jen had come along. He knew he shouldn't dabble in such sentiment.

He walked up the stairs to the police canteen. He'd pick up a playpen on his way home for Maisy – she was such a handful at the moment. Maybe that would give Jen time for herself. Time to think, reflect, and talk to him.

'Omelette and chips,' he said.

'Do you always have to be so bloody difficult? Can't you just have something off the board for once?' said the usually jolly kitchen assistant.

Difficult. Is that what he was, difficult? Maybe Jen daren't tell him she knew Shaun Turner because he was difficult?

'Difficult's my middle name, didn't you know?' he replied, with half a smile. 'You should know that by now.'

'You'll have to wait,' the counter assistant said, mopping her brow with the back of her hand before stuffing the tea towel she was holding back in the string of her apron.

'No problem, I just thought I'd try an omelette, like you've advertised on that banner up there.'

'It says, *Please Put Used Crockery Here*, over yonder, but nobody ever does,' she said nodding her head in the direction of the condiment section.

'I'll just sit over there quiet then. Give us a shout when it's ready.' Ten minutes later he walked past the counter, dropped his crockery in the elected spot and threw a forced smile at the counter assistant. She grimaced. 'Lovely omelette,' he said. He let the door of the canteen swing noisily behind him.

The afternoon was an arduous one of paperwork that needed decisions and signatures. It appeared to him that more and more people were frightened to death of doing what was required of them, terrified of making a decision in case it came back to haunt them. He wasn't cavalier, but he did what he got paid for, which was taking charge and making decisions and he wished others would do likewise.

'Dylan,' he said, his voice sounded odd to his own ears when he answered his phone. He hadn't spoken to anyone for hours. He coughed to clear his throat.

'Detective Inspector Dylan, it's Stewart Viney from HQ Fingerprints. DC Hardacre, Vicky, asked me to ring you when I had news for you in respect of my examination of the biscuit wrappers from the Harwood girl's motor vehicle.'

'Yes.' Dylan was all ears.

'We've identified some marks on the wrappers as the girl's, but we have also found a partial left thumb and forefinger on the foil wrapper too, which makes me think that someone held it and maybe offered it to her.'

'Is it the boyfriend, Matt Prentice?' Dylan asked.

'Definitely not, we have eliminated him.'

'Her mother?'

'We've eliminated her too.'

'It looks like this person may have a very slight blemish on the thumb. I can't be too exact... but it's a mark that stands out, although it may not be very visible to the human eye. It may be an old wound.

'That's good news, right?' Dylan said. For the first time in the investigation, he had hope and evidence that would put a person into the enquiry.

'Yes, it's good. However, the downside is that it's not good enough for a database search.'

Dylan's joy was brief.

'But we can check it against any individual you put forward, providing of course whoever takes the prints gets a proper roll on the thumb,' he said. 'Whether or not it would be good enough to put before a court I can't say for sure at this time, but that's for the future.'

'I understand. That's great work, excellent news Stewart, thank you.'

'Kit Kat's are better than Ginger Snaps.'

'My favourite too,' Dylan couldn't stop the smile.

'No, you're missing my point Inspector I meant the quality of the marks are better on the foil of a Kit Kat than the wrapper of the ginger biscuit that was also there.'

'Yes, I know Stewart. It was a joke... never mind.'

'Oh yes. Right,' said the serious young man. 'I'll send the report out to you. If you require any marks to be checked, send them to me. If the person is recorded with us we'll have the prints to eliminate them or bring me the prints over I can quickly eliminate them for you while you wait.'

'Thanks again, that's excellent. We will be in touch as soon as we have some prints to be checked.'

'Thank you sir, it's a pleasure.'

Dylan had wondered where the biscuits had come from. They had been eaten, so the wrappers were the only thing left for them to examine. It was positive news and he was looking forward to updating the team at debrief with the latest revelation.

Was this the day that moved the enquiry forward? Oh, he hoped so. The team meeting was planned to go ahead in the next five minutes. Should he ring Jen? And say what? He decided to text instead. *I've got that surprise for you. I hope it will make you smile,* he texted. He half closed his eyes and looked up to the ceiling. He pressed SEND before he could change his mind.

His phone bleeped as he walked out of the door. He hesitated, should he go back?

'Boss,' shouted Vicky bouncing in front of him. 'Good news about the fingerprints!' she said thrusting a half cup of coffee in his hand.

'Do you have to?' moaned Ned.

'Have to what?'

'Be so bloody cheerful,' he said, holding his head in his hands.

'Takes longer to get over a hangover when you're old I've heard, old fella.'

'Whatever.'

Dylan's office phone rang on an external line. Lisa looked at him.

'Shall I get it?'

'No, it's late, we need to get this debrief over so we can all get to our homes tonight. Barrowclough's telephone?'

'I can't get the billing information until the supervisor in Intel gets back to me – he's floundering, tells me there is a lot of intelligence to assess on the system.'

'Tell him I want it and I want it now, otherwise I will speak to him tomorrow.'

Dylan looked at him pensively.

'I already told him it was a matter of life and death.'

'It will be – his – if he doesn't come back to us tomorrow morning.'

Ned yawned. 'Too old for these late nights are we Ned?' Vicky said her flaying arm cutting very close to his ear.

'Get off my case, will you?' he said, dodging the slap.

'Vicky,' Dylan scolded. The CID office phone rang. Lisa once again looked at Dylan, who shook his head. 'Andy, anything?'

'Apart from him securing a date with the lovely Marlene, boss, haven't you pal?' said Vicky winking at her blushing colleague.

'I don't want to know Andy,' said Dylan. 'What's up with you Vicky, have you been on the Red Bull again?'

Vicky wrinkled her nose.

'I have spoken to Marlene today sir, but sadly she has

nothing to add other than Mavis Beanland, Kayleigh's last customer had a suitcase with her when she came for her hair doing. It seems she was going to stay at her sister's. She promises to ask her to contact us when she calls to make her next appointment on her return,' said Andy.

'And that's it? Doesn't anyone know where the sister lives?'

'No sir.'

'Do we know how long she's gone for?'

'No sir.'

'Can we try to find out where Mavis Beanland lives, please? Someone must know.'

'Yes sir,' said Andy.

'Okay. Come on then Vicky, what have you been up to, apart from teasing the hell out of the lads?'

'You'll be glad to hear PC Jackie May will be back with us tomorrow and I have arranged for us to see Kim Harwood and Matt Prentice already.'

'Excellent, the bike bell Andy?'

'The expert had a hospital appointment today and forgot about me. Seeing him now tomorrow, first thing.'

'Joy! Okay, thanks everyone. I'll speak to you in a minute about the skull enquiry John, but before I do, Stewart Viney rang me from SOCO. They've managed to lift some fingerprints, from the eaten biscuit wrappers in Kayleigh's car.' The room fell silent. 'Don't get too excited, it's only a partial left thumb and forefinger print. The quality isn't great, he tells me, but it's as valuable as gold dust to us right now. Maybe it will put someone else in the frame for us and we can check this print against elims taken from any suspects that come into the enquiry. Sadly they're not good enough for a database search, he doesn't think. We need to know where the biscuits came from, home, work maybe? It's a long shot, but it is just about the only substantial evidence we've got so far. Her boyfriend is eliminated and so is her mum, but we need elims from the salon owner, Andy, and I'd also like you to ask Mrs Harwood and Marlene if they have Kit-Kats or Cafe Bronte Dunking Bars Ginger Snap at home or at the salon.

'They have the Bronte biscuits at the salon,' said Andy. 'I've had one.'

'Right, we need to seize the rest. We will also need elims from Barrowclough and Regan. Someone is going to have a lot of questions to answer – and hopefully it's someone in the frame already. I'm sure Stewart will give any fingerprints we get priority, as he reckons he can do them quickly because there is some sort of blemish on the thumb. So, once you have them, take them across to him A.S.A.P. He will check them for you while you wait, if he can. Okay people, let's have this enquiry moving forward in the next twenty four hours. I want an early start tomorrow. John, what've you got for me?'

'Well I think you'll be pleased we have got an agreement from the Council to move the rock salt to the other side of the lay-by to check for further human bones.'

'Timescale?'

'Tomorrow. You wanted it doing sooner rather than later, boss?'

'I wish they were so quick repairing bloody potholes. Can you arrange then tomorrow to get one of the search team and a dog handler to have a walk around the field below once it's done? Especially at the corner that is now directly beneath the grit where our skulls were found.'

'Will do, boss'

'If the person moving the grit or the dog man isn't aware of the discovery, will you fill them in? Let them know we are actively looking for other evidence – skeletal remains that may have been buried there for some years – but that the severe weather may have also just washed them up onto the road from the stream.'

'There's been enough publicity surrounding the skulls, they should be aware.'

'Never assume anything, John,' warned Dylan. Instantly his remark came back to haunt him – for isn't that what he was doing with Jen and Shaun?

'I've made a start with the dentists, boss.'

'Oh, yeah, any luck?'

'No, not yet.'

'Keep at it. That would be a good job to find out just who the skulls belong to.'

Dylan had a feeling that things were going to move forward and he was pleased with today's progress. He kept that feeling to himself as he strolled about the office. It was too late to get a playpen tonight but tomorrow it would be the first thing on his list of things to do. He picked up his mobile phone. The message was from Jen.

Max has had a fit and we're at the vets, can you come? I've tried ringing. Where are you?

He looked at his watch. That was an hour ago. He rang her

mobile, he rang home, but there was no answer.

Which vets Jen? Where are you? he texted.

Chapter 31

Max lay still, on his side, on the table. His breathing was laboured now that the vet had administered the drugs. His filmy eyes looked up at Jen, who'd had to leave Maisy outside the surgery with the receptionist. She could hear her daughter sobbing as if her little ribs had been crushed. She spoke to Max gently.

'Good boy Maxy,' she said, putting her face to his. 'I love you, please don't leave me,' she whispered.

Jen's coat in which they had carried Max into the surgery lay on the lino floor at her feet. It was badly stained as he had lost control of his bodily functions.

'A dog can be often go blind following a seizure. Don't worry though, Mrs Dylan, it may just be temporary,' said the vet when she walked briskly back into brightly lit room a few moments later. 'Keep talking to him. He'll be in a state we call postictal for a few hours, maybe longer. It probably didn't help the poor fella with your baby crying and screaming like that,' she said with a jerk of her head towards the door. 'Noise can often agitate animals in this state,' she tutted.

Jen didn't take her eyes off Max. She nodded at the vet and made soothing noises to him as she held his paw gently in her hand.

'Seizures are seldom fatal but if the possible cause can be determined, it will help us treat him. Has this happened before?'

Jen sighed. 'It's the first time I've seen him like this,' she said, her words catching in her throat.

'Good. Successive seizures and prolonged oxygen deprivation can cause permanent brain damage over time.'

Max struggled to raise his head to her face. His tongue came out and he licked her. He started to shake. Jen eyes flashed up at the vet who got a towel and put it under his head.

'Don't worry, he won't swallow his tongue. Keep your hands away from his mouth, he may bite you and be unable to release your hand,' she said.

The door was slightly ajar but the house was silent. Jen's car was gone off the drive and there was no sign of Maisy and Max. The pram was at the foot of the stairs and Max's lead was still on the hook. Were they still at the vets? Dylan opened the lounge door. All was as it should be. He went through to the kitchen. A chair was overturned and he picked it up. There was a vile smell, which he discovered was a pool of vomit and diarrhoea near the back door.

'Which damn vets Jen?' he said out loud as he read her text message again.

Just as he finished cleaning up, Jack heard the front door open. Dylan's eyes were fixed on the sleeping bundle in Jen's arms as she emerged through it. His sleeves were rolled up and he held a cloth. The house stank of bleach. He looked past her.

'Where is he? Where's Max?'

'They're keeping him in,' she said, her face was red and tear-stained, her eyes big and black.

'What happened?' he said putting the cloth down and taking Maisy.

'I tried to get hold of you. The vet says he's had a seizure. He was just lying on the floor. I noticed him start to tremble, he tried to get up but couldn't. I went to him. He was trying to crawl to the back door; he must have known he needed to go out. I was so scared. He looked so disorientated. Then he lay down and stiffened.' Jen looked at Jack, her eyes were wide and staring. 'Max might just be just a dog to you – but for a while, when I left the Island,' she swallowed hard. 'I had nothing. He was my whole life and all I had when...' she said, her eyes filling with tears. Her hands trembled as she wiped her eyes with the tissue that she had screwed into a ball. She took a big gulp of air.

'When what?'

Jen shut her eyes and shook her head. Jack opened the lounge door and laid Maisy on the settee. He pulled a cushion from its arm and gently placed it under her head. She had been sweating with the exertion of crying and her hair curled at her temples and the nape of her neck. He kissed her gently on her forehead. Jen watched his tenderness with his daughter and her face screwed up as she fought back the tears.

Jen sat down. Jack sat beside her. 'When he was a pup he wouldn't ever come to me to say goodbye, you know,' she said, with a sigh. Jack took her hand in his and watched her intently. 'If I was going out he would always know, even before I reached for my coat and he'd flop down under the kitchen table with a groan,' she smiled through her tears.

'Will he be okay?'

'I've got to ring in the morning.'

'And I've got an early start,' Dylan said, uncomfortably. Jen shrugged her shoulder with an acceptance of the situation.

'Am I difficult to live with, Jen?' he said.

Jen smiled weakly. 'Difficult no, wrapped up in your work that leaves no room for anything else, yes, but I knew that. I've no complaints,' she said touching his worried face.

Dylan's office faced north and looked out over the secure back yard of the police station. Police files requiring attention cluttered his desk as usual the next morning. There was also an old knife, a blotting pad, an 'in' and 'out' tray which sat on top of one another, an old wooden ink stand with pens, pencils and a ruler and a glass paperweight, his computer and his phone. Each object had its appointed place. His phone rang and he quickly snatched it up.

'Mr Dylan, I had to ring you, I've been seeing a mountain of skulls all night. You've disturbed an ancient burial ground and the spirits are not happy with you,' said a woman, in a high-pitched, sing-song voice.

'Sorry, who is this?' Dylan said, somewhat bemused.

'Rosie, Mr Dylan. The tea leaves tell me you will find more bodies, I have had the visions.'

'I'm sure you have, Rosie. And your last name would be?'

'Lee,' she said.

'I also had a vision you were going to say that and that we were going to be cut off,' he said, slamming the phone down. Dylan picked up the glass paperweight, tossing it in the air with one hand and catching it with the other. People had often asked if it was a crystal ball, by God, he wished it was right now. Dylan got up from behind his desk and walked into the incident room where the staff were busy at their terminals.'

'No news yet?' asked Lisa.

He shook his head.

'Kettle's just boiled sir, do you fancy a cuppa?'

'Yes please, better make it a strong coffee.'

'Why?' she asked.

'Well it appears our local Rosie Lee has predicted an uncovering of a burial ground,' he said, nodding in the direction of his office.

'Oh Jesus, what if we do find an old graveyard now?' she

said.

'I don't need a graveyard to find numbskulls, just look over there,' he said. 'We already have dead men walking in here.' The pair watched as Ned strolled towards them.

'What you laughing at?' said Ned, looking uneasy.

'I got the elim prints from Marlene,' said Andy. His face had a rosy glow.

'Charging the date as overtime?' said Vicky, who walked in behind him. Andy threw her a look that said the comment wasn't worthy of a reply. She smiled sweetly.

'How'd you get on with Regan?' asked Dylan.

'He didn't want to give them to us, until Vicky used her womanly charms,' said Ned. 'Got to give it to her boss, she's a right dick tease.'

'I did what I had to do to get a set of elimination prints off him, boss,' she said indignantly.

'What a bloody martyr,' said Ned dramatically.

'Look here though, the thumb on his left hand has a blank patch, there is a break in the ridges,' she said. 'Cut it on a corned beef tin, he says.'

She passed the piece of paper with his fingerprints on to Dylan to see. 'Interesting, let's get them over to Fingerprints with the others straight away.'

'If I have to go to that house again boss, I'm wearing overalls.'

'We might all well be Vicky, if the marks are his,' he said. 'We're going to be having the briefings and debriefings in the incident room now that more information is coming in. I want to keep the HOLMES staff up to speed too.'

'And talking of speed, come on Ned, get your fat arse off that chair. There's no time for drinking tea,' said Vicky.

'I've only just sat down,' he protested.

'I'll tell them to ring you A.S.A.P boss,' said Vicky.

Dylan nodded and went back to his office. He looked over the overnight reports on his computer and The Chief Constable's Log. Sadly, it showed that Sergeant Maude had been found dead in his vehicle by officers from the St Leonard's Police Station in central Edinburgh. If he hadn't been a copper, would he still be alive? wondered Dylan. He hadn't been worried about the threats made towards him, neither had he mentioned them to Jen, now there was no need. He switched the screen off and glanced out of the window.

'Hey, don't be doing that so early boss,' said John from the doorway.

'Eh?' said Dylan.

'You know what they say, you'll have nothing to do this afternoon,' he laughed.

'Oh, yeah,' Dylan smiled half heartedly.

'It's Maude, they've found him dead.'

'They have? Sadly, he won't be the last bad egg, I guess,' John sighed.

'Jackie May's back and Vicky has gone to see Stewart Viney at Fingerprints. Could you see to her 'til Vicky gets back for me please? I think they're off to see Kayleigh's boyfriend and her Mum later.'

'Yeah, sure. Are you having a briefing?'

'I'm not having one for the sake of it, we'll have an update about two o'clock today if you'll put a note in the book for the others.'

John sat down.

'The Council have started moving the grit from one side of the lay-by to the other this morning. It shouldn't take them long, I'm told, as they used a vast amount over the last few weeks Usually they would have replaced it, but they're waiting for new financial year – how time flies.'

'Time seems to pass much quicker when you're older?' said John. 'When I was a child it seemed like I was forever waiting for the Christmas or the summer holidays, but now...'

Dylan stood at his filing cabinet, tense with expectation. His office phone rang. 'Will you?' said Dylan as his mobile vibrated in his shirt pocket at the same time. He put his hand in to retrieve it.

'It's Stewart Viney, they've got a match,' said John eagerly offering him the receiver.

His mobile screen flashed 'Jen calling!' Dylan took the phone off John.

'Inspector! First time, that doesn't happen very often!'

'Whose?' Dylan said impatiently.

'Norris Regan, no hesitation whatsoever.'

'Say it again. He had definitely touched a biscuit wrapper that was found in Kayleigh's car?'

'The Kit Kat wrapper, the prints the officer took were good. I'll go over them to see if they are of a sufficient standard for Court purposes. I think they actually might be...'

'That's excellent news,' Dylan said smiling with relief. 'I'll pass on your comments to the officer.'

'Yes please do. It's a rare thing, quality prints, and people don't always co-operate when they are having them taken. I'll be sending the report through to you.'

'Thanks again, Stewart.'

Dylan put down the phone and dialled Jen's mobile. 'I'll be with you in a minute John,' he said.

John nodded. Jen picked up immediately. Her crying was more of a wail.

'Is it bad news?' Dylan felt his stomach tighten. Her answer felt like a lifetime coming.

'No good, it's good,' she sobbed. 'He's going to be alright.'

For a moment he couldn't say anything but felt a lump in his throat and he put his head in his hands. He could hear Maisy screeching in the background.

'No, Maisy,' Jen called. 'I'll have to go. She's just opened the cupboard under the sink.'

The line went dead. 'I think I might be fitting latches to off-limits cupboard doors on my next day off,' said Dylan with a tired smile and tears in his eyes.

'Ah, I remember it well,' said John. 'Max going to be okay?'

'Yes, it appears he will be, thank God,' said Dylan. 'I don't think Jen could have coped with losing him right now. You okay for a bit? I've just got a personal phone call to make.'

'Yeah, sure. I'll leave you to it.' John said, closing the door behind him.

Dylan climbed the stairs to the canteen and grabbed a sandwich out of the vending machine. Dawn beckoned him from a table near the window and as he ambled over she watched how disoriented her friend looked.

'I've had a word with Jen's dad. It appears that not only did Jen know Turner, but she was engaged to him once upon a time,' said Dylan. On speaking the words out loud, the colour drained from his face. He opened his mouth to say more but shut it again.

'And she never said?' Dawn said shaking her head.

'I guessed she'd moved away for a reason when she left the Isle of Wight but running away from a broken heart – no I never guessed that,' he said in a raspy, barely audible voice. 'Then again, I never asked her either. At our age we've obviously both got history.'

'Or in your case, another enquiry,' Dawn scolded.

Dylan looked wounded. 'Do you think I'm difficult?' he asked his old friend and colleague.

'Cantankerous,' she said. 'Bloody stubborn, but not difficult, and neither of us would have you any other way.'

'That's what Jen said. So, if I surprised her with the tickets, she won't be able to say she's not going then, will she?'

'Are you stark raving bonkers?'

'If she hasn't told me about Shaun Turner, then there must be a good reason.'

'Don't you see, you could be sending her right back into his arms, you bloody idiot? She's lonely, not surprisingly, struggling to cope with a baby on her own while you work long hours. She misses her mum, who's only been dead for just over a year, and her dad is three hundred miles away and has been ill. You need to hold her close, not send the poor girl to the other side of the country where she might be comforted by an old flame, especially one who seems to want their relationship to rekindle.'

'You don't know that. You don't get it do you? I told you. I trust her. There must be a perfectly good explanation why she hasn't told me. My mum used to say if you love something, let it go. If it comes back to you, it was meant to be. If not, it was never yours to keep in the first place.'

'No matter what my mother said, much as I loved her, God rest her soul, I wouldn't be sending my Ralph away into a lion's den. If Shaun Turner hasn't told you about his association with Jen then he's sniffing around, you mark my words.'

'If she's having any doubts about me – us, then maybe it's for the best anyway... I know what I'm doing. She'll be back if it's me she wants.'

'And if not?'

'If not, I can't bear to think about it,' he said, his eyes downcast. 'I'll be putting her on that train, no one else, and she'll be in no doubt how much I love her before she leaves and all I can do then is wait.'

'Well, I guess you know what you're doing but it's beyond me, I thought you had more bloody sense,' Dawn said.

It was two o'clock and everyone had assembled for the briefing.

'Kim Harwood was hoping for some news... but she seems to be coping. It was a shock to see her. She's lost a hell of a lot of weight,' said PC Jackie May.

'It's nice to have you back on the team, Jackie,' said Dylan. Her cheeks flushed.

'The Kit Kat didn't come from the Harwood house. Kim had been trying to slim at the time, ironically, and biscuits were off limits,' said Vicky, biting into a custard cream from the packet on the desk. 'We weren't able to locate Matt Prentice, so we left a note through his letter box to contact us.'

'Good work,' said Dylan.

'Some of you already know, but for those that don't we have a positive identification on the marks lifted from the Kit Kat wrapper.'

All eyes followed him as he walked to the dry wipe board. Dylan made them wait a little longer. 'Stewart Viney tells me that the person who took the prints should be complimented, the quality is excellent. Well done Vicky and Ned. Okay, okay, for those who don't know, they are Norris Regan's.'

There were mumblings of, 'Yes,' all around the room.

'I knew it,' Ned said.

'One step at a time, Ned. We now know he's lied to us. He did see her and what the marks suggest is that he was at her car and gave her a biscuit, nothing else. Off the record, Donny Longbottom has told his solicitor that he saw someone talking to Kayleigh at her car that night – looks like Norris Regan is now that man. We need to get a statement to that effect. It's a positive connection, and as far as we know he was the last person to see her alive. But we still have a lot of unanswered questions. Did she go to his house? So this time we go and arrest him on suspicion of abduction and murder and we'll bring him in for questioning. While he's here, I want his house taking apart, firstly to make sure that Kayleigh isn't there and secondly, if she isn't, to find evidence if she was there. My intention is for that to happen at 7 am tomorrow, but we need to put together a package in the meantime for searching the inside and outside of his premises. Also, we need to put together an interview strategy. While it's great news, I'm conscious we have a lot of work to do. Once he's in the net, we want him to stay.'

'Perhaps boss, we could nominate a team for each room or a team to take the upstairs and a team to put onto the downstairs?' suggested Andy.

'You'll need the Operational Support Team with scythes for the outside, boss. It's a real mess and he has a dog there too, which isn't a problem, it's not vicious, but we'll need to give some thought as to what's going to happen to it when he's locked up,' said Ned.

'Oh, what a softie,' said Vicky. Ned stuck one finger in the air at her.

'Vicky?' said Dylan.

'Someone needs to access his sense of humour today,' Vicky whispered in Jackie's ear. 'Glendene Kennels is on the rota and will take it unless Regan can nominate somewhere or someone to look after it,' she said loudly.

'We don't have a lot of time and a hell of a lot to do, so let's get on. Does anyone have anything to add?' said Dylan.

'Do you want me to make one in, just for tomorrow boss then go back to the skulls enquiry?'

'Please, John. We need all hands to the pump, we're only gonna get the one shot at this and, according to a telephone call I got this morning from a certain Rosie Lee, we will be uncovering a burial ground there,' Dylan said, which prompted a lot of eye rolling in the room. 'Anything on the bell?'

'No, not yet. The expert, he's a nice enough old chap, but his eyesight isn't good – hence the hospital appointment and him missing our appointment that was in his diary. I've left him a blown-up picture of the item and he's going to show a friend. In his opinion it's one of the first models that Raleigh made but of course there are no markings.'

'Phone bills, Ned?'

'Got the clearance from supervision in Intel and the phone companies have told me that the first batch will be here shortly.'

'And you believed them?'

Ned sniggered.

'Interview: Vicky and I will start, seeing as Norris appears to like her,' Vicky winked at Dylan. 'Once he's been certified as fit for interview that is, and we've got his solicitor organised. We'll see how that first interview goes – and Andy and Ned, you can be our back-up once the searching is complete inside his house. Just on that, I want SOCO there and if we find anything which requires an in depth examination we'll get Forensic out at that point, from the lab. I want everyone suited and booted. The last thing we want is any suggestion of contamination.'

'Exhibits boss?' said Vicky.

'Is there anyone free?' Dylan said.

'Leave it to me, boss,' said John.

'Okay, everyone. There's a lot to arrange before tomorrow, last-minute checks at 6.30 am and I want us away from here by 7 am I want our movements kept tight. I don't want the press knowing anything yet. When the time is right, they'll be updated. We will also update Mrs Harwood and Matt Prentice first thing on any developments but only when we have something positive to tell them. Now for the paperwork, I'm going back to my office to write the Operational Order with a section for each search team in there for you to see quite clearly. Each one of the team's criteria will be stipulated. Remember read it and take heed, we don't want any excuse for Beaky coming back at us on the Health and Safety front.'

'I thought you'd called a truce with the Divisional Administrator,' said Vicky as she followed him into his office.

'Mmm... Jen might have, but I still have my misgivings about what Avril Summerfield-Preston does actually do for this Division, apart from suck up to Chief Superintendent Walter Hugo-Watkins. I still don't trust her.'

Vicky giggled. 'It has been rumoured that they were caught in an uncompromising position in his en-suite last week.'

'Nothing surprises me. Pity they don't put their passion into their work,' he said.

It had been a while since Dylan had felt the buzz from the team. He could sense their eagerness peaking and knew he would need to harness it tomorrow morning.

'Jen,' Dylan said. 'Most likely I won't be home 'til you're in bed tonight and most probably be off before you get up in the morning. I'll sleep in the spare room,' he said. He could feel the tension over the phone.

'Thanks for letting me know. I won't wait up but I'll leave you a dinner plated up so you can warm it in the microwave when you get in,' she said. 'You okay?'

'Yes, fine You?'

'We're okay, could just do with a little sun I guess and I'll be glad to get Max home.'

'Well you never know your luck,' he said, his voice sounding a little brighter for her sake.

'What do you mean?'

'Oh nothing, just the little surprise I've got planned.'

'Come on, tell me,' she said, with an excitement in her voice he hadn't heard in a while.

'No, you'll have to wait,' he teased.

'Maisy's been trying to pull herself up on the furniture today. I wish mum could've seen her... I wish dad could see her. I could do with a playpen.'

'I was going to pick one up the other day before...'

'Before?'

'Something important must have come up,' he said.

'Yeah, I guess so...'

'No really. I know, it was the day we got the hit on the fingerprint.'

'You mean the day that Max had his seizure?'

'Yes..,' he said softly. 'She'll be walking before we know it, won't she?' he added sadly, realising how much he was missing out on his daughter's little milestones. 'Just think, if you still lived on the Isle of Wight you'd be taking her to the beach soon for her to play in the sand. Do you miss it?'

'Yeah, Mum used to take us to the beach no matter what the weather. I've dug in the sand with snow all around me. Hey ho, well I'm not there, am I? And unless you solve this case, I guess none of us will be going soon,' she said.

'I'd better get back to work,' he said. 'See you later.'

'Love you,' she said in a whisper as she heard the phone click.

'And I love you too, more than you'll ever know,' he said to himself.

Jen got Dylan's suit, shirt and tie out and hung them on the spare bedroom wardrobe door before she went to bed. His underpants, socks and handkerchief lay on the corner of the pine dressing table next to his aftershave. She knew he'd want to look smart for his big day tomorrow.

It was 5.30 a.m when she heard the persistent ring of the alarm and rolled out of bed. Sleep had evaded her. She heard Dylan go into the bathroom. Jen padded softly, bleary eyed in her dressing gown, downstairs towards the kitchen. It felt strange for Max not to be laid at the bottom of the stairs where he would normally greet her no matter what time of day or night she descended them, usually to make Dylan a drink when he was called out. Coffee and toast were soon on the kitchen table and, whispering goodbye to Jack, she once again climbed the stairs to bed.

'I slept in the spare room so as not to wake you, nothing more,' Dylan said, putting his hand on her arm and kissing his wife on the cheek.

'I know, I was awake. Thankfully Maisy hasn't woken, so I'm going back to bed.'

'You do right,' he said. Reaching out for her hand, he squeezed it tight.

Jen pulled the duvet above her shoulders and closed her eyes, snuggling into Jack's pillow. His masculine scent was soothing.

The roads were quiet as Dylan drove to the nick. A red sun was coming up when he arrived at the police yard. His eyes were red, his hands were cold, but it was 'game on' and the adrenaline was already pumping.

At first Jen couldn't sleep and her eyes were still open as the morning dawned. She saw the walls and furniture start to clearly define in the dim half-light through the bedroom curtains as she lay thinking. She had noticed a cobweb hanging where the window frame met the wall yesterday, but couldn't see it now. She listened, but there wasn't a sound, and she must have drifted off to sleep. Her reccurring dream was of Shaun, his behaviour and their parting which seemed like another lifetime, a different dimension. But although pictures were of Shaun, her feelings were those she had for Jack. It was he she was searching for, him she couldn't reach. Her anxiety rose as to her horror she couldn't find his phone number in her mobile phone. She was on the street where he lived but she couldn't find his front door. She woke with sweat on her brow and her heart racing. She sat up quickly, but the cries she heard this morning were those of her daughter, Maisy, who had roused her from the nightmare.

Chapter 32

Briskly, Dylan rubbed his hands together in an attempt to warm them. It was a dry but cold morning as the convoy of police vehicles travelled to Ivy Cottage. The horizon was clear on this windless day. Everything appeared vivid and tranquil. The trees were a slowly sliding curtain in his path as he drove along Manchester Road.

The officers were quickly and quietly out of the cars. The silence was overpowering, but then, under the officers' feet, the dry twigs, leaves and small stones on the pathway were reassuringly audible. Before Dylan knew it, they were in the vestibule and he was rapping the heavy, black, iron door knocker. A blind hung awry at a window, creating a strange and sinister expression. The knocking seemed to vibrate across the open grassland like a moorland breeze, but Dylan could also hear bird song.

The dog inside started to bark incessantly and soon Norris Regan appeared with a dressing gown over his everyday clothes, his wig askew on his head.

'Mr Regan. I am Detective Inspector Dylan, from Harrowfield CID. You are under arrest for the abduction and murder of a Kayleigh Harwood.' He cautioned Regan and, stepping forward, grabbed the startled looking man unceremoniously by the collar of his dressing gown. He would have pulled him off the ground if it hadn't been for the weight of the leg irons which were now visible. Handcuffing him, Dylan pulled Regan from the house before passing him over to two uniformed staff waiting to transport him to the cells. The arrest was so swift that if you had blinked you would have missed the action. Regan didn't speak. His mouth was an ugly slit in a face full of bleached fury. Dylan was in no doubt that they had taken him by surprise. This suited him fine, the last thing he wanted was to be standing having a discussion with the perpetrator. One thing he had learned over the years was to never tell the person he was arresting that he only 'suspected' them of the charge. The doer would always insist that they hadn't done the crime if the police only 'suspected' them of it.

By the doorway, Norris Regan's dog whimpered as she cowered in the corner. The kennel staff would look after it – after all, Tess had done nothing wrong.

Outside the house, the teams were getting into their protective clothing and face masks. The police presence was a quiet hive of sustained activity. Dylan put on his own protective clothing and retrieved some latex gloves from the box. He would walk around the house first. He needed to see the layout for himself before he talked to Regan in an interview room back at Harrowfield station. Vicky would be interviewing with him, but at the moment she was struggling to get the zip of the paper suit past her cleavage.

She saw Dylan's look. 'Not a word boss, not a word,' she said, her face red and contorted. 'I am in a Small, I am...'

'Would I dare disagree?' he said, laughing as he watched Jasmine climb the path. A size six, Jasmine he knew, would never have the same trouble. She was trailed by Louisa Edwards, another dedicated SOCO officer.

'I don't know about police officers looking younger,' commented Vicky. 'Now then you bright, skinny, tart,' she called, 'what you up to?'.

'Hi Vicky,' said Jasmine, smiling at her colleague and friend. 'I'll never lose the nickname Dawn christened me with, will I?'

'It's your own fault for being so darn smart,' Vicky chuckled. 'I hear your department is going all American on us soon?'

'They're threatening to call us Crime Scene Investigators. CSI to you, Vicky.'

'You'll always be bloody SOCO to me,' she said with a toss of her head. 'Just like you'll always be a bleedin' bright, skinny, tart!'

'Come on you lot, let's get this over with,' said Dylan as he blew his rubber gloves up like a balloon to make them easier to put upon his large hands. Talc filled the air and he coughed. 'Think on, hands in your pockets until we have perused the scene. If you came to a house as a visitor or guest, it's most likely that you would use the hallway, lounge and toilet, I would have thought, wouldn't you? So let's start there first.'

He turned to see his suited followers nod the affirmative in his direction. 'We need to concentrate on those rooms.' Dylan spoke his instructions as loud and as clear as he could from behind his face mask. He walked to the furthest point of the hallway.

'The bathroom is very small and there is no lock on the door,' he said, opening and closing it. 'To keep it closed you could use a hand or a foot while sat on the toilet.'

'A man might not bother, but a woman would, maybe?' Vicky said. 'And I speak from experience. It's only a fraction better in there than the public loos in Tin Can Alley down town.'

'Take the door away Jasmine and this handrail on the corridor. Let's check for fingerprints, Louisa. Make sure you check the underneath of the rail as well as the top. If you held this, your fingers are going to wrap beneath it, aren't they?. And if someone was trying to erase prints, they might only dust above. I know it's a long-shot, especially after all this time, but we need to take every opportunity we have to put Kayleigh in this house.'

'Already made a mental note to do that,' said Jasmine. 'It doesn't look like the occupier is up on his cleaning sir, luckily.'

'Sorry Jasmine, I'm teaching you how to suck eggs, aren't I? Just thinking aloud.'

'Told you she was smart didn't I?' whispered Vicky to Louisa.

'It's a team effort,' she said, eyes smiling. 'Kayleigh was wearing a white fur jacket when she went missing, so I'm also thinking that we should take tapings from the furniture,' said Jasmine. 'If she's been here, it might put her here for us.'

'Take the cushions, the furniture, whatever you need. If she was here, we need that evidence. Regan is not going to offer us the information unless we can substantiate it. Okay...' Dylan said eventually, as he stood staring into a used cess pot in the bedroom. 'We'll be interviewing after lunch. Let me have an update about two o'clock, Jasmine, unless you find something damning beforehand.'

As Dylan left the scene he spoke to the others. He needed to be armed with all the information possible for the interview.

'Right Vicky, you and I need to get back to the nick. Let's hope the press don't get wind of what we're doing just yet. We might just be lucky with this one. It is a bit remote up here.'

'As remote as you can be on a main road I guess, but you know how the media have got the ability to scan our police radios better than us. I can't think it'll be long before they'll be sniffing around. When I was a rookie I always wondered how the press got to the scene on occasions before we did. I thought there was someone in the Control Room tipping them off. I always suspected Donald Irvine. You remember him don't you boss? Piggy eyes that were too close together for my liking and them eyebrows... joined in the middle of his forehead.'

Dylan laughed, 'If that's your scientific approach to assessing people, Regan won't stand a cat in hell's chance.'

'Well, I did tell you he was involved right from word go didn't I? His eyebrows are almost nonexistent come to think of it.'

'So that's another tell-tale sign I should be aware of in your book, is it?'

'It helps if we can prove he's lying, of course,' she said.

'You think he's going to lie to us in interview?'

'He's a man and he moves his lips, doesn't he?'

Dylan shook his head. 'You never cease to amaze me.'

'Then I rest my case and my job is done,' she said.

Dylan laughed at his colleague.

'What's your fella done now?'

Vicky screwed up her face and shook her head. 'What fella?' she said. 'and for that very reason.'

'I might have guessed.'

Dylan checked with the Custody Sergeant that Regan had nominated a solicitor on his arrival in the Custody Suite.

'He's having the duty solicitor sir, Yvonne Best from Perfect and Best,' he said. Dylan wasn't displeased.

'Before you go sir,' said the Custody Officer. 'I should tell you that the prisoner was wearing women's underwear beneath his attire and is insisting that he wears his wig when he is not in his cell. I've placed him in an all-in-one paper suit so he had nothing to self harm himself. But he is insisting on wearing them leg irons, therefore he's on open door watch,' he added out of the corner of his mouth.

'Good, I want an officer outside his cell at all times.'

Vicky walked in Dylan's office with two cups of coffee in her hands and kicked the door shut behind her with a booted foot.

'Duty Solicitor Yvonne Best,' said Dylan without looking up from his computer. 'And we need him examined by a doctor to ensure he is educationally, as well as physically, okay for interview. I'd like to get the first interview arranged for as soon as we can after lunch, so I've got Lisa ringing her office.' They settled down to work on the questions for the interview, and agree strategy. 'We'll need his background history before we start,' said Dylan.

Lisa brought the pair a bacon sandwich. It was going to be a long day but the team spirit and buzz in the CID office was exhilarating. 'Yvonne Best is in Court 'til lunch time, but will be free for you for one o'clock,' she said. 'In the meantime, she has got one of the clerks in her office to attend, get some background information from Mr Regan and fill out the legal aid forms, no doubt.'

'After the first interview, I intend to get updates from the officers at his home address and then we'll continue. I just hope that there will be something else by then that we can drop on his toes,' Dylan said to Vicky pensively as they walked down the corridor to the interview room.

Dylan's first impression of Norris Regan, sat in the white coverall suit and ill-fitting synthetic wig, was of a pathetic individual. Yvonne Best was sitting as far away as she could manage in the confined space. His legs, in leg irons, were outstretched at the side of the table. Dylan and Vicky went through the administrative procedures and identified themselves and the others for the purpose of the recording tape. Dylan explained on the tape about the leg irons which the prisoner wore – that they were not prescribed for him medically, but because he had worn them for a number of years, it was likely Mr Norris Regan had suffered muscle wastage and was advised to wear them.

'That's right,' Regan said.

'Tell me, whose leg irons were they?'

'Mother's,' he replied.

The interview could now begin in earnest.

Chapter 33

It made sense to Dylan for Vicky to start interviewing, as she had already formed a rapport with Regan.

Formalities, caution and introduction over, she started on their planned interview strategy.

'When I spoke to you at your house about the missing girl, Kayleigh Harwood, you told me and DC Granger that you had only thought about taking hot drinks out to people who were stuck in the heavy snow on White Wednesday, is that right?'

Norris Regan looked at her and nodded.

'Mr Regan is nodding in the affirmative,' said Dylan. 'Would you please speak out for the purpose of the tape?'

Regan nodded, his movements jerky.

'Could you tell me again what happened that night?' said Vicky.

'Hell fire! I haven't killed anyone. If you're looking for someone to blame you, should be talking to them I saw damaging that car.'

'That's right. If I remember rightly you told me you were just about to go out with a warm drink for the stranded motorists when you saw and heard some young lads making a bit of a commotion, so you decided to go back inside. You said you didn't go out again that night, is that right?'

Regan appeared thoughtful.

'Is that right? Just tell us how it was, in your own time. In your own words, what did you do that night?'

'I thought it would be a nice thing to do. There was a blizzard. I thought the motorists might be stalled, hungry and cold so I made drinks and was going to go out in the heavy snow when I saw two lads banging on a car and shouting; I went back inside sharpish.'

'And you didn't go out again?' said Vicky.

'No,' he said nodding his head.

'You mean yes? You're nodding your head.'

'I mean no,' he said nodding his head.

'Okay... Did you have the leg irons on that night? Because no doubt that would have made it much more difficult for you to walk in the snow, wouldn't it?'

'These are neither use nor ornament in the snow,' he said, patting the irons. 'Are you're trying to catch me out.'

'Not at all, we're just trying to seek the truth.'

'I'm not a liar.'

Vicky raised an eyebrow. 'So we've established you had every intention of being the Good Samaritan that night, but you were put off by the actions of the two young men you saw?'

'They sounded drunk.'

'If what you're telling us is true, why do you think we would bother arresting you for abduction and murder?' Vicky said, thoughtfully.

'Because you've got it wrong.'

Dylan cleared his throat. 'Tell us what we've got wrong, Mr Regan?'

'You're looking for someone to blame and I'm not what you see as your average looking man am I? I'm not as daft as I'm cabbage looking though, either. She's the good cop and you're the bad. You can play your games all day but you'll get the same answers to your questions from me.'

'Nobody is playing games Norris, I can assure you, and your solicitor will confirm it. This is a very serious investigation and we believe that you were the last person to have contact with Kayleigh Harwood before she was reported missing.'

'You've got me flummoxed. You and your officers can search my house 'til they're blue in the face but you won't find ought.'

'Oh aye, so where is she then?' said Dylan.

'I've no idea.'

'You're lying. We know you saw her that night.'

'He's a one your gaffer, isn't he?' Norris Regan said to Vicky. 'He's got that bit between his teeth alright, and he's not going to drop it, is he?'

'Your fingerprints were taken before your arrest and we have your marks on an item found in Kayleigh Harwood's secure vehicle, how do you explain that?' said Vicky.

He took the wig off his head and his pallor changed. 'Ah'll go to t'foot of arh stairs, you've gone and fitted me up,' he said. 'They must have been planted,' Norris said, raising his voice as he turned to face Yvonne Best.

'Mr Regan, please,' Yvonne Best said.

'We are simply trying to find out what happened to the young lass that went missing near your house that night. We know you saw Kayleigh, but what we can't understand is why you're lying to us about it. What happened to her Norris, did you abduct her?' Vicky said.

'Pack it in.' Regan was on the edge of his seat. 'Now do I look as if I could abduct a fit young girl in my condition?'

'It'll be easier if you just tell us the truth. Your fingerprints have been found on a biscuit wrapper found inside Kayleigh's car. Explain to us how they got there?' said Dylan.

Head bowed, Regan gave Yvonne Best a slanting look. His face appeared to go slack and his mouth opened but he didn't speak.

'It's no good looking at her, she can't help you. Mrs Best wasn't there, but you were. I'll ask you again, do you admit seeing Kayleigh Harwood, in her car, on the evening of White Wednesday? Did she come to your house? Where is she now?' Dylan pushed on.

'Inspector Dylan, multiple questions,' Yvonne Best said wagging her finger at him. 'You know my client can only answer one at a time. Do you have evidence? If so, can you disclose that evidence to me?' she said.

Regan had the smug look of a toad breakfasting on fat marsh flies as he stared back at Dylan.

She was right. 'Noted,' Dylan said, directly dismissing Yvonne Best's comment like he would return a ping pong ball in a game of table tennis. 'Is it right Mr Regan that you have told officers on previous occasions that you wear your mother's leg irons because they sexually excite you?'

Regan appeared tongue tied.

Mrs Best's face was a picture. Vicky had difficulty stifling a smile.

'Is it also right that you have magazines of a sexual nature alongside calliper devotee literature at the side of your bed?'

Regan looked up at the corner of the interview room ceiling and and declined to comment.

'Is it right that you slept in the same bed as your mother, when she was alive?'

His head shot towards Dylan and his eyes met his.

'What's that got to do with you?' he said.

'Well there is only one bedroom in your house. Was your relationship with your mother a sexual one?'

'No,' he said nodding his head.

'You're nodding your head. Do you mean yes Norris?'

'No, I mean no,' he said and continued to nod his head in the affirmative.

'Have you ever had a real girlfriend?' asked Vicky.

'No,' he said, shaking his head.

'So you must have thought all your Christmases had come at once when you found a pretty young girl stranded in the snow, Norris? I think that was just too much temptation and you couldn't control yourself,' said Dylan.

'You don't know what you're talking about,' he mumbled.

'Explain to us how your fingerprints got onto the Kit Kat wrapper inside Kayleigh's locked car?'

'I want to talk to my solicitor in private.'

Dylan slammed his pen down on the paperwork in front of him on the table and leaned forward. His chair legs scraped on the interview room floor tiles. 'Okay, that's perfectly within your rights to do so. We will terminate the interview and allow you to speak to your solicitor,' he said, shuffling the paperwork on the table into a neat pile before picking it up.

Dylan took big determined strides down the corridor. Vicky ran to keep up with him. This was going to be a long day of tension, and of waiting. Would Regan eventually tell them anything without them finding the evidence?

'He's saying one thing but his body language is telling us another.' said Dylan.

'He's a stubborn bastard,' Vicky said, through gritted teeth. Dylan pushed the CID door open and walked in to the busy office.

'Not as stubborn as me though Vicky? I haven't even started yet.' Vicky grimaced at Lisa who was sitting at her desk outside Dylan's office as he stomped past. 'Let's see if the others have any ammunition for us to use when we resume the interview.'

Jasmine was sitting at a desk in the office, smiling. 'You'll be pleased to hear we've got some interesting finds for you, sir.'

Dylan raised his eyebrows and he heard Vicky take a sharp intake of breath. He looked around the CID office. 'Lisa, Andy, John, Jackie, here,' he called.

Jasmine flicked over the pages of the reports she had been reading.

'We've lifted a few white fibres from the settee in the lounge for comparison against Kayleigh's jacket,' she said as she looked up at Dylan. 'And before you ask, yes, we've checked and there is nothing in the room, that we could find, which would shed such fibres. Also, interestingly enough we found a piece of thread, whitish in colour, snarled in the toilet chain pulley and there is a small partial footmark indent in the grime on the inside of the toilet door.'

Vicky smiled at Dylan, 'What did I tell you?'

'Are you suggesting to us that Kayleigh has been inside his house?'

Jasmine took a deep breath, nodded and bit her bottom lip. 'And, that's not all,' she said screwing up her eyes. 'We've unscrewed the hand rail in the hallway and Louisa has lifted some finger marks. She's preparing them now and John has arranged for Traffic Sergeant Wilson to take them over to HQ for checking. He should be here any minute to collect them.'

'Oh, joy,' said Vicky. 'I'm out of here.'

'What?' said Dylan.

'Wilson. We finished, I told you! I'll get you a brew and see you back in the interview room,' said Vicky, exiting the room swiftly.

Dylan shook his head.

'Again? What's she like, how long this time for do you reckon?' said Lisa with a groan.

'She gets a good 'un and she freaks out,' said Jasmine. 'Will she ever learn?'

'I guess we should never assume, but it does appear some women are only attracted to the ones who treat them badly, sadly,' said Andy.

'Yeah, you only have to look at all the domestic violence jobs we go to, don't you?' said John.

Dylan looked thoughtful for a moment. 'And why's that, do you think?' he asked, seriously.

'God knows,' Jasmine said, wide eyed. 'Do you?'

'Ask me one on learning to fly.'

'You're taking flying lessons sir?' said Jackie.

'No, and I know about as much about women and their choice in men,' he said with a frown on his face. 'Are the marks reasonable?' he said, his mind turning back to the job in hand.

'Yes, they appear to be,' said Jasmine.

Dylan sat down.

'Why didn't I call for the in-depth examination of the house nearest to her abandoned car sooner?' he said pensively.

'Does that mean we've lost evidence, do you think boss?' said Jackie.

'No, it doesn't,' said Jasmine with a shake of her head. 'He's just being hypercritical of himself, as per usual. We didn't have the information before.'

'Can anyone else follow Jasmine's good news?' Dylan

said, not so reassured.

'Sorry boss, there's nothing come from our search. A few pictures of naked girls secreted but the close ups aren't focused on the faces, if you know what I mean,' said John.

'Ned's just checking out a partial telephone number that was written some time ago by the look of it on the wallpaper above his telephone in the hallway though,' said Andy nodding in the officer's direction. Ned was talking intently on the phone. 'It appears it could be Barrowclough's.'

'Blood and sand,' Lisa said.

Dylan smiled. 'Nothing of interest from outside the property?'

'No, the search is still ongoing but we're only turning up piles of dog shit, household rubbish and more shit,' he said with an air of distaste.

'Messy job I know, but it is necessary, just to be sure,' said Dylan. 'We've had just the one interview so far with Regan and he's not admitting to even going to her car yet, so round two looks like it's going to be interesting when we tell him we can put her at his house. Keep me updated, especially in relation to the examination of the prints and that telephone number.'

Chapter 34

Norris Regan sat in the chair in the interview room, his back straight and rigid, with eyes that were wide and empty and did not meet Dylan's. Dylan sat down opposite him, cool and assertive.

Vicky closed the door before sitting to face Yvonne Best. The light in the room seemed toned in anticipation of the telling of things to come.

Dylan could feel a coldness that he knew in this interview was about to change to a flame.

For the first time Regan looked at Dylan as he finished reading the monotonous introductions before the interview could commence. His eyes were a dark blaze.

'In the last interview, we told you that your fingerprints had been found on biscuit wrapper in Kayleigh's secure car and you requested a private consultation with your solicitor, which you've now had time to do. Do you have an explanation for the revelation now?' he said.

With an abruptness that was like the breaking of brittle wood, Norris spoke. 'Yes, I lied. I'm sorry,' he said sullenly. 'I did go out again that night. It was later when the lads seemed to have gone. I saw the flicker of a light in a car and so I did give the young lady a warm drink and a biscuit and she was fine when I left her.'

'Why lie if you have done nothing wrong?' said Vicky, speaking softly.

'I expected to get the blame.'

'Why?' asked Dylan.

Regan didn't answer.

'What sort of biscuit did you take this young lady?'

'Kit Kat.'

Dylan could feel his legs stiffen. 'We didn't find a cup at the scene. Did you return for it later that evening?'

Norris shook his head. 'No, she drank it straight away and I took the cup back to the house with me.'

'Did you sit in her car?'

'No.'

'What were you wearing?'

'Coit, gloves, hat... a balaclava.'

'Can you recall what she was wearing that night?' asked Dylan. The two men were now eyeing each other like a couple of hostile dogs. A tingling sensation went through Vicky as she watched the performance.

'A short skirt,' Regan said, his eyes half closing. 'A fluffy jacket.'

'What time was it?'

'I don't remember exactly, it was dark,' he said.

'Do you remember if she said anything about what she intended to do, given her situation?' said Dylan.

Norris avoided direct eye contact. 'No.'

'Do you think she was thinking about staying in the car all night?' said Vicky.

He shrugged his shoulders. 'Yes, I think that's what she said she was going to do.'

'Weren't you just a little bit concerned for the young girl's welfare?' said Dylan.

'It was nothing to do with me,' he said.

It seemed to Dylan that Regan was more at ease now answering the questions put to him. He turned to look at Vicky.

Vicky took over.

'That doesn't sound like the Norris Regan I know. You were considerate enough to take her a hot drink and biscuit. Surely, you'd not leave her there?'

'Well, I did.'

'So you went home, to your nice warm house and forgot all about the poor young girl who was sat practically outside your door, alone in her car with not a cat in hell's chance of getting home that night in the snow?'

'Yes.'

'Did you offer any other motorists a drink that night?'

'There was no one else about.'

'How did you know Kayleigh was there?'

'I told you I heard the men banging on the car, then I saw a flickering light so I went to see if anybody was stuck and needed anything like a warm drink and a biscuit.'

'Exactly. And now you're telling us once you found a young vulnerable girl stuck in her car, you left her there alone, without finding out what her intentions were? She'd already had drunken men banging on her car. Was she not scared or you frightened for her?'

Regan shrugged.

'I don't think your mum would've been very pleased with you, if she knew you'd abandoned a young girl so easily, do you?'

He looked up to the ceiling but remained silent.

'You're lying to us again, aren't you?' Vicky said quietly.

'I know what you're doing. You're being the nasty cop now, aren't you?'

'No, I'm asking you questions that'll help me understand why, if you were caring enough to take beverages out to Kayleigh, you weren't also bothered about her staying out all night in her car in what you describe yourself as blizzard conditions. You'd heard on the radio that more snow was forecast. It just doesn't make any sense.'

'Well, that's what happened.'

'That's a lie Norris. Did she go to your house willingly, did you entice her there with promise of a nice warm bed or did you drag her there?'

'What? Me? Have you felt how heavy my leg irons are?' Norris Regan faltered.

'But you said you weren't wearing them that night because you couldn't walk the snow in them. Make your mind up,' said Dylan.

'She was in your house!' Vicky snapped. The room went quiet.

'Oppressive,' said Yvonne Best, leaning towards the officer.

'No, I saw her in her car when I offered her a drink and a biscuit, that's all,' Norris said.

'I think he's answered that question quite a few times now. Can we move on?' said Yvonne Best.

Vicky stared at Norris Regan long and hard.

'You are aware that, as we speak, officers are searching your house, aren't you Norris?' Dylan said, as he took over the questioning from Vicky.

'Yes. She's not there, they're wasting their time, I told you. She didn't come to my house,' he said, lifting his head slightly and jutting his chin out.

'I was going to say if you hadn't rudely interrupted me, that they have come across some secreted, naked pictures of women, are you aware of them?'

'You've no right to look at my personal things. People go missing all the time but you lot shouldn't be allowed to go through my private things.'

'So you are aware of them? Was your mother aware of the extent of your calliper devotee obsession?'

Yvonne Best's breath hitched in her throat. She looked at Vicky through her eyelashes.

'From what I hear, I don't think your relationship with your mother was what people would consider to be quite normal, do you?' said Dylan, suggestively.

'My mother has nothing to do with the missing girl, so why don't you just leave her out of this?' Regan spat.

'Perhaps the way she brought you up means your mother has a lot to do with this. We believe Kayleigh Harwood was at your house, but what we want to know is was she there willingly and where is she now?'

'How many times do I have to tell you, she wasn't there?' Regan shouted.

'Who're you trying to convince – us, or yourself?' Dylan continued to push his prisoner.

'I haven't killed her. You've got the wrong man.'

'Who says she's dead Norris?' he said cocking his head in Regan's direction. 'From the settee in your lounge and in the toilet area of your home, we have found traces of white fur, similar to the jacket Kayleigh was wearing. There is also a footmark of a small boot at the back of the toilet door. We have lifted fingerprints from under the handrail in the hallway, too. All these are being checked by experts as we sit here talking to you. Are they going to prove you're lying to us again Norris?'

Norris Regan looked stunned.

'Were you in the house on your own the night of White Wednesday?'

'Yes, who else would've been there?'

'Just asking. Just giving you the opportunity to tell us what really happened that night. Because the evidence will only continue to build.'

Norris Regan got to his feet. He tried to push the table. It was screwed to the floor. 'I didn't do it,' he shouted.

'Sit down,' Dylan barked at him. Yvonne and Vicky jumped in their seats.

Regan immediately sat. The atmosphere in the small room was electric. A loud knock at the door bounced off the grey gloss painted walls.

Dylan got up and walked slowly to the door. Opening it, without speaking, he accepted a folded piece of paper from the Custody Sergeant. Vicky, for the benefit of the tape, spoke out loud as to what was taking place.

All eyes were on Dylan who looked at the content. His face didn't give away what he had read and, folding the paper to hide the information, he placed it on the table in front of him.

'Calmed down a bit now, have we Norris?' Dylan said.

Regan sat perfectly still. His solicitor and Vicky looked at Dylan in expectation, but they were disappointed if they thought he was going to share what the note said.

'We've already proved you've lied to us. Now why not make this easier for us all, save us time, tell us the whole truth – because I know, and you know, you're lying through your back teeth,' Dylan said.

'I'd like to go home now,' said Norris.

'I bet you would,' said Dylan with a throaty laugh. 'So would I, DC Hardacre and Mrs Best, but you see that piece of paper I've just been handed,' he said, lifting it from the table. 'They,' he said, looking at the two women, 'and you might wonder what it's all about? Let me tell you,' Dylan said, passing the paper to Vicky who discreetly opened it and read it, in silence. Furtively she looked across at Yvonne Best. All eyes were now on Dylan.

'That piece of paper confirms to me that you have done nothing but lie to us since being arrested. It tells me that Kayleigh Harwood was most definitively in your house.'

'No,' he said.

'Oh yes. We found her fingerprints on the handrail in your hallway.'

Regan's expression didn't change.

'There can be only one explanation for that, can't there Norris? But then you already know that, don't you?'

Regan stared with emotionless eyes at his interviewers and remained silent.

'Could we terminate the interview after this recent disclosure please? I think I need a private consultation with my client,' said Yvonne Best, breaking the silence.

The second interview was terminated.

Vicky and Dylan sat either side of the desk in the CID office checking their mobile phones for messages. There was one from Jen for Dylan to say Dawn was calling to see her. Dylan smiled, he knew he could count on his old friend.

'Why would Norris keep Barrowclough's number written on the wallpaper by the phone?' Vicky said, thoughtfully.

Dylan put his phone down.

'Do you think that Regan and Barrowclough could be in this together?' she said, biting the inside of her lip.

'Don't know. Keep doing that and your lip will look like Regan's.'

'Him and Barrowclough together?' she said, screwing up

her face. 'But they're like chalk and cheese, what would those two have in common?'

'Sex?' said Dylan.

Soft lines crinkled around her blue eyes and the corners of her mouth turned slowly upwards into a broad smile. 'Boss,' she said, shaking her main of messy long blonde hair. 'Not the right time or place,' she whispered, looking over her shoulder.

'You know perfectly well what I meant,' he said chuckling at his young colleague as he picked up his ringing phone and spun it around in his hand to answer it. Vicky sat back in her chair giggling like a schoolgirl.

'Ned?' said Dylan.

'The number on Regan's wall, it's Barrowclough's.'

'Have we received any billing information for the number yet? I'm desperate to see if those two have had contact lately.'

'No, I can't confirm anything yet. It is possible the paperwork is in the incident room on my desk, though.'

'I'll get Vicky to check now,' he said, waving his hand at her to go. She waved back, absorbed in typing a message on her phone. Dylan pointed to Ned's desk and scowled. Vicky looked up and pulled a face. He leaned forward to stand up and she got up and ran out of the office. He needed to give some serious thought to the strategy for the next interview – and Barrowclough – but Barrowclough would have to wait for now. The door opened.

'They're ready to resume, boss,' said the custody officer.

Dylan got to his feet. 'Vicky!'

'Nothing there yet,' she Vicky, running to keep up with him.

'Think we've made him sweat enough,' he said. 'It's time to sort this motherfucker out once and for all.'

'Yes, not quite politically correct, but you could say that,' she said as they arrived at the interview room door.

Chapter 35

The formalities over, Dylan was ready to start nipping at Norris Regan's heels. At only forty five minutes' long, the tapes didn't give the interviewers much time to get stuck in the prisoner's ribs and it was getting late. 'Now you've had time to think about what evidence we've found and now you've consulted with your solicitor, is there anything else you want to tell us?'

'She did come to the house. But to use the toilet, nothing else.'

'Ah, so she used your toilet and then she went back to her car?'

Regan nodded his head. He really did have a revolting looking, bulbous mouth.

'You have been lying to us throughout, but is this now finally the truth?' Dylan said.

'Yes. She followed me back to the house, used the toilet and then went back to her car,' he said.

'So let's be absolutely clear about this. You're saying Kayleigh Harwood followed you back to your house, she walked through the front door and down the hallway, which is when she might have held onto the rail you think?'

Regan nodded.

'Norris Regan is nodding his head in the affirmative. Please, for the sake of the tape, could you confirm your actions please Norris,' said Vicky.

'That's right,' he said.

'She used the toilet, which is when, of course, she might have put her foot up against the door so that no one came in. I see,' said Dylan.

Regan nodded again. 'Yes.'

'I get it. Then she walked back to her car? She never went anywhere else in the house?'

'No, that's right, that's just what happened.'

'If this is as innocent as you're making out Norris, I just can't understand why you haven't come forward before with this information. You have had plenty of opportunity. You knew we were looking for her...'

'Because no one would've believed me. Would you?' Norris Regan looked hurt.

'But why wouldn't we, if it is the truth?' Dylan frowned.

Regan sat very still and quiet but the look of smug self-satisfaction was almost immediately wiped off his face.

'Did she go back to her car alone?'

'Yes.'

'Why didn't you walk her back to her car Norris? Anything could have happened to her, and maybe did,' said Vicky.

'I told her she could stay.' Norris fussed. 'But she didn't want to. She said her boyfriend and her mother would be worried about her and she wanted to ring them. Like I told you, my phone wasn't working.'

'Did she say that, or is that something you've just made up?'

'No it's true, it is,' he said nodding his head vigorously.

'So let me get this straight. The weather conditions were horrendous. She was dressed inappropriately for the weather. You went out to take her some refreshments. She came back to your house to use the toilet and then she went back to her car, alone?'

Regan nodded his head.

'For the purpose of the tape, Mr Regan is nodding his head in the affirmative,' said Vicky.

'Weren't you a bit concerned for the young girl?'

'How was I going to stop her? She was not my problem,' he said, looking down at his callipers.

'But you have been portraying to us all along that you are the Good Samaritan who took beverages out to a young damsel in distress. Now you're saying she was not your problem?' Dylan said. Vicky took a sideways look at Dylan, she knew he was building up to a tongue lashing.

'That was before.'

'Before what, she rejected you? Wouldn't play your sordid little games? The truth, Mr Regan, is that you were outside that night as a predator weren't you? Just looking for that helpless victim, and when you heard the drunken young men banging on the car of what appeared to be a female's car. You thought your luck was in, didn't you? You frightened them off, or at least you thought you had, but one of them saw you go to her car with your honey trap. Kayleigh Harwood was young, pretty, dressed inappropriately for the weather and even better for you appeared stranded and vulnerable. You really must have thought all your birthdays had come at once. Did you ever stop to think she would feel like an animal in a trap?'

'It wasn't like that! It's not true.'

'Which bit isn't true Norris? She wasn't pretty, because she was, wasn't she?'

'I don't remember.'

'You don't remember if she was young and pretty but you remember that she had a short skirt on. Okay.' Dylan's voice was getting louder and louder.

'You took her to your house, didn't you? She thought she had found a safe haven, didn't she? But the truth is you're a sex fiend, aren't you? You couldn't keep your hands off her, could you, and she rejected you, didn't she? That's why you...?'

'I didn't kill her,' Norris screamed.

'I was going to say abducted her,' Dylan said softly. 'Where is she now Norris?'

'I don't know where she is now and that's the truth.'

'Lies just roll off your tongue don't they? If you had one ounce of decency about you, you'd at least tell us where she is.'

Norris Regan looked up to the ceiling in exasperation.

'Kayleigh's mum is out of her mind with worry. Just think how your mum would have felt if you had gone missing when you were a lad?' said Vicky.

Dylan nodded to Vicky, who took over the interview.

'How could you do this to her, Norris?' Vicky pleaded with him.

'I wouldn't have got myself into that sort of situation, would I?' he said matter of factly.

'Come on Norris. She's a young girl. Kayleigh is her mum's best friend, like you were your mum's friend. You know what it was like to lose your mother, so just think how hard it is for Mrs Harwood to lose her young daughter. Because Kayleigh is missing, Mrs Harwood doesn't know if she's alive or dead and that's a thousand times worse for her.'

Norris didn't look at Vicky but at the hands clasped on his knee. She could see he was seething inside. The muscles in his neck were taut, his breathing heavy. 'Is what you've told us now the absolute truth?' she said.

'Yes, how many times do I have to tell you? That is my final word,' he said shuffling to the edge of his seat.

Vicky continued to put questions to him but he remained silent. The officers collected their paperwork from the desk.

'Just one last thing before we end the interview, Mr Regan. Do you know a Mr Paul Barrowclough?' Dylan said.

Regans jaw dropped open, revealing a lower lip that looked

like some red fungus growth. He didn't reply but looked from Dylan's face to Vicky's.

'Well, do you know him or not? It's a simple question.'

'No, no,' he stuttered nodding his head in little jerky movements for a second or two.

'Mr Regan is nodding in the affirmative,' Dylan said for the purpose of the tape. Was his body language giving him away?

'Okay. What you haven't explained is the white fibres on your furniture in the lounge to us.'

Regan was silent.

'Okay, well I'll leave you to think about that for now. Interview over,' he said.

Dylan walked slowly back to the CID office, he opened up his shoulders, stood tall and breathed in deeply.

'You okay?' asked Vicky.

'Nothing I can't handle,' he said, opening the door for her to enter the incident room ahead of him.

'When you mentioned Barrowclough's name you would have thought you'd touched the back of his hand with a hot spoon. He was quaking in his frigging boots... well, his leg irons,' Vicky said.

'The mention of his name certainly came as a bit of a shock to him, didn't it? I don't think he expected that. But he can't stop himself lying, can he? I'm convinced Kayleigh is dead and he knows something about it – but where the hell is she?'

Vicky shook her head. 'God only knows.'

'By the way, look in Ned's tray again to see if the billing enquiry results have turned up. We could do with knowing if there has been any contact between them before the next interview. If there is, as well as that little nugget of information about Barrowclough's phone number written on his wall, we can also drop on his toes any contact that they had.'

'We're close... I just know it.'

'The bastard is hanging on for dear life, I can tell,' said Dylan.

'Humans do that don't we? We hang on for dear life when we think we're losing something precious?' Vicky said thoughtfully.

Dylan looked at her. 'For someone so scatty, you talk a lot of sense sometimes,' he cocked his head sideways and half-smiled at her.

'Cheers boss. That's a compliment, right?' Vicky said sticking out her tongue. Her mouth wide, she yawned like a lion.

'Lisa will you get this one a strong coffee please,' Dylan said. 'She's obviously lost the plot.'

'Make it a stiff gin,' she said.

'In your dreams. Once Regan gets his sleep time tonight his twenty-four hour custody time limit will be up, so we have to get back in there and get some answers. I'll prime the Divisional Commander – no doubt we're going to need the twelve hour extension – while you look for those billing results. We're going to be here for a few hours yet today lady, so I hope you're match fit.'

Dylan picked up his phone.

'Jen!' he said.

'Guess that's, Jen I'll see you tomorrow,' she said, before he had got the words out of his mouth.

'Ah, yes,' he said. 'Don't wait up. We can put Kayleigh in Norris Regan's house and we know he's lied through his back teeth, but we don't yet know what happened to her. We're taking his house and garden apart. The surprise...'

'Yes?' Jen said, sounding brighter.

'The surprise is, I've got tickets for ...'

'Us to go on holiday when it's all over?' she said.

'Not quite... you and Maisy to go to see your dad.' The line went silent. 'Jen? Are you still there?'

'When?'

'Tomorrow. Look, it's all sorted,' he said hurriedly. 'I wanted to tell you face to face. I hoped you'd be pleased. I've arranged for your dad to collect you from the ferry. I wanted to tell you earlier. It just never seemed the right time.'

'I can't,' she said flatly.

'Of course you can.'

'How can I get everything ready by tomorrow? You can be so damn thoughtless sometimes! I want to wait, we'll go together... in a little while. Cancel the tickets,' she said, a rising panic in her voice. 'What about Max?'

'I know what you're saying, but I'm about as useless as a bucket with a hole in to you and Maisy right now. Think about it. It's all booked and me and Max, we'll be good.' He didn't realise how nervous he had been about her reaction until he put down the phone, but she didn't jump at the chance of a visit to the Isle of Wight to see Shaun Turner again, and that had to be good news.

Jen put her hand to her chest. Her heart was beating fast. 'Please Jack,' she said quietly, 'Please don't send me away. Please don't do this to me.'

Dylan was writing his policy log as Vicky scanned the telephone information.

'Bingo Boss, we've got contact. Regan rang Barrowclough and visa versa. Checking times and dates now to see if they're relevant,' Vicky added excitedly.

'Fantastic,' he said picking up his ringing telephone.

'Sergeant Languard, cells, boss. This isn't good news, Regan has had to be sent by ambulance to Harrowfield General with a Police escort, he's complaining of chest pains.'

'Fucking hell!' said Dylan, thumping the desk.

'His custody clock has stopped until he returns, sir.'

'Of course, yes. Thanks. I hope... he's going to be alright.'

'You do?' he said.

'We don't want the bastard taking an easy way out now, do we?'

'Ah, no. Well, there's been nothing wrong with his appetite. He had a big plate of curry and chips for his tea.'

'Curry?' Dylan said, as his taste buds took a roller coaster ride. 'And guess what, we'll have to go without, since our canteen is closed. Where's the justice there then?'

'No sir, there isn't sir. I'll keep you updated.'

'Vicky, you sorted that little job yet?' Dylan shouted as he replaced the receiver.

'I'm going as fast as I can,' she said. 'You don't need to rush... Regan's on his way to hospital, chest pains,' Dylan said as he stood at his door.

'Oh my God,' said PC Jackie May.

'Don't worry, paramedics are fantastic these days, I've got faith they'll save him for another interview,' Vicky said, biting into a Crunchie bar.

'He could be at the hospital for a while though, maybe all night for observations. He doesn't have a history of heart problems that we know of, does he?'

'No, probably bloody guilt.'

'More like heartburn, he's just had a plate of curry. But the delay might just work in our favour, especially if we can get a dawn raid together to do on Barrowclough's place tomorrow morning?' said Dylan, raising his eyebrows.

'Now you're talking boss, we're on a roll – and don't forget he's my number-one suspect,' Vicky smiled a Cheshire Cat smile.

'You're not going to let me forget, are you? But if it all goes pear-shaped, I won't let you forget either,' he said, with a wink.

'From what I can see from this information, Regan telephoned Barrowclough the night Kayleigh went missing. There are a cluster of calls to and from that night and the day after, then nothing until around the time we did house to house enquiries.'

'Thought he said his phone wasn't working the night she went missing?' said Dylan.

Andy, Ned and the rest of the team filtered into the incident room. It was late, they were all pale and tired and most couldn't wait to get into a nice hot shower, but the debrief and update had to be done first.

The hospital confirmed that Regan would be detained overnight for observations. He hadn't had a heart attack as suspected but they needed to rule out an infection, although the likeliest cause was indigestion. The drain on uniform staff to guard him was necessary but frustrating.

'We've secured the house and the garden is over seventy five percent cleared, sir,' said Andy. 'And there's been no further information or evidence discovered.'

'Nothing much new this end either, since Regan has been whipped to the hospital. The cluster of calls shown on the billing information between him and Barrowclough are interesting, especially as Regan denied knowing him in interview,' said Dylan.

'Do you think Regan might have rang Barrowclough when he found Kayleigh in her car and continued to update him as the situation unfolded?' said PC Jackie May.

'Don't know, but it looks almighty suspicious, don't you think? What I do know is that we need to strike while the iron is hot. I've arranged with the HQ support team to send us twelve officers tomorrow morning to help us with the raid on Barrowclough's address. I need you all there but we need to be extremely cautious about cross contamination. Our main objective is to arrest him, and to search for Kayleigh or evidence of his involvement in her disappearance.'

Dylan looked grave. He knew the team were exhausted, but he also knew they had to make a move sooner rather than later. The adrenaline rush would give them enough energy to do what was necessary with the next address – it had to, for the sake of the enquiry.

Briefing over, and everyone's roles sorted for the next morning, it was off home for a few hours' sleep, ready for the next phase of the investigation.

Chapter 36

'Talk about ships that pass in the night,' Jen said under her breath as she turned to the dressing table to pick out a handkerchief. Dylan's suit and shirt was on the rail and she was choosing his tie when he walked in. Her heart melted at the sight of his tired, pale face – tonight was no night to give him a hard time, and although it was difficult she kept cool and calm. Dylan didn't notice. His mind was elsewhere but something in her eyes made her appear more mysterious than any police enquiry.

As Dylan shaved the next morning, Jen placed a cup of coffee on the corner of the sink. 'You tossed and turned last night.'

'Yeah, I know, I'm sorry if I kept you awake. I tried to shut down, but my mind was buzzing. You know how it is love,' he said, lifting his chin to shave underneath.

'I've put some sandwiches and fruit on top of your briefcase. Go and do what you have to do at work, then you can come home with a clear head. We can talk before I leave,' she said.

'No, we'll talk when you get back. You go home and catch up with your dad,' he smiled. Patting his face with a towel before taking her head in his warm hands, he leant forward and kissed the top of it, like a child.

Jen looked up at him, about to protest. Dylan put a finger to her lips. 'Shhh.. It's okay. I'll pick you up at six to take you to the train station. We'll have plenty of time to talk then. I'm not taking no for an answer.' He turned away from her and splashed cold water in his face to stop her from seeing the tears burning in his eyes.

She reached out and her fingers lingered against the skin on his bare back for a moment or two before she turned and left.

'Don't forget to give Maisy a kiss from me when she wakes up every morning and tell her how much her Daddy misses her every night, yeah?' he called. His voice was muffled. Through the half-closed door, she saw him splashing aftershave on his face.

'I will,' she said, quietly. He studied her reflection in the shaving mirror and walked into the bedroom, caught up with her and embraced her from behind. He could feel her warm naked body beneath her thin dressing gown. 'Just remember how much I love you, Miss Jones,' he said, nuzzling his face into her neck. 'Much more than anyone else ever could – and don't you ever, ever forget that.' She turned to face him. He touched the tip of her nose with his finger. She looked longingly into his eyes and felt a deep stirring within her.

'Better go, otherwise the raid will be over before I even get there,' he said clearing his throat as he tore himself away to shrug on a crisp, clean shirt. 'I've got some interviewing today that will produce some fidgety backsides.'

Jen smiled despite the situation and Dylan grinned back. 'Yes, you'd better go,' she whispered, pulling her dressing gown around her. She held out his handkerchief. 'That won't wait.'

Maisy stirred. 'You're a good man Jack,' Jen said, lying down on the bed.

'If I was a good man, I'd be jumping back into bed with my wife,' he said with a deep groan.

Maisy's murmurings became a cry that increased in volume.

Dylan silently watched Jen walk from the room and heard her singing to Maisy a few seconds later in a soft, calming, reassuring tone. He knew he would need every bit of energy he could muster over the next forty eight hours – this was no time for distractions. The pressure today would be intense and any mistakes would be put down to him, no one else. It was a relief to feel everything appeared okay between the two of them, which meant he could focus on the task ahead.

'I'll be back to take you both to the station, I promise,' he called from the nursery door.

Jen looked up, her eyes searching his face for a clue as to why he was sending her away, but she couldn't find one.

The office was a noisy place. So much so, that Dylan had to close his office door to answer his telephone. Claire Rose from the Force press office was being harassed by journalists to confirm or otherwise the arrest of someone on suspicion of the murder of Kayleigh Harwood, and that the perpetrator was under police guard at the hospital.

'I'm sorry Claire,' Dylan said. 'You're going have to hold them off for a little while longer, but I'll give you a full update later today. The family are unaware of the Police activities, so they will have to be updated before we divulge any information to the media.'

As the clock struck 7 am everyone was ready. Dylan had made arrangements for uniform to remove the prisoner from the scene, assuming of course he was at the address, and once the arrest had been made he had told the cell area staff at the police station to expect another prisoner in for murder. Arrangements had also been made for Barrowclough to be placed in the female cell block away from Regan, ensuring there could be no contact between them.

Vicky travelled with Dylan.

'They're calling me sir's pet, because I'm travelling with you,' she said.

Dylan smiled at his companion. 'Does it bother you?'

'Nah, if they're talking about me, they're leaving some other poor bugger alone,' she said.

'That's true.' Dylan nodded. 'You're interviewing with me, so I need to make sure you don't get bogged down with anyone else's work.'

It was cold and there had been a sharp frost overnight. Slowly, the police vehicles crunched down the unmade track to Railway House, avoiding the pot holes where possible. The house was enclosed by a rotting fence. Alighting from his car, Dylan pulled back the catch of the gate – even though he could have easily walked through the broken boundary, he took the preferred route. He closed it behind him before walking down the cracked and uneven flagstone path. He could see the cows in the adjacent field and smell wood smoke. The officers passed a dog handler, stood with his hand against the trunk of a big old oak tree with branches that appeared to penetrate an open upstairs window of the residence and emerge some feet later through a hole in the tiled roof. Tiles lay on the ground. The dog handler gave Dylan a wincing smile as Bite leapt forward on his chain. Dylan and Vicky stood still. Bite's owner brandished a pole and a noose – there would be no risks taken with vicious dogs that were reported to live here. An old ramshackle kennel stood empty in the yard. All was silent, expect for the odd bird trill.

'Where's his German Shepherd?' Vicky whispered.

'Don't know.' Dylan said with the shrug as he scoured the rest of the cluttered courtyard with keen eyes.

A uniformed officer could be seen in the marked police car

out of sight of the house, and another stood beside the door. A rush of OSU officers rolled quietly through the wood and around the house in sequence, hidden in the shadow of the trees. There was a raw north-easterly wind blowing up. Soil that had been mud and sludge not so long ago bore the scars of heavy vehicles being recently driven over it.

The house itself looked very forlorn. Up close, Dylan could see the peeling wall, and the woodwork of the windows showed through the perished paint. There was a greenish-brown streak down the corner of the building where a gutter had been blocked, with leaves and rainwater spilling over. Slates were loose and hung over the guttering. If the house had blinds or curtains, they were drawn. A dim light could be seen and a dog began to bark.

Dylan turned at the old weather-beaten stable door to see his officers in position. His blood pumped and he felt breathless as adrenaline raced through his veins. There was nothing like feeling a collar.

He knocked, and the door was answered almost immediately by Paul Barrowclough. He was fully dressed in long-worn, unwashed clothes. The house smelled of old cooking fat and heavy smoke. He held the German Shepherd dog by a thick, worn, leather collar.

'DI Jack Dylan, Harrowfield CID,' he said, showing his warrant card. 'Put the dog in another room.'

'What the fuck's this?' Barrowclough demanded. The dog lunged forward, barking and baring its teeth at Dylan. He didn't flinch. Vicky came from behind and bent down, talking to the dog in a friendly manner. He quietened, but his eyes remained fixed on her face. Barrowclough pulled back the choker and the dog growled, but its eyes had lost their mistrust.

'Move the dog and I'll tell you, or we'll remove it for you,' said Dylan, in a calm voice. The Police dog man, with a padded sleeve on his arm and a pole in his hand, was prepared to move in at Dylan's nod. He walked slowly into view.

'Why the fuck should I? Tell me what I'm supposed to have done, or piss off,' Barrowclough shouted.

Dylan stepped forward and pushed the door open with the toe of his boot, with such force that the handle stuck into the wall. The dog was ripped from Barrowclough's grasp and Dylan could hear the floorboards complain as Barrowclough was knocked to the floor by four uniformed officers. His large frame blocked the hallway as he swore and cursed.

'Now then, where was I?' said Dylan. 'Oh yes, you wanted to know what all this is about, didn't you?' he added, as the officers unceremoniously pulled Barrowclough to his feet and secured the handcuffs on his wrists.

'You're under arrest for the abduction and murder of Kayleigh Harwood. You do not have to say anything, but it may harm your defence if you do not mention when questioned something you later rely on in court. Anything you do say may be given in evidence.'

'Bollocks!' Barrowclough said, spitting in the direction of Dylan's face. The spittle landed at his feet. Dylan looked down at the floor and then at Barrowclough, his face expressionless.

'Your little mate from Ivy Cottage is already locked up.' Paul Barrowclough gave him a hostile look. 'Take him away.' Dylan told the officers holding him. A struggle ensued and it took six officers to get him into the waiting van. Once he and his dog were out of the way, the team could start the meticulous planned search.

'Protective clothing,' Dylan shouted. Jasmine held open the SOCO van doors and threw Dylan a plastic bag containing suit, boots and mask.

'Not sure we'll both fit in the interview room with him boss,' Vicky said, as she shrugged into her gear.

'With all that grease on him, he should bloody slide in,' he said.

'First impressions?'

'We're on the right track Vicky, I can feel it,' he said, excitement rising like bile in his throat.

The visual check of the house to ensure that no one else was inside was made easy by the fact that many rooms were relatively unused except for the odd empty cardboard box or wooden crate. These rooms smelt of damp, mothballs and mildew. Footsteps echoed nosily throughout as officers trampled the uncarpeted wooden floorboards. There were no curtains or blinds, but old threadbare cotton blankets and towels were draped untidily at the side of the decaying box sash windows. A pattern stained the aged wallpaper at the foot of the stairs where a clock or barometer had once hung, and likewise in the lounge where mirrors and pictures had once been on display. What had happened to them all? An old oil stove stood in the kitchen with a drum of paraffin, a funnel stuck in its pourer. A clock perched on the high old mantelpiece and there was a mug, a dirty plate with cold potatoes in congealed butter on it and assorted crockery on a little square card table that was covered in chequered plastic, standing on a filthy, antique Persian rug. A milk bottle with sour milk solidified at the bottom was on the metal drainer. It didn't look as if anyone had been there for days, perhaps even weeks. The flagstone floor downstairs held a dampness that sent a chill through the footwear and up to the knees.

Suddenly there was a loud clang as the clock struck half past seven. Vicky looked as if she was about to jump out of her skin. Dylan laughed.

'What the fuck?' she said, as she raised her hand to her chest. Ned sniggered. She stuck a finger in the air at him and moved on to the next room.

The rooms that were used were full of stuff that looked as if it came from a car boot sale. Clothing and rubbish adorned every inch of floor space in the room Barrowclough obviously used as his bedsit. There was a double bed settee in front of a large TV, at the side of which were piles of videos and DVDs. Closer examination showed they were pornography, depicting all kinds of sexual activities and behaviour.

'Enough to make you puke,' said Vicky. 'The thought of that grotesque man laid there watching these things...'

'Don't go there,' said Dylan. 'Come on. Leave it with you guys, Ned, Jackie.'

The rest of the team moved from the house to the overgrown garden and then to the wagon-shed. The doors were heavily padlocked.

'Get the bolt croppers over here, will you?' Dylan yelled. He stood patiently waiting for someone to respond. Roses that hadn't been pruned for several years had taken over the south wall, and a water-butt was buried inside a blackberry bush to the left of the doors. Dylan stood and looked at the green moss that covered most of the roof. The officers designated to search this building stood eagerly waiting alongside him.

Once inside, Dylan scanned the makeshift garage, searching for anything that would help the investigation. The soft morning light illuminated the dark room.

A wagon filled most of the floor space. Although it was old, it still had much of the original paint and lettering. To their surprise, the vehicle's doors were unlocked and the keys were in the ignition.

'Kind of him.' said Andy. Dylan nodded and continued his tour. The workshop beyond was covered in debris of a thousand old motors: gearboxes, wheels, wire spokes and mudguards lay piled on top of one another. Dust and cobwebs coated the roof and the high wall beams.

Hard hats, dirty overalls and fluorescent jackets were hung on pegs neatly behind a door. Paperwork and maps littered the floor and there were tools left here and there. Oil and grease residue had been splashed on the walls and ingrained black, thick patches on the floor. It was a mess but amid the rubble of wire, screws and bolts there was also a pile of wagon tyres. It was obvious the shed had a further room beyond. How deep were these tyres and why were they not outside?

'Sarg,' Dylan shouted, to Simon Clegg, 'Get someone from OSU to clamber up and see what's at the back will you?'

A clean, tall, fair haired lad in overalls and boots gingerly scaled the tyres and Dylan heard him drop to the other side.

Dylan stood beside a shelf with jars on it. Old nail, screws, bolts, metal, they were labelled, neat and tidily, totally out of place in this disorganised building. He picked up one and screwed off the lid, 'Gold & Silver/Jewellery'.

'There's two old chest freezers here,' came a shout.

Dylan handed the jar to Vicky who took a look and gave it to Louisa.

'Can you open them and have a look inside?' he called back.

'I'll have a go.'

'Never mind trying Goddamn it, just do it,' said Dylan, holding his breath.

They listened as the officer pulled and pushed at the lid, but it wasn't for shifting.

'Can someone pass me a wrench?' he shouted.

With the aid of the tool, a seal was heard to pop. All was still. 'I need some light,' he shouted. A torch was passed over the wall of tyres. Again, all was silent for a moment or two as a ray of light flickered from one side of the garage ceiling to the other.

'Well?' shouted Dylan.

'Bits of scrap metal, boss, and rubbish as far as I can see,' he said. His voice echoed. 'Looks like no one's been in here for donkey's years.'

Dylan breathed a sigh of relief but also felt a sense of disappointment. He heard the lid slamming shut. Dylan could see the ray of the torch moving.

'I can't open the other, it's solid,' the officer panted.

'Do you think it's working?' said Dylan.

'Yes, yes it is, there's a light.'

Dylan looked up to the ceiling. 'You're thinking what I'm thinking, aren't you?' he said to Vicky. 'Come out,' he shouted.

The young officer climbed back over the tyres and dropped with a thud at Dylan's feet.

'We need to move the tyres, sir,' he said.

'Okay, listen up,' Dylan said to the small team. 'Firstly, I want everything photographing in situ before we disturb anything. If the wagon starts, let's carefully drive it outside, then I want the interior searching and printing. Our priority is to see what's inside those freezers.'

Dylan was conscious of movement around him as Jasmine put her team to work. Dylan had to wait 'til they were finished before the next phase of the operation could start.

'It's at times like these, I wish I still smoked,' said Vicky pacing the yard. Dylan tossed her a mint.

The atmosphere was tense and fifteen minutes seemed an eternity. Vicky looked at her watch. A video camera was placed on a tripod and a 360 degree scan was started by Jasmine.

She gave the nod. They could begin.

'We're going to need someone to drive the wagon out,' Dylan said.

'Sergeant Wilson's working in Traffic sir?' said Andy.

'Oh, no,' groaned Vicky. 'That's all I bloody need.'

'I've got my HGV licence sir,' said Stewart.

'You have? You've just saved the day, son,' said Dylan.

Dylan watched Stewart climb into the wagon's cab. He walked to the rear with the rest of the team. There was stillness; a moment of anticipation. Stewart turned the key and waited for the start light to come on and go off. He turned the key again and revved furiously as the engine started up. It was imperative that he kept it going. The team stood watching at the rear and were rewarded with a cloud of thick, grey smoke from the exhaust. So many thoughts were flashing through Dylan's mind. As soon as it was moved, anything under the wheel arches would be dislodged. Samples would be needed from the tyres. A low loader was an option to take it to the garage but, due to its size, work might have to be done in situ – a delay they didn't want. Coughing and spluttering, the team were deployed around the yard, their backs turned to the vehicle as it was steadily brought out of the garage with the expertise of someone who knew the importance of creating as little disruption to the scene as possible.

Stewart jumped down, job well done. Dylan patted him on the back.

'In the cab, Louisa,' said Jasmine. 'You do the necessary on the interior.' Louisa climbed in, her tiny frame disappearing into the scruffy compartment.

'Form a line,' said Dylan. 'We need to move the tyres from the garage to the yard.'

'That's going to take some time.'

'And time is what we haven't got, Vicky, so roll your sleeves up.'

The support team were fit and seeing them relish their work with a shared goal was impressive. Photographs were taken at intervals.

The chest freezers became visible as tyres were removed one by one. Further photographs were taken. A light could now be seen on the second freezer, indicating there was power to it from an electric socket.

'I think we are going to need to move the first freezer slightly to get better lighting into the scene sir,' said Jasmine.

'Agreed, let's empty the first freezer and move it to the side.'

'What do you want us to do with the contents?' said PS Clegg.

'We don't know what we might find, or how relevant it might be yet,' Dylan said.

'We've got some protective sheeting in the van. We can spread it out and throw everything on that,' suggested Stewart.

'Be careful, just in case, eh? We might have to record and retain it all yet,' said Dylan.

'Sure thing, boss.'

'Vicky, we'll need tea and coffee flasks brought in. Can you arrange? It's going to be a long and painstaking search.'

The process of unloading the first freezer began. Dylan strolled to look at the big wagon where the SOCO officers were working away.

Vicky appeared glued to the spot, mobile in her hand,

staring at the unopened freezer. 'Hey, Dolly Daydream, you done that bit of a job for me yet?'

Vicky nodded the affirmative but didn't speak.

'There is a hell of a lot of lead and copper pipe boss in this one. Ouch! And bloody sharp some of it is too,' yelled Andy.

'Just be careful I don't want any injuries. I've enough bloody paperwork to do.'

Dylan looked at the huge pile of metal, 'You sure all that's coming out of one freezer?'

'Yes – and there's still some debris inside, but if we put those two planks of wood against it we can slide it over to get into the second freezer easier and get direct lighting into both.'

'Okay, Stewart? Can you get your back behind it? Carefully!' he yelled.

Collectively they managed to push it and without much effort it slid, jerkily, to enable them to move forward.

Andy and Stewart carried the planks back. Dylan peered inside. It was scattered with bits of rusty, dirty metal garbage. Jasmine turned the spotlights that she'd erected on tripods to the ON position.

'Sir, look, bones?' said Andy.

Dylan looked more carefully as his eyes became accustomed to the light – and yes, in among the residue of metal were what appeared to be slivers of smashed and powdering bone.

'It needs photographing and bagging,' he said pointing inside the freezer to Jasmine.

Dylan could wait no longer. He now had access to the second freezer. Stepping forward eagerly, he attempted to open the lid with his bare hands, but it wouldn't move. The garage was eerie, the officers still. Vicky looked up at her boss's calm face, fearing that the knocking of her knees would betray her feelings. Little did she know that he was shaking inside like a jelly. Andy passed him a jemmy and held one himself.

'You take that end boss, and I'll take this,' he said.

The men prised the lid open with brute force and peered inside.

Chapter 37

'I think we've just found our missing girl,' Dylan said as he looked down on the naked frozen body that was squashed inside.

Vicky turned and walked outside. She felt hot and dizzy. 'I'm going to be sick,' she said. Dylan followed her a few minutes later. 'Here,' he said handing her his handkerchief to wipe the bile from around her mouth. 'Beware of the bogies.'

It was just the sort of light touch she needed. She looked up at him from where she was squatted.

'Sorry boss, must have been all the anticipation. Poor, poor kid,' she said shaking her head.

'No need to apologise. Just glad you didn't throw up over me.'

'You should be used to that with Maisy.'

'True,' he conceded, putting another mint in his mouth and offering the packet to her.

'Thanks,' she said.

'For what?'

'For not laughing at me,' she said.

The fact was, he knew exactly how she felt. It was a sad, sorry sight and the only positive he could take from the find was that they now knew where Kayleigh Harwood was and could move forward in the investigation to find out what happened to her on White Wednesday.

This was a scene within a scene for the investigation team.

'I want necessary examination and photographing to be carried out before anything else is moved, Jasmine,' he said. 'I don't want to lose any evidence that's available to us here and now.'

The news of the find spread quickly around the search team inside the house and they came out in force.

Decisions had to be made – and quickly. Should he switch off the fridge? Would he need it defrosting to get her out?

'How quickly could they get us a hot air blowing heater to the scene to release her from the ice?' he asked.

Arrangements were made. Once they managed to lift the body out of the freezer, it would be put into a body bag and taken to the mortuary.

'Not only have you a body sir, some of the bits of smashed up bones from the other freezer are human too,' Jasmine

said.

'So we're looking at a double murderer?' PC Jackie May said. 'I guess I'm glad you left me inside with Ned and the search team now,' she said, looking at Vicky's ashen face.

Jasmine nodded, 'Or a serial killer; there's more... Inside an old sleeping bag under the driver's seat is a pair of girls knickers and there's a couple of rolls of masking tape.'

'From having bugger all this morning, we now appear to have a vast amount of exhibits. And before you say anything Vicky, I can see by your face...'

'I told you so? To be honest, it's taken me aback too. Barrowclough was cocky enough to think that nobody would go looking in there. And even if they did, he didn't expect them to find the freezers or look inside them.'

'A good job we're thorough, then. You'd think people would know these days that we remove patios, extensions and dig up gardens if need be.'

'Talking about gardens, those markers in the garden are where we've found further bits of bone,' said Jasmine. 'Some look like they might be human. Maybe he fed bits of his victims to his animals?'

'Grotesque!' said Vicky, covering her mouth with Dylan's hankie.

'One thing for sure, there's a hell of a lot of work to do here. We're going to have to protect this scene for a few days and get some more staff to assist until we are satisfied we have gathered all the evidence. So can you speak to the Divisional Inspector with my compliments Vicky, and tell them from this evening it needs to be secured, guarded and preserved around the clock.'

'Consider it done, boss.'

Dylan sat in his car with the door open. He was writing his policy log book – a job which was not easy at the best of times, but he wanted to write this one up immediately, regarding the decisions he had made and the reasons why. He was interrupted by a call from the cells to say that Regan was being discharged from hospital and they were expecting him back within the hour.

'Barrowclough's housed in the female side of the cell block as requested, so there's no chance of them seeing each other,' said the Custody Sergeant.

'He needs to be on an open door policy. I want an officer sat outside his cell at all times. One of my officers from CID will be coming to bag his clothing so he'll have to go into a paper suit.'

'You've got to be joking? We don't have suits in his size. He only just fits through the bleedin' cell door.'

'Well I'll have to leave that with y' kid, as they say. I'm sure you'll use your imagination and come up with something. Get hold of the Divisional Administrator and see if she can get locate an extra large paper suit. She won't have anything else to do.'

'If I said that about Beaky, I'd be hung, drawn and quartered,' he said. 'I just saw her as a matter of fact, trailing the Chief Supt.'

'Oh, what a surprise. They'd be going for tea and cakes with someone, no doubt?'

'Actually I think you might be right. I've just seen Janet with a family size custard pie. I think they're entertaining Eddie Thornton.'

'Now why doesn't it surprise me that they're courting the Assistant Chief Constable?'

'You do create me some problems Dylan, but I like challenges. They make the shift go quicker.'

Dylan put the phone down. If Billy Burns called that a challenge he should be sat where he was right now. 'Vicky,' he called across the yard. 'Once the body has been removed from the freezer and is en route to the mortuary, we need to get back to the nick. I've confirmed with forensics, her removal is the best way to retain evidence. We need to sort Norris Regan out and then we'll have Kayleigh's post mortem to attend, so get cracking. Oh, by the way, have you heard anything about a time for the forensic pathologist, or who it is that might be attending the mortuary?'

'Yes, it's going to be this evening at the earliest. They're trying to get hold of Daniel Jones.'

'Great, he's good. Keep on it will you? And let me know what time.'

'Will do, boss.'

The temperature of the freezer slowed down the decomposition process to a minimum, but formal identification of Kayleigh Harwood would still be necessary.

'Careful,' Dylan said to the team. 'I want the actions videoed for evidence – who knows, perhaps we could use this for training officers in the future?' he said to Jasmine.

Heat was used to ease the body out. It was midday before Vicky and Dylan left the scene, knowing that Kayleigh's body was recovered and safely on its way to the morgue.

Officers from the Forensic Science lab were on their way to the scene to liaise with Jasmine, Louisa and Stewart. The freezers would be scrutinised inside and out for evidence, as would the garage, HGV, house, garden and the yard. Whatever experts were necessary, Dylan would consider using. This sort of enquiry needed to be a joint effort of the West Yorkshire Police Force. He didn't want to lose any data, accidentally or otherwise, and so he left the professionals at the scene. The cost had just begun to spiral, but expenditure was essential – although, no doubt, Dylan would be facing some wrath from his bosses in the future. Even though there was the suggestion of other human bones littered about the location, he would concentrate on the body recovered for now and retain the rest for later. There was only one way with a murder enquiry and that was one step at a time.

Vicky yawned. 'Keeping you up, are we?' asked Dylan as they drove into the police station's yard.

She looked sideways at him. 'No,' she said, swallowing hard.

'Good, you've got a long day ahead of you yet. Better get some food in you. Remind me to speak to Claire Rose at the press office and the Coroner's Officer will you?'

'You won't forget though will you? You never forget anything, so why do you always tell me to remind you when you don't forget?' she moaned.

'Because one time I might,' he said. 'I want to talk to Kayleigh's mum too and her boyfriend this afternoon, update Hugo-Watkins and get him to do the necessary for the custody extension for Regan. Although,' he said with a wry smile. 'If he's been in the company of the ACC for an hour or two, he'll still be floating on a cloud somewhere, dreaming about when he gets the invite to Bramshill.'

'You think he will?'

'What, get ACC? Well he's kissed enough arses in the process to get where he is now – so who knows what dizzy heights he'll end up at? But these things are definitely not for mere mortals such as us, Vicky.' Dylan grimaced. 'He's not going to be pleased today when he finds out his division is going to be invaded by the world media. The satellite vans will start arriving as soon as they hear, with their live transmitters... I hope they don't ask him to comment before I get to him. I must tell him, I mean advise him, before he does

– since people are under arrest for the murder – or he could prejudice the case.'

'We've got one body boss, but since there could be others, I wonder if Barrowclough will speak to us?'

'Time will tell,' he said pensively. 'Let's get something to eat first, because before long it'll become so manic we won't manage a cup of tea.'

Their meal was consumed quickly, and in silence, as they filled up with the fuel to get them through the long journey ahead. Dylan's mind was focused on what needed to be done. He was confident that his team of officers at Paul Barrowclough's address would be meticulous in their search and everything would be recorded, ready for disclosure to the Courts or any future defence teams, which was one less thing for him to worry about.

'Post mortem arranged for six thirty this evening, sir,' said Geoff Painter, the Coroner's Officer, as he sat discussing the next interview with Vicky in his office.

Dylan groaned, leaning his head back against his chair and closing his eyes for a moment. 'Damnation,' he whispered under his breath.

'Is there a problem? It's the only available slot today for the Home Office Pathologist Daniel Jones, I'm afraid.'

'No, no, it's fine Geoff. I'm supposed to be somewhere else...' he said, looking at the silver haired, bearded ex-police officer.

'Can I do anything to help?' Painter asked.

'No thanks mate, leave it with me,' he said with a sigh.

Dylan picked up his phone and dialled, his head was buzzing.

'Claire Rose, Press Office.'

'You've been chasing me?'

'Ah! Dylan.'

'Listen Claire, the family haven't been notified yet, so what I am about to say must under no circumstance be released until I let you know. Do you understand?'

'Of course,' she said, seriously.

'Okay. Yesterday, police arrested a fifty nine year old local man in connection with the disappearance of the nineteen year old hairdresser Kayleigh Harwood. He remains in custody. As part of that ongoing enquiry, this morning police have arrested another local man, aged fifty five years, and the body of a female has been discovered. The enquiry is in its infancy and once identification and other important issues have been resolved, a further update will be given and that will be within the next twenty four hours. Thank you for your co-operation.'

'Can we not give them anything to keep the wolves from the doors?' she pleaded.

'No, absolutely nothing. It is likely to be late tonight before I get back to you, so please do not release what I have just given you until then.'

'Okay,' said Claire, 'whatever you say,' she sighed. Dylan knew the press wouldn't like it but he had no choice. He had to keep all the plates spinning, otherwise they would start to fall and break.

Vicky watched Dylan put the phone down and pick it up again, never taking his eyes off the paperwork on the desk in front of him.

'Is Chief Superintendent Hugo-Watkins there, Janet?' Dylan asked the Divisional Commander's secretary.

'He is just in a meeting with Beaky... I mean the Divisional Administrator,' she said. 'And I was told not to disturb them. They're going over next year's budgets.'

'Yes, I'm sure they are Janet, but will you get him on the phone and tell him it's urgent please?'

Vicky sat next to him, doodling on a blotter. The office phone rang and she answered it. Her hand seemed to take on a life of its own as it scribbled notes.

Dylan could hear a lot of scuffling going on in the Divisional Secretary's office. He heard Janet rap on Hugo-Watkins' door, open and then shut it again. 'He will take your call now, Dylan,' she said after a moment or two, 'Just putting you through.'

'Hugo-Watkins,' said with a little dry cough and a clearing of his throat.

'We've made the discovery of a body and other human remains this morning. I've got two men in custody and I might need your authority to extend the custody time limits,' he said.

'The missing girl?'

'Kayleigh Harwood? Yes, I'm afraid so.'

'My word Jack, whether we want it or not, it appears Harrowfield has a massive investigation on its hands,' he said. Dylan could imagine him going to the wardrobe in his office to check his best uniform was there indeed and the buttons polished. He heard him open and shut a drawer and he couldn't help smiling.

'I presume the television crews will be milling around,' he said. There was the sound of him pulling his Venetian window blinds. Dylan shook his head. 'Better get the best uniform out,' he said.

'Oh, I'm sure they'll want to speak to you in due course sir, but we are very restricted at what we can say at the moment with people in custody etcetera.'

'Of course, I understand Dylan. Please keep me updated. I had better speak to the Chief's Office to let them know what's going on. All eyes on us then, Dylan. Leave it with you,' he said before hanging up. He couldn't help himself could he?

'What you got to smile about?' asked Vicky.

'You really don't want to know,' he said.

'Forensic are at the scene with Jasmine and looking closely at the bone remnants that they've uncovered.'

'So the suggested plan of action for us is?' he asked.

'See if Barrowclough has got a solicitor. We need a time scale for the first interview. We'll see if he's talking. We will arrange to get all the relevant samples from him, such as hair, DNA, nail scrapings etcetera and everything must be checked for comparisons, boss and then we'll go into interview with Regan and drop it on his toes about the discoveries this morning, the arrest of Barrowclough and ask him about his contact with him via the telephone to see what reaction we get?'

'Well done! I'm impressed,' he said.

'Yeah but with our luck he'll probably have a proper heart attack then.'

'He's been examined, he's okay,' Dylan grinned. 'We'll also need to arrange a debrief, or at least an update with the team, before we knock off, so everyone is up to speed before tomorrow. We must speak to Mrs Harwood and the boyfriend. I'll get them brought down here to save us some time after the post mortem.'

'And you never know, if we're lucky we might just catch the pub before it shuts,' Vicky said with a false smile. 'I'll need a double by then.'

'I need a drink now,' he said.

'Dylan?'

'Yes.'

'Is it just me, am I just weird?'

Dylan cocked his head. 'Do you want me to answer that truthfully?'

'Serious.'

'Go on.'

'I always come out of a post mortems feeling hungry.'

'Yes, me too, I guess it's because we don't eat before we go in, for obvious reasons, and then we're usually stood about for hours – so we're bound to be hungry aren't we?'

'Or it may be that I'm just glad it's all over and thankful I've got through it,' she said. 'Isn't it funny how most people think that once a body is found and someone is locked up, the job's over? My mum always says, 'Well you've got them now love that's a good job done.' Done? Done? The general public don't know the half of it, do they?'

'Perhaps better they don't. Once it's out of the news it's out of sight for many, unless of course they're involved. Truth be known, it's only then that the work really starts isn't it? Well, obviously with the file preparation and the court case later. Like I said before, let's just take it one step at a time. For now we have to concentrate on the two fish we've got already in the net and getting Kayleigh's body formally identified.'

'And the other remains, boss?'

'They're not going anywhere, are they? We'll deal with them later.'

Chapter 38

Dylan and Vicky walked into the cell area interview room. Barrowclough was already there with his solicitor, who had a back as straight as a poker. As predicted, the prisoner took over a vast amount of space in the little room and there was a distinctive strong body odour. Vicky covered her mouth, breathed in deeply and gagged, the smell couldn't be absorbed by her mucus and it felt like there was something stuck in her throat. Dylan looked at her for reassurance that she could continue. She nodded. 'He reminds me of a block of lard,' she whispered.

Barrowclough must weigh over twenty stone, Dylan thought, and the muscles on him made him look like a heavyweight wrestler. He had an unpleasant face, Dylan noted as he took the seat opposite, with red patches over his nose and cheekbones, and his little angry eyes were indeed close together. His beard made him look like a tramp who had not shaved for many days. In contrast, his solicitor was a little, squat, bullet headed man with a very red face. He wore a pin stripe suit, with a silk tie and hanky to match, peeping out of the top pocket.

The solicitor stood, held out his cold, chubby hand and introduced himself. 'Marshall Richmond,' he said. The skin over his face was taut and he had an aggressive stare. Richmond sat down with his head thrust forward on its short truculent, neck.

After the mandatory introductions for tape followed by the caution, Dylan made a start.

'Earlier today you were arrested for the abduction and murder of nineteen year old Kayleigh Harwood,' he said, solemnly.

'No comment,' said Barrowclough, staring straight ahead, his hands clasped tightly together.

'Since your arrest, we have discovered the naked body of a girl in a freezer in your garage, would you like to explain that?'

'No comment' he said, seemingly unmoved, but Dylan caught him taking a sly glance towards his solicitor, who remained stony faced.

'We will be able to positively identify the body in due course. Is it Kayleigh Harwood?'

'No comment,' Barrowclough said, his eyes cold.

'If I may intervene, my client has requested that on his behalf I make the following statement at this time,' he said. Richmond's face remained wooden as he put on glasses taken from his breast pocket and picked up a sheet of paper from the table in front of him. 'I have not abducted or murdered anyone. However, I do own up to concealment of a body on behalf of a friend, who informed me that the person had died accidentally. I realise now that this was a totally stupid thing to do. I realise that I have been naïve and acted insanely.'

'Okay,' Dylan said. 'Now would you care to enlarge upon that statement for me, Mr Barrowclough?'

'No comment,' he said remaining outwardly calm, cool and collected – although Dylan had a feeling behind that cold exterior, white fat was boiling inside.

'Are you going to name your friend and tell us when this took place?'

'My client has named his friend as a Mr Norris Regan. He called upon Mr Barrowclough in January, on the night of the heavy snow fall when he was out working.'

'I think your client, Mr er...'

'Richmond.'

'Mr Richmond. I think your client is more than capable of answering for himself, don't you?' Dylan said.

'After this morning's events, as you can well imagine he is still in a state of shock – and like I said I have taken instruction from him to speak on his behalf, Detective...?'

'Detective Inspector Dylan,' he said. 'Well, to give your client more time to come to terms with his situation, we will terminate the interview for now,' Dylan added with a half smile. 'But we would like your client's consent to a medical examination and to provide us with the necessary samples.'

Mr Richmond looked at his client and Barrowclough nodded.

'He can go back to the cell,' Dylan said not taking his eyes off the monster of a man before him. Barrowclough struggled to get to his feet and slowly walked towards the door of the interview room.

'Mr Richmond, a word please,' Dylan said.

Dylan told the solicitor about the other human bones found at Barrowclough's property, and he could see that Mr Richmond was taken by surprise. He wiped his large roman nose with a pristine handkerchief from his pocket.

'I will make myself available for what will no doubt be quite a few more interviews then, Detective Inspector,' he said.

'Well, put it this way, I wouldn't plan anything for the near future, Mr Richmond,' Dylan said, leaving him in the cell area.

A short break and he and Vicky would be going into interview with Norris Regan.

'Do you want a brew, boss?' shouted Vicky as she rushed ahead of him down the corridor towards the CID office. He nodded.

Dylan was stood with his back to the filing cabinet in his office, reading, when she walked in with two steaming mugs in her hand.

'Pilsbury Dough wasn't up for saying much, was he?' Vicky said.

'Pilsbury Dough?'

'Barrowclough. Rolls of fat? Dough?'

Dylan rolled his eyes. 'Not for the moment, but he was quick enough to come up with a reason for the body being there,' he said, taking the drink from her.

'Yeah, a fucking crap one,' she said, sitting down on the corner of his desk.

'True. If we give him enough rope, he'll hang himself,' he said wafting the papers in front of her. 'They always do.'

Dylan was outside the big grey fire door of the interview room again thirty minutes later. He put his hand on the handle, felt in his pocket for his phone, looked at the screen and switched it off. He turned the door knob and pushed the heavy door open to allow himself and Vicky to enter. Yvonne Best was sitting with her client Norris Regan beside her. Dylan checked that Regan was feeling well enough to continue before they began.

'I think it is only right to inform you that, since you have been in custody, Paul Barrowclough has been arrested and his home and outbuildings have been searched. In a concealed chest freezer we discovered the naked body of a female which we believe is Kayleigh Harwood. Formal identification will take place later today. We have at this stage only had a brief interview with Mr Barrowclough and he tells us that he hid the body for a friend, naming you as that person. He says he was told by you that she had died by accident. Is he telling us the truth?'

Dylan had Regan's full attention. He was silent as tears ran unchecked down his face.

'He's lying,' he said. 'She came to my house. I lied to you. She did sit on my settee. Barrowclough had been working on the Manchester Road that night and he came into the house after I left her sleeping on my settee. He went into the front room. When I heard the commotion that followed, I came downstairs to find him on top of her. Her clothes were hung off her and he was knelt across her, shouting at me to have a go. I was excited,' he said.

'And?'

'Yes.'

'Yes, you raped her?'

Regan nodded. 'For the purpose of the tape, Mr Norris Regan is nodding in the affirmative,' said Vicky.

'His hands were around her neck. She was trying to scream. He told me to shove her coit in her mouth to stop her making a noise.'

Dylan raised his eyebrows.

'I panicked. The next thing I know her clothes were off. She'd gone quiet. He told me to fetch him a drink.'

'Alcohol? He was drunk?' said Vicky.

'No, tea. He wanted a cup of tea. He said she'd seen us, we couldn't let her go.'

'And?'

'He told me to put my hands over her mouth and nose and he knelt across her neck. Her head flopped to one side...' Tears were rolling down his cheeks unchecked. Yvonne Best sniffled into a tissue that she pulled from the sleeve of her cardigan.

'Then what?' Dylan said.

'He said he would get rid of her. No one was out to see and nobody would ever know. He took her and her clothes away but I found one of her boots in the house and her coit so I called him. He came and took them away.'

'So you killed her?'

'No. I didn't kill her, he did.'

'But you tried. You've admitted to us that you were the one who stuffed her coat in her mouth, then put your hands over her airways so she couldn't breathe. She was strangled, suffocated. You may have broken the poor girl's neck. You both killed her.'

'I didn't mean to kill her. I just wanted her to be quiet.'

'So what you're telling us is, this version of events is the truth and the other stuff, lies?' said Dylan.

'On my mother's life, that's what happened that night.'

'You obviously have no morals whatsoever have you Mr Regan? You're lying again.' Vicky spoke for the first time.

Norris Regan looked shocked. 'No, this time I really, I swear I am telling you the truth.'

'Then why did you ring Barrowclough that night?' she said.

'I didn't. The phone was dead, I told you.'

'Not at your house. Your phone was not dead. Not unless you unplugged the phone, because we have proof that you made a call from your telephone that night. Barrowclough's number was written on the wallpaper next to the telephone in your house. You called him because you had a young girl in your house and you fancied the look of her. You wanted his help, didn't you?' Vicky said.

'No, that's not true.'

'The truth is you weren't strong enough alone were you? The books, the magazines, the photos and even the leg irons weren't enough any more, were they? How did you get her to your house, Norris? Did you drag her there?' Vicky continued.

'She came of her own free will, to use the toilet. To get warm.'

'Into your trap, then you terrified her, viciously raped her and when you were done, you killed her. You were nothing more than animals toying with their prey, were you?'

'No! I had sex with her. I admit that. But I didn't kill her. She enjoyed it.'

'What?' Vicky said, shaking her head in total disbelief, 'She told you that, did she? She actually said she'd enjoyed having sex with you?'

Dylan looked anxiously in his partner's direction. Her eyes were slightly glazed.

'Since your arrest, you've done nothing but lie to us about Kayleigh Harwood, who was tragically stuck in the severe weather on White Wednesday outside your home. When, and only when, we could prove it, did you come clean to us that you had seen her that night, been to her car and offered her a drink. Then when, and only when, we could prove it did you admit that she had been in your house to use the toilet. Again, only when we can prove beyond doubt, did you confess that she had indeed been in the lounge. When asked if you knew a man called Paul Barrowclough, you told us you didn't. Then when we verify you do, you admit it. Now we have found a body and Mr Barrowclough is accusing you of her death. Now you decide to tell us what you say is the truth?' Dylan leaned forward and didn't move his stony eyes from the man's face. 'What do you want to lie to me about now Norris?'

Regan leaned back in his seat as far as he could. The men's hackles were up. It reminded Vicky of a cock fight. 'I've told you I had consensual sex with her and I tried to keep her quiet.' Regan said quietly.

'Is there anything else you wish to say?' said Dylan with an air of finality.

'Sorry?' Regan said.

Dylan wanted to rip the evil, twisted man apart, but somehow he controlled his emotions.

'There will be further interviews in the not too distant future about other matters.'

'There will?' said Yvonne Best.

'There have been more human remains discovered at Barrowclough's address.' he said coldly and clinically. 'I am now going to conclude this interview – and Norris Regan, you will be taken back to your cell.'

'Are you okay?' Dylan asked Yvonne Best as they stood in the corridor afterwards.

'Thank you. Yes, I'm fine now but I have to admit that for a minute I got drawn into all the sadness and fear for that poor girl. What must she have gone through that night?'

'It's understandable. Are you sure I can't get you a cup of tea or a drink of water?'

'No, no really, I'm fine,' she said. 'Don't fuss. By the sound of it, you suspect this might not be their first murder?'

'Sadly not, but once I have more information and the confirmation of some tests we're running I'll let you know.'

'In the meantime then, I'll see if there is anything else he wants to tell me now,' said Mrs Best.

Dylan and Vicky left the cells.

'That poor kid, she must have thought she was safe from the freezing cold weather by going to his house. It doesn't bear thinking about what she went through, does it?'

'And the frightening thing is it's looking more than likely that she wasn't their first victim.'

'Quick cuppa to keep your strength up before we go to the mortuary, and then we'll go to see Kim Harwood and Matt Prentice eh? You sure you're okay to carry on?'

'Most definitely boss. I want to make sure we absolutely

nail this fucking pair.'

Dylan smiled. 'There is one thing I must do though before I do anything else,' Dylan said picking up the phone. Vicky nodded.

'Dawn, is that you? Can I ask you a huge favour,' he said.

'Oh no. Most definitely not...' she said.

'But, I've a post mortem to go into,' he exclaimed.

'And the body isn't going anywhere Jack, Jen and Maisy are.'

'But the Home Office Pathologist isn't going to wait 'til I take my wife and daughter to the train station, now is he? Please? I have no one else to ask.'

'You should do this.'

'I wouldn't ask if it wasn't absolutely necessary. I never wanted this to happen.'

'Okay. But don't blame me when this ludicrous idea of sending Jen away blows up in your bloody face.'

'I won't. Jen will understand, you'll see,' he said, breathing a big sigh of relief.

Chapter 39

Mortuaries are places most people wish to avoid, but Dylan couldn't, it was a big part of the investigation process. As SIO, he had to see and know first-hand the extent of the victim's injuries, how they were caused and, most importantly, the cause of death. The same old smell greeted him – a mixture of stagnant water, damp, mouldy room and a butcher's shop, combined with a refuse tip. It seemed to be absorbed in the dull white tiled walls. He knew the odour would remain on the clothes he was wearing until they were dry-cleaned. Putting a hand in his pocket, he pulled out his packet of extra strong mints. 'Here, take one, they always work for me,' he said to Vicky.

Now dressed in a green overall and plastic apron, they were joined by Stewart Viney from SOCO and the night Detective, who had been called in early for his shift to be exhibits officer at the mortuary.

Daniel Jones, the Home Office pathologist, had arrived and Dylan outlined the disappearance of Kayleigh Harwood to him. He went on to explain the discovery of the female body, the circumstances and the fact that he believed it to be Kayleigh, but that formal identification was to follow the post mortem. He also told him of the two arrests and the recent interview with Norris Regan and briefly what he said had taken place.

Daniel Jones started the examination. He was a strong, athletic young man with a steadfast hand and although he was quick with his examinations, he was very thorough. Dylan was impressed.

He spoke into his hand-held recorder as he surveyed the body laid out before him. 'Initial visual check of the body is that of a female, around twenty years. She is well preserved, due to being kept in an electric chest freezer, which is where she was apparently found.'

The running commentary went on as he took relevant tapings, internal swabs and asked for close-up photographs by SOCO where necessary. Once he had completed the external examination, he prepared to remove the skull cap. The surgical saw whirred. The skull's crack could only be likened to taking the top off a boiled egg. He examined the skull and the brain before opening the chest cavity and examining her internal organs. The examination lasted for two and a half hours. Dylan was grateful for Daniel's swift hand and expert eye.

Once over, Daniel took them into the mortuary office and sat with them over a hot drink to talk through his findings. 'As you are aware, she has bite marks to her breasts which I had photographed. These, I am confident, were inflicted some considerable time after her death. You will need teeth impressions from your suspects. She also has bruising to her arms and legs which appear to suggest she has been pinned down or held against her will. I removed some strands of material from the inside of her throat. There has obviously been a tremendous effort to stop her breathing with some type of material. There is bruising around her nose and mouth where intense pressure has been applied. The petechial haemorrhaging in her eyes means she was possibly strangled. Petechia occurs when the pressure in the brain causes the blood vessels to burst, and this is why her eyes appeared bloodshot and were bulging. The bruising around her neck is also consistent with strangulation. I think that she was probably rendered unconscious through strangulation at the same time of suffocation, there is also a fracture to her neck. This was a really vicious and sustained assault, in my opinion. The strangulation is the cause of death, and I think that the pressure over her mouth and nose simply delayed the last bit of oxygen leaving her lungs. However the pressure was such that, independently, either would have proved fatal.'

'This was more than someone trying to stop her screaming or shouting, then?' said Dylan.

'Most certainly, whoever did this to her were out to kill her in my opinion. By the way, I've taken swabs as you are aware from her vagina, anus and mouth. I think looking at the bruising that someone has had sex with the body since her death which may also explain the bite marks I mentioned earlier to her breasts.'

'I can't thank you enough for your thoroughness,' Dylan said.

From what the Pathologist had just told them, he knew when it went to trial at the Crown Court the defence barristers would each blame the other perpetrator for causing Kayleigh's death. Now Dylan needed to prove that it was a case of joint enterprise, used in murder cases where more than one defendant is involved, intent on carrying out a common purpose.

Jen stood on the platform, her suitcase at her feet. 'No, no, don't wait with us, I understand,' she said to Dawn. 'Of course you must get back to relieve Ralph of Violet before the restaurant opens.'

'It's the damn job, love. Dylan's under a lot of pressure right now,' Dawn smiled at her friend, feeling her pain.

Jen nodded. It was a cold evening and easy to make the excuse that her tears were from the cool night air. She returned her friend's kindly kiss on the cheek. Before Dawn left Jen reached for her hand and held it for a brief moment. Dawn answered with a little reassuring pressure of her fingers. 'He would be here if he could, you know that,' she said. Jen forced a smile and her teeth chattered as the cold wind whipped her. Dawn walked down the steps, looking back to wave before she turned the corner and vanished into the underground tunnel. The train pulled in. A guard stepped down. He pulled out his pipe, knocked it against a wall, stretched his legs and began to walk down the platform towards her. Jen took one last look up and down the empty dark platform. With a lump in her throat, she swallowed hard and struggled onto the train with her suitcase and a crying Maisy who was rested on her hip. The guard blew the whistle. The train jolted. She stumbled into a seat with the screaming child – and a foreboding that had followed her into the busy carriage.

Fortunately Kayleigh's body had not decomposed and although she had extensive bruising to her mouth and nose, Dylan knew that make up would cover it, and minimise the shock that Kim and Matt were going to soon encounter. The mortuary attendant would see to this procedure before the viewing took place. Kayleigh was being prepared and her mutilated body would be carefully concealed with a starched white sheet, with the exception of her face.

Dylan looked at his watch. Jen and Maisy would be on the train. He sighed, his face grey and serious. 'Come on Vicky; let's get on with this bloody awful task.'

PC Jackie May's job had been to bring Kim Harwood and Matt Prentice to a private room at the Hospital. She had, as instructed, only disclosed to them that the body of a girl had been found and they needed them to confirm whether it was Kayleigh.

Dylan and Vicky entered the room and saw the sudden relief on Jackie's face. It was the most difficult of situations. What did you say to the bereaved family? What could anyone say?

Kim Harwood looked up. Her face was a wretched mask with shadowy holes for eyes. Painfully, for Dylan, it seemed as if Kim came to life when she saw him, as though he might offer her some hope. He nodded and when she saw his sombre expression she looked back to her hands that she continued to wring in her lap. She sat in silence, unmoving. Dylan had asked the Coroner's Officer to attend to support the family and to guide them through what would happen. Retired policeman Geoff Painter was tall and wiry and didn't need a uniform to look like a stereotypical police officer. The family would have many questions for him after they had identified her body and Geoff would deal with this admirably, Dylan knew.

Dylan quietly and sensitively told Kim and Matt what had happened in the past twenty four hours without going into any details. 'Yesterday, we arrested a man from a house in Manchester Road after we uncovered that he lied to us about Kayleigh going to his house in search of shelter. While he was in custody, our enquiries led us to another house away from the area, the home of an acquaintance of his. He has also been arrested this morning and both men are, and let me assure you will remain, in custody. While searching an outbuilding at the second address, we found the body of a young girl hidden. We believe that to be Kayleigh.' Kim gasped and inhaled deeply before letting out a wail.

'No! Please,' she cried.

Matt, appeared to freeze and Dylan couldn't see him breathing, but then he saw the shock melt away and the young man stared at something in front of him that no one else could see. His face drained of all colour. Slowly everything seemed to return to normal and his eyes that were deep, dark and comprehending met Dylan's. His mouth opened, then snapped shut. He gulped, 'Who are they?'

'It would be wrong of me to tell you now, but I promise you that I will let you know later. I understand that they are complete strangers to you and to Kayleigh,' he said. Matt nodded.

After a short while Dylan asked if they felt up to looking through a glass screen at the girl they had found.

'There is a table behind that window,' he said nodding at

the curtained windowpane. 'The girl we have found is on that table. She is covered in a sheet up to her neck, so all you will see is her head. She looks serene and at peace.'

'I think we need to get this over with as soon as possible,' Matt said, finding his voice. He grabbed Kim's hand.

They stood in front of the glass, then the drapes were pulled back. Kim let out a cry and a hand flew to her mouth. The scream ripped through Dylan's heart and soul, bouncing off walls, ceilings and floor. It flooded the corridor and gushed like a tidal wave through the building and out into the yard beyond. Kim's face was red, angry and contorted and then the tears came, streaming down her face as she pressed it against the cold glass. 'Did he? Did they... rape my baby?' she cried, her eyes searching Dylan's face. 'Don't lie to me, please,' she whispered.

Matt took a step back and put his head back against the wall, panting, hands hanging. Geoff Painter stepped forward and grabbed him under the arms.

'You're okay,' he said. 'Just a little light-headed and disorientated, it's not unusual,' he added, helping Matt to a chair and guiding the young man's head between his legs.

'If only I'd gone to meet her that night,' he cried a few minutes later on the shoulder of the Coroner's Officer.

Dylan put his arm around Kim. Her face was the colour of milk. 'She's safe now and nobody can hurt her any more. Just look how peaceful she is.'

Kim was shivering, and her trembling seemed to go far beyond her power of self-control. He could hear her teeth chattering and she looked very small and frail, like a frightened child. All the days and weeks of worrying, and her worst nightmare had come true.

'We were the best of friends... you know. I miss her so, so much,' she said, struggling with her words.

'I know, Vicky said. Do you want to go inside to be with her?' asked Dylan, kindly.

'Am I allowed?' she said but made no movement. He pushed her gently forward. 'Come with me,' he said taking her arm. 'She's your daughter, of course you're allowed. Let me show you how at peace she is.'

Dylan opened the door and went inside with her to stand at the side of the table. Lavender oil had been sprinkled on the tired potpourri in a dish on the table and the smell was pungent. Unaware of anything but her daughter's body, Kim put out her hand gingerly and tenderly stroked Kayleigh's face. Kayleigh's head was covered in what looked like a nun's habit. Dylan stepped back and put his face closer to the glass, which reflected the ghostly flame of the candle lit in the opposite corner of the room. Kim bent to kiss Kayleigh on the forehead. 'Mum's here love. You're safe now in Dad's arms. No more pain. You'll be safe now until we meet again.'

How the hell did anyone cope after something as horrific as this, he wondered. The family and friends were victims too. They lived the trauma, day after day. He knew the smallest thing could trigger off a memory. They had the life sentence, not the offenders.

Kim kissed Kayleigh once more on each eyelid, took a deep breath, wiped her eyes and then stepped away. 'Night darling... for now,' she said, kissing her finger tips and putting them to Kayleigh's lips. She looked back at Dylan. 'I'm ready now. I know where she is and that she's safe in God's hands with her dad,' she said. 'Tell me, what did my little girl ever do to anyone to deserve this?' she added with a sob that caught in her throat.

Jen watched the lights of the railway stations float past the train's windows, like shooting stars low in the night sky. Maisy thankfully slept. It was a small consolation. Once or twice she gave Jen a dreamy little wet smile and, with a tissue she had used to dry her own eyes, Jen patted her daughter's face lovingly.

'I just hope they suffer,' Kim said, gritting her teeth as she and Dylan returned to join Matt and the others.

'We'll need a statement from you, but the Coroner's Officer will explain everything and be there for you now. Once we have gathered all the information about what took place and what is happening to the two men we have in custody, I will come and see you to go through everything with you and answer all your questions. Please don't believe everything you read in the papers. If you want to know anything at all, contact me and I will tell you the truth. I promise you. I will hold nothing back from you – but for now, I think you've had enough to deal with.'

Leaving them in the safe hands of Geoff, it was time to go back to the police station. It was late, and time for that debrief.

'It's the first time I've been there when the family have done an identification like that, boss. It was heart wrenching, even for me, and poor Jackie couldn't stop crying.'

'And no matter how many times you see it, it doesn't get any easier, not one damn bit,' Dylan said with a lump in his throat. His eyes looked glassy.

'No, I bet it doesn't,' she said.

'Go charge Norris Regan with murder, that'll cheer you up,' Dylan said.

'Are you serious?' she said wide-eyed.

'Deadly.' he smiled. 'We've got enough evidence now. Let them know in the cells that Barrowclough won't be interviewed again until tomorrow, will you?'

'Will do. See you at the debrief boss,' she said She left him sat at his desk and walked briskly to her work station in the CID office. She picked up her phone with one hand and ran her finger down the contact details on file with another. 'Yvonne Best, please?' Dylan heard her say with new vigour in her voice.

'Speaking.'

'Just for your information, I'm about to charge your client Norris Regan with murder.'

'Thank you for letting me know. It's not a great surprise, is it? I won't be attending tonight, but I guess I'll see you at Court tomorrow for his appearance?'

'You will that,' said Vicky before she hung up. 'Fait accompli!' she said under her breath.

The fatigued team gathered in the incident room. Dylan looked around him and saw more than one set of red, tired, bleary eyes. They looked like Dylan felt. 'Get a drink, we'll wait 'til DC Hardacre gets back before starting,' he said from his office door.

Dylan sat back at his desk, his whole being ached. He shook his head, looked down and stared at his phone disbelievingly. Jen's dad's car was broken down. She would be expecting him at the station.

'Jen?' he shouted into the mouthpiece two minutes later. 'Can you hear me?' He heard the rush of a train. The phone went dead.

He sat with the phone in his hand for a while and reluctantly he eventually dialled the number. 'Shaun, Shaun Turner?' he said. 'It's Jack Dylan will you could do me a favour?'

It wasn't long before Vicky returned. 'That felt so good,' she said with a satisfied sigh. 'Believe it or not, he wanted to put his bloody wig on while I charged him.' She smiled candidly. 'But I wouldn't let him,' she said fingering the papers in her hand.

'Vicky...,' said Dylan.

'Okay, okay so he's making an official complaint about breaching his human rights but...'

'But, nothing, you've got to remain professional. How else are you going to get them stripes?'

'He said he was sorry anyway... before faking another heart attack.'

Dylan winced. 'What?'

'It's okay. The Custody Sarg is Billy. He told him that he'd already pulled that stunt once on him and to go back to his cell – and guess what? He did without another word.'

Dylan smiled. 'Good old Billy Burns. Right guys and gals, ready for the scrum down,' he shouted from his office as he walked to the door.

'I know you're all knackered. First, let me say thank you all for your efforts today, they haven't gone unnoticed and I am very grateful for your dedication and commitment. The updates that follow will hopefully bring you all up to speed with everything that has happened. We have managed to get through an awful lot of work and tomorrow will be just as intense, so I'll get this over with as quickly as possible and we can all hit the decks for some much needed sleep,' Dylan said, nodding in the direction of a yawning PC Jackie May. 'The drinks will have to wait,' he said without emotion. 'Norris Regan, you will be pleased to know, has just been charged with the murder of Kayleigh Harwood.

'Yes,' came the collective cry.

Fifteen minutes later the group was disbanded. Dylan's next job was to update the press office, to tell them that they could release the information regarding the discovery of a body which had now been formally identified as that of Kayleigh Harwood.

'Not often we get such good news on the graveyard shift, Dylan. Is there a charge to be announced?' said Claire.

'You on a split shift?'

'Yes, I had to go somewhere this afternoon, so I've been lucky enough to follow the day through with you.'

'Good. Yes, one man has been charged and will appear

before the Court tomorrow but we are still questioning another and he remains in custody. The investigations into him are in their infancy and continuing.'

Jen settled into the corner of her window seat. Her arm had gone dead with the weight of Maisy on it. Would this journey never end? She reached into her handbag and took out her phone, two Paracetamols and a bottle of water. It was eleven thirty. When did the train become so warm and stuffy? she thought, as she adjusted her sitting position and loosened her clothing around her neck. There was a missed call from Dylan. The consolation – she knew he was okay. She looked out of the window and sighed. The train was passing Fratton Park, the home of her dad's beloved Pompey. At that moment she felt suspended between two worlds. The train slowed down and stopped at the station. Jen looked on longingly. She couldn't count how many times had she disembarked here as a child, hand in hand with her dad, to walk through the mock Tudor facade building guarding the entrance to the ground, full of excitement. A warm pork pie at half time was always her treat, she remembered fondly. She looked down at Maisy. Would she have such memories of days out with her daddy when she grew up, she wondered?

It was time to go home. Dylan climbed into his car and let his head fell back against the headrest. He inhaled deeply through his nose and could feel the cold air filling his lungs. Closing his eyes, he exhaled slowly through pursed lips, until there was no more air to expel. He opened his eyes, leaned forward, turned on the ignition and the lights guided him through the back yard gates and out onto the street. Who did the other bones that they had discovered belong to? Were they human? he wondered. He needed to get Regan and Barrowclough both remanded for Kayleigh's murder before he did anything else, then he would speak to them again when they had gathered the evidence and he had it before him.

Jen descended the steps from the creaking train. Her back ached and her head was thumping. The station was relatively quiet, but then it was very late. She walked gingerly, jostling her luggage and Maisy down the platform to the tunnel that led to the Wightlink terminal. A few slightly inebriated students were left on the platform, as aggressive drunks boarded the train for London. No doubt the compartment would be soon filled with beer, and some poor unsuspecting guard who wouldn't have the knowledge or get paid enough to challenge them.

The best thing about landing at Portsmouth Harbour train station was that the Wightlink terminal for the passenger ferry was only a stone's throw away. Not having to venture outside meant a lot to her – Dylan had thought her journey through. A kindly guard asked if he could help her with her case. Gratefully, she accepted, and walking down the centre of the aisle she let her hand run along the railing – perhaps to steady her, or maybe just to get the sense of something textured and cool, after sitting on the train for such a long journey. She smiled excitedly at the lady behind the desk in the ticket office. There was a little girl in her yet.

The guard wheeled her case to a handy spot. 'Can you manage from here?' he asked.

'Maisy is heavy but the luggage...'

'It's light, I bet in comparison. You not staying long?'

'An open ticket, so who knows,' she said with a half-hearted smile. 'Thank you.'

'She's been a joy to watch on the journey,' he said, nodding towards Maisy. 'Make your arms ache when their little and your heart when they grow up.'

'Yeah, so I keep getting told.'

'Enjoy her while you can, she won't be like that for long, mark my words,' he said.

'I will,' she said.

Always a pleasure when she woke, Maisy was happily kept amused by the twinkling of the lights of the boats in the harbour that could be seen from the waiting room.

Jen's phone rang .'Jack, at last,' she said warmly and with relief.

'It's Shaun.'

Jen closed her eyes and looked up to the ceiling, tears springing to her eyes. She bit her lip. 'Wait, Jack asked me to pick you up from Ryde Pier. I've been waiting,' he said. 'What time you in?'

'I thought Dad was... How did you know? Oh, never mind,' she said crossly.

'His car's in the garage,' he said.

The sea was calm, and the boat was almost empty, apart from a couple of girls who giggled and sang songs from a musical they had just seen and a young couple who nibbled away at each other like rabbits, oblivious to anyone else. An older man in a beret with binoculars around his neck came to sit in a seat directly behind them. Maisy clambered over Jen's shoulder, fascinated by the pale, ghostly green glow of the apparatus.

'Night scope,' he said to Jen when she turned to see what was delighting her daughter. 'I study bats.'

'Oh, will you be going to see the people who run the bat hospital on the Island?'

'Yes, that's where I'm heading, Sandown.'

'You've not been to the Island before?'

'No, but since the Island attracts fourteen of the seventeen species found in England, and some of these are very rare ones too, I was thrilled when the Streets invited me to visit. Archie,' he said holding out his hand.

The radio bleeped.'The captain of this vessel would like to draw your attention to the following safety announcement...'

Archie pulled a face at the startled Maisy and she grinned and hid in Jen's shoulder, only to periodically peep out at her new-found playmate before she hid again.

'We hope you enjoy this vessel, and thank you for travelling with Wightlink,' the man said before turning off the tannoy. It whistled loudly and Jen covered Maisy's ears. Jen felt the captain open the full throttle at the black mouth of the harbour and the craft forged ahead at speed.

Looking out of the window towards Ryde Pier, Jen started to distinguish the dimly-lit outlines of some Island residences rising out of the swell of the sea. Maisy settled on her knee with her dolly.

Twenty five minutes later, the captain slowed the boat down and cut the engine. He reversed it slowly and berthed it with skill.

'Can I take your bag for you dear?' Archie said as Jen balanced Maisy proficiently on her hip, grabbing hold of the back of her seat to stop herself from falling.

'That's very kind of you,' she said.

Jen followed Archie across the ramp and up the tunnel. He placed her case on the floor at the Ryde Pier Head train station adjacent to terminal. The old red London underground train to Shanklin was waiting for the passengers of the ferry to take them on their onward journey. 'Would you be kind enough to direct me to the taxi rank please?' he said.

'I can do better than that...,' she said, pointing towards the man walking across the foyer of the station entrance to meet them. 'Shaun'll give you a lift.'

'Are you sure it's no trouble dear?' said Archie.

'None whatsoever. You don't mind dropping Archie off at the Bat Hospital, do you?'

Shaun winked at her. 'No not at all mate,' he said, amicably to Archie. Jen frostily grabbed the handle of her suitcase, refusing to surrender it to Shaun.

'He'll be driving past the Bat Hospital after dropping me and Maisy off at my father's, won't you Shaun?' Jen said. 'Tell you what Archie, you sit in the front with Shaun. We'll be okay in the back,' she said throwing her luggage in the back seat of the car before getting in.

Shaun turned and looked at her. She saw the disappointment in his eyes.

Jen's dad's face was a picture as he embraced his daughter and his grand-daughter at his door.

'I'll see you then?' said Shaun as he wheeled her suitcase to the gate.

'I doubt it, but thank you for the lift,' Jen said, waving at Archie who smiled and stuck out his tongue at Maisy. She laughed.

'Dad you're cold,' Jen said. 'Let's get you inside,' she said, with an arm around his shoulder. 'I bet you've been waiting out here for us for ages, haven't you? Go in and get warm before you get pneumonia.'

'You know me too well,' he said hugging them both. Tears sprang to his eyes. 'I couldn't come for you. I had to leave a message for Jack. My car's in the garage,' he said regretfully. A ham sandwich, and a tea cup with the tea bag in ready to steep, sat waiting for her on the kitchen worktop next to the kettle. Jen put Maisy on the rug among toys and she played happily in front of the roaring fire.

'That was your safety gate, got it down from the attic,' he said proudly. 'And the toys, do you remember Julie?' he said, picking an old doll whose eyelashes were missing.

'How could I forget? You raced to town, the minute you were paid, on the eve of my first birthday to get her,' she said, picking her up and stroking her hair fondly.

'Yes, and can you remember your mum spending a week's housekeeping on those red tap shoes so you wouldn't be the only one in the class in black plimsolls?' he laughed.

'And I never went again... God, she never let me forget that, did she?' said Jen.

Maisy yawned. 'Come on little one. It's very late and time to get you into your jim jams,' she said, stroking her daughter's head.

'Look I bought her a book. Friends of mine are writing a cartoon series about alpacas,' said her dad, excitedly handing it to his grand-daughter.

'She'll love that. Dad, can I ask you something?' she said seriously.

'That sounds ominous,' he said, taking a sip from the glass of whisky he'd poured himself. 'I know what you're going to say and I apologise,' he added, looking sheepish.

Now it was Jen's turn to frown. 'Apologise, whatever for?'

'I just presumed that Jack knew.'

'Knew what?' she said, shaking her head.

'About you and Shaun, of course.'

'Jack knows, about Shaun?' Jen said sitting back down on the settee.

'You didn't know? Jack rang... He wanted to surprise you, buy you a ticket to come stay. Don't look so worried, he was concerned about you. I told him that I'd bumped into Shaun, who'd just returned ...'

Jen held her head in her hands. 'Oh no, go on.'

'Well, we got talking. You know how it is... and,'

'No, I don't, tell me,' Jen looked composed and unruffled but her eyes and trembling hand betrayed her. 'How much does he know?'

Jen's dad winced. 'Everything,' he said.

Jack Dylan checked over the remand file for the morning's court to ensure that Norris Regan was going to be kept in custody. The press would be present, but there would be restrictions on what they could report upon, now that someone had been charged and another person was under arrest in connection with the same incident. He would send Andy and Ned round to the courthouse to listen to the remand hearing. He needed Vicky at the station.

He switched off the light at the side of him and for a moment looked at Max who was curled up on the hearth rug in front of the fire. 'Good job your mum had the sense to ring Penny to walk you, eh mate? What would we do without her, eh? Don't look at me like that. At least you're looked after, what about poor Regan's dog then?' he said putting down the note that Penny had left for him. Dylan knew that if Regan couldn't nominate anyone to take care of Tess, via his solicitor, then she would be dealt with as a stray, and might even be put down. There was a daily charge from the budget and realistically they couldn't pay for it in the kennels indefinitely. No matter how you looked at it, Norris Regan was facing life imprisonment and he was the real animal.

'Not fair, is it mate? They should put Norris Regan down and let the dog spend the rest of its life in the kennels, shouldn't they? It'd be a darn sight cheaper.'

Max struggled to his feet and sat resting against Dylan's leg, with his head upon his knee. 'Come on mate, let's go to bed eh?' he said, rubbing the dog behind his ears affectionately. He got up and stood by the fireplace, holding the clock to the fire, he found the hands were at seventeen minutes past midnight.

He hadn't spoken to Jen; it was too late to call now. He was no nearer to knowing what she would be thinking or feeling. The ultimate decision lay with her and her alone. Her choice between him and Shaun would have to be made and that would be final. For he and Jen were alike, and there would be no going back once she had made a decision. While she was away, he could somehow hold off on the reality of the situation between them, like a man with his shoulder against a door. He was helpless.

It was time to go into the interview with Barrowclough.

'Ready?' Dylan said at the interview room door. Vicky took one look at him, stretched her arms wide and yawned loudly.

'Ready as I'll ever be,' she said, standing up straight.

'Regan might be a little lying bastard, yet his account of what took place is corroborated by the post mortem, so let's see what the big fella's got to say to us this morning – or not, as the case may be,' he said, raising his eyebrows.

The air conditioning was on in the interview room. There was only just enough space for the officers to stand between the desk and chairs in the middle and the wall with a touch-sensitive panic alarm strip around the centre. Marshall Richmond sat away from his client. Dylan wasn't surprised, the body odour oozing from what seemed like every pore of Barrowclough's body was even more overpowering today, but it was nothing compared to the sickening smell when he opened his mouth to give his name for the voice recognition on the tape recording. There were no windows in the room except for a small, integral window at head height in the heavy fire door that had to remain closed.

'Since your arrest yesterday, as you would expect, a vast amount of enquiries have been made and an identification and post mortem of the body, found in a freezer in your garage, has been carried out. It is confirmed that the body is that of Kayleigh Harwood. Now, Norris Regan says that you came to his house, raped the girl and then proceeded to strangle her. He admits to having sex with her but says that you took her dead body away afterwards.'

'Evidence of co-accused, Inspector, is worth very little, as you are well aware,' his solicitor said.

'Mr Richmond you are here to advise your client, not answer for him. I am relating to him what the other person present at the time of Kayleigh's death says took place, which gives Mr Barrowclough an opportunity to comment on this, if he so wishes.' Dylan turned to the defendant. 'Mr Barrowclough, do you wish to make comment?'

'No comment,' he said.

'Yesterday, you told us that you had removed the body after an accident on behalf of a friend. Can you tell us what this accident was?'

'No comment.'

'Surely if someone had died and you were involving yourself, you would want to know what had happened?'

'No comment,' said Barrowclough. He yawned. Vicky put her hand over her mouth and retched.

'Keeping you up, are we? Well, if you answer our questions you can go back to your cell for a lie down, how does that sound?'

No emotion showed on Barrowclough's face.

'There is apparently evidence of semen both in the girl's vagina and anus. Did you have sex with her, because DNA will confirm in due course if you did?'

Barrowclough sat unmoved, staring down at the table in between him and the officers.

'Do you want to make comment?' asked Dylan.

'No comment.'

'There are bite marks on the breasts of the deceased which

were inflicted after her death and it is believed that sex took place also after her death. Since you were in charge of the body, were you having sex with her dead body?'

Barrowclough looked up to the ceiling and gazed indifferently around the room.

'It's only a matter of time before we know the truth. This is an opportunity to put your version of events forward, we are simply trying to find out what happened.'

'No comment.' Barrowclough said. He sighed.

'While it's your choice to 'no comment',' Dylan said making quote marks in the air. 'That can sometimes be very unhelpful to you.'

'No comment,' he said, inhaling deeply.

'Norris Regan is a feeble little disabled man. You're a lot taller, bigger and stronger than he is, so therefore I put to you that you were the instigator and the physical force behind this murder?'

'No comment.'

'The truth is he telephoned you, told you a young girl was at his house, didn't he? And you went round there, attacked, raped and strangled her?'

'No comment.'

'That suggests to me that it's perhaps not the first time you have done this?'

'No comment'.

'You can't control your sexual urges, can you?'

'No comment.'

'Is it all about sex, or is the killing more important?'

'No comment.'

'Can you not, or have you never had a normal relationship with a woman? Is that why you have to render women unconscious and then kill them?'

'No comment.'

'Are the knickers hidden in the sleeping bag under your seat in the wagon Kayleigh's?'

'No comment.'

'Of course Forensic will tell us, but this as I said before is your opportunity to explain to us your involvement and actions on these findings.'

'No comment.'

'I believe that it's not the first time you've had dead bodies at your home. You knew very well that we would find other human remains, didn't you? You've killed before, haven't you?'

'Really Inspector, there has been no disclosure about any other remains found at my client's address. How can he possibly comment as to whatever the remains may be? I would suggest at this moment in time that those findings are irrelevant. My client is here in respect of the discovery of the body of Kayleigh Harwood at his home, so could we focus on that please? My client is not under arrest on suspicion of any other murders,' said Mr Richmond.

He was right of course, but Dylan knew his client was going to no reply and he needed to say it, so he went ahead. 'No, I totally disagree Mr Richmond. They are highly relevant because it shows me that Mr Barrowclough's story is utter rubbish. He's killed before and I believe that he keeps the dead bodies to continue to carry out his sexual perversions until he gets another. The pattern of which perhaps has repeated in respect of Kayleigh.' Dylan turned to Barrowclough.

'Is there any comment you would like to make about this?'

'No comment,' he muttered once more.

'You Mr Barrowclough are a dangerous sexual predator, who kills for pleasure and Regan's nothing but your monkey, I suggest. He gets to have sex when the victim is alive, doesn't he? But not after death, because that's your turn on, isn't it? That's why you keep the body preserved for as long as you can. Otherwise, why would you keep the body in a freezer?'

'No comment.'

The interview was terminated.

Dylan leaned back in his chair in the office. The fire doors were open into the yard. It was cold, but Vicky stood relishing the fresh air.

'Do you think he'll talk to you?' said Lisa, placing a cup of coffee on his desk as she pulled her cardigan around her tightly. She shivered.

'Doesn't look like it at the moment, but who knows? He may want to tell us about everything once he knows his hopes of freedom are futile. That would make things a lot easier for us, wouldn't it?'

'Life's optimist, he is,' Vicky said, joining them and taking her cup of coffee from Lisa. 'I wonder if Regan knows a lot more than he's saying too?'

'Well, we'll give him another interview later to give him opportunity to talk to us. In the meantime, I need to get the Chief Supt to extend Barrowclough's detention for a further twelve hours and we'll chase Forensic for priority on the swabs. If they show it is indeed his semen, that will destroy his story of just moving a body for a friend and clarify for us who bit her.'

'Yeah, man and van for hire to shift dead bodies, Barrowclough would have us believe, Lisa.'

'Remind me to ask him about his dog.'

'You don't think he's been...?' Lisa said with a gasp.

'Well you never know with perverts like him but no, I meant we need to find out if there is anyone that will give it a home or, like Regan's dog, Tess, it may find itself receiving the death penalty, instead of the owner.'

Lisa looked sad. 'More victims...' she said. 'Barrowclough's dog was in such a state he has had to been put down.'

Andy and Ned walked in. 'Put wood in t'hole lass will you, its bloody freezing in here,' said Ned.

'Moron. You mean please close the door Vicky,' she said. 'You should have been in the interview with Barrowclough, you wouldn't have been saying that then about good old fresh air,' she said.

'Regan's remanded boss, no application for bail, Mrs Best says she will ring you later today as she has some other matters to bring to your attention about her client and Barrowclough.'

'That's good. It would be good to have something else to put to Barrowclough in interview, he's not commenting.'

'Early days though boss eh? It's not like the telly would have us believe. Criminals don't just roll over and accept their fate,' said Andy.

DS John Benjamin knocked at his open door. 'The bones at Barrowclough's, boss, suggest not one but at least two other bodies – and guess what? There are no skulls.'

'There is a message on your desk from the Council offices and a dentist, John,' said Lisa.

'And look at this – a fax from Jasmine about the jar that was marked gold and silver we found in Barrowclough's shed. Some interesting items, she says and one of the jewellery items has a name etched upon it.'

Dylan looked heavenwards. 'Thank you God,' he said.

Chapter 40

Dylan was standing next to the filing cabinet in his office when his phone rang.

'Yvonne,' he said.

'I've got some information from my client that might be of interest to you,' she said stiffly.

'Go on.'

'Norris Regan has confessed to me his involvement with Barrowclough that spans back over a number of years and admits to being involved with previous incidents with young girls.'

'Any in particular?'

'One that happened about twenty years ago that I remember well was a girl that went missing on her way back from her work at a mill in Harrowfield. Barrowclough knocked her off her bike with his wagon and took her to Regan at Ivy Cottage.'

'Tina Walker..,' Dylan said in a whisper as his eyes wandered over to Barry Sharpe's file.

'Another he brought from over the border... He can't give me specific names but he says there were others. Look, I'll fax over a copy of the signed admission. He's expecting further interviews in due course. I don't think you'll have any problems with him, he's singing like a canary.'

'That's excellent news. Thank you, it's really appreciated Yvonne.'

'I've explained the likely consequences of his admission, but I think he's just determined not to go down for them on his own, to be honest with you.'

'Blimey, that's a refreshing change. I think we may have discovered the remains of at least two of the girls in question, therefore it would help us to interview him about these other two murders as soon as possible.'

'Will you have him produced back to the police station or interview him at the prison?'

'I think it would be easier all round if we get a production order for him to be in our cells for forty-eight hours, don't you?'

'I agree. Let me know the times and dates. Either myself or Lin will make one in.'

'I owe you.'

'I'll remember that,' she said. He could hear her smile in her voice.

'Yes!' Dylan shouted. Replacing the receiver he punched the air.

'Yes!' he heard Vicky shout from in the CID office.

Dylan got up and hurried to the door. 'What's happened?'

Vicky stood up and walked towards him her arm resting around Jackie May's shoulders. 'Our little treasure PC Jackie May has only got a statement off Mavis Beanland, who puts Barrowclough in the gritter the night of White Wednesday and shows him being introduced to Kayleigh and her car, inadvertently by Mavis while he was carrying her as a passenger to the station. She is Regan's next door neighbour and has known him for years so she also give us the association we need from a third party with Regan and Barrowclough.'

'You little beauty,' he said. 'And I've got some other news...' The staff in the office looked on with expectation. 'Regan has put himself and Barrowclough in the frame for a least two more murders of young women.' Dylan patted Jackie May on the back. 'Well done you.'

'I only took the statement as directed sir. It could have been any one of us taking the action,' she said shyly.

'But you did it Jackie, you did it girl!'

'With the confession from Regan to his solicitor and the statement from Mavis Beanland, we have them both.'

The fax machine jolted into action. Dylan took the papers as they came off. 'Perfect and Best,' he said as he scrutinised the content. 'While Regan is admitting involvement with two other deaths he doesn't go into any detail, it's merely an outline,' he said.

Vicky saw Jackie's face cloud over. 'Don't worry kid, we'll get that from interviews with him in the future, I'm certain.'

'The skulls and human remains are a start. Andy, speak with the prison and get Regan produced to the police cells will you? Let them know he will be arrested for two more murders after the recent disclosure to his solicitor. Vicky, you and I have another interview to carry out.'

'Ready and willing boss,' she grinned.

Ten minutes later, the two were sitting in the interview room with Barrowclough and Mr Richmond. Dylan opened the interview and put questions to him about Kayleigh Harwood, but he was sticking to his previous stance of no comment.

Dylan closed the interview. 'Norris Regan is talking to us

quite openly, via his solicitor, about other incidents that he tells us you have been involved in over the years, so no doubt we will be speaking to you at a later date, Mr Barrowclough.'

A few minutes later Vicky read out the charge of murder to Barrowclough in the presence of his solicitor and when asked if he wished to reply he said, 'No Comment,' which was recorded on the charge sheet.

'Well he's consistent, if nothing else,' said Vicky. 'He'll be at Court tomorrow,' she said to Mr Richmond as she escorted him to the door.

Back in the office Ned sat slouched over his desk.

'What's with the long face? 'Dylan asked.

'Don't shoot the messenger, boss. I've been speaking to the prison. Regan is at present in theatre at Harrowfield General, having been attacked by his cell mate.'

'How bad is it?'

'They say it's pretty bad. His throat's been slashed open, cutting through the artery. Once they have an update, they'll let us know.'

'He could have bloody waited until we'd interviewed him,' said Vicky despondently.

'Yeah, well we've got two charged with Kayleigh's murder and now we need to update Kayleigh's mum and boyfriend. Then I think we all deserve a drink, don't you?' Dylan sighed. 'Anyone got anything else for me?'

'The bicycle bell boss,' said Andy. 'It's the right era but nothing to prove it was from Tina's bike. Could have been, the expert tells us, but that's about as close as we're gonna get I'm afraid.'

'Where's John? I think we've had about as much luck as we can expect today don't you,' he smiled. 'Let's go get that drink.'

Dylan stood at the bar, wallet in hand. The team were grouped in a corner, taking over a number of tables. The banter was noisy and boisterous.

'Everyone got a drink?' he shouted. Those that heard him raised their glasses in the air.

'Where's John?' Dylan said taking a seat next to Andy, whose mobile rang. He stood up and went outside to take the call. As he went out of one door, John walked in. Dylan got up to get him a drink.

'The mystery of what happened to Tina Walker looks like getting solved after all these years,' he said.

'It does?' said Dylan.

'We've a positive ID by way of the teeth from one of the skulls,' he said, smiling broadly.

'Wooh! Can today get any better?' Dylan said, raising his glass towards John's, 'Cheers mate.'

'I can't wait to tell Barry Sharpe and Norman Tempest.'

'It'll be good news for Norman. He's just been told they're retiring him out.'

'You're joking.'

'No, an award one day for outstanding work and his ticket the next. There's no justice in this job, is there?'

'Well, you can be assured when my thirty years are up you won't see me for bloody dust, John,' he said pensively. 'We've still a lot of work to do, but well done mate.'

Andy came back into the bar and walked towards the pair. 'The prison,' he said, his mobile phone still in his hand. 'Regan's out of theatre but he's on a life support machine. The next twenty four hours will decide his fate. Apparently they lost him in theatre, but managed to revive him.'

'As long as he stays alive long enough to confess, that'll do for us, won't it boss?' Vicky said putting her arm around Andy and Ned's shoulders. 'I think that drink might have gone straight to my head.'

'Make sure we have an officer with him at all times,' said Dylan, shaking his head at Vicky.

'Boss, we've found a necklace with a pair of scissors on it,' said Jasmine.

'Was it in that jar in his garage?' Jasmine nodded.

'Kayleigh's,' said Vicky.

'And a gold bangle with the inscription Diffy inside.'

'The traveller from over the border,' said Dylan. 'Defiance, her name was Diffy for short. I remember Barry Sharpe telling me she had gone missing around the time Tina Walker disappeared, but it was assumed she had moved on. I guess it's too much for us to hope we'd get some low copy DNA?'

Jasmine hunched her shoulders.

'Maybe we could get familial DNA...?'

'We can try to find a family member. One good thing about the travelling fraternity in my experience is that they can get the word out far, wide and fast.'

Chapter 41

A tame Robin came and hopped about their feet and under the seat, hoping for crumbs.

'You can't spend much time at Seaview Wildlife Park without being struck by their friendliness, can you?' said Cyril. 'Even the wild ones.'

Jen saw the bird had a black eye fixed on her.

Cyril went down on his haunches and whistled to the bird. Much to Maisy's amusement, it came to him and took food from his hand. They strolled over the bridge. There was a freshness in the air.

Jen sat very still for a moment, gazing at her daughter from across the table in the cafe.

'How do children manage to eat ice creams at this time of year,' Cyril said with a shudder as he pulled his hankie out of his trouser pocket and wiped around his grand-daughter's mouth. She protested.

Jen cupped her chin in the palm of her hand and turned to look at her daughter, then her eyes went back to the landscape as her mind whirled.

The journey home was a quiet one, with Maisy falling asleep before they had driven out of the car park, and carefully Jen extracted her from the car seat when they got home. Holding her daughter in her arms, she waited at the edge of the pavement until the traffic gave them an opportunity to cross to their front door. Shaun pulled up in front of them.

'Dad. Will you take Maisy inside please? There's something I have to do,' Jen said, nodding towards Shaun's car. She gently handed Maisy to Cyril, then kissed her daughter's forehead and her dad's cheek before slipping into the passenger seat of Shaun's car. 'Drive,' she said.

'Where to?'

'Anywhere but here,' she said, staring straight ahead.

Shaun pulled into the car park at Culver Downs. 'Do you remember, we were sat right here in my clapped out old banger the first time I ever told you that I loved you,' he said as he turned off the ignition and swivelled in his seat to face Jen, an air of surety about him. 'Here our love story began,' he said contentedly, reaching out for the hand that lay in her lap. 'I come here often and think of you.'

It was as if a hand had removed a piece of tissue paper from a picture. She looked at him. 'And most apt,' she said with a forced smile. 'As this is where it has to end,' she added, pulling her hand away.

'But, I don't understand?' he said, his hand halfway to cupping her face.

'Well, let me spell it out for you, shall I? Once and for all,' she snapped, knocking his protesting hand away. 'I don't ever want to see you again as long as I live. Is that clear enough?'

'But...? I'm glad I chinned him.'

'You did what?'

'Planted one right there....' he said pointing under her chin. 'He was pissed off with you that night. What right has he?'

'Look,' she said shaking with anger. 'I'm truly sorry if your life hasn't worked out just as you'd planned, Shaun, but mine is complete. I'm not surprised Dylan was mad at me, I deserved it. I love Jack with all my heart and I know he loves me unconditionally – which is more than you ever did, if you're honest. Right now, I can't stand to be here. This isn't my home any more. I can't wait to get back to Harrowfield,' she said.

Shaun's face turned sour. 'If I can't have you then...' He turned on the ignition and revved the engine.

Jen laughed in his face. 'Then what Shaun? You don't love me, you never did. We were young – and now you just like the thought of being young again. Maybe you like the idea that if you snap your fingers I'd come running, just like I used to. Might it also be because your marriage isn't all you want it to be? There's someone else for her?'

Shaun looked downcast. 'No, we can't have children.'

'Her fault?'

'No, ironically, it's me.'

'I'm sorry. What goes around comes around?'

'But I thought, when I came to your door that night, you were...'

Jen smiled. 'Tempted?'

'No,' she said shaking her head. 'Surprised, shocked,' she added, biting her bottom lip. 'Flattered, maybe, but cheat on Dylan? Never in a million years. He's a good man Shaun, worth a hundred of you.'

Jen got out of the car and walked away. The tyres on Shaun's car crunched on the gravel as it sped off.

'Dad,' she said into her mobile phone. 'Can you come pick me up please?'

Dylan took the call. 'He's dead, sir.'

'Dead?'

'Norris Regan died half an hour ago,' said Vicky.

'Damn, before we got his confession.'

'What will we do now?'

'Thank God his solicitor got it. Her notes won't have as much detail as I'd have liked, but we'll be able to use them. I'm sure they'll be enough with everything else we've got.

'Do you think the other convict killed him for his leg irons, boss?' she smiled. 'He did tell us they were like gold dust these days.'

'Trust you...' he said.

'Well, it'll save the taxpayer a lot of money, won't it? Good riddance to bad rubbish is all I can say.'

Jackie May shouted to Dylan from the office. 'Maggie Jones on the phone from Forensic, sir.'

Dylan put his phone down and headed for the CID office.

'Maggie.'

'Dylan, we've got some test results for you. You'll be pleased to know they confirm your thoughts about Paul Barrowclough.'

'Go on,' he said, sitting down.

'Firstly, the knickers found in the cab of his wagon have been identified as Kayleigh Harwood's through DNA.'

'Yes.'

'And secondly, the semen samples from the recovered body's anus were also his and the bite mark comparison has been confirmed by forensic odontology.'

'Absolutely brilliant, thank you,' he said before putting down the phone. 'Well, Jackie,' he said smugly. 'We have evidence against Paul Barrowclough in abundance. In fact, I can't remember a case where we've had so much corroboration.'

'What will happen now?' she said.

'We'll get him convicted and sentenced for Kayleigh's murder while enquiries continue into the other remains found. It would be nice to get a conviction for the murder of Tina Walker and the Difiance girl too and maybe they'll be more off that missing from home list. When all the relevant evidence is secured, it will be reviewed, involving the Crown Prosecution Service.'

'And then?'

'Then Barrowclough will be produced, arrested and interviewed and hopefully charged with at least two further murders. And now we have the pleasure of going to see Barry Sharpe, to tell him after all these years we have solved the murder of Tina Walker. Do you want to come along?'

'Do I just, I'll get my coat,' she said, beaming from ear to ear.

'And then lady, I suggest you get them forms filled in to apply for a CID course.'

'Too right,' said Vicky putting an arm around her shoulders and giving her a squeeze.

'And you Vicky, the Sergeant's boards lady!'

Vicky nodded.

Looking at the joy, happiness and excitement on Jackie's face made him think of Jen. His heart felt heavy.

'You okay sir?' Vicky said as she looked at his tired, pinched, grey face. His phone bleeped.

'I'm coming home,' he read. *'I know why you sent me away but you can't make me stay away. I love you.'*

'I am now,' he said, beaming from ear to ear as he sent a text back. *'Can't wait! I love you too! x'*

The End

CPSIA information can be obtained at www.ICGtesting.com
Printed in the USA
BVOW02s2152290514

354917BV00001B/12/P